THE BEACHEAD
PRINCIPLE
ARTHUR PHILLIPS

THE BEACHEAD PRINCIPLE

ARTHUR PHILLIPS

Simon & Pierre Publishing Company Limited
Toronto, Ontario, Canada

We would like to express our gratitude to The Canada Council and the Ontario Arts Council for their support.

Marian M. Wilson, Publisher

ISBN 0-88924-063-9
1 2 3 4 5/81 80 79 78 77

Canadian Cataloguing in Publication Data

Phillips, Arthur, 1921 –
    The beachead principle

ISBN 0-88924-063-9
I. Title.

PS8581.H546B43   C813'.5'4   C77-001471-2
PR9199.3.P45B43

Simon & Pierre Publishing Company Limited
Order Department
P.O. Box 280 Adelaide Street Postal Station
Toronto, Ontario, Canada
M5C 2J4

Printed and bound in Canada by The Bryant Press Limited.
General Editor, Rolf Kalman
Designer, Catherine P. Wilson
Typographer, The Bryant Press Limited

". . . there are now powerful forces, powerfully aided from outside, that would divide us as a people and destroy us as a state . . ."

from an address by
the Honourable Lester B. Pearson
The Prime Minister of Canada
Montreal, 1968

PREFACE

The *beachhead* principle, as old as history itself, is as necessary for conquest today as it was when the Greeks used the legendary wooden horse to establish their beachhead in Troy, or when the Allies established their beachhead in Normandy on D-day.

The only difference today is that there are newer and more peaceful ways of establishing a beachhead.

Researched in the mid-sixties, the original version of this book was completed in 1969. In view of the FLQ incidents that took place in the early '70s, it was updated in 1973. But even then the manuscript was not taken to a publisher until 1977, when the imaginary events depicted in the story had started to become frighteningly real.

Is a beachhead about to be established for another ideology in a separated Quebec?

Arthur Phillips

1

Pierre LaPointe eased the old Chevrolet convertible to the curb. He reached into the back and lifted a leather briefcase from the floor. Slowly, cautiously he placed it securely on the front seat between himself and Paul Flambeau. He then drove off, entering the highway and passing a sign reading *Au revoir, St. Hyacinthe — Montréal, 37 milles.*

"It made me nervous — that thing bouncing around in the back," said Pierre. "I'll be glad when we get rid of it."

Paul looked at him, but did not speak.

Pierre wondered how his friend could be so cool. Paul sat there as though nothing was going to happen, as though they were just going for a drive. But it was not like that for Pierre. His mind raced in tormented circles. His hands, wet with perspiration, slipped on the steering wheel and he coughed frequently; a dry nervous choking kind of cough. Like a boy playing truant from school for the first time, he felt excited and scared. Scared enough that he wished he could get out of what he was going to do, turn the car around and head straight back to the home of Emile and Yvonne in Rivière du Loup, which he had left only yesterday. But he couldn't. Not if he wanted to look Paul in the eye again.

How I envy Paul! *Mon Dieu*, I wish I was like him. Not afraid. No feelings. Nothing. But he's always been like that. He's always had guts. Maybe that's why I look up to him.

Pierre's mind flashed back to the events of the last two days. Emile had driven him in his old truck to the railway station at Rivière du Loup where he boarded the train. Paul had been waiting for him at Lévis, and together they had driven to the ferry which took them across the St. Lawrence River to Québec City. Then they had travelled to the outskirts, to an aristocratic old mansion perched on a hill overlooking the broad valley of the St. Lawrence. Flanked on the east side by a long row of elm trees, the house stood majestically before a wide green lawn, broken only by a circular driveway which led to the front door.

Along the west side, opposite the elm trees, was another gravelled driveway which stopped at a converted two-storey brick coach house.

Paul had taken Pierre through a side entrance of the coach

house, and up a flight of stairs to a large den-like room. The smell of gun oil saturated the stuffy air, and when Paul switched on the light Pierre could see why. A selection of rifles, shotguns and automatic pistols hung on three of the walls. They were highly polished and obviously well cared for. Against the fourth wall was an old-fashioned dresser topped with a large mirror. Beside it was a small window overlooking the driveway.

A man, who had apparently been sleeping on one of two cots in the cluttered room, rose quickly to a sitting position and reached for a Browning automatic from a wooden box beside the cot.

"It's okay, Roger," Paul said, and the man lay down again muttering an unintelligible phrase.

"You can sleep on this one," said Paul, pointing to the other cot. "I'll pick you up in the morning." Pierre had gone directly to bed, slept fitfully, and was glad to see Paul when he returned at daybreak. Roger, the man on the other cot, was still sleeping when they left.

Each involved in his own thoughts, they drove silently to rue Belvédère where Paul stopped at a grey brick, three-storey apartment building. He entered, reappearing moments later with a leather briefcase. Then they had driven down Grande Allée through Ste. Foy to the bridge which crosses the St. Lawrence, and soon were speeding down Highway 9 toward Montréal. Pierre drove while Paul slouched on the seat, his hat tilted over his eyes as though he were asleep. He didn't speak until they were a short distance from St. Hyacinthe.

"I have to talk to Henri Bédault," he said. "Take the next exit." Pierre obeyed without question. Paul was soon directing him through a maze of city streets.

Eventually, they arrived at a new brick bungalow in a middle-class residential area of St. Hyacinthe, and Paul entered the house by a side door. It was almost ten minutes later when he opened the door and beckoned Pierre to come into the house. A balding, middle-aged man stood in the shadows.

"Henri, this is my new assistant," said Paul in a sophisticated manner that impressed Pierre. "And," he added with a broad smile, "soon a very useful member of the Movement."

Henri shook Pierre's hand as Paul continued. "Henri is our public relations man," he said to Pierre in a confidential tone. "He's the man who makes sure that everybody gets the right slant. And you can take it from me," he added with a laugh, as he slapped Henri affectionately on the back, "he's the best in the business." Henri smiled and motioned them to follow him up the few steps to the kitchen, where a pot of coffee sat on the stove. They remained silent while Henri poured the steaming liquid into three large mugs. Then he spoke.

"I don't know what I can do to help you," he said, as he passed the sugar bowl to Paul. "I need time to prepare press releases, I can't dream them up over a cup of coffee. Until you walked in that door ten minutes ago, I'd never even heard of this operation. No one has consulted me. Are you sure Bordeaux has approved it? I thought he'd sworn off this type of thing, especially after that FLQ fiasco."

"François made all the arrangements." Paul looked at the wrinkles of displeasure on Henri's forehead. "I'm sure he checked with Bordeaux. He always has before."

"Sometimes I wonder about François," said Henri with a shrug. "Sometimes I wonder who gives the orders any more."

Paul smiled. "Things are happening and happening fast in the Movement, Henri. You've got to be on your toes to keep up with the changes. But look! François wants you to make whatever you can out of this. Whatever is good for the Movement, of course." He looked at his watch and stood up. "We've got to go, we haven't much time." Henri nodded and walked them to the door.

And now they were speeding along the highway again to Montréal. Past the farmhouses spread out on the flat countryside, past the numerous villages easily seen across the almost treeless meadows, and past the substantial churches dotting the fertile lands of these South Shore parishes.

In the distance another church spire pointed to the sky, hinting at the existence of another village still unseen. But Pierre knew that a village lay beneath those spires, as surely as if he could see it. For every village, no matter how small, had its huge church with its impressive spire, a symbol, an emblem, a monument to the simple faith of the people of Québec.

Pierre stared at the broken white line in the middle of the highway. He found it hard to concentrate. Without realizing it, he pushed his foot down on the accelerator and the speed increased with his thoughts. I wish he'd say something — anything. I wish he'd tell me what I should do if anything goes wrong. But no! Paul won't admit that anything can go wrong. He thinks everything's going to be perfect. But something will go wrong. I know. I can feel it in my bones. But isn't that just like me? Why do I always look on the bad side? I guess it's part of my makeup. I can't help worrying. I know I'd feel better if he'd only talk to me instead of just sitting there. But I guess that's a weakness too. I want to lean on him. That's the way I am. When I'm scared I want to lean on somebody. I want somebody to tell me things are all right, that I shouldn't worry. But why should I feel like this? We've rehearsed this whole thing a hundred times and nothing can happen. Absolutely nothing! If anybody gets hurt, if anybody gets killed, it's not going to be us. It's going to be some damn fool that's hanging around and not doing what he's told. It's just like Paul says. As long as we phone the police and give them a warning after we've planted this thing, then it's not our responsibility. It's theirs.

"You're driving too fast, Pierre. You'd better slow down. We don't want to be picked up for speeding." Paul's voice was matter-of-fact and had a calming effect on Pierre. He slowed the car quickly.

"I'm sorry," he said. "But I was thinking, daydreaming I suppose."

"What about?"

"I don't know." Pierre was embarrassed and didn't want to admit his fears. "I keep thinking that something's wrong."

"Wrong? Everything is going perfectly. Why should you think something's wrong?"

"You're so damn quiet, that's why. It makes me nervous."

"There's nothing left to say, Pierre. We've gone over it all so many times." Abruptly Paul stopped talking and looked at Pierre, who was nervously licking his lips, faint drops of perspiration showing along his hairline. Paul knew only too well what was going on in Pierre's mind. He knew instinctively what he must say and do. "You're hardly scared at all. I can tell." He laughed loudly and the laugh had a ring of practised sincerity. "You should have seen me the first time. *Mon Dieu*, I was scared. It was a long time ago but I can still remember. Let's see now, it must have been ten years ago. And was I scared! Nobody could be more scared than I was. But after it was all over, I realized how stupid I'd been. Yes, after it was all over I went out and sure tied one on!"

Pierre had heard this story before. About all the fun, the women, the drinks, the laughs, and the excitement! He had heard it in minute detail from Paul, especially about the women. It used to be about many women, but lately, the story featured one in particular, Giselle. Paul carried a picture of her in his wallet, and one day he had shown it to Pierre. She was beautiful, Pierre had thought, and he hoped he would meet her some day. Sure, she was Paul's girl but then Paul had so many girls, he mightn't mind if. . . . But on the other hand, thought Pierre, Paul was a funny guy and maybe he would mind when it came to Giselle. Sometimes Pierre wondered if Paul was really the idealist that he seemed to be or the patriot that he claimed to be. Or was he in the Movement just for the kicks, the money and maybe the women? But as soon as the thought crossed his mind, Pierre chided himself. Of course Paul's a patriot! How can I think otherwise? Wasn't it Paul who got me that iron pit job in Labrador? Wasn't it Paul who made life bearable in the long winters of Rivière du Loup with his many visits, his gifts and his laughter? He made me feel good, he was almost like a father to me. Paul's a patriot all right. He only turns to the booze and the women as a release. He has to have something.

"Are we going right back to Québec City when we've finished?" Pierre felt better now that they were talking.

"As fast as we can," Paul replied good-naturedly. "We'll be back there before the action really gets started."

"Then we'll haul out the booze and really tie one on," said Pierre. "Won't we?"

The remark stopped Paul. He had made plans only for himself. He really didn't give a damn about Pierre's plans as long as they didn't interfere with his, which included jumping in the sack with Giselle. He was about to remind Pierre of this, when it suddenly occurred to him that his stories of ribaldry had been believed, and that this was no time to disillusion his friend. "We'll find something really big to do, Pierre," he said, "something really big!" Paul could sense an immediate change in Pierre's attitude.

"Does Giselle have a girlfriend? Maybe she's got a girlfriend for me. Maybe we could go out and really have a ball. How is Giselle? Does she . . .?"

"Does she what?"

"You know what I mean? Does she — huh?"

Paul was surprised at the question. Pierre had never been a ladies' man; in fact Paul had never seen him with a girl. There was vague talk of marriage a year ago but the idea had died a quick death when Pierre went to Labrador. Pierre was a rough-and-ready outdoors type with the boys: shy and retiring with the opposite sex. Why the hell am I surprised, Paul asked himself, he's grown up now, he's not a kid anymore. Let's see now, how old is he? Must be about twenty-two. Old enough to be a problem when sex rears its ugly head. No, it wouldn't be wise to tell him about Giselle. "She's not like that," he lied. "Giselle's a nice, clean kid. We can't ask her to any wild parties. She keeps strictly to the business of the Movement."

"I didn't know she worked with you," said Pierre with a hint of disappointment in his voice. But his interest was unabated. "Does she live in Québec City?" he persisted.

"Sure."

"Where?"

For a moment Paul felt angry with Pierre. He didn't like being cross-examined and he resented Pierre's curiosity. Then he realized that Pierre was asking a natural question. "She lives in that apartment where I picked up the briefcase this morning," he said.

"On rue Belvédère?"

"Hey, you're not trying to cut me out, are you?" Paul laughed.

"*Sacre coeur!* I wouldn't want to do a thing like that."

Silence fell between them as they neared the end of their journey. The spires of Nôtre Dame Cathédrale and the silhouette of downtown Montréal were plainly visible against the backdrop of Mount Royal in the distance. They were not far from their destination, Central Station, the railway terminal at Place Ville Marie. Paul directed Pierre to leave the highway and drive along the banks of the St. Lawrence.

Paul pointed to the powerful current. "Look at the river, Pierre," he said. "Look at it, study it, think about it. It carries the waters of ten thousand streams, it drains the lakes from half this continent and it carries the trading ships of a hundred nations."

"I've never thought of it like that," said Pierre, his country mind overwhelmed by the sights of the Montréal waterfront.

"But think what it could mean to us. Think about that, Pierre. Think about that and you'll understand why your future must be with the Movement." Then they swung onto the Jacques Cartier bridge, and entered Montréal.

"It'll just be another couple of minutes." It was Paul's voice and his excitement was well controlled. "Now you watch exactly what I do. First of all, you'll notice that I'm very nonchalant. Everybody will be carrying a briefcase or a suitcase or some kind of bag, so there's nothing unusual about me carrying one. Then I pick out a locker as close to the centre of things as I can. Nobody will notice me. I put the briefcase in the locker, set the timing mechanism, put a quarter in the slot and lock the door. Then I come back to the car and we drive away. The only thing left to do is phone the police. It's as simple as that."

"But there's enough explosive in that case to smash fifty lockers. I know. I've used that stuff enough times in the pits. It could kill!"

"Pierre!" Paul's voice was stern. "The explosive is not meant to kill. How many times do I have to tell you? It's only intended to frighten. The noise we want to hear will be from the press, the television, the radio. They'll get the message that we're back in business. And that's the object of this exercise."

"I still can't understand why we have to use the real stuff. Why can't we put in a dummy charge?"

"And screw up the whole deal? If we do that everybody will know we're bluffing. They won't take us seriously. But the real thing — that's different! It'll put the edge back on. People will sit up and take notice again. But remember, Pierre, this time the strategy's different. This time the bombs are only a small part of a big plan. A plan that should work. A plan that'll finally make us free."

"Are you sure the timing device is set properly?"

"Of course I'm sure. It's set for five hours."

"How do you know for sure?"

"I was in the room when François set it."

"François? What does he have to do with bombs? I thought he was the top man."

François! *Enfant chien!* That was exactly what he considered himself to be. The top man! The big man with the big plan. Paul hated him and he was just about to say so when he realized the negative effect it would have on Pierre. He'd tell him later. Besides, there wasn't time now.

Ahead of them was rue Lagauchetière and the entrance to Central Station. "Turn here," he commanded and Pierre drove the car into a circular driveway crowded with vehicles. He stopped in front of the centre doors to let Paul leave the car. Then he gingerly pushed the innocent-looking briefcase toward Paul, who picked it up and walked jauntily into the railway station.

Pierre drove the car part way around the circle and, seeing an empty space, he pulled in and stopped.

Although it was against orders, his nervousness prompted him to remove the keys from the ignition, open the door, and stand on the pavement. Curiosity lured him along the sidewalk to the entrance and drew him up the corridor to the interior of the station. He was drawn by an overwhelming urge to watch Paul as he planted the bomb. Robotlike, he walked into the main section of the ultra-modern station. Straight ahead of him was the information booth. On the right were ticket vendors. In the centre were the entrances to the various tracks. To the left and at the far end was a restaurant and a group of stores. Pierre looked over his shoulder toward the line of lockers opposite the booth. There was Paul opening the door of a locker. Pierre watched as he reached down and pulled a tab from the centre of the briefcase. This was the method of setting the timing mechanism, a device that would detonate the bomb in exactly five hours. Paul lifted the case waist high and pushed it into the locker.

Pierre glanced at his watch. It was almost noon. Then he watched Paul reach into his pocket, pull out a coin and insert it in the locker. Then he closed the door, removed the key and half turned to leave.

And then it happened!

Paul was less than two steps from the locker when the explosion ripped through the encompassing metal. Like a cannon shot off at close range, the sound echoed and re-echoed through the spacious chambers. Although Pierre was halfway across the building, the concussion deafened him. He fell to the floor while jagged pieces of metal, stone and plaster flew by. A hush followed the holocaust, but only for a moment. Then screams and hysterical shouts rang through the building. Like the mad, unreal noises of a circus chamber of horrors, the screams reverberated against the stone pillars and walls. Pierre rose to his feet and raced across the marble floor toward the exit. His thoughts were of himself, and not for his friend Paul, whose broken body lay on the floor.

Pierre had to get away! That was all that mattered. He could think of nothing else. There was no logic. Just a wild feeling inside him as he raced desperately to the car.

He searched frantically through his pockets, but he couldn't find the keys. He opened the car door, looked in. They weren't in the ignition. Again, he dove his hands into his pockets and finally, his fingers closed around the keys. He fell into the driver's seat, his hands palsied with fear, and found that even the simple action of putting the key into the ignition required his complete concentration. When he succeeded in starting the car and was about to ram it into gear, a wild banging on the opposite window caught his attention. Without looking, for he was sure it was the police, he pushed the accelerator to the floor. But he pushed too quickly, the motor stalled. Then he looked. It was Paul.

He pushed the door open. Paul fell in, blood streaming from his left arm, his face pitted with pockmarks of blood. His coat hung from him in shreds and Pierre could see that his left arm, almost completely severed, was caught in the sleeve. How Paul could still be conscious was beyond imagination. That he could have carried himself to the car was unbelievable. But Pierre had no time to think of this. Without closing the door, he again started the car and drove it forward. The momentum made the door slam shut as he sped through the entrance into the street, burning rubber as he skidded around the corner.

In the distance he could hear the sirens of police cars and ambulances. Screaming and screeching, their noises frightened him. He pushed the accelerator to the floor, racing through the crowded streets. Paul tried to raise himself to a sitting position. "No!" he mumbled, and Pierre realized that his actions were attracting far too much attention. If he continued this way he would surely be caught. He swung around a corner and slowed down abruptly, then turning again quickly onto another street, he continued at a moderate speed. No one seemed to notice him and although his teeth were chattering and perspiration dripped freely from his forehead, he forced himself to continue at this slow rate toward Boulevard Métropolitain, the tunnel under the St. Lawrence River and the highway back to St. Hyacinthe.

2

The highway from Montréal to St. Hyacinthe is wide and straight, one of the best in the province of Québec. It begins as an extension to Boulevard Métropolitain, an elevated freeway which crosses the city. When the highway reaches the St. Lawrence River in the downtown section, it enters a tunnel, one of the first of its kind in the world. Constructed of prefabricated concrete sections, carefully lowered to the bottom of the fast-running river, it was ingeniously locked together and braced against the shifting sands. On completion, it became the most direct route between Montréal and the Eastern Townships.

A few miles from the tunnel the road divides, one section turning south to enter the United States, the other branching north and east to parallel the river's shore to the Gaspé.

As Pierre reached this intersection he looked closely at Paul. Paul sprawled against the door, his clothes blood-drenched, his glazed eyes showing no form of recognition as he stared straight ahead. "Can you hold on for fifteen minutes?" Pierre asked.

There was no reply; but Pierre was glad to see Paul's eyelids closed and opened in an effort to communicate.

"I'm taking you to St. Hyacinthe," Pierre said, although he didn't know whether Paul could understand. "I'm taking you to Henri. He's smart. He should know what to do. He'll be able to get a doctor. He'll know somebody."

Still no reply.

Pierre turned on the radio. A group was singing a song obviously translated from English to French. He looked ahead. The long ribbon of road stretched mile after mile in front of him. He looked at the speedometer. Eighty miles an hour. Too fast! He eased off. Just in time. Coming from the opposite direction was a police car. Fear stabbed Pierre's chest but the police car continued on its way. Pierre kept his eye on it through the rear-view mirror until it was out of sight.

The music stopped. "About ten minutes ago," interrupted the announcer, "an explosion at Central Station ripped through a locker on the south side of the main rotunda. According to an eye-witness report, three people were killed in the blast. The victims are reported to have been bystanders who were in the vicinity of the lockers when the explosion occurred. A fourth man, who appeared to be badly hurt, was picked up by a man in a white convertible, and apparently taken to hospital. The police are anxious to locate the victim, and hospitals in the Montréal area are asked to contact the police when this man is brought in. There are several theories as to the cause of the explosion. One is that it was caused by a leaking gas main. Another, more readily believed by the police, is that it was caused by a bomb planted by a separatist group. Stay tuned to this station for up-to-the-minute reports."

Pierre felt numb. The newscast had only one meaning for him. A murderer! That's what he was. A murderer! "Three people killed." The words numbed his mind. *Mon Dieu!* No!

How could Paul have been so wrong? At this very moment they should have just completed their phone call to the police who would run around in circles, as Paul had laughingly said, until all the lockers were opened and searched and the mechanism defused. The bomb would then have fulfilled its purpose: to have public attention focussed on the aim of the Movement.

But this! Oh Jesus, Mary and Joseph. I pray this is not true. I pray it's only a dream!

"Did you hear that, Paul?" he asked, looking over. "Paul, did you hear that?"

Paul was grey, his eyelids drooping. Perspiration bubbled on his skin.

"Can you hang on for another five minutes, Paul? Please." The look on Paul's face was frightening. "Please try to hold on, Paul, please. I'll get you to Henri's place. It'll only take a few minutes. Please hold on, Paul. Please try to hold on."

Above Pierre's numerous fears and phobias, there stood one spectre he could not reconcile — the spectre of death. Thoughts of death held such horror for him that he could not bear to lay his eyes on a dead person; he could not bear to be alone in a room with a corpse. His thoughts of death were weird and horrible and hopeless and sick.

One time when he was a boy, a friend, René, had drowned in the St. Lawrence River. They were both only ten years old and Pierre had never been closely associated with death. But now that his friend was dead, his mother had told him that he should go to see him. And he had gone. The custom at that time was to keep the body in the house. He walked to the door where the wreath was hung. It was a cold January morning and a chill gripped him to his bones. But he knocked on the door and René's mother opened it. She led him to the living room. And there he saw the coffin against the wall and René was lying in it, as still and silent as a statue. A baby cried in the kitchen, and the woman ran to it. Pierre stopped just inside the doorway, as though his feet were frozen in his boots, and his boots were glued to the floor. He could not force himself to go ahead. There was his best friend lying there, a waxen image. There was something morbid and evil, and he could not stay in the room. He had to get away. Quickly he backed from the room, ran down the hall, and left the house. He was almost a block away before he stopped running.

The thought of his friend's death never quite left him. For months afterwards, he was afraid to be left alone and was terrified of the dark, plagued with the thought that the spirit of René would appear to him. As time went by, he began to wonder why he was afraid of anything so ridiculous. It never occurred to him that the fear was deliberately planted in him; that he had been educated in fear. He had never quite fathomed the mystery, and he would never discuss it because of his shame. He only knew it was quite possible for a spirit to appear to him. Hadn't the nuns at school and the priests at church told him so? Hadn't the Virgin Mary appeared many times to many people? Hadn't the talk of apparitions been constantly repeated during his youth? Yes, there was a great fear of death in Pierre's mind. It was all mixed up with mortal sin, confession and heaven and hell — especially hell.

Pierre knew that his friend René was in hell, as surely as he knew he was dead. For hadn't both of them, only two hours before René's death, sworn and told dirty jokes, and even stolen some licorice from old man LaCourte's grocery store? Three mortal sins! Each of them punishable by eternal damnation in hell. Each of them unresolved by confession to a priest — for René had not gone to confession before he drowned. And the last rites of the church were not given to him either. It had been a full day before René's body had been found. And everyone knew that his soul had left his body only minutes after his death. Father DesMarché, the parish priest, had verified this. René was in hell. Pierre knew. Because he had been taught. And ever since then he had been filled with a morbid fear of death. And no matter how he tried to reason it out, the strange unnatural fear still haunted him.

Paul was shaking convulsively. The pupils of his eyes were dilated and his skin was putty grey. "Oh, Jesus, don't let him die." Pierre's utterance was a prayer. "Oh, Jesus, don't let him die."

Finally, they arrived at the access road to St. Hyacinthe. Pierre drove directly to Henri's house.

With barely a glance at Paul, he parked the car in the driveway, leaped out, ran to the house and banged on the door. A moment later, Henri appeared.

"Henri, you must help. Paul's hurt bad."

Henri ran to the car, quickly assessed the situation, then slid into the back seat. "Get in," he hissed. "Hurry before we're seen." Pierre jumped into the car. "Drive," said Henri with authority. "I'll tell you where to go."

Pierre followed his rapid-fire instructions as they drove from the neighbourhood.

"You're taking me back to the highway," he protested. "Isn't there a doctor in town?"

"Don't be a damn fool. We can't take him to a doctor."

"But he'll die."

Henri looked at Paul, slumped in the seat. "I don't think a doctor could do much for him anyway."

"Where are we going?"

"Never mind. Do as you're told."

They drove for over twenty-five miles, up parish roads and across the flat countryside, until they came to a large, beautiful church, built of solid rock, with a huge spire topped with a golden cross. Beside the church stood the rectory, beautifully constructed of matching stone, a marked contrast to the shanty-like frame houses which clustered about it.

Henri left the car, entered the side door of the rectory, and returned with a priest. After looking at Paul, the priest told the two men to carry him into the sacristy. When they had done so, the priest quickly donned vestments, brought out candles and oil, and began a ritual over the body.

"What's he doing?" Pierre was puzzled by the actions of the priest.

"He's giving him the last rites." Henri's voice had no emotion.

"The last rites! Why doesn't he call a doctor?" Pierre advanced on the priest. "Why are we wasting time, Father? Why can't you call a doctor? My friend needs help."

The priest answered with a stern look. "Quiet," he ordered. Then he looked at Henri. "Get him out of here."

Pierre left the sacristy and walked slowly down the hallway toward two doors, one of which led outside, the other into the church where the familiar fragrance of incense and burning wax filled the air. Walking through the portal he found himself in front of a life-size statue of the Virgin Mary at a side altar. Between himself and the statue, which was mounted on a circular globe with a serpent crushed beneath its feet, was the communion rail. Pierre knelt down and, laying his head on the rail, prayed. The serenity of the church relaxed him and the burden he was carrying seemed lighter. "Holy Mary," he prayed, "Mother of God, pray for us sinners, now and at the hour of our death. Amen."

For how long he was there he did not know. He was so absorbed in his prayers that he didn't hear the priest as he walked up behind him and placed a hand on his shoulder.

"My son," said the priest. "Come with me." Together they left the church and walked across a well-manicured lawn to the rectory. They entered and went directly to the study.

"I'm Father Moreau," said the priest. Pierre introduced himself. Then impatience gripped him.

"How is he?" he blurted out.

"My son, I have done everything I can for your friend." The priest's voice was quiet now and full of pity. The stern expression was gone and in its place was compassion.

"Is he — is he all right, Father?"

"He is all right," the priest said simply. "He will no longer have to face the trials and tribulations with which we are beset. No longer will he have to fight for his rights. He has gone to eternal glory, to sit at the right hand of God the Father Almighty. You did the right thing, my son, bringing him here so that he could receive the Last Sacraments and have the door to Paradise opened for him. It was your duty and you did it well."

But Pierre was not listening. Paul dead? Impossible! Paul couldn't be dead. A fury rose in him. "What do you mean 'opened the door to Paradise'?" he shouted. "Why didn't you call a doctor?"

Horrified, the priest looked at him. Then Pierre realized what he had said. He was accusing the priest! He was accusing the authority of the church. "I'm sorry, Father," he said. "I didn't know what I was saying."

Immediately the priest's expression changed. "I understand, my son. Events have unnerved you. Come, have a drink of wine. It will calm you." Father Moreau poured two glasses of wine from a bottle produced from his desk. Pierre sipped the wine, although he felt like gulping it.

"I listened to the newscast and I know how you must feel. I

know that in addition to your friend, there were three others killed. Innocent people. We know that this is against the commandments of God. But we also know, my son, that it was not your intention to kill." He stopped, then questioned Pierre. "It wasn't, was it?" Pierre shook his head. Father Moreau looked relieved. "I know it was simply your intention to protest. The voice of a man crying for his rights. The voice of Québec crying for her rights. After all, my son, we are only asking for what is justly ours. We are only asking for our God-given rights to rule ourselves, our rights to utilize our own language and our own customs." The priest strode to the window. "For two hundred years, my son, we have fought this battle, this incessant war against the overwhelming flood of English-speaking people on this continent. We have tried to preserve our heritage, and we have tried to do it without violence. But we have failed, my son." He flung his arms in a gesture of despair as he turned from the window. "We have failed miserably. We have only gone deeper and deeper into the abyss. We are a defeated people," he said solemnly and dramatically, "a defeated people." The priest stopped for a moment but began pacing back and forth in front of Pierre who stood motionless, the empty glass still in his hand. "But defeated or not," Father Moreau continued, "we must never give up." He studied Pierre who returned his gaze with a questioning look. Pierre had never thought of himself as a defeated man!

"I remember a time when I was a youth," the priest went on, "and full of all the impudence and vitality of the young." He stopped to think for a moment. "It was at a place near Mont Joli and we had found an old brown bear and cornered him in a stable. We wanted to lasoo him, tie him up and cage him. But the bear would have none of it, and suddenly, while three of us were prodding and pushing him into position, he stood up on his hind legs and roared in defiance. Then advancing on us, he knocked me to the floor and scattered my friends. Although my arm was broken, I soon learned to forgive the bear. I reasoned that he did not want to hurt me; he was only trying to stop us from hurting him."

With that the priest stopped momentarily. "Do you understand, my son? We, the French people in Québec, are like that bear. Cornered, bullied, discriminated against. And like that cornered bear we must rise to our feet, we must growl in defiance and we must fight." He stopped again and walked back to the window. "What happened today was an accident, a terrible accident but nevertheless an accident. You must not worry. You must not feel responsible. Someday it will not be necessary to employ the tactics we are forced to use today."

Pierre could hardly believe what he was hearing. He had never known a priest to speak this way. Yes, he had heard the priests talk of the value of the French language, the Catholic religion and the customs and culture of Québec. But he had never heard words uttered so frankly from the mouth of a priest.

Father Moreau continued: "We have preserved the culture and the language of Québec for two hundred years. We, the clergy, have worked to protect it for you. We have been the guardians, the keepers of the faith. But now it is up to you. In the past few years, the government of Québec has seen fit to limit our powers, to take away our responsibility to educate and rule. They have set up a Ministry of Education. The Church's hands are tied. We can do no more. We are looking to you to carry on the fight. The fight that can no longer be waged from the pulpit."

Puzzled, Pierre began to realize that he was mixed up in something far bigger than he had imagined. The way Paul had explained it, there was nothing really serious or complicated about the separatist movement. As Pierre understood it, the English-speaking Canadians and Americans wouldn't give the French-speaking people their rights. He never was quite sure what rights were involved, but he was certain there were plenty. People spoke about them everywhere. It was on the radio and television and in the newspapers. Pierre had long been convinced that the English-speaking people were his enemies. Because of this, he kept away from anyone who spoke English. In all of his life, he had never been out of Québec. Never even across the border into Vermont, or across the Ottawa River into Ontario. Once, he had driven as far as Ste. Anne on the Restigouche River, but he had not crossed it into New Brunswick.

The priest's words shocked him. How big the Movement must be to have the Church behind it! Pierre wished he knew more, wished he could understand it all. The priest noticed his bewilderment.

"Did you not know it was the French Jesuit priests who forged through the Canadian wilderness and the valley of the Mississippi long before others came?" Pierre said nothing but listened intently. The priest went on. "Did you not know that it was the French priests who taught the word of God to the savages, who founded great cities like Québec, Montréal and New Orleans, great forts like Louisburg and Duquesne?"

"Yes, I know," said Pierre. "I learned that in school, but I don't know what happened to make it so bad for us."

"You must learn, my son, you must learn. When this affair has blown over, you must come to me. I will put you in touch with the people who can teach you. You owe it to yourself to learn. But I must warn you of one great danger."

Almost mesmerized by the priest's long discourse, it took Pierre a moment to ask the question.

"Warn me? What danger?"

"You must be careful to get the facts straight. You must get them from us. The great danger is that you will listen to the English-speaking deceivers, that you will be influenced by their words, and that your loyalty to our cause will be weakened."

"Never! I will always be strong."

The priest smiled. "Shall I hear your confession?" he asked.

3

The gurgling of the draining bath water muffled the music from the living room as Giselle LaFlesche pushed back the shower curtains, stepped gingerly onto the bath mat, grabbed a towel from the rack and patted her slim, well-rounded body dry. Then, draping the towel sarong-like around her, she danced to the soft lilting music of an accordion band that drifted lazily through the small, old-fashioned, one-bedroom apartment from a portable record player in the living room. Giselle hummed with the music as she pirouetted her way into the bedroom, where a small electric alarm clock beside the bed told her she'd better hurry. Paul would soon be there.

Her humming stopped, as if cut off by a switch deep in her subconscious mind, as she thought of why she must hurry. Her boss! He had deliberately kept her late at the office again, finding a trivial excuse to keep her there when all the others had gone. Why does he keep up the charade, she wondered. Surely he must know by now that I'm not available. Why doesn't he give up? He's so goddamn obvious. If I could, I'd quit. I'd tell him where to go. Back to New York or Washington or wherever the hell he comes from. And one of these days, I will. She sighed as she adjusted her pantyhose, stepped into her dress and turning to view it in the mirror, reached her arm in a contortionist gesture and zipped it up.

If only Paul would see it her way. She could do so many other things. She could make more money working for a big company. Now she was back on her feet, her old confidence restored and her abilities unimpaired. She could do so much better than working for this boring office. No matter what François said, no matter how much he went on about her importance, she wanted to quit. This time she would. If Paul doesn't like it — well, he isn't the only tree in the forest! Why he wants to stay in the Movement is beyond me! It hasn't done him a damn bit of good so far, and the future doesn't seem to be studded with anything but hopes. Oh, what the hell's the use. I'm not going through another argument over that.

In the dinette, she rearranged the candles on the small table, checked the wine glasses and puttered with the silverware. The kitchen clock must be fast. Either that, or Paul was really late.

In the kitchen, she double-checked the oven, opened the refrigerator, touched the bottles of red wine, then impatiently walked into the living room. The telephone was not off the hook as she had imagined and it was not out of service. She had checked it. He must be with François. But why didn't he phone this afternoon if he was going to be tied up? What the hell! That's Paul. There was a sound of knocking on the door.

"Paul?" No answer. She opened the door. A man stood there dumbly, a helpless expression on his face. "What do you want?"

"Giselle?"

She studied his face. It was a mask of despair as his brown eyes pleaded. She could see that his front teeth were slightly crooked, his ears too large for his slender face, his body strong and obviously well developed beneath his unfashionable clothes.

"What do you want?" she repeated.

"I must talk to you."

"I'm busy. I'm expecting company. Come back later."

"Now! I must talk to you now!"

"What about?"

"Paul."

"Paul?" What could this rough-looking country bumpkin want with Paul? She stifled a smile as the thought crossed her mind. Maybe he was a federal cop. Surely they couldn't sink this low. "Who are you?" she demanded.

"Pierre LaPointe. Please. Please let me in."

"You'd better go away. There's nobody by the name of Paul who lives here." Maybe he was a cop. "You're looking for Paul. Paul who?"

"Paul Flambeau. Haven't you heard?"

"Heard what?"

Pierre's hands reached up in a beseeching gesture. He tried desperately to speak but the words caught in his throat. "You're his girl," he mumbled, "and you don't know. You don't know that . . ." He stopped. He could continue no longer. Giselle watched as tears formed in his eyes. Then he broke down, tears streaming down his face as he choked out, "He's dead. Paul's dead."

Stunned by the words, Giselle opened the door. Pierre followed her into the living room where she turned on him with blazing eyes. "What kind of a trick is this?"

He pulled a big, blue handkerchief from his pocket, wiped

his eyes and blew his nose. "It's not a trick. I wish it was. But it isn't. Paul is dead. He was blown up by a bomb in Montréal this morning."

"How do you know?"

"I was there."

Pierre recounted the details of his involvement, of the three men killed, of his escape, his attempt to find a doctor and of the eventual meeting with the priest. At first Giselle would not believe him. "It's impossible. Paul could never make a mistake like that."

"Didn't you hear it on the news?"

In answer, Giselle rejected the record of the accordion band that had been repeating itself, turned on the radio and disappeared into the kitchen. She returned moments later with a bottle of wine and two glasses. The glasses tinkled in her shaking hands, betraying her emotions. She poured the drinks while Pierre stood awkwardly beside the radio. "You'll see!" she said with finality. "When the news comes on, you'll see. Then you'd better get the hell out of here in a hurry."

But it was all in the news. Spelled out so clearly that Giselle could not deny it. It had happened. The truth, the plain, dirty, hurtful truth flooded into her mind, the realization, the real meaning, the consequences, began to dawn on her. Too shocked to show emotion, she sat down on the sofa. She knew some day this had to happen. His luck couldn't hold out forever. But why now? Why not at some future date, way off in time when his going would not be so important?

Paul's effect on Giselle had been magical. He was more than a lover, even more than a husband could have been to her. Paul was an image, an idol, a thing to worship when there was nothing else left.

And she had worshipped him with all her heart, all her mind and all her body. He couldn't be dead! There were too many things between them, too many things that were destined to be part of them both. He could not be dead!

The announcer continued, recounting each detail, following up with eye-witness accounts. "The police," he said, "have not been able to find the man in the 1964 Chevrolet convertible as yet. They are convinced he is implicated. A province-wide search for him is underway."

Pierre took a cigarette, one he had rolled himself, lit it and gave it to Giselle. There was no visible display of emotion that would release the torrent building up inside her; there was only the awful whiteness of her skin and the irregularity of her breathing to reveal her pain and her tormented thoughts. When she finally spoke, it was as though she was directing a servant. "Take me to him," she said, rising.

"I can't."

"You can't? Or you won't?"

"The priest made me promise I wouldn't betray him. I can't go back on my vow to a priest."

"The doctor. Take me to the doctor who looked after him."

"There was no doctor."

"No doctor?" Her voice was flat, unbelieving, cynical, hardly that of a girl of twenty-one. Paul was her life. Without him she was nothing. Although he was almost twenty years her senior, she had gone along with him, had loved him and helped him, had sheltered him and at times, kept him. Now it was over and she was again nothing, as she had been before they met. "Why didn't you get a doctor?" she asked.

"I couldn't. I went to St. Hyacinthe. I saw Henri. He couldn't get one." His voice caught on the lie. "I took him to a priest. He gave him the Last Sacraments."

Giselle viciously butted her cigarette. "To hell with the last rites," she screamed. "To hell with the priest. Do you know what I believe? I think you're a dirty, stinking, little coward. You ran out on Paul. You left him lying in his own blood. Your best friend! What kind of a creature are you?"

Pierre hung his head, thoughts of cowardice and shame stilling his tongue as Giselle ranted on. "A sneak! Running away, afraid to risk your own neck. You didn't kill three people today. You killed four. Instead of taking him to a doctor, to a hospital where he could have been helped, where did you take him? To a stupid little parish priest. And what did he want to do? Give him the last rites? What the hell good did that do?"

The provoking words had the desired effect on Pierre. He felt sick and dizzy under the onslaught. If it had not been for the fact that he had gone to confession and had been assured by the priest that he was not a murderer, he would have crumbled under her words. As it was, her accusations that he had killed Paul made his knees feel weak. He gulped his drink, was glad to see Giselle pouring herself another and without being asked, held out his glass for her to fill it. She did.

"I drink to you, a coward. I drink to Paul who was a patriot and you, a coward."

He knew she was hurt, terribly hurt. He couldn't blame her. In spite of the insults, he felt sorry for her. Father Moreau had told him of the torment, the hurt, the abuse suffered so long by the French Canadians. He had said that some day it would be different. When we rise up and fight the injustices, like that old bear the priest had talked about, then things would be different.

His compassion made him feel better. He wished he could put his arms around her, let her cry on his shoulder, comfort her. But he couldn't. So he said nothing, and together they drank until the bottle was empty. When it was, Giselle replenished it from the kitchen.

Although her attitude toward Pierre was one of hostility, she wanted him to stay. Who else could she turn to? François? Jacques Ginette? Charpentier? No! Not one of them would care. Maybe Madame Hébert. But no, not even her! After all, who am I to them? A cog in the Movement's wheels? Paul's mistress? An ex-prostitute? On the other hand, what was I to Paul or he to me? We were lovers, and yet we never spoke of love. He was never true to me, but I was true to him. So that makes me a fool? Why can't something good happen to me? Am I being punished for my sins? No! It's just stinking fate, that's all. Things will change for me. I'll get over this. I'll find something else to do. After all, I wasn't in love with Paul anyway.

"How long did you know him?" she asked.

"Ever since I can remember," replied Pierre with feeling. Then, like a flood bursting a dam, he told her how he had known Paul since he was a child; how Paul had helped his mother fight the poverty that had been their inheritance; and how Paul had convinced him to join the Movement to protect his language and culture from the Americans.

Heavy smoke from the kitchen interrupted their conversation. The dinner she had so carefully prepared was burned to a crisp. She turned off the oven, opened a window to let out the heavy vapours, then stared helplessly at the still smoking remnants of Paul's favourite meal.

"It was what he really liked," she said wistfully. "I cooked it specially for him." Her hands rose in an impotent gesture. "He asked me . . . he asked me this morning . . ." And then it came. The tears, so long held back, welled up and like a spring flood streamed down her face.

Pierre moved to her, gently touching her shoulders, tenderly holding her in his arms.

4

The telephone rang incessantly. Giselle lay sleeping on a chair and Pierre was sprawled on the sofa. Finally, Pierre shook his head, as though to force out the effects of last night's wine. Standing over Giselle, he nudged her gingerly at first, and then with greater force. The telephone continued to ring as she became conscious. With an unsteady hand she lifted the receiver.

"Hello."

"Giselle?"

"Yes."

"This is François."

"I know."

"Then listen to me. The police are on their way to your apartment. They'll be there within the next ten minutes. They've been tipped off about your connection with Paul. They think he might be with you. I suppose you know something went wrong yesterday? You know what happened to Paul?"

"Yes."

"I'm sorry, Giselle. I'm very sorry. But I haven't time to discuss it now. We'll talk about it later. In the meantime, I want you to tell the police that you quarrelled with Paul. The federal police know that you've been close to Paul. They don't know how close, maybe, but they know you've been friends. There's no use denying it, Giselle. It'd only make matters worse. You might as well admit knowing him, but at the same time tell them you've broken up. Say you had a fight. They'll believe you. But don't admit anything. You understand?" He waited for an answer. There was none. "Some innocent people were killed, Giselle. Paul could be in a hell of a mess if they catch him. I want to help if I can." He stopped. "Are you all right, Giselle?"

"Yes, I'm all right." Her head was throbbing. They had consumed too much wine. They had been drinking half the night, she and Pierre. But now she was waking up and remembering again. The shock, the fear and the hurt began to flood back. "You want to help Paul?" she asked.

"Of course I do." François sounded sincere.

"You know where he is?"

"No. I haven't heard a word from him. All I know is what I've heard from the news. That kid he had helping him drove him away somewhere. He's probably holed up somewhere. I phoned Bordeaux, but he's as much in the dark as I am."

"I know where he is."

"You do? Where?"

"He's dead."

"How can you be sure?"

"The kid who was with him came to see me last night."

"Where is he now?"

"Here."

There was silence at the other end. Giselle could hear François breathing, but nothing else. Then he spoke, slowly and deliberately. "Look, Giselle, you have only minutes to spare. You must get him out of your apartment. If they find him there, they'll question him until he breaks down."

"He knows nothing."

"He was with Paul?"

"Yes."

"Then for Christ's sake, do as I say. No arguments, just do as I say." He gave her explicit instructions and hung up.

Jumping to her feet, Giselle brushed some loose strands of hair from her face and shouted to Pierre.

"Hurry," she cried. "Hurry! You must get out of here."

Pierre found himself again in front of the aristocratic old house overlooking the St. Lawrence. Behind it was the coach house where he had slept only two nights before. It seemed so much longer than that; so many things had happened. But it was true, it was only the night before last. Circling the driveway, Pierre was chauffeured past a parking area where a lone Ford station wagon stood. He had expected to be taken to the coach house. Instead they drove to the front door of the big house.

On either side of the entrance stood two grotesque gargoyles mounted on stately marble pillars. The gargoyles, grinning their insipid smiles, looked straight at Pierre and an uneasy feeling swept over him. The feeling was omen-like, almost nightmarish. Something like walking into a room, one in which you know you have never been, yet which seems strangely familiar, eerie and repulsive. He stopped a moment as the apprehension washed over him, and then as quickly as it had come the fear receded. He followed the chauffeur into the house.

He had left Giselle's apartment in the nick of time, ducking out the side door at the very moment the police were coming in the front. He met his escort, Roger Flynn, at the corner of the street as Giselle had said he would. A sly-looking man in his early thirties. Together, they had driven for almost thirty minutes without a word between them. Pierre thought he had met Roger before, but could not recall the occasion. When the old mansion presented itself, Pierre remembered where he had seen him before. He was the man in the other cot that night in the coach house.

"Come in." A very fat and very friendly woman in her mid-fifties stood in a wide hallway beyond the vestibule. "You do look pale," she said with concern, as she took Pierre's coat. "Do you feel all right?"

"Yes," said Pierre with hesitation. "I feel okay."

"Then you will breakfast with us," his hostess declared as she escorted him down the central hallway and past a circular staircase.

The thought of eating made Pierre feel squeamish. The excitement and shock of the past two days, the wine last night and the fear that now enveloped him left butterflies in his stomach.

"Only coffee," he said when they reached the dining room. "I don't feel hungry. I'll accept your invitation for coffee only, if you don't mind."

She stopped and looked at him for a moment. "Very well," she said with a sigh. "I'm not really hungry myself, either."

It was only after they had finished their first cup of coffee and his hostess was pouring the second, that she introduced herself. "I suppose you are wondering why you are here," she said in a well-articulated voice. "There's no use keeping you in suspense. My name is Eloise Hébert. I'm a widow. I own this house. I want to help you."

Pierre looked at her in surprise. Everyone seemed anxious to help him: Henri, the priest, Giselle. And now this woman. "Why?" he asked. "Why do you want to help me?"

"That was a very direct question, young man, and it deserves a very direct answer. I want to help you because I believe you can be of service to us. And," she said slowly and deliberately, "you must not question our motives. You need our help. You are an accessory to murder. Is that not correct?"

Pierre shuddered. "I suppose I am," he mumbled. He felt like telling her that he was not really guilty, that it was all a terrible mistake. That he was only helping a friend. But he didn't. For this gracious person suddenly changed into a forceful, dynamic and direct businesswoman.

"I want you to understand, Pierre, that we don't consider you a murderer as do the police. I consider you a patriot. I consider you a hero." Pierre winced as he thought of his lack of courage the previous day when he ran from the railway station. Madame Hébert continued. "I have a strong admiration for you and other members of the Movement," she said as she stood up, her head held high, her eyes turned upward. "I suppose I admire you so much because you are like my late husband. There was a man! And his father before him, and his grandfather before that. A long, strong line of patriots. Men that held this country together. Men that kept it from being swallowed up. Yes, Pierre, I mean swallowed up. Swallowed up in the English flood. Do you know, Pierre, that one of my ancestors fought in the Citadel? Yes, the Citadel, against the British, and later on against the Americans. And we've kept our dignity and our language and our customs since that time."

It was hard for Pierre to concentrate on what Madame Hébert was saying. His mind worried constantly about the events taking place in Giselle's apartment. Then he'd think with remorse of Paul's death, and the frightening experiences that had been his for the past twenty-four hours.

"Where is your home?"

"Uh?"

"Where are you from?"

"Rivière du Loup."

"A magnificent town! So quaint! Truly French! You have maintained the culture and the language there. You must be proud!"

Except for the times when Paul had sounded off about French pride, Pierre had never really thought about it. He had only thought that Rivière du Loup was a dirty town. Old and dirty. Nothing else! He had been glad to kick the dust of Rivière du Loup from his boots, and when he compared it to Montréal or Québec City, his thoughts were far from being proud. Nevertheless, it was nice to hear a woman of such obvious stature praising the place of his birth, and it was nice to hear her flatter him. It helped to take his mind off his problems.

Madame Hébert continued. "I want to make myself very clear, Pierre. I want you to know that I admire what you have done. I have a feeling for people." She laughed. "I always go by my feelings. They are so much more reliable than logic. My grandfather always said, 'You can trust your heart but not your head.' I suppose that's what makes me truly French. We're different from the others, you know, so dramatically different." She thought for a moment and then continued. "We must treasure our links with the past, Pierre. This is so important. We must uphold our traditions. We cannot discard them. We cannot forget that we are members of the founding race. The race that founded Canada. This is our country. We own it. No one can take it from us. It belongs to us." She walked to the bay windows which overlooked a green meadow beyond the elm trees, and said nothing for a time.

Then she turned toward Pierre, who still sat at the table sipping his coffee. She sat in a chair on the opposite side of the table. "Pierre," she said, "our culture is of such importance that we cannot let it be taken from us." Her eyes, which had been glistening with idealism, suddenly narrowed and focused on Pierre. "We have suffered indignities and injustice for too long. We will fight against them and we will win." She stood up and slapped her hands together. "You have performed a courageous act and we will help you. And God will help us all. For as sure as God helped David fight Goliath, He shall help us in our fight against the Goliath of the English and the Americans. Yes, Pierre, we are proud of you for what you have done. But there is something far more important that I wish to impress on you."

"Far more important?"

"We will expect loyalty from you, Pierre. We will expect loyalty and obedience. And we will expect more and more. You are only the beginning of a long line of heroes and patriots."

"Heroes? Patriots? What more can I do?"

"You will see," she replied nodding her head, "you will see. We will talk again."

Pierre's thoughts spun. What had he gotten himself into? Surely he had been influenced by Paul to become interested in the Movement. He wasn't quite certain what the Movement was all about, but Paul had assured him that it would be good for Québec. "And what's good for Québec," Paul had always said, "is good for you, Pierre." And Paul had told him too, that he should hate Canada and the United States. "France is our mother country," he had said so many times. "We are French, not American." This kind of thinking had appealed to Pierre and he had gone along with it, mostly because of Paul. But now! This was something else. This woman, from an old French family, was expecting so much. And the way she was talking, she thought he was a male Joan of Arc.

"May I leave now?" he asked. "I want to go back and see how Giselle made out."

Madame Hébert walked to the door and opened it. "Roger,"

she called, "Come here." Then she returned to Pierre. "I'm sorry," she said.

"Sorry?"

"It's for your own protection. I'm thinking only of you. You must remember that. For your own sake you must stay here for a while. Just until things quiet down."

Roger entered the room. "Come with me," he said briskly. Pierre instinctively disliked him. He didn't want to obey, and was about to say so when the truth hit him. He was in one hell of a mess! There was no doubt about that. He needed friends. He needed help. And here was this woman offering it. He'd better do as he was told. He followed Roger through the hallway to the kitchen, out the back door and along a pathway to the coach house.

Giselle had little time to think before the police arrived. When the loud knock sounded at the door, she waited as long as she could before opening it, and gave the appropriate sounds of surprise when the police introduced themselves. One man was in plain-clothes, the other in the uniform of the Québec Provincial Police. The man in plain-clothes seemed to be senior. "I am Detective Genou. May we come in?" He made an attempt to step forward, but Giselle stood firm.

"What do you want?" she demanded. "I didn't call the police."

"We simply want to talk to you. You are Giselle LaFlesche?"

"I don't know that that's any of your business."

The detective looked at the constable and nodded his head. The constable placed his hand against the door and pushed it hard. Giselle could not resist the pressure and it opened wide. The detective's voice hardened.

"We have a search warrant, Miss LaFlesche. You can either invite us in or . . ."

Giselle looked at him contemptuously. She knew by his attitude that he was not fooling, but she didn't want to give in too easily. "Show me the papers," she demanded. He did. They looked official and Giselle knew there was no use resisting. "Come in," she said, as she turned and walked into the living room.

Once inside the apartment, the detective surveyed the living room, the kitchen and the bathroom, while the policeman searched the bedroom, checking the clothes closet, under the bed and behind the draperies. Then, apparently satisfied that no one was hiding in the room, he returned to the closet where he shuffled through the assortment of clothing. He continued until his hand fell on a man's suit. Paul's suit! The cleaners had delivered it only yesterday. Giselle's breath caught in her throat. Why hadn't she thought ahead? Surely she must have known that Paul's clothes would link her to him. But so much had happened. The shock, the hurt and the despair had loosened her wits. And the wine of last night hadn't helped either. She felt suddenly weak as she stared at the policeman, still thumbing through the clothes. He had found a dressing gown with Paul's initials monogrammed on the pocket and had removed it from the hook along with the suit.

His actions were disturbed by a call from the living room. "Have you found anything?" It was the detective. The constable motioned her to go first. He followed a moment later. Giselle was surprised to see that he did not have the suit or dressing gown with him. The two men walked to the far corner of the living room and held a whispered conversation. After that, Detective Genou confronted her.

"Where is he?"

"Where is who?"

"You know exactly who I mean, Paul Flambeau."

"The name sounds familiar, but I'm afraid I don't know him."

How many times had she been briefed by Paul on this very question? How many times had he told her what to tell the police? Yes, Giselle had been well trained for this game. If nothing else, she was not going to make it easy for them.

"Do you want to talk here or would you prefer to come with us?" persisted the detective. "In any case, we'll find the truth. You can count on that."

"I don't understand what you are doing in my apartment. What is the reason for all this? What do you want from me?" She asked the questions with such innocence and sincerity that the detective showed signs of weakening.

"You're entitled to an explanation, Miss LaFlesche, so I'll give you one. Approximately three hours ago, a white convertible, parked less than a block from this apartment, was found by the police. The front seat was soaked with blood, Miss LaFlesche. Pools of human blood."

Giselle steadied herself.

"The car is registered in the name of Paul Flambeau of rue St. Jean." The detective studied Giselle's expression as he spoke. "We checked the rooming house where Mr. Flambeau lives and the landlady hasn't seen him for a week. Further to this, we discovered a photograph of yourself on the dressing table in his room. Your address was on the back of an envelope you had sent him some weeks ago when he was in Montréal. And now we are here,

Miss LaFlesche. It is rather obvious that you know him."

Tears formed in Giselle's eyes and trickled down her cheeks. "I don't know where he is." There was a plaintive note in her voice.

"You must come with us," the detective said. "Please get your coat."

At the station, she was ushered into a sparsely furnished room where a third man waited. "I am Inspector De Roche," he said, smiling broadly and offering her a cigarette. She accepted and he lit it for her. Then, talking as he moved, he sat down in a wooden chair behind an old dilapidated desk. "This is only a routine investigation, Miss LaFlesche. I hope my men have been polite?" Giselle said nothing, so he continued. "I might add, Miss LaFlesche, that it is extremely important that we find Paul Flambeau. In order to do this, we need your co-operation."

"What makes you think . . .?" Giselle stopped for a moment, then continued. "What makes you think that I know where Mr. Flambeau is?"

"Didn't my men explain?"

"Not really. I have no idea how I could have broken the law."

The inspector smiled again. He was hardly what Giselle had expected. She felt compelled to trust him, tempted to tell him everything. He acted as though he was a good friend. Giselle felt that he wanted to help. Impossible!

"You showed an interest in Flambeau's well being."

"Is there a law against that?" she asked defiantly.

"Then you admit you know him?"

"I wish you'd get to the point, Inspector. I'm very confused and becoming more than a little annoyed with this badgering."

"Miss LaFlesche!" The inspector leaned across the desk and drew hard on his cigarette, blowing the smoke out slowly. "Miss LaFlesche, I assure you, we have no intention of badgering you! We have no intention of causing you any unnecessary inconvenience. Nor do we suggest there is any law against knowing Mr. Flambeau. May I make it very, very clear to you. We have only one motivation in asking for your help. Whatever the involvement of your friend, Paul Flambeau, in the Montréal incident yesterday, there is one thing we know for certain. We know that your friend is badly hurt. There is another important fact, Miss LaFlesche. We know that he has not been admitted to a hospital. Every hospital in the province has been checked." The inspector butted his cigarette, walked around the desk and squatted on his haunches in front of her. "We want to help, Miss LaFlesche. He is badly hurt, desperate . . . and not being in a hospital . . . Think!

Think! Miss LaFlesche. Who will look after him? Who will care for him? Who will help him?''

Tears of pain and despair formed in Giselle's eyes. She tried to stop them, biting her lip in a vain attempt. "I admit I know a Paul Flambeau," she said through her tears. "My relationship with him," her voice caught, "was only casual." Then she stopped and a wild thought flooded into her head. Perhaps the policeman knew more than Pierre. Perhaps he was right. Perhaps Paul was only hurt. After all, Pierre had left him in the sacristy of the church, but had not seen him die. Had he? No! Pierre had only accepted the priest's word that Paul was dead. Hope welled up in her. Maybe the inspector was right. Maybe Paul was only badly hurt. Not dead.

The telephone rang, interrupting her thoughts. The inspector moved from his squatting position in front of her and picked up the phone. He listened for a moment then said, "Thank you," replacing the receiver slowly. Then he turned to Giselle. "I'm sorry, Miss LaFlesche. I don't like to make this more difficult. You realize that I am only doing my job. I am quite convinced that you do not know where Paul Flambeau is."

Giselle looked at the inspector pleadingly, hopefully, beseechingly. "Do you know where he is?" she asked.

"Yes I do." The inspector's voice was solemn. Giselle's heart leaped.

Perhaps Paul was all right. Perhaps he had been given the attention he needed. Oh, God, if he were all right! Her face brightened. "Where is he?" she asked.

The inspector was slow in replying. "In the morgue at St. Hyacinthe," he said. Then he added, "I'm sorry."

Numbly, Giselle grasped the back of the chair to keep from falling. "Oh, God," she moaned. "Then it's true! He's dead."

The inspector squatted again in front of her as she sat, sobbing hysterically, wiping her eyes with a white lace handkerchief. He took her hand. "I'm sorry, Miss LaFlesche. I'm sorry that I've had to tell you this. But I'm certain that if Paul were here he would be proud of you. Proud of you as . . ." He stopped abruptly. Giselle took the handkerchief from her eyes and stared at him. He turned away refusing to answer the unspoken question on her lips. But there was something about his manner, the inflection in his voice when he referred to Paul, the genuine sorrow which showed on his face that convinced Giselle. Inspector De Roche must be one of them.

5

Pierre walked across the thickly carpeted master bedroom of Madame Hébert's house, threw himself onto the canopied bed and looked up at the fringe. It must be at least two hundred years old, he thought. I wonder how many people have rested here. Despite the heat of the afternoon sun, it was cool in this old house; the spreading branches of the elm trees hung like protective wings over the gabled roof and added a serenity to the place.

As a youth, Pierre had often wondered what it was like in a grand house like this, but he had never imagined himself in one of them. He had seen the inside of a number of priest's houses, and marvelled at their elegance, but had never envisioned himself in the life there. The house furnishings of rural Québec are usually plain and practical and Pierre, well accustomed to this sort of environment, was fascinated by the ornate decor which now surrounded him. In addition to this, he had been wined and dined regally for the last three days and this introduction to luxury appealed to him more than he had ever dreamed possible.

The shock of Paul's death was wearing off. There was still a certain numbness, a vague feeling of guilt and a generous amount of sorrow, but now it was a fear for himself that was most prominent. In the first place, Pierre rationalized, in times like these wasn't it natural that someone was bound to get hurt or killed? Secondly, his guilt feelings had rapidly subsided as a result of his discussions, not only with Father Moreau, but with Madame Hébert as well. He was convinced now that the responsibility was not his. If I were to get killed, Pierre thought bravely, I wouldn't want anybody feeling guilty about it.

Pierre's mind refused to think about it any more and his body felt the relaxation of the big, soft bed, the quiet of the room and he soon fell asleep.

When Pierre LaPointe was a boy of twelve in Rivière du Loup, he used to refer to Paul as his uncle. Pierre's father had died when he was very young, and his widowed mother, far from unattractive, was never without suitors. But it was Paul Flambeau, the sophisticated opportunist from Québec City, who monopolized her favours. The adolescent Pierre was always glad when Paul arrived at the house; he could go out with his friends, and return as late as he liked. It seemed as though his mother didn't care if he came home at all, when Paul was there. Paul usually arrived unannounced and left with no goodbyes. Often, he would arrive in the middle of the night, but always bearing gifts for Pierre and his mother.

Pierre's high school days were a disaster. He had failed miserably and finally quit. Paul had consoled him. "It doesn't matter. School is just a waste of time." But it was Paul who got Pierre a job as a lumberjack deep in the Gaspé woods. There in the logging camp, Pierre would fell the trees which would be sent down the chutes into the fast flowing waters of the upper Restigouche. From that point they would float down the river to the great paper manufacturing plants at Edmundston on the New Brunswick side of the river, the bustling, energetic plants owned by the Americans. Pierre used to look across the river from Québec and wish that he was part of that life, the group that worked in the giant mills. But Paul discouraged him. "Don't involve yourself with them, Pierre. They'll rob you of everything you have. They'll laugh at you because you speak French. They'll try to force you to speak English. But you're too smart for them, you won't let them. Live in the woods, Pierre. Live in the hills of Gaspé and breathe the fresh air of your homeland. For I'll tell you, Pierre, as truly as I would tell my own son, if you involve yourself with those English-speaking people, they'll ruin you. They'll take away what we're fighting so hard to preserve."

At no time did Pierre question the fact that Paul himself spoke both French and English. He took Paul's word as gospel. It was only natural that he would, for Paul held emotional bonds on Pierre as strong as those of a blood relative.

And so Pierre had retreated back into the hills of Gaspé, and although he had never once considered himself to be one, he had become a prisoner of his own land and of his own people.

One time on a visit to Rimouski, a town on the banks of the St. Lawrence, he was walking down a side road when an American tourist, in a new Buick sedan, drove up beside him and stopped. He called to Pierre in English and seemed to be asking for directions. But Pierre could not understand a word that this foreigner said. He looked questioningly at the man, a look which turned to contempt as he studied the car, a beautiful expensive piece of machinery. His eyes turned back to the well-dressed man and the woman who sat beside him, but he said nothing. He could not answer because he didn't know what had been asked. Then the American, detecting the obvious dislike and mistrust in Pierre's eyes, mumbled something in English and drove off. The only thoughts Pierre had as he looked at the disappearing licence plates were ones of hatred. Why should he have a big car like that when I have none? Where did he steal the money to get things like that? Why should others have money when I have none? Later, Paul had explained. "They exploit us. But don't worry, some day things will be different."

When Pierre was seventeen he idolized Paul, and when he was twenty-one his feelings had only strengthened. Paul's relationship with Pierre's mother had ended. Paul moved to Montréal while Pierre's mother had gone to live with her sister in Connecticut. But Paul still had an interest in Pierre and looked him up whenever he was in the Gaspé.

One day Paul turned up at the lumber camp where Pierre was finishing a hard day. It had been one of those long, blistering, August afternoons. Paul opened the trunk of his car and exposed an ice bucket stacked with beer.

"Come on, Pierre, let's relax. You've worked hard enough today and so-help-me-God, so have I. Have a beer." Without waiting for a reply, Paul snapped the cap from a cold, sweaty bottle and handed it to Pierre who lustily drank it down.

After the usual formalities, Paul got to the point of his visit. "Do you know anything about explosives?" he asked.

Pierre took a long gulp from the bottle, finishing it. He handed the empty to Paul. "What kind of explosives?"

"Plastic, dynamite, TNT, nitroglycerin. Hell! Anything! Any kind of explosives." Paul opened another bottle and handed it to Pierre.

"I've fooled around with some of it. Not on my own, but I've helped some of the guys when they wanted to blow up a tree stump or maybe level off a rock. Why do you ask?"

"Just trying to help, Pierre, that's all. Just trying to help." Paul looked at Pierre. He had finally grown into a man. An obedient man, the church had taught him that. A stubborn man, Paul had taught him that. But above all, he was a man of faith. When once he believed in someone, his loyalty was unshakable. And he believed in Paul, and Paul knew it, and was determined to take advantage of it. He had finally found a way to use Pierre. And on this hot August afternoon, he would start the wheels in motion.

"I've got an excellent opportunity for you, Pierre," said Paul, still gulping his beer. "I've got a real big opportunity for you in Labrador."

"Labrador? Who wants to go there?"

"It's a big country, Pierre. It's the biggest. If you think the Gaspé has something, you should see Labrador. But that's not why I want you to go. I want you to learn about explosives."

"*Mon Dieu*! Paul, I don't want to go. I got a girl in Rimouski. We might get married."

"*Maudit Calice*!" With the curse, Paul jumped to his feet. "Get married? You? Like hell, you're getting married." He threw his half-empty bottle at a rock and the resounding crash and the splinters of glass showed his anger and disgust. "You're going to get married? After all the plans I've made for you!" Paul quickly composed himself, sat down again and opened two more beers. Then he laughed. "I'm sorry, Pierre. I didn't really mean it. But damn, that's a real surprise to me. After all the trouble I went to, getting you this job." He eyed Pierre.

Pierre felt as though he was being ungrateful. He was quick to apologize. "*Sacré Coeur*, Paul, we're not engaged yet. We were just talking." Paul was relieved.

"Well if that's the case, there's nothing to worry about. It'll only be for a short time and you can make so much money up there that you'll be able to get married as soon as you come back."

Pierre's face had brightened and the two of them continued their conversation in good spirits. Paul explained that in the pits of the Labrador mines, they had a constant need for explosives experts. "It'll be the quickest and easiest way for you to learn all the tricks, Pierre," he had said. Eventually, Pierre agreed that it was a good idea. He could not resist Paul. Paul, who was so persuasive, so dynamic, so much like the person Pierre had always wanted to be.

Paul was constantly on the lookout for new talent, especially in explosives. The Movement needed more and more if they were to succeed. "Get me some guys that can be led around by the nose," François had once said to Paul. "They're the best kind. Not those smart-aleck bastards from Montréal. They've got too many ideas. They're too hard to handle. If you can get me one real good, reliable kid, I promise you I'll make it worth your while."

Paul had not been getting on too well with François and he knew that it was only a matter of time before the bitterness would boil over. Pierre would make a good ally then, thought Paul, and when Pierre shook his hand on that fateful day and promised to go to Labrador, Paul was very happy. Pierre was happy, too, for now he had found a way of repaying his old friend, his adopted uncle, and he didn't harbour any suspicion about the devious plans which Paul had in mind.

A knock sounded at the door. Madame Hébert entered the room without a word. Pierre, shaken from his sleep, quickly jumped to his feet. She looked through the chintz curtains for a moment before she spoke. "Sit down," she said pleasantly.

Pierre obeyed and sat on the side of the bed. Madame Hébert opened a gold cigarette case she had been holding in her hand, lit a cigarette and offered one to Pierre. He fumbled in his pockets. "I like my own," he said. "I roll them myself."

"I see," said Madame Hébert as she watched him draw on his cigarette. "There's something I want to say, Pierre." Madame Hébert's voice was warm. "I am sure you are anxious for an explanation. I know you weren't too happy when I asked you to stay here three days ago, but as I said before, it was for your own good. We can appreciate what you have been going through the last three days and our sympathies are with you." She placed her hand on his shoulder. "I know what it is like to lose someone close to you, for after all, it is not so long ago that I lost my dear husband, Alphonse. But we cannot live in remorse and sorrow. We must go on," she sighed. "Yes, we must go on."

Pierre wished she'd get to the point, tell him what she'd done. He studied her. She had a full face, broad through the cheekbones with a well-padded jaw line. Her hair seemed falsely red, but the clear green of her sparkling eyes detracted from the harshness. She was a handsome woman, and Pierre could see that the solid lines of her now heavy figure revealed what must have been a very attractive buxomness in her youth. Here was a woman, a kind of woman that he had never known. He had seen women like her, but he had never experienced such a closeness. She inspired him. He felt a sense of encouragement from her very presence. But he still wished she would tell him what was on her mind.

Madame Hébert looked at her watch, then she switched on a small portable radio. It was the beginning of a newscast. "In Montréal this morning," the announcer said, "funerals were conducted for the victims of the recent bombing." Lengthy details followed, giving the names of the unfortunates and the cemeteries where they were buried. Then came the startling news. "In Québec City, meanwhile, comes an unexpected end to the search for the white convertible and its driver who disappeared shortly after the explosion. The man, who police did not identify, turned himself in. An innocent victim of the incident, he had been forced at gunpoint to drive to Québec City. The man was released. No charges were laid."

Madame Hébert turned off the radio. "Well . . .?"

Dumbfounded, it took Pierre some time to realize the significance of the announcement. Until this moment, he had been the quarry in a country-wide police hunt. Now, as if by magic, the hunt was called off. Because somehow, somewhere, someone had concocted this story for the police. The case would be closed. There would be no need for him to run, no need for him to be afraid. His heart began to pound wildly in the emotional release from the fear and torment of the last few days. The terror of being hunted down like a dog, trapped by the police in a shoot-out or, almost as bad, being caged like an animal for years.

"But how?" he asked, the startled expression still on his face.

"Does it matter?"

"I guess not."

"Now do you understand the power of the Movement?"

"I'm beginning."

"You have just experienced a very small sample of our influence, François' and mine."

"François? I've heard of him. He's one of the top men, isn't he?"

"Not one of them, Pierre. He will soon be the only top man. He is a very brilliant man, completely dedicated to our cause, unflinching in his devotion. A truly great man. History will some day record his achievements and they will link his name to Garibaldi, Gandhi, Lenin . . ."

6

Because Roger didn't like being a chauffeur and Madame Hébert insisted he drive Pierre, all speed laws were broken and the trip back to Giselle's apartment took less than fifteen minutes.

Pierre felt pleased with himself. Gone was the deep depression of the last few horrible days; gone was the shock he had felt for Paul's death; gone was the fear for his own safety. In their place, he was filled with a new-found arrogance, a feeling of importance. He thought of Madame Hébert's statement as he left. "We need you, Pierre. We need men like you more and more. We need you to accomplish the goals we have set for ourselves. But always remember, Pierre, you need us. Don't ever forget that, *you need us!*"

It occurred to Pierre that he would have to learn more, do more thinking, more studying about the history of Québec, and the reasons for the existence of the Movement.

When they arrived at Giselle's apartment, he jumped from the car and waved a friendly goodbye to Roger. "Thanks for the lift," he said. Roger drove away without a word or a nod.

Pierre found himself alone at the entrance of the old apartment when a sudden thought struck him. He stopped abruptly, took a cigarette from his pocket and standing at the doorway, lit it. Drawing deeply, he recalled Giselle's anger at their previous meeting and a worried frown crossed his forehead as he remembered her words, "You're a coward, a dirty coward." He took another drag on the cigarette, then on an impulse threw the almost unsmoked butt onto the small patch of grass at the entrance. "*Sacré Coeur,*" he muttered to himself, "she seemed all right when I left." But he was not really convinced until Giselle had invited him into the apartment, offered him a cup of coffee and said, "I might as well say it, Pierre, I'm ashamed of myself for the way I treated you the other night. I do hope you'll forgive me."

He was relieved and happy that she wanted to be a friend, perhaps a very close friend, or something even more. She still looked sad and morose, he thought, and that was to be expected. But now she was calm, and she impressed him as a thoughtful, intelligent girl.

"Did you go to the funeral?" She was staring at the cup of

coffee she held in her hands, when he asked. Slowly, she raised her head, caught his eye and then with no change in her expression, nodded in assent.

"What was it like?"

"Just like any funeral." Her expression still did not change.

"You know what I mean. Did they have a Requiem High Mass for Paul?"

"Everything!" She looked bitter, but she repeated it. "Everything! The whole thing."

Pierre shifted nervously in his chair. He wasn't getting very far with his attempt at conversation. "I wanted to go to the funeral," he said. "But they wouldn't let me."

"I know."

"Look, Giselle, I'm not complaining. I know they did it to help me." She didn't reply so he continued, "Another thing I want you to know is that I was thinking about you a lot when I was at the Hébert house. I was worried about you. You can ask Madame Hébert if you like. I really bothered her with my questions until she finally told me you were all right."

Giselle looked at him quizzically. Although he was probably a year older than she, he looked like a child to her. She was used to mature men, men at least fifteen years older than herself. Men with none of the idealism of Pierre, men of the world. Men like Paul. This crazy, mixed-up kid from the backwoods was almost unbelievable. He was so eager to do something. He wanted so desperately to help and yet, Giselle knew that he didn't really know what he was supposed to do. He didn't understand the cause, he didn't understand the Movement. And yet, as she looked at his glistening eyes and listened to his eager voice, she felt that his enthusiasm would carry him a long way. She began to understand why Paul had tried to bring him into the party. She forced a smile. "You must learn to be careful who you talk to, Pierre."

"What do you mean?"

"I mean you should never tell anybody what you really think. You should never show your true feelings. You can never tell, Pierre, who are your real friends. Your best friend of today can be your worst enemy tomorrow."

"Madame Hébert?"

Giselle nodded. "Anybody," she said. "And possibly everybody."

"Aren't we all working for the same cause?"

"I suppose so."

"Well then, everybody in the Movement will be my friend,"

he said with finality. "I'll trust them all and I won't care how many of them know that Paul was my best friend and," he added in a quieter voice, "that I was worried about you."

How long ago? How dreadfully long ago had it been since Giselle had experienced this sort of belief. Ages ago. A lifetime ago. And yet, it couldn't have been that long. She was only twenty-one. Maybe it was her days at the Abbey School. The rules were severe and the life was rigid, but it was there that the idealistic spirit had first invaded her soul.

"Sister Thérèse," she had said one day to her catechism teacher as they walked together through the blossoming garden at the back of the Abbey. "Sister, I want to be just like you when I grow up."

"Thank you, my child. That is a great compliment," said Sister Thérèse, putting her hand on the shoulder of the young Giselle who was only fifteen.

"I am going to live up to all the rules. Just like the saints. Just like the Blessed Virgin Mary. Just like you." Giselle had looked up at her teacher, wide-eyed and serious. "I want to be a nun."

Sister Thérèse's face brightened. "It is a wonderful vocation, Giselle, being called to do God's work," she said. "Surely it is a demanding vocation, but very rewarding. But I must tell you, Giselle . . ." Sister Thérèse turned around until they faced each other and then tucking her finger under Giselle's chin, she lifted her head and they looked at each other intently. "You must think very carefully about it, Giselle. It is not a decision to be lightly made. You must be certain. Absolutely certain."

"I am certain," said Giselle as she broke away and with a spring in her step, bounced along beside the nun. "I am very sure. In fact, I am positive."

But by the time Giselle was seventeen, she had left the security of the Abbey School. She had moved back with her Aunt Rita in Montréal's east end and soon fell in love — desperately in love, she thought — with a boy of eighteen, Armand. Maybe this was the turning point, maybe this was the death of her idealism. Giselle was not sure. She only knew that her lover had suddenly lost interest when he learned she was pregnant. By the time the baby arrived, her idealism was gone and bitterness had taken its place. It almost killed her to give the child away. It was like giving away part of her own body, a fragment of her own life and a disastrous share of her soul. She was constantly tortured with ugly thoughts. Men are no good! They are animals. They want a woman for only one thing and after that there is nothing. So finally, in desperation, she went back to Sister Thérèse and told her everything. "I want to join the Order," she pleaded. "I want to wait no longer."

Graven-faced, Sister Thérèse listened to her. "Come with me," she said and together they strolled through the familiar garden behind the Abbey as they had done so many times before. "You know how much I have always loved you, Giselle," said Sister Thérèse. Giselle said nothing. The Sister continued. "Listen to me, Giselle, for I want you to know that what I am going to tell you is for your own good. You will make a dreadful mistake if you join the Order under the present conditions. You have been very disappointed. You have been disappointed because you have sinned."

Giselle looked at Sister Thérèse in surprise and shock. She had never heard her talk like this before. She had always been kind and understanding. But the Sister continued. "You have broken the Commandments of God, Giselle, and you have reaped a just punishment for your sin."

"Oh, no, Sister Thérèse! It wasn't like that at all." Giselle's heart pounded and her throat ached. If only she could tell Sister Thérèse the truth. How she had loved Armand and how she had given herself to him for love. It had been so beautiful. It could not have been a sin. But Sister Thérèse looked straight ahead, speaking more like a lecturer than a friend. "You must not interrupt," she said when Giselle tried to speak. "You must let me finish. You must listen and then make up your own mind. If you should join the Order now, you would be doing so only as a reaction to your guilt. You would neither be joining the Order to serve Jesus Christ nor would you be joining the Order to do His work. You would simply be trying to escape, trying to make up for your sin. I'm not telling you what you must do, Giselle, I am only advising you. Always remember that. If you were to make an application to the Mother House they would probably take you in. But you have come to me for advice and I must give it to you honestly and sincerely. Go and make peace with yourself, Giselle, and then with a pure heart, you can return to serve the Lord."

After the initial disappointment, Giselle had thought deeply and on her return to Montréal had taken a secretarial course, determined to get a job and follow Sister Thérèse's advice. But her Aunt Rita died unexpectedly while on a trip to Europe. Giselle found herself alone in the city of Montréal where the French and

English languages meet head-on, sometimes complementing one another, but more often than not creating unnecessary antagonisms and deep undercurrents of hate.

Giselle found it impossible to get a good secretarial position, as she could speak only French. To her, there was no reason to learn English except to satisfy the domineering egos of the English-speaking businessmen. She would not accept the explanation that English was of necessity, the language of business. Instead, she took the request to speak English as a deep personal affront, an insult she would not accept. She fought back violently, but it was a losing battle and a great resentment built up in her mind. Like twigs, each insult thrown on the smouldering fires of hate within her, ignited. Finally, the intensity became so great that she quit her job and vowed she would never work for anyone who spoke English. Never would she degrade herself by learning it. Her resolve was steadfast despite her unsound reasoning, for she could still not get a good position as a secretary.

"There are easier ways," a new-found friend told her one day, "and a hell of a lot more pleasant ways to keep from starving to death than working in a damned office."

Giselle was hungry, sick at heart, worn thin by fighting the inevitable. She did not question her acquaintance who worked in a night spot on rue Ste. Catherine. Giselle just looked at her. "Come on, honey," her friend had said, "I'm going to introduce you to Harry. He'll see that you get fixed up."

Two months later she was a prostitute working for the pimp, Harry. But she soon tired of giving the lion's share to him and, within a year, had become a call girl working under the guise of a public stenographer. She had grown into a beautiful woman and was never without eager clients. Another reason for her popularity was the delightful accent she acquired since learning to speak English. She remembered her vow, but recalled as well that she had made only a hundred and thirty dollars a week as a stenographer, while now she was making six to eight hundred a week as a call girl. Hell, she reasoned, I'd speak Chinese for that kind of money.

But Giselle did not have the heart of a whore. She deplored the perversions to which most harlots degenerated and their escape into the false and pitiful world of drugs frightened her. The constant stream of faceless men sickened her and she wished she could quit. But she couldn't until Paul, whom she met as a customer, entered her life. He talked constantly of the Movement to which he belonged, and of his ambitions.

"We believe," Paul had emphasized, "that now is the time

to strike. We've got everything to win and nothing to lose. Everything is in our favour. It's like a game of poker and the cards are all in our hands."

Although Giselle was not in love with Paul, she liked him and leaned heavily on him for companionship. But she had heard the old story of the French defeat by the British so many times as a child, she could almost recite it verbatim. All about a sickly Englishman named Wolfe who attacked Québec City, God knows how many years ago, and laid siege to the Citadel, and a stately Frenchman named Montcalm who valiantly led his people in an heroic defence of the old fort. It was only by traitorous help, so the story went, of a farmer named Abraham Martin, whose property adjoined the south-west wall of the fort, that the English invaders could scale the heights from the St. Lawrence River to win the battle which followed. Yes, Giselle had heard this. How the English oppressors had deprived them of their pride and how, only by the continual efforts of the clergy, they had been able to maintain their religion, their customs and their language. But it had also occurred to Giselle that millions of other people outside Québec, both in the United States and Canada, had also maintained their rights to be Roman Catholics, without the help of the patriarchal bishops of Québec. With her new-found knowledge of the English tongue and the ability to communicate which it afforded her, it occurred to her as well, that the cultures of over fifty different racial groups had melted together, all of whom had accepted the English language as a common tongue for the sake of easy communication and understanding.

Yes, Giselle had thought often of these things and it was because of them that she now preferred to speak English. It was a complete reversal from her original thoughts, but she felt her reasoning was sound. No one is going to shackle me to a language spoken in only one isolated section of this continent, where only one person in two hundred can understand me. No! It would have been foolish for anyone to expect Giselle to harbour such shallow thoughts anymore. She was reaching out now, trying to understand why the leaders of Québec constantly insisted that French Canadians were different. It seemed to her that it was a lie, a false belief instigated by leaders who would use their people, rather than help them; who would plant seeds of hate, instead of understanding; who would build walls of pride around an impoverished people to isolate them in ignorance, and therefore to control them.

But in spite of Giselle's beliefs, she agreed to work with Paul. She needed help. She could not hope to break from the confines of harlotry without someone's help and so, she elected Paul to be her benefactor. Besides, she reasoned, I like him and I understand how he feels. Didn't I feel the same as he, not so long ago? Her sympathy for his beliefs drew them together and they became close friends as well as lovers. Finally, Paul convinced her to leave Montréal and go to Québec City with him. "Leave your past behind," he had said. "I'll get you a job and you can make a new start." She agreed, and Paul did as he had promised and more. Before Giselle realized it, Paul had her deeply involved in the Movement. And now it was very clear that Pierre was being caught up as well. The only difference between the two was that Pierre had his heart in it, while Giselle had done it only for Paul.

"I've been doing a lot of thinking these last three days," said Pierre, "and there's one thing I'm certain of. Paul died for something bigger than you, or me, or anybody else in Québec." He stopped for a moment. "There's something else I've been thinking about, Giselle, and it's been eating away at me. I never thought that Paul would make such a damn stupid mistake like he did."

"A mistake?"

"Yes! Setting the dynamite blast the way he did. I never thought he could be so careless. Even when I was learning, I never did anything that crazy. And," continued Pierre slowly, "I always thought Paul was smarter than me."

Giselle listened as Pierre droned on and on, recounting the many technicalities required in making a successful bomb. But she did not listen. Her thoughts raced back to that night less than a month ago, when she was to pick up Paul at François' basement workshop.

It was in the evening dusk. She parked her car in front of the dilapidated four-storey tenement house which housed François' workshop. Walking to the metal staircase which resembled a fire escape, she made her way down the six concrete steps to a door opening into a long narrow hall. She moved quietly along the dimly lit corridor and was about to knock on François' door, when she heard a loud voice from inside. It was Paul.

"I've sat in the background long enough," he shouted. "I'm not going to stay there any longer."

The resounding voice of François was the next she heard. "And how long do you think I've been waiting?" he retorted angrily. "Look at this dump. Look at the conditions I tolerate. For a man of my breeding, my experience, my intellect . . . It disgusts me."

Then Giselle heard Paul speak again, more softly this time.

"I've worked like a dog for ten years, François. You've only been around for two, and now you're trying to tell me what to do. But let me tell you this, and you'd better listen. At our annual meeting in October, I'm going to challenge Bordeaux. Not you! I'm going to tell them what to do. I'm going to be the new leader — the new president. I'm not going to be ploughed under. Not by you or any other son-of-a-bitch." There was a firmness in Paul's voice that Giselle had never heard before, and when François spoke again, his voice was quieter. Much quieter.

"There's enough in this for all of us, Paul. There's enough in this for thousands of men like you and me. Listen to me, Paul, ever since I arrived in this country, ever since I came here from Paris, how my heart has bled for your people. You, who have been ignored by the mother country for so long. Ignored by France. I'm with you, Paul. I'm not your enemy, I'm your friend. You look at me as though I had a selfish interest."

Giselle could hear footsteps moving back and forth in the room. Then François continued. "Do you want to know why I've taken such a firm stand, Paul?" There was no reply. "I'll tell you anyway. I'll tell you because I have to tell you. Ever since our association, I've been appalled by your small thinking. I've listened patiently while you rambled on about your outmoded culture. I've stifled my boredom while you've gone on and on about your precious language. But do you know what impressed me? Do you know what I've been thinking?"

Giselle waited to hear Paul's reply. Finally he answered, "What?"

"You've been raving on about your culture and your language for so damn long, you believe it yourself. But in the meantime, you're ignoring a gold mine. The power that'll be in our hands the minute we become a separate state."

"What power?"

François' voice rose in confidence. "That's what I mean, Paul, you're not aware of the potential. You're like a poker player with a royal flush. And you want to be dealt out. You don't seem to realize what you've got."

Footsteps inside the room indicated to Giselle that it was François who was walking back and forth. He must have walked closer to Paul because when he spoke again, his voice was low and confidential. Giselle put her ear to the door and listened carefully. "The point is," François said in a dramatically loud whisper, "that we hold a dagger pointed directly at the heart of the United States and you don't realize it."

"A dagger?" Interest rose in Paul's voice. "A dagger pointed at the United States." Then he laughed, a low, contemptuous laugh. "You're crazier than I thought you were, François."

"Crazy like a fox," François replied smugly. "Crazy like a fox. I know you're too slow to figure it out for yourself, so I'll explain it simply to you." The words of insult reverberated about the room and Giselle, who still held her ear close to the door, could feel her heart pounding. She knew that Paul would not take much more without exploding.

François continued. "Before I tell you of your potential power, Paul, let me explain your weakness. Let's look at your culture and let's be realistic. You don't think like a European Frenchman. You think like every damn North American I've ever seen, or smelt, or talked to. Your television programmes are the same, your music is the same, your art is the same. You like the same cars, the same type of houses and the same entertainment. Do you know what the word culture means, Paul? It means the way you think and the way you feel. It means the things you enjoy and the way you live. And you'll never convince anyone that you are any different in these matters than any of the other two hundred and twenty million people in North America."

"We are different." Paul was defiant. "There are a great number of differences in the way we think."

"Name one."

"We love our families. We love our church. We love our country — Québec. We love our language."

François laughed. "Paul, you don't make sense. You really don't. There isn't a human being alive that doesn't love his family and his church and his home and his language and his country. But I'll tell you one way you are different."

"How?"

"You are stupid."

"What?"

Giselle could hear a terrible anger in Paul's voice.

"I said stupid! Ignorant! Dumb! Compared to a sophisticated Parisien, you are a farmer. You are not a leader, you are a follower. You believe the absurdities that are only meant for the masses. You believe that all your problems are the other guy's fault. You really believe that everything will be perfect when you secede from Canada. You think you can survive alone, you think you can prosper as a sovereign state. You think that five million French-speaking people can survive in the English-speaking sea which surrounds you. And you think you can do all this without outside help — without an ace in the hole. That is why I call you a fool!"

Suddenly he stopped talking. Then a curse from Paul. "*Maudit enfant chien.*" Then, just as suddenly, Giselle could hear the crash of a bottle as it hit the wall. Panic seized her as the sounds of upsetting furniture, smashing glass and lunging bodies filled the air. She hit as hard as she could on the door but the bedlam continued. She screamed louder. Then finally the noises stopped. "Who is it?"

"Giselle."

The door opened and Paul, dishevelled, his face and body splattered with blood, stood there. "Go away," he commanded. "I'll talk to you later."

"No!" Giselle pushed herself against the door. At first Paul tried to stop her, then realizing she wouldn't go away, he let her in.

François sprawled on the floor, his back propped against the wall. The room was a shambles. "What are you trying to do?" Giselle addressed herself to the two. "Do you want to kill each other?"

A curious expression formed on François' face. "Kill each other?" he asked. "We're not fighting! We were only having a little roustabout." He looked at Paul. "Weren't we?"

Paul pulled a handkerchief from his pocket and wiped the blood from his forehead. "You're hurt!" Giselle tried to help him, but he turned to a small mirror and looked at himself closely.

"It's nothing," he said. "It's nothing at all."

Giselle had put the incident from her mind, but she couldn't help thinking about it as she listened to Pierre expound his theories on explosives. Giselle had already formed a theory of her own on the explosion but it wasn't based on technicalities. As far as she was concerned, Paul had been murdered. And the murderer was François.

Pierre lit a cigarette and forgot to offer one to Giselle. He moved about the room, scratching his head. "You want to know what I feel about the Movement? I'll tell you. I believe in the Movement, not because of what I know about it or what I think I know, but because of what I feel." He stopped and thought for a moment. "I guess I'm just like Madame Hébert. I want to believe in something. I want to believe in somebody I feel is good."

Giselle was touched by the statement. Like all uneducated people, like all inexperienced people, like all the child-like people she had ever met, Pierre wanted to think with his heart instead of his head. She reached out and touched his hand. "I'm glad I know you, Pierre. I'm glad you came to me and I want to know you better. I want to know you so that we can help one another. So that we can work together and think together and learn together." She looked directly into his eyes. "It'll be good for both of us, but I think mostly for you, Pierre. You must learn to believe only because you know what you're doing and why you're doing it. Your feelings aren't reliable, you can't count on them."

"What do you mean, not reliable?"

"I mean, Pierre," said Giselle quietly and slowly, "Your feelings are too easily ignited and too easily influenced by those who wish to use you."

But she could see he didn't understand so she dropped the subject. She would pursue it another time. In the meanwhile he'd be a good ally. Perhaps he could help her find out more about François; why he killed Paul and how he intended to plunge his dagger into the heart of the United States.

7

Giselle decided to take the long way to François' workshop, partly to show Pierre the city, but mostly, because she wanted time to think. She'd lain awake half the night soul-searching and had come up with the only sensible solution to her problem — get out of town. She'd reasoned her only alternative to disaster was to leave the Movement: stop her growing involvement with Pierre, ignore Paul's death, and tell François to do his own dirty work.

But that was last night. Now with the courage of a new day, her mind was changing as she drove Pierre through the narrow, winding streets of Lower Town. She was troubled with vagrant thoughts.

Everything that's logical, she reminded herself, tells me to leave. I don't believe in the Movement. I think the idealists like Bordeaux, Charpentier and that melodramatic fossil Hébert are just bloody fools; I think François, Roger and Ginette are a bunch of bloodsuckers. I think Pierre is a weakling. Or do I? Maybe he's just like most people. The trusting people who only want to live out their lives, who are only looking for a better way of life. She glanced at Pierre, busily taking in the sights; the sparkling waters of the river on their right, the long row of seventeenth-century houses on their left, and the cliffs behind that rose to the Château and beyond to the ancient ramparts of the Citadel, a solid-rock reminder of the colourful history of Québec and the glories of this one-time French colony.

Nobody can force me to stay in the Movement. Bordeaux is still president. He's harmless. François would be different but he's all mouth. Not if he gets his way, of course. He and his psychopathic shadow, Roger, they'd be a couple of proper bastards if François gets to be president. But hell! What have I got to worry about? He doesn't know I suspect him of murdering Paul. I wouldn't tell that to anybody. Not even Pierre! I've never even knocked the Movement to Pierre. Or to anybody else as far as that's concerned. Then why the hell do I have any doubts?

They passed the ferry docks to Lévis, the elevator, called the Ascenseur, that carried tourists from Lower Town to the Terrace on top, and the car shuddered as she drove up the steep cliff road.

How did François get his power in such a short time? He appeared from nowhere, took everyone by surprise, leap-frogging over all the hopefuls that wanted to take Bordeaux's place. Even Paul!

They passed the statue of Samuel de Champlain, one of the greatest of the early French explorers, overlooking the eastern battlements. Then turning abruptly, they arrived at Place d'Armes around which mustered a group of horse-drawn carriages.

François had picked up with Jacques Ginette first. They hit it off right from the start. Then Madame Hébert started having François' meetings at her house. That gave him the big image. How François had managed to do that buffaloed everybody, except me, I guess. That horny bitch! She's too obvious. But nobody seems to notice the way she fawns over him. My bet is that he's paying off between the sheets for every favour she does him in the drawing room. But hell! There goes my dirty mind again.

They drove down rue St. Jean and through the gates of the ancient walled city.

I wish I could tell Pierre. I like him. But God, I can't take the chance. He's got to make his own decisions. I'm not his guardian angel. But I still wish to hell I could tell him to get out without getting in dutch myself.

They drove up Grande Allée.

I'll stay. But only for a while. I'll stick around long enough to find out if that bastard really killed Paul. Then I'll take off for somewhere — Montréal, Toronto. Christ! Even the States if I can get the papers.

They arrived at François' basement workshop. Pierre was surprised when they walked into the old building. Nothing like Madame Hébert's house, he thought.

"Isn't François the chief?" he asked in amazement as he looked at the old frame house with its rickety stairs leading up to open verandahs on each of its three floors.

Giselle had often asked herself the same question, and the answer was always the same. François was not head of the Movement. He was a pretender. A small man with big ideas. A man with no principles, no ethics, no morals. Just a common criminal, hiding behind the mask of a patriot. But she couldn't tell Pierre what was on her mind — not yet. "He's somebody you have to know," she said as she knocked on the door.

A small man with a commonplace face, greying hair and slightly hunched shoulders greeted them. If it were not for his eyes, small, black and penetrating, he would go unnoticed in a group.

His smile had the slightest hint of a sneer as he glanced quickly from Giselle to Pierre.

"Come in, come in," he said in an impatient manner. They followed him through the door into his workshop.

François Lallemont, who travelled with a French passport but whose mother was Yugoslavian and his father Belgian, was not an imposing man. But he was a cunning man, a conniving man who had decided his future lay with the separatists of Québec.

François' first association with the underground had been in World War II when he had fled to France from his home in Brussels following the German invasion. He had found refuge with the French Maquis, an underground force in France which harassed the German occupiers. He had spent almost five years there, sabotaging railway trains, factories, ammunition dumps and anything else he was ordered to destroy. The imaginative qualities of his devious mind served him well, for over and over again, he miraculously escaped detection by the Nazis. His exploits were legendary and his cunning admired.

But fate had made him different from so many of his comrades. His father had been a member of the Belgian Communist Party before the war and when François fled to France, he sought out a friend of his father who introduced him to a group of Communist members of the Maquis. Because of this, François' exploits were not recognized as patriotic actions by non-Communist members of the organization, and he felt like an outsider with almost everyone but his own comrades. The rejection, or at least the feeling of rejection, made him draw into himself, becoming tight-lipped and moody.

When the war was over, he went to Moscow for a short period where he was mildly commended for his work against the Nazis. Too mildly, François thought bitterly. It was a time of reconstruction in the Soviet Union and the country was overflowing with war heroes.

But François did not appreciate what he considered a rebuke. He had worked hard and diligently, had risked his life many times for the Party, and now that it was all over, he felt cheated. However, his circuitous mind was not long in finding a way to strengthen his position. Armed with the fact that he had been a loyal comrade during the war and backed up by many of his Communist friends, he was successful in being retained as an agent for the Soviet Union in France. It was in this capacity that he had served until the Algerian uprising in the 1950's.

It was only after a series of bombing incidents in Algeria

and a close call with death, that François began to analyze his life and a new bitterness came over him. Had he not spent the bulk of his life fighting for the Communist Party? Had he not risked his life, followed orders and devoted himself to the Cause? No matter what he did, wasn't there always more expected of him? There was no future. There was nothing to look forward to. No wealth. No reward for accomplishments. No recognition. Only the constant fear of being expelled from the Party or losing his position because of failure. He had lived like a pauper these last twenty years and unless things changed, he would fare worse than a pauper for the next twenty. But what else was he trained to do? Nothing!

It was during this period that he read about the trouble in Québec. The more he read, the more he wanted to study and learn. What interesting developments were taking place in Québec! Bombings. Riots. Even General de Gaulle had become involved in a separatist rally.

At first François had only glossed over the situation and laughed. It was the same old hassle that had gone on for two hundred years; a small group of backwoodsmen trying to fight off the overwhelming cultural trend of a continent. A minority of radicals trying desperately to hold on to their old customs and language while at the same time complaining of the hardships brought on by their ways. What fools, thought François. What bloody idiots! How could a group of people fight so hard and so long for such a worthless purpose? Then came the profound realization. Hadn't he spent the greater part of his own life doing exactly the same thing? It was unfortunate that he had drifted into it, but it was pathetic that he had remained in it. After all, what had Communism done for him? What had it meant to him? Nothing! And yet he had worked for it so many years. Just like those people in Québec. They were just like him. So he continued to study the situation and soon began to see the overwhelming possibilities that existed for a revolutionary like himself.

There was great promise in Québec. He could see an opportunity so fantastic, so rewarding, that he wondered why no one else had seen it before. There were the circumstances, the temperament of the people. Yes, there was everything in Québec, everything necessary to serve his purpose. And so, he had quit the Communist Party, left his assignment and went to Québec.

The first step of his plan had already been accomplished. In the past two years, he had become an invaluable and necessary part of the Movement. He knew all the important people, his influence was felt in all the important places. He had surrounded himself with the nucleus of his future power, he was accepted as a Frenchman, a radical and a potential leader.

The second step of his plan was to take over the leadership of the Party. But to do this he needed more help and he had decided that two of his pawns were to be Giselle and Pierre. It was to stimulate Pierre's interest that he had asked Giselle to bring him today to his basement workshop.

François walked directly to a cabinet from which he produced a bottle of Grand Marnier, an orange cognac, his favourite drink. Then, without asking, he took three small glasses from the right-hand drawer of an old desk, and filled them with the sweet-smelling liqueur. He handed one to Giselle, the other to Pierre. "Do sit down." He pointed to three chairs, two of which were close together. Giselle took the one by itself. Pierre sat down and François seated himself beside him.

Giselle listened to François as he talked glibly and convincingly to Pierre. His words, like seeds, reached fertile ground, for Giselle could see that Pierre was listening intently, the expression on his face mirroring understanding one moment and complete mystification the next.

"You must learn to do exactly as you are told, Pierre. You are like a soldier. I am the General and you are the soldier. We must work together, we must all do our part."

To Giselle, François sounded like a broken record. She had heard all this so many times before. François bragging about his ideas that he claimed were so much better than Bordeaux's. It was the same sales pitch François had given her so long ago. It was the same line François had given Paul only a few short weeks ago. It had been in this same dingy place and the conversation revolved on the same old theme.

"We mustn't disagree," François had said as he shook Paul's hand that evening. "We are looking for exactly the same thing. You know it and I know it." Then François had turned to Giselle. "Why can't he understand me? It's so simple. Maybe it's because you've been too close to it. Maybe you can't see the forest for the trees. But believe me, Paul. Listen to me. Canada is a tenth-rate power. There's no use denying that. Canada is nothing. It's not a nuclear power. It's nothing!"

Paul lifted his head in resentment and Giselle could feel her heart pumping faster in fear of what might happen. François continued. "Paul, you hate only Canada. But I say it's foolish to think that way. It's short-sighted. It's impractical. Can't you see that the target must be the United States? How many times have I told you?'' Paul looked at Giselle and winked as though to say ''Here we go again.''

''The target must be the United States,'' François repeated. ''Until you can see that, you'll never understand my theory on separation.''

''François, you're crazy! The United States? Why do you always fall back on that old chestnut? Sure, I know the United States has a lot of capital tied up in Québec. Everybody from Montréal to New York knows that. But how can you say the United States has anything to do with our problem of language and culture?''

François put his hand in his pocket and pulled out a package of cigarettes. Then, reaching into his vest, he produced a gold cigarette holder. Slowly and methodically he pushed the cigarette into the holder, placed the holder in his mouth and lit it. Then he spoke.

''I thought you understood, Paul,'' he said, with a tinge of exasperation. ''I've been trying to tell you for two years and I thought you understood, but it's obvious you don't. I can't see how anyone can overlook the possibilities. But then everybody does.'' François blew a smoke ring into the air before continuing. ''Let's review your plan, Paul. Let's forget mine for a minute. Let's review yours.''

Paul nodded.

''Your only desire, Paul is to maintain the French language and the French culture in Québec?''

Paul nodded and smiled.

''In order to do this, you feel you must build a wall around Québec. You must isolate yourself from the rest of the continent. On top of this, you feel you must establish close economic ties with France.''

Paul nodded again. François had a perfect understanding of his plan.

''But there is a flaw, Paul. There is a flaw that you don't see. A fact that you ignore.'' Paul's face clouded. ''Economics won't let you. What you want is impossible. Your plan would bankrupt Québec in a year.'' François searched Paul's face for the frown he tried to hide. He knew it bothered Paul to hear anyone say that Québec could not survive as an economic entity on the North American continent.

''That's the greatest enemy of your plan, Paul, lack of money. If Québec ever separated on your terms, the standard of living would drop fifty percent overnight. That's why those two-bit politicians jump on and off Bordeaux's bandwagon. If they thought the money was good, they'd stay on. But, your plan? Hell, Paul! It just isn't practical. It's too idealistic. The hard facts are that you'd lose your supporters one by one when they found they were starving to death."

François stopped and toyed with the cigarette in his vest pocket. He knew he had Paul confused and he enjoyed it. "Paul, you know it's a gag. I know it's a gag. Everybody knows it's a gag. That's why they all scoff at the Movement. Don't you see how they know it's a gag? They know you're just playing games because everybody suspects Québec would go down the drain economically, the minute we became a sovereign state. And you've got to remember something else, Paul. Québec can't break away from Canada without a damn good reason. The rest of Canada and even the United States might not agree to Québec separating. They could become quite difficult about it. Look what they did when the FLQ got out of hand."

Paul didn't like François and had often told Giselle so. But this time he had controlled his antagonism and answered soberly. "I agree with you, François. I don't like to admit it, but I agree with you. It's going to be a long, hard road, the one we're taking. But a few minutes ago, you said you had a better plan. A bigger plan. You've hinted about it a dozen times in the last year. Why don't you spit it out? Tell me about it. I'm interested."

François smiled. "Suppose," he said slowly and then repeated himself. "Suppose I could show you how you can get everything you want and not suffer the economic problems everyone says we must?"

Paul's face lightened. "That'd be like cake with ice cream," he said, but quickly added, "We'll be lucky to get a slice of bread."

"Why don't you let me finish?"

"Okay."

"What country is the greatest single power on earth?"

"The United States," Paul was quick to answer, "or maybe Russia. But what's that got to do with us?"

"Which is the wealthiest country?" asked François, ignoring Paul's question.

"The United States," Paul said again with no hesitation. "But..."

"And do you know ...?" François asked, "Do you know

where the strength of the United States lies?"

Paul scratched his head. "The strength of the United States? What do you mean?"

"I mean the economic strength," answered François. "Where is their concentration of heavy industry? That's what I mean, friend Paul. Where are the biggest American factories?"

Paul thought for a time. François waited patiently. "I'm no expert on the United States, but I don't think the big factories are in the south," Paul said finally. "I'm sure of that. My guess is the north — probably the north-east."

"Precisely!" François' eyes sparkled. "And how do they transport the raw materials to their factories? How do they send the finished product to their foreign markets?" François was too filled with enthusiasm to wait for an answer. "I'll tell you how, Paul, through the Great Lakes and through the St. Lawrence Seaway. Last year over fifty million tons."

"I know," said Paul. "I know that, François. Everybody knows that. It's an international waterway."

François stubbed his cigarette. "I know it's an international seaway now, Paul. But it doesn't have to be forever."

Paul laughed. "It probably will be," he said. "But what's that got to do with your plan?"

"Here, let me show you." François went to his desk and unrolled a wall map. "Here is North America," he said pointing to the map. "The United States and Canada divided by water — the Great Lakes. Look at the huge cities centred on them, Paul. Chicago." He pointed at Lake Michigan. "Detroit." His finger moved down Lake Huron. "Rochester, Toledo, Buffalo. Need I go on? They fill the boats here for every port in the world. A hundred million tons of it every year. Tankers, freighters, from everywhere. And look where they take it?" He ran his finger along the map. "They float it through Lake Ontario; through the St. Lawrence Seaway to Montréal. Then what happens to it? Look, Paul. Look good. On both sides of the river — what do you see? Québec! For over three hundred miles, Paul, it's Québec on both sides of the river. As a separate state — our river. Ours to control. Ours to command. Ours to do with as we please. Ours to blockade. The hundred million tons would rot in their holds if we bottled up the river."

"There's one snag."

"What's that?"

"If they let you get away with bottling up the river, they'd send their hundred million tons by some other way."

"What way?"

"Railway. Transport. By some other river."

"There is no other river that can handle the ships. It'd cost them twenty dollars a ton to transport it by road or rail. Do you know what that means? Two billion dollars a year."

The unbelieving Paul just stood there.

"They'd pay our tolls, Paul. If they didn't we'd have them right by the nuts."

"What makes you think you could get away with it? It's impossible. The Americans aren't fools. They must have agreements. There must be a treaty."

"You follow my plan," François said smugly, "it's not only possible — it's guaranteed."

"You figure on starting a war?"

François shook his head. "It won't be necessary."

"They'd never let you do it."

"They won't have a choice."

"You're crazy!"

"Like a fox."

"Jesus Christ, François! If you expect me to believe that bullshit, you'll have to spell it out. What is your plan? How do you expect to make it work?"

"My plan," said François simply, "is a secret. You'll have to think about what I've told you. Then you'll have to believe me, have faith in me. Before I tell you any more, you'll have to show me your faith, you'll have to prove your loyalty! You'll have to do exactly as I say."

"Blind faith? You're talking to the wrong guy, François. I haven't had that since I caught the parish priest playing games with my school teacher, and I was only fourteen then."

"I want you to come along with me, Paul, but it's got to be on my terms."

The conversation had ended abruptly. François had ushered them both to the door without further formalities. In the car Giselle had asked Paul, "Do you really believe he's got a workable plan or is he just plain crazy?"

"I believe," Paul had said, and Giselle remembered his exact words, "I believe he has a plan and I think he told us the whole thing. He plans to tell the United States that if he gets elected, he'll charge tolls on the river or close it up. He figures that the Québécois will eat up the idea and vote him in. That's his plan, Giselle. That's it, and I think that's all there is to it."

But Giselle wasn't so easily convinced. She was sure that François had something more up his sleeve.

This incident had taken place only six weeks ago. But Giselle shuddered as she realized that although Paul was dead and buried, François was still pushing his plan.

Pierre was listening intently to François' every word. François realized he had a better dupe in Pierre than he had ever had in Paul, a more easily convinced client for his ideas, a more naive, trusting individual, one who had the makings of a devoted pawn.

Finally, François was finished with Pierre. He stood up and in his customary manner, placed a cigarette in his holder and then with great precision, lit it. "I want you and Giselle to work together," he said in a decisive tone.

"Work together?" Pierre looked at Giselle and his heart leaped. "With Giselle?" He had been dreaming of such a prospect, but hadn't held out much hope.

Giselle turned quickly to François. "Work together on what?" she demanded.

"On a project, Giselle. On the biggest project ever to hit North America. And," François went on with a laugh, "I'll guarantee it'll be the biggest bombshell in both of your young lives."

The restaurant, with its typical French atmosphere, blended almost unnoticed into a line of quaint, old buildings that lined the narrow, cobble-stoned street.

Opening the door, Pierre found himself in a dark, intimate vestibule where rich aromas of cooking delicacies welcomed him. The darkness of the place, after the bright morning sun, blinded him momentarily and he squinted, studying the faces at the tables. But there was no sign of François. A waitress approached. "Table for one, m'sieu?"

"I'm looking for François Lallemont," said Pierre.

"Come with me."

He followed her through a room, a set of French doors, down a hallway and into a meeting chamber. There they found François, seated at a long table with a group of men. Pierre recognized two of them, Henri, the public relations man from St. Hyacinthe, and Roger Flynn, Madame Hébert's handyman, who sat apart from the others at the door, as though on guard. He showed no sign of recognition or friendliness. François, however, beaming, stood up to welcome him. Then, turning to Roger, he said, "Give him your chair."

Anger played in Roger's eyes but his expression did not change. He stood up, gave his chair to Pierre and left the room. François began the introductions. "I want you to meet Pierre LaPointe. I'm expecting big things from him. He was brought into the Movement by Paul. And if that isn't enough, I can tell you that Pierre has already proven himself magnificently." Henri Bédault jerked his head noticeably. He'd been there and didn't swallow the story, but the others remained poker-faced. François continued.

"This is Jacques Ginette, our politician." François patted Jacques on the shoulder. He smiled broadly and reached across the table offering his hand to Pierre.

"Glad to meet you," he said.

François pointed to the next man. "Jean Petrie, our student organizer." Pierre's confidence was increasing rapidly. "Monsieur Charpentier," continued François, as he directed his attention to the man at the far end of the table, "our legal expert." Charpentier nodded but didn't stand or offer his hand. François gestured to the next man. "Henri Bédault, our propaganda expert."

The waitress arrived with a tray of fine crystal glass and filled them with the same orange-coloured drink François had given Pierre at their first meeting. She set one in front of Pierre who might have wondered why he, a simple boy from the backwoods, was being given this VIP treatment.

The luncheon was served almost immediately: Acadian clam chowder, snails garnished with butter sauce, filet mignon and coffee. The rich food impressed Pierre who had been bred on the simplest fare.

In fact, almost everything that had happened during the past few weeks had affected him, awakening interests he had never known, inspiring idealisms that he had never even suspected.

Pierre was certain that François liked him. They were constantly together after their first meeting in François' workshop. Every day, Pierre would report to him, follow his instructions, run errands and, most important of all, discuss the problems of Québec in minutest detail. "You've been terribly abused," François kept reminding him. "Look how poorly you've been treated. Just like all French Canadians, you've been pushed around, betrayed, robbed of your heritage and worst of all, humiliated. And why? Because the English defeated you, forced their ways on you, and now walk over you as though you were a piece of grass."

At first, Pierre hadn't really understood, but as the days wore on and the discussions became more involved, he began to see more clearly what François was getting at. "There's no reason for you to live in defeat, Pierre," François said one day. "We have it in our power to throw off this yoke of oppression. We have the methods to be free. All we need is the will. And when enough of us get that, we'll have our own language, our own culture, our own pride."

Pierre was convinced that François, too, had been Paul's best friend. "We worked together, Paul and me. We worked for a new Québec, a new system, a new justice." Then François would sit down, light a cigarette for himself and, offering one to Pierre, would say, "And now Paul's gone. Killed like a true soldier. A martyr in the cause of freedom."

They spent time in the workshop assembling strange gadgets, driving to out-of-the-way places to procure pieces of equipment François said were essential and, almost always, ending up at Madame Hébert's rambling house in the country where they would sit and talk, waiting for Giselle to pick him up and take him back to his rooming house only a few blocks from her apartment.

One day, while they were waiting, Madame Hébert entered the room and plunked herself on a huge chair beside François. After a few pleasantries, she studied Pierre, then turned intently to François. "Well," she said, "have you decided?"

"Yes," said François solemnly. "I have."

"And you?" She turned her gaze on Pierre. "Are you determined to be loyal to the Movement?" To François? To me? Are you convinced of the righteousness of our cause?"

Pierre felt awkward under her gaze and looked at François who spoke for him.

"He is," he said firmly. "Pierre's a good boy. He believes firmly in our cause. He's shown me his loyalty. He's the man for the job. He loved Paul as much as we, didn't you, Pierre?"

"He was like my father."

"And you'll carry on in his place?"

"I'll try."

"Then it's settled," said Madame Hébert, pushing herself out of the chair.

François hurried up to help her. Pierre stood.

She took his hand, then kissed him on the cheek. "Welcome to the Movement, my dear son," she said tenderly. "We shall see to it that you are well rewarded." She looked affectionately at François who stood beside her. "Won't we, François?"

"Of course, my dear. Of course we will."

With that she left the room. Shortly afterwards Giselle arrived to drive him home.

Pierre was equally convinced that Giselle liked him. He had been glad to spend almost every evening with her and was pleasantly surprised to realize that she enjoyed his company. One evening, just for the sake of something to say, he had said he was thinking of going back to Rivière du Loup or maybe even Labrador. Giselle had shown disappointment and pleaded with him to stay. It sounded as though she wanted him, not for the Movement, but for herself. His hopes brightened considerably after that.

Pierre's reveries were jolted back to the meeting by the sound of his name. François was speaking intently to the group. "Pierre is getting impatient for action," he said jovially. "I wish we were all as impatient. Pierre has the right essentials. New blood! Young blood! Impatient blood! That's what we need. The winds of change are blowing our way, but unless we play along with them, unless we unfurl our sails and use the winds for all they're worth, we'll drift in the doldrums forever." He turned his attention to Jean Petrie, the student activist. "We must work harder on the students," he coaxed, "get better organized, more enthusiasm. Make more demands. Time is running out. We have no more time for academics, no time for red tape. Like a welder moulding iron, we must fashion our plans while the climate in Québec is hot. Once the heat has died, it will take a thousand times more pressure to turn circumstances our way again. Now is the time to fire the furnace of Québec; now is the time the country must be bent to our will." François stopped abruptly, individually scanning their faces. He smiled, realizing how he held them all in the palm of his hand, all except Charpentier. "What have you done, Petrie?" he demanded, pointing his finger. "In two minutes, tell us what's happened since our last meeting."

Petrie smiled confidently. "We've organized Québec into communes and have commanders for each area. Each commune is divided into four cells and they, too, have leaders." He looked at the group for approval. Jacques Ginette's smile was the broadest. "Each cell commander deals individually with the schools in his area," Petrie went on. "When student councils co-operate, we deal directly with them. If not, we organize opposition to them." He laughed. "We're not having much trouble. Most councils are easily sold. They're enthusiastic. In fact, I believe they're our strongest weapon."

"Where's your greatest strength?" asked François.

"Montréal," replied Petrie with no hesitation.

"Can we rely on them for support?"

Petrie nodded.

"What do they think of violence?"

"Not too much. They're leery of it after . . ."

"Are they convinced that we're non-violent?"

"I think so."

"Will you have all the commune members at our leadership conference next month?"

"Yes."

"Good!" François slammed his fist on the table. "That's what I like — action." He turned to Jacques Ginette. "And what about you, Jacques? What's happening in your department?"

Jacques' face beamed with his ever-present smile. "As you know, gentlemen, we now have candidates in every riding, and I know they'll all be at the conference, rooting for you, François, as the new president of our Movement. In the meantime, they're working hard in their constituencies, building a strong, grass-roots machine, explaining the merits of our philosophy and gaining new supporters, day after day."

"Good." François seemed delighted.

"There is one major problem I must explain, if I may, gentlemen," Jacques added quickly. "In the political sphere we're having more difficulties in recruitment of candidates, than, perhaps, Jean is having with the students. Not in quantity, mind you, but in quality. You see, most sophisticated politicians feel they can't win on a separatist ticket. The failures of the past have discouraged them, and, after all, every politician wants to win. So, in some areas we have to compromise, take a candidate whose experience is limited, who is politically naive. However, when some of Petrie's students graduate, I'm sure this problem will be solved."

François interrupted. "We can't think that way, Jacques. We can't sit around and wait. The time to act is now. This year. This month. This week."

Jacques was unruffled. "I didn't say impossible, François. I said more difficult. What we need is a good slogan that'll catch on. Something like the Americans had in the Japanese war. What was it — 'remember Pearl Harbour'? Or maybe something like Hitler's 'guns before butter.' We need something to unite every French Canadian under our banner."

"We'll get one. We'll have one before I've warmed up the presidential chair." François' voice was low and sincere. "We'll focus world attention on us and our problems. We'll show the world how we've been mistreated. We'll prove beyond a doubt that our destiny must lie in our own hands. The British and the Americans must get out of our affairs. We are Québécois, not Canadians." He cut his voice to a whisper. "The world will agree that the St. Lawrence belongs to us. Our river must be returned to us."

The room was quiet. It was obvious that the reference to the St. Lawrence produced skepticism. No one really believed that a sovereign Québec would own a sovereign St. Lawrence.

The obvious lack of enthusiasm did not appear to affect François. "And what have you to report?" He directed his question to Charpentier who was caught off guard. He sat quietly for a moment, fingering his beard, composing his thoughts. When he spoke, his well-trained voice was firm.

"In the first place, I feel that this meeting is out of order. It should never have been called without Bordeaux. He is our president and until someone succeeds him, I feel it is our duty to follow his directions only."

François leaned across the table, his face breaking into what he hoped was a smile. "You know I called this meeting, Charpentier. As well, you must know why Bordeaux is not here. He knows I'm opposing him in the presidential elections next month. He's leaving the field wide open for me. You knew too, Charpentier, that I want your support. That's why I called this meeting." He sat back in his chair and shrugged. "However, gentlemen, we live in a democratic society. I can't tell you what to do. I can only ask for your support. We're all working for the same cause, the freedom of Québec. Whether it's me or Bordeaux as president, really doesn't matter. I suggest to you that I will make a better leader than Bordeaux. If you follow my plan, Québec will be ours within the year. Can Bordeaux promise that?"

Charpentier ignored the question. "You asked for my legal opinion, our rights to seize the river," he said. "I'll give you my opinion, frankly and honestly. We have no rights of seizure. We could never take the river. We'd be playing with dynamite if we tried."

The reference to dynamite brought a rise out of the group. Even François smiled momentarily, but hastened back to the subject.

"Why?" he asked.

"Because of the international treaty," responded Charpentier. "The rights to use the river are controlled by the treaty."

"Treaty? Whose treaty?"

"Canada and the United States."

"And Québec? Did Québec sign?"

"Yes," said Charpentier sadly. "Signed by Canada on behalf of the province of Québec. It may not be to our liking, but that's the way it is. That's the law. And if we try to break the law, we may have to accept some rather dire consequences. In plain language, we'd better not interfere with the right of American ships to use the river." With that he was finished and a marked silence followed, finally broken by François.

"Not even if they present a danger to our citizens?"

"A danger?"

"A terrible danger."

"How?" asked Charpentier with exasperation.

"The horror of a nuclear holocaust," François stated dramatically.

Charpentier shrugged. "I don't understand."

"By transporting nuclear bombs through our river, past our cities, beside our villages."

"Nuclear weapons! How do we know they transport nuclear machinery through the St. Lawrence?"

"How do we know they don't? Do we inspect their ships, or are they so invincible, we don't dare?"

"We don't inspect American ships. Why should we?"

"You mean why shouldn't we? If one of their warships carried a bomb and it exploded, it would kill thousands of our people."

"If it did have a bomb, why should it explode?"

"An accident. A collision. A miscalculation. Anything could happen. Something will happen, unless we stop it. The Americans use our river as if they owned it. Québec must inspect all ships on our river. It is our right. I demand it!"

"Ridiculous!" scoffed Charpentier. "The federal authorities have this well in hand."

"What do they care for us?" demanded François. "What do they care about the safety of Québécois? They only care about contraband. They leave the American warships alone. They're pawns for the Americans."

"Nonsense!" Charpentier cut in. "The Americans have used the river peaceably for decades. They've always respected the treaty."

"A one-sided treaty, signed in the gun-powder era," shouted François. "Now we're in the atomic age. Have we forgotten that? An accident today would be a disaster."

Charpentier lashed back. "And what would you do, if you found an atomic bomb in the hold of an American destroyer? Even when we are a sovereign state. What would you do?"

"We would seize it," François retorted.

"What good would that do?" said Charpentier. "The Americans would simply come and get it."

"Would they?" François laughed. "Would they?"

"Of course," replied Charpentier. "Do you think they'd put up with that kind of nonsense?"

"They'd have to," laughed François. "They've been running scared ever since Vietnam. Look what they did to get out of that mess. You don't think they'd risk another situation like that, not on their own doorstep."

"I can't believe you." Charpentier was more serious now. "International law would back them up. The United States is the mightiest nation on earth. It would be like a mouse challenging a lion. You're playing with fantasies, François. Your plan sounds like the illusions of a madman and I, for one, cannot follow a madman."

François jumped to his feet, his face crimson. "You call me a madman? You dare to say that!" Then his voice changed quickly and he pointed his finger at Charpentier. "If I can give you an example of how a mouse tweaked the lion's nose and got away with it, will you listen to me then?"

"Perhaps."

"I'll use only one name," said François. "I'll use only the name San Pueblo and I'll mention only one country, North Korea. When they seized the Pueblo, my friend Charpentier, they were as small as we, like your mouse. But did the lion pounce on the mouse? Did the mighty American fleet sail into the North Korean harbour to retrieve their ship? No! No! No! They huffed and they puffed and they threatened and they pleaded. But they didn't attack."

Silence fell over the room. Everyone had heard of the North Korean seizure of the American ship on the high seas and the imprisonment of the crew. It had been front page news for months. Now, here was François suggesting the same could be done in Québec. Not on the high seas, but in territorial waters of an inland trade route.

Charpentier was momentarily stopped. But he soon regained his wits. "There was one factor that was present in North Korea that is not present here, François," he said. "If the United States had gone into North Korea and seized the Pueblo, they would have had Russia and China to contend with. But it's different here, François. When Québec separates, we'll stand alone with no power in the world that could come to our aid."

François couldn't argue this point. Not yet. Not in the open. He'd have no scruples when he was leader of the Movement; when the Movement was the Government of Québec. And when Québec was a sovereign state, he'd use whatever possibilities existed at that time. He wouldn't hesitate to accept the help of Russia, China, Cuba or France. Anyone! As long as they'd pay the price. He wasn't like Charpentier with his ethics and principles. He wasn't like any of the others. But now wasn't the time for open discussion on this crucial issue. Not even with the most trusted members of the Movement. "You're a very intelligent man, Charpentier. And I bow to your knowledge of international law and to your observations. But I'm sure you do agree on one point — the nose of the lion has been tweaked by one mouse. Do you not consider it feasible that it could be tweaked again by another?"

Everyone laughed; even Charpentier smiled, and François had won his point. The eyes of the men had betrayed their hopes. All of them, except Charpentier, welcomed the power-play approach even if they didn't quite understand it.

François turned to Henri Bédault. "Will you see that my fears are reported in the newspapers?" he asked. "At least, I want the Québécois to know of my suspicions. I want them to know that, at least, one man in Québec recognizes an existing danger. I want everyone to known that François is thinking ahead. Thinking of the welfare of our people along the banks of the St. Lawrence. I want it to be said when disaster comes that 'François prophesied this. François could see it while all the others were blind.' "

Henri looked at Charpentier. "Unless Bordeaux okays it, I can't represent your statements as party policy." Then he hesitated. "Why not publish it as your own personal view? It would still be on the records."

"Do what you can. Do the very best you can." François looked at his watch. "I know how busy you are, gentlemen, and I won't keep you any longer." He lifted his half-filled glass. "*Bon santé.*" They lifted their glasses, drained them, then, one by one, left the room. Pierre and François were left alone. François poured another drink.

"You wanted action," said François as he raised his glass. "You wanted action and you're going to get it. I want you to begin preparations. Get your mind in tune. Think of the need for perfect timing. This is important. Do you understand?"

"I think so," lied Pierre.

"You heard our discussions. You can see they need my leadership, can't you?"

"Yes."

"Then, Pierre," said François lifting his glass slowly to his lips and sipping it, "it's up to us to create a danger."

"How?"

"An incident, Pierre. An incident is the technical name. Since fate hasn't been kind enough to supply us with a danger, then we must take matters into our own hands."

"But?"

"A collision with an American warship," said François casually, "would be an incident. Blowing up an American warship as it passes through our river."

"But what good will that do?"

"Try to understand. People let a situation go on and on without doing a damn thing. Then something happens. They try to make up for their previous neglect. They over-react too hastily. What I mean is this. Today when I pointed out the danger on our river, they scoffed at me. But, once the danger shows itself, then

I'll be a hero, and everything I say will be accepted. Wait and see, Pierre. For you and Giselle are going to make it happen and everything will change quickly, just like you want it to. It won't be like it is now: dormant, inert, inactive. The Movement's been stagnating under Bordeaux's leadership. Under my leadership, we'll make quick, decisive actions. We'll move again. Hit the headlines.''

"How will we . . . what will happen . . . if we bomb an American warship?''

"We'll only scratch it.'' François carefully inserted a cigarette in his holder and lit it flamboyantly. "We'll make a big noise. People will talk. Then, everyone'll run around like chickens with their heads cut off, racing in all directions, demanding this and that. And then I'll say 'I warned you,' and then, our people in the Movement will insist that I be their leader. The people of Québec will rally around me and say 'François was the only man who saw the danger.' The people of Québec will call for me. We'll topple the government. We'll be the new power. And then, Pierre, there's only one more step. We'll say to the whole world 'We're separated from Canada.'' We'll seize what's rightly ours, Pierre. We'll seize Québec and later on Labrador and the North Shore of New Brunswick. It's all rightfully ours. It's all ours. Our river, Pierre! Remember that. It's our river and when anybody says 'you shouldn't have done that,' we'll point to the explosion and say 'there was a danger we couldn't tolerate.' And they'll understand and agree. Take my word for it, Pierre, it's a foolproof plan.''

Pierre nodded in assent, but his brain was whirling. He knew he should have run away before, but now, *Mon Dieu*, is it too late to run now?

"Pierre,'' François went on. "The timing of the explosion is of vital importance. You must follow my every order to the letter. After all, Pierre, you owe me a lot. If it wasn't for me, you'd be in jail. You know that, don't you? You needed my help then, I need your help now. But you still need me, Pierre. Remember that! The case isn't closed. You still need me. You can't escape that.''

Pierre's heart beat wildly as he fought to maintain his composure. It was almost as though François had read his mind. It was almost as though François knew that he wanted to run away. What a stupid fool he'd been. He'd forgotten the time would come for action. All his talk and bravado in front of Giselle! Sure, he'd wanted action. But not to bomb a warship!

"Remember your promise to Madame Hébert. It was like a solemn vow, Pierre. Working for me is like avenging Paul's death. If you were to betray me, it would be like betraying Paul. Like running out on everything you believe."

Pierre fought the urge to turn and run, to get out, to get away from François and the rest of these people. To get back to the security of his home near Rivière du Loup and his friends, Emile and Yvonne. But he couldn't go. He couldn't be a coward in front of François. On top of that, Giselle would find out, and Giselle was becoming more important to him with each passing day.

François leaned across the table. In a whisper he continued. "It isn't the Movement you're working for, Pierre. It wasn't the Movement that saved you from the police. It was me! You're working for me. Maybe I should say, you're working with me. Just like Paul."

"Paul? Wasn't he in the Movement?"

"Of course he was, Pierre. But he was planning on bigger things. We were going ahead together, me and Paul. He should have been the next president. I was going to support him."

"I didn't know."

"He was too modest to tell."

"I thought he was only . . ."

"He was a leader. You know that. Wasn't he like a father to you? Weren't you like his son? You said so. He wanted you with him, didn't he?"

"Yes."

"Why?"

"I don't know."

"I'll tell you. He wanted you in the Movement. Like I want you. You can't betray Paul. You can't betray me."

"I won't." Pierre licked his lips.

"Good. Now I'll tell you what was on Paul's mind just before he died."

There was no response.

"He wanted you to contact your friend Emile. He wanted you to get more explosives from him. Even more than you've got before."

"But . . ."

"No 'buts,' Pierre. That's how you got the explosives before?"

"Yes."

"Then you'll get them again. We'll need about ten boxes."

"Ten!"

"The sides of that American destroyer are made of ten-inch steel. We've got to have enough to bend it a little. What good would it do if we didn't make a big noise or bend it a little?"

"But ten boxes would sink it."

"Okay, Pierre. You're the expert. We don't want to sink it. Just dent it. Make it six or eight boxes, if you think that's enough." François studied Pierre's reaction. He was scared and confused. That was obvious. Like a fish trying to spit out that hook, he was trying in his inexpert way to beg off. But François, the skillful angler, had him well secured. All he needed now was to net him. "Working with Giselle on Madame Hébert's boat will be fun, Pierre. This little job is only the beginning for you. Mind this, Pierre. I don't think we'll be able to spare you for any more of this kind of work. With explosives, I mean. You're far too important for that. You'll have earned it too. You'll deserve the position Paul wanted you to have. A top position of trust in the Movement."

Pierre's defences crumbled under François' onslaught. How could he deny Paul? Or even François or Madame Hébert who had both been such good friends. Then there was the pleasure of working with Giselle. His pride. His hopes for Québec. Yes, that was something he'd forgotten lately — lost in all the facts and ideas presented to him by François in their daily meetings — his hopes and dreams for his people.

He thought of Father Moreau's story of the bear. How it had been cornered and fought back. There was no question in Pierre's mind any more. Québec was like that bear and the Americans were its tormenters. Québec would have to fight back. That meant Pierre. He was Québec.

"I'll ask Emile to get the dynamite."

"Good!" François was glad to get the commitment. "You will contact Emile immediately. Tell him nothing about its use. In three days' time, you will tell me when the explosives will be ready." With that, he left the room, leaving Pierre sitting alone at the deserted table, his right hand still holding the half-filled glass of liqueur.

When Pierre left the café, he was confused and strangely depressed. It was still very early in the afternoon, and he had almost three hours before he could meet Giselle at her apartment. He wandered up the narrow street to the Place d'Armes where he sat down beside the fountain in the centre of the square. Giselle had told him of the significance of the square. It was a scene of military parades and public meetings when the French had owned all of Québec and half of the United States. Even when the English took over, they had continued the tradition, but later the people of Québec had erected the Monument of Faith which stood in the centre of the square.

Pierre looked at the Monument of Faith and wondered how much faith he had in himself. He thought of the faith of his fore-fathers. He thought of his people's faith in the church. He thought of the faith which he held in his heart. Yes, it was faith. Faith, that what François was going to do would be good. Faith, that this land would be returned to the French to whom it belonged. It would be taken from the hands of England forever, and the despised English would suffer the indignities which the French had endured for so many centuries. And then, Pierre realized what it was that was bothering him. What was making him depressed. All his life he had despised the English, and now today, François never mentioned the English and placed the blame instead on the Americans. Why? Why was the blame gradually being switched from the English to the Americans? It didn't make any sense.

The thought disturbed Pierre and he stood up and walked around the fountain and across the square. In front of him was the imposing sight of the Château Frontenac Hotel, to his left was the giant statue of Champlain, behind him were four roads leading to Lower Town. He wandered across the square, but stopped short when he saw a life-size statue of a British Redcoat. He studied the sign below it. "The Redcoats are coming," it said, "a show every thirty minutes." The sight of the seventeenth-century British soldier, commonly known as the Redcoat in historical documents, interested Pierre. He stuck his head inside the door. There was a girl standing behind a counter. "What is this?" he asked. "What do you mean 'The Redcoats are coming'?"

The girl smiled and spoke to him in French. "It is for the

tourists," she said. "It is the story of Québec and its battles. It is very interesting."

"Is it a movie?"

"No."

"Is it a stage play?"

"No."

"Then what is it?"

"It's just a model of old Québec," said the girl. "It tells the story of what happened here."

"You mean when the English came?"

"And the Americans," the girl said, to Pierre's surprise.

"And the Americans?"

"Sure."

"I didn't . . ."

"Don't you want to go in? It only costs a dollar," said the girl.

"I'd like to, but I don't have the money." With a shrug, he turned to the door.

"Wait a minute. We're very quiet right now," said the girl. "If you don't have the money, you can go in for nothing." Then she added, "The next show starts in fifteen minutes."

"Thanks, I might take you up on that."

Outside in the clear September air, the sun streaked down on a cobblestone walk. Instead of turning left and taking the road to Lower Town, he crossed the street, walked past Champlain's monument and then across the Terrace. There were many people strolling on the Terrace, on one side of which stands the Château Frontenac, on the other, a sheer precipice dropping to Lower Town. From the Terrace can be seen the historic old buildings of Lower Town, the churning, relentless waters of the St. Lawrence and the rising hills of Lévis on the opposite bank.

Pierre looked at Champlain's monument, high up on a stone column. The plaque on the base of the monument gave notice that this was the exact site of Fort St. Louis which Champlain himself built in 1620. Pierre stood there, hat in hand, before the monument, and a thrill of pride swept over him as he read the legend of this great French explorer.

He must see the show, he must see what happened here. He must see what happened between the Redcoats and the Americans.

From the Terrace, he walked quickly past the monument, crossed the cobblestone street, and into the Fort de Musée, directly to the girl. "I appreciate your offer," he said. "Can I still take you up on it?"

The girl smiled. "Go ahead," she said.

Pierre walked through the curtained doorway and found himself in a small theatre. The seating arrangement was such that he looked down on the stage which held a model of the St. Lawrence River, Québec City and the surrounding countryside. It was as it was in 1759. Soon the lights dimmed and the show began.

The recorded narrative told of the ancient fortified village, the building of the Citadel, and finally, of the City of Québec. Then it went on to explain the six sieges of Québec; some of them were small and insignificant, Pierre had never heard of any. As the narrator described the events in the battle, a map on the front of the stage lit up. "In 1759, Louisburg, the French fortress guarding the St. Lawrence, was besieged and taken by the British. Fort Duquesne, now the site of Pittsburgh, was also captured. At almost the same time, the British General Wolfe defeated the French General Montcalm and occupied Québec. From that moment, the English controlled the North American continent from Labrador to Florida, from Hudson Bay to the Gulf of Mexico, and from the Mississippi Valley to the Atlantic. As a result, the British ruled Québec and its defeated French colonists. However, they did not interfere with the customs of the French inhabitants, and, indeed, did not impose a government upon them. Instead the seig-neurial system, the rule by the leaders of the Roman Catholic church, was allowed to continue."

Pierre could not believe what he was hearing. This was impossible. Or was it? The hated English had invaded and con-quered Québec, and had allowed them all the privileges they had enjoyed before? This was not what Pierre had been taught. But he listened, as the story continued.

"The next invasion of Québec," the narrator continued, "was by the Americans." Pierre leaned forward in his seat and listened intently. "The Americans invaded Montréal and defeated it under the command of Generals Montgomery and Benedict Arnold. At this time, the British and the French, as allies, defended Québec." This statement completely shocked Pierre. Never, never had he heard that the British and the French had been allies. The voice continued. "The Americans besieged Québec City and, on the last day of 1775, the Americans launched an attack in a blinding snow storm. So strong was the defence by the heroic British and French inside the fort, that the Americans were driven off and their leader, Montgomery, killed. The Americans continued to harass

Québec City, until the arrival of ten thousand British troops in May, 1776, which relieved the fort and guaranteed the freedom of the French inhabitants."

The show was finished, and Pierre left the theatre quickly. He nodded to the girl as he went out. She smiled back. Pierre was confused by what he had just seen. Ever since he could remember, his teachers in school and the priests in church had taught him that the English would stop him from worshipping in his own church, and deny him the right to speak French. Pierre had faith in his leaders and believed them. But it didn't really make that much sense, not if the story he had just heard was true. Not if the English had been the allies of the French against the Americans.

Pierre wandered back to the Terrace. Maybe François is right, he mused, maybe the Americans are the real enemy of Québec. They were in 1776 and maybe they still are. Suppose, he asked himself as he leaned on the Terrace rail and looked down the cliff to Lower Town, suppose the Americans had defeated the French and English in that last battle. Suppose General Montgomery had not been killed but instead, had taken Québec. It looks like that would have happened, if the French and the British had not been allies. And if they did, would they have been so lenient as the conquering English had been?

Perhaps François was right, thought Pierre. Perhaps François is more intelligent, smarter than the seigneurs and the priests. After all, hadn't Paul often insisted that the Americans exploited the Québécois? Pierre remembered the time when he wanted to go across the border and work in the log mills. What had Paul said? He had told him not to bother with the Americans. "They are no good," he had said. "They will rob you of your language and your culture." Yes, thought Pierre as he walked along the heavy wooden planks of the Terrace. Yes, I must listen more closely to François. The Americans are our real enemy. It is the Americans that we must fight.

Pierre looked down onto the long stretch of the St. Lawrence River, reaching as far as his eyes could see in both directions. He caught sight of a great, ocean-going ship, loaded to capacity with a cargo destined for far-off lands. It had come from the very centre of the continent, and was now steaming its way toward the broad Atlantic. Pierre looked at its flag streaming in the wind. It was the Stars and Stripes.

He looked at his watch. He had to meet Giselle. He turned and hurried toward the bus stop outside the Château Frontenac.

10

He missed the bus by inches. It pulled away, leaving its acrid exhaust hanging in the air, just as Pierre rounded the corner. He yelled, but the driver ignored him. It would be ten minutes before the right bus came again. He could walk it almost as quickly.

Pierre seemed able to think better when he walked, and now was the time for thinking. Everything's at stake, he reminded himself. I'm either in or out. I've got to do what François says, or run away. But, my God! What am I getting into? How'd I ever get into this thing? Paul! He got me in. But now he's not here, how can I get out? I'm not even sure what's going on. Madame Hébert says I need the Movement. François says I owe him something because he kept me out of jail. They're right. I heard the newscast myself. I owe them something. But holy Christ! An American warship! How? Jesus! I could get killed!

He felt sick and ashamed when he thought of his fear. It was the same fear that had stopped him from helping Paul in the station. Made him run to Henri instead of to a doctor. And now that stinking guilt! It was just like when René got drowned. The same fear was there then, the same quaking that had stopped him from jumping in to help, maybe to save René's life. But Christ! If I'd jumped in, I'd have got drowned myself.

That's why Giselle called me a coward. Because I'm gutless. Maybe I could've saved René, maybe Paul. But how do I know? I'll never find out. I can't change the past, unless I can make up for what I've done.

Paul was working with François. He told me. He must've liked François' ideas. Maybe that's why he wanted me in. To help him with this big job. Like François says, if I run away, it'll be like I ran away at the station. Just like I'm running out on Paul again.

He turned the corner. The apartment was only a block away.

Giselle wants me to stay. When I told her I was going back to Rivière du Loup, she almost cried. She likes me. I can tell that. She liked Paul too, but he was like her father. Not like me. I'm her age. We think the same. She's innocent. It must have been tough for her. An orphan. He aunt dying like that. Paul getting her a job. No wonder she liked him. I'd better talk to her. I'll ask for her advice.

He flicked his cigarette into the gutter at the front of the apartment, opened the outer door with the key Giselle had given him, and walked up the hall. Maybe I should get a real job. Maybe we could get married. Maybe I could get out of this mess.

Noises from inside the apartment made him stop before he inserted the key — raucous, loud, drunken noises. He listened. A woman's shrill laughter echoed through, followed by two men's guffaws. Pierre inserted the key and opened the door.

The noise stopped abruptly as all eyes turned on him. It was a tall, heavy-set man beside Giselle who spoke first. "Come on in," he bellowed. "Come on in and join the party." Pierre's face darkened as the man grasped the resisting Giselle around the waist, and drew her close. Pushing herself away, she said in French, "These are my friends, Pierre. I'd like you to meet them. My employer, Max Friedman." She pointed to the man who had just spoken. "This is Bill Jackson, and this," she led him to the girl, "is Gloria." Then, directing her attention to the three, she introduced Pierre, ending up with, "He was a friend of Paul's."

"Paul!" Max retreated to the alcove where he poured another drink. "You mean that separatist you were hanging around with?"

A quick glance from Giselle told Pierre to be quiet.

Max handed Pierre a drink. "You're a hell of a lot younger than that clown. I hope you've got more brains." Pierre felt his anger rising at the man's attitude even though he didn't understand the full gist of the remark spoken in English.

"Paul was his best friend, Max. You shouldn't speak like that." It was Giselle and she put her hand on Max's shoulder.

"Why not? Since when can't I say what I'm thinking?"

"He's dead," Giselle reminded him.

"Good riddance," laughed Max returning to the alcove for two more drinks. He handed one to Giselle and took a large gulp from the other. "Let's dance." He increased the volume of the record player. "Let's dance," he said again as he took Giselle in his arms.

Pierre felt angry and uncomfortable as he watched. Unconsciously, he moved back into a corner where he stood sipping his drink. Why was Giselle making up to this pig? How could she stand having his hands on her? The hatred in Pierre's eyes showed clearly. How he'd like to beat this son-of-a-bitch to a pulp. Him and his filthy roving hands. For the first time in years, he wished he could understand English better. Just so he'd know what they were saying. The few necessary words he'd learned in Labrador weren't enough. They were talking too fast. He didn't want to drink with these people. Just like all the damned English! Walking into someone's home and taking over. Ignorant bastards with no culture.

The music ended and Giselle extricated herself from Max's reaching arms. She sat beside Gloria. Max brought another drink to her. "Drink it down, honey. You're too sober." Together they drank and talked, hardly noticing Pierre, who still stood in the corner. Despite his antagonism, he envied the way these two men carried on. He envied their way of telling jokes and evoking squeals of laughter from the girls. One moment he wished he could be like them, the next he felt a deep resentment. He wished he could join them. Wished he had something to offer. But he didn't and he knew it. Like a little boy afraid to join an adult group, he just stood there, not knowing what to say or do. Finally, Max looked across the room.

"Hey!" he pointed to Pierre. "What's the matter with you? That's no way to act at a party. Come on over here and join the happy throng." He laughed loudly. Pierre forced a smile. Max motioned to him again. "Come on," he said. Pierre stood his ground.

"What's the matter?" Max chided. "You don't *parlez-vous* the English?"

This brought a rise out of Pierre. "I *parlez-vous* French. It's good enough for me."

"Then you can talk!" said Max in French as he turned to Giselle. "I thought he was a separatist," he said. "But he can't be, he actually spoke English."

"Stop it," ordered Giselle. "Stop it, or I'll have to ask you to leave."

"Leave?" Max's back was up. "Now look here, Giselle, that bottle's only half gone and I'm not leaving here until it's empty."

"Well then, behave yourself. Pierre's my friend."

"Well any friend of yours . . ." Max turned again to Pierre. "Where're you from, boy?" he asked in French.

"Rivière du Loup."

"Rivière du Loup. River of the wolves?"

"Wolf River," corrected Giselle.

"Where is it?"

"On the St. Lawrence, about a hundred miles down river."

"Oh, I see," said Max. "You must forgive me, Pierre. I'm not from around here. I'm from the big city. New York. I'm sorry. It must be terrible coming from a place like that, with people ribbing you about it all the time."

"It's not so bad."

But Max Friedman, co-ordinator of American shipping on the St. Lawrence, was not to be put off. "Are you a separatist, boy?" he asked, still speaking French.

Pierre gulped. He had never been asked this question before, and he didn't really know what to say. He looked nervously at Giselle whose face was blank. "Yes," he said, "I am."

"Well, I've finally met one who admits it." Max stood up, towering six inches over Pierre. "Tell me all about it," he said. "What are you planning to do and when are you planning to do it?"

Pierre surprised himself with his reply. "We're going to separate," he said, "and we're going to do it by 1979."

"Who are you going to separate from, boy?"

Pierre remembered François' words and was glad now he had listened so intently. "We're going to separate from Canada and we're going to be by ourselves. We don't want the United States telling us what to do anymore. We want to be alone."

"Well that's very interesting." Max returned to the alcove. "So you're going to live by yourselves, way up here in the big north woods? What'll you say if I tell you, you'll never do it? It's all a pipe dream. You haven't a Chinaman's chance. Hell, boy, look what you've got up here. You've got ice and snow for nine months of the year and a hell of a lot of nothing for the rest of the time. Look fellow, I'm old enough to be your dad and I tell you this. You don't know what you're talking about. What you should do is join the good old United States. That's what side your bread's buttered on. You should join the United States and really be something."

"Like you?"

"Sure, fellow. And let me tell you something else. If it weren't for guys like me, you'd still be living in log huts up here."

Pierre stopped thinking. "Get out of here," he said in a low voice.

"Get out! Go to hell."

"I said get out. Get out before I throw you out."

Max shrugged his shoulders and looked at Giselle.

"How can you be so rude?" she cut in.

Pierre ignored her. "Get out," he yelled, and pushed Max who began to realize that Pierre meant business. He backed off. "Let's go," he said to his friends who seemed quite willing to leave. Max finished his drink and said goodbye to Giselle with the pretense of a smile. Giselle protested, but it was no use. Pierre wouldn't listen to her and herded the three out the door.

When they had gone, Giselle turned on him. "You stupid, ignorant ass," she screamed. "Do you realize what you've done?"

The fury in Pierre's eyes abated momentarily, but then it returned. "You heard what he said. He can't talk to me like that in my home."

"Your home? I was under the impression this was my apartment."

"I mean in Québec."

"You fool! You bloody fool."

"A fool? I'm a fool because I want to stand up and fight for my country? I'm a fool because I won't be insulted by a foreigner? Giselle, you are the fool. You play along with these bastards. You pretend to like them when you hate their guts. You've told me you do. So, if I'm a fool, then I'm an honest fool. I tell them I hate them. I tell them I'll fight them. And I'm not fooling. I'll fight. I'll die and I'll die gladly, if I have to. But I won't give in to them."

Giselle heaved a sigh, sat on the chesterfield and lit a cigarette. "Do you know who he is?"

"Of course I do. He's an American."

"Do you know that he's my boss? Do you know he signs my pay cheque? Do you know that I get shipping information for the Movement? Do you know that if he fires me, there's no other way to get the information?"

Pierre ignored her questions and crouched to a kneeling position before her. "Giselle, do you know what I'm thinking? I'm thinking François is right. The Americans are our enemies. We've got to help him. And the Movement. It's our only way to help ourselves. We'll work together. Won't we? We'll do what he says. That's why I came over early. To talk to you about it."

Giselle changed the subject abruptly. "Will you do me a favour?" she asked.

"You know I will. I'll do anything for you. You know that."

"Then leave me alone. Get the hell out of here."

"Why?"

"Let's just say I can't stand the sight of you right now. Let's just say that I don't want to be bothered any more. I just don't give a good goddamn any more."

But when Pierre had left, Giselle wearily poured herself another drink. "Why do I bother with this fool?" she asked herself. "He's so damn serious. Why don't I meet some people that are fun? But maybe, that's what's been wrong with my life. Too much of the wrong kind of fun. Have I ever been sensible about men? Certainly not with Armand. I loved him but he was only after me for what he could get. Maybe with Paul. He helped me. Or did he? He got me off the street. But in return, he got me mixed up in this thing. And which is worse?"

Suddenly, the realization hit her that it was Pierre, and only Pierre, who had ever reached out his hand to help and had asked for nothing in return. "I'll do anything for you." And he had meant it. Meant it sincerely and openly and honestly. But the thought disturbed her. "To hell with him," she said to herself as she poured the rest of the bottle into her glass.

Pierre walked home, partly because he didn't have the money for a cab but mostly to think. He lingered by the telephone at the rooming house. Then he picked it up and called Madame Hébert's house. The maid answered, but soon François was on the line.

"I need some money if I'm gonna call Emile. And I'll need more if I have to go and see him."

"Of course." François accepted the call as a commitment. Pierre had decided to do as he was told. He'd been too sheepish about it earlier at the café. But now, he sounded as though he'd made up his mind to go all the way. Something must have happened to change his mind.

"Don't worry about the money," François said. "Charge the phone call to my number and as far as going to Emile's, I'll get an advance for you, as soon as you confirm the need for a visit to your friend."

When Pierre hung up, he felt sick and wished he had the money for a bottle. He'd kill it quick. Anything to numb this lost and lonely feeling. This feeling that it was the end of the world.

"Who was it, darling?"

"Just business. Nothing for you to bother your pretty head."

"Oh, you silly boy! Just for that I'm going to surprise you."

"Surprise?"

"Yes, you naughty boy. Saying those foolish little things. Just at the right time. You don't know how it pleases me. Come with me."

François followed Eloise Hébert into the dining room of her old house, where two candles flickered on the classically set table. The silverware sparkled in the wavering light as she led him to the cane-backed, upholstered armchair at the head of the table. A single red rose greeted him as he stood there, its long stem holding it high in the crystal vase. Eloise picked up a gaily decorated box and handed it to him. "For you, my darling. For your birthday."

He took the box and opened it. A gawdy red vest met François' disappointed eyes. He lifted it, inspecting it against the flickering light. "Beautiful, my sweetheart! Beautiful."

"Try it on."

Careful to hide his feelings of disgust at the cheapness of the gift, François put it on, smiling as he did. Madame Hébert buttoned it, rubbing her hands on his chest in a loving caress as she finished.

"You look elegant, *cheri.*" He kissed her on the cheek. She answered with a body gesture that took him by surprise, lunging her huge bosoms at him while, at the same time, grasping him tightly with both her arms. Then kissing him passionately on the lips, she held on until he pushed her away.

"François!"

Realizing his mistake, he salvaged the situation quickly. "My darling Eloise. You arouse me so quickly. We must be careful. It's not fair of me to take advantage. Someone might find out. Your reputation. . . !"

"How sweet, François. But I've dismissed the servants. There's no one here."

"Roger is in the coach house."

"Roger! How much longer do we have to put up with that

man?" She grasped François' hand and led him to the highback chair. When he sat down, she sat on his knee, the chair groaning under the weight. He wished her romantic urge would die. But it didn't. She leaned her head girlishly on his shoulder. "I've been meaning to talk to you about Roger, darling. He's been positively boorish with the servants lately. Yesterday, he sent Annette out crying, after I'd sent her especially to clean up that untidy room in the coach house. Then, when I went to see him, he was uncivil to me." She stood up and moved away from François. Her anger removed the last vestige of romance from her mind. For the first time in weeks, François appreciated Roger. At least his action, this time, had served a useful purpose. It had extricated François from hours of sheer boredom, caressing this creature.

"I'll speak to him."

"You'll have to do more than that. You must get rid of him immediately."

"I can't, my darling. It won't be possible until after the expedition on the Sans Souci."

"I will not go with him on the Sans Souci. I positively refuse."

François stifled a curse. He sat thinking, staring at the fire. Roger was indispensable to his plan.

"It's the way he smells. That room is absolutely rank. Besides, I don't trust him."

There was no other way. François would have to play out the game. The hard way, he thought, as he stood close to her, touched her hand, and holding it bent his head and kissed it. "I can't deny you, *cherie*, you are so beautiful when you are happy. I can't bear to have anything happen that will interfere."

"Oh! François!"

"I have a confession to make."

"A confession?"

"Yes, I'm jealous."

"Jealous? Of whom?"

"Pierre."

"Pierre? Don't be silly. He's just a boy."

"I know. But he has such a fondness for you. A loyalty almost as strong as it used to be for Paul. I'm almost afraid to send him with you on the Sans Souci."

Eloise took the bait. "He likes me? I thought he did. I was sure of it in fact. The dear boy." She leaned her head again on François' shoulder. "I like him too. But you mustn't be jealous, you silly boy."

François kissed her forehead. "I want you to be happy, my

dear. I've asked Giselle to go with you as well."

"Giselle! Why? She's so coarse."

"But with her and Pierre, my darling, you won't be bothered by Roger."

"But I said . . ."

His kiss silenced her. There would be no more talk of this, if François could help it. Eloise groaned with delight as the thoughts of Roger, the Sans Souci, and the insurance she had planned to discuss tonight, were lost in the joy of being loved by François. The only man in the world who had ever loved her, except for her dear departed husband, Alphonse.

"We'll go to bed," she said finally.

"I'll be up in a few minutes, sweetheart. I'll give you time to freshen up." He kissed her again and led her to the central staircase. Then as she went up, he turned abruptly and walked to the rear door, where the cool night air greeted him as he walked briskly to the coach house.

"Did you get it?"

"Yep."

"Where is it?"

"In the barn. With the rest."

"How much do we have now?"

"About a hundred boxes."

"That'll make mince-meat out of it."

"You're not tellin' me something I don't know. There's only one thing bothering me."

"What's that?"

"Aren't they gonna be suspicious? The old lady and those two dummies. Won't they ask what's in the boxes? They're so heavy, they'll damn near sink the thing. They gotta notice."

"Can't you mark the boxes? Mark them 'fragile,' breakable items or something like that. Tell them it's ballast. By the time they find out, it'll be too late."

Roger laughed. "Yah. Too late for sure."

"I'm in a hurry." François turned toward the door. "Madame Hébert is really upset. Roger. She demanded I get rid of you."

"Get rid of me! That'd be a switch. I think I'll mess her up a little."

"Patience, Roger, patience! It will get you farther than bluster. Think of your reward. Think of the end result. That'll give you the strength. You'll enjoy Cuba. You'll learn a few more tricks."

"I'd enjoy knocking her goddamn head off. That's what I'd enjoy."

"Do as I say. You don't have long to wait. By the way, there's been a slight change of plans."

"Change?"

"Giselle will be going with Eloise."

"Really going?"

"The whole way."

"That'll be fun. But why there? I'd like to do her when I have a bit more time."

"Do as I say. She goes with Eloise. That's the deal. One other thing."

"What's that?"

"Pierre comes back."

"What! You said he went the same route as the old biddy."

"Never mind what I said. I told you plans are changed. You screwed it up with your surliness. She won't sign the papers with your name on them. She hates you but likes Pierre. So, Pierre comes back. Or, you don't get the money. No Cuba. Nothing." Roger sulked. "Cheer up." François turned at the door. "I didn't say he was coming back to stay." François smiled. "Just for a little while."

Roger's mood lightened noticeably.

François left the room, walked down the steps, and forced himself to return to the house, where an expectant Eloise waited for him in the big canopied bed in the master bedroom.

12

The hard knock on the door startled Pierre from his sleep. When it sounded again, he half sat up, shook his head, listened, then called out, "Who is it?"

"You're wanted on the phone." The gruff, unfriendly voice was that of his landlord.

Pierre jumped from the bed, grabbed a dressing gown from the back of a chair, stepped into his slippers, opened the door and hurried downstairs to the old-fashioned wall phone.

"Hello."

"Pierre?" It was Giselle.

"Yes."

"Pierre, I don't know how to say it. I had to call you. I felt so bad. About last night, I mean. I was terrible. I'm ashamed."

"It's okay," he said, but his voice caught. Giselle's scorn of last night had really stung. After his commitment to François, he had gone to his dingy room and laid awake, smoking all night. It was only when the first streaks of grey cut through the jet black of the night sky that he finally fell into an uneasy sleep.

Giselle recognized the hurt. "I must see you, Pierre. Will you meet me?"

She wanted to see him. And Pierre knew that he wanted to see her. "Where?" he asked.

"I've got to attend a meeting in the Château," she said. "Could you meet me in the lobby? We could have coffee in the Place de la Fontaine."

"What time?" Pierre looked at his watch. It was 8:30. "Would 9:30 be okay?"

"Okay, 9:30." She hung up.

Pierre forgot his tiredness. All of a sudden he felt great. As though he'd slept for a week, as though he'd kicked a ton of lead off his back. Gone was the despair of last night when Giselle had called him a fool. In its place were thoughts that made him feel like singing.

Giselle was waiting for him when he walked under the medieval archway and into the well-appointed lobby of the hotel. When they entered the Place de la Fontaine, Pierre could feel her warmth and friendliness; this was the Giselle he loved and wanted. She held his arm as he led her to an intimate corner. Giselle spoke as soon as they were seated. "I'm glad you came, Pierre," she said as she grasped his hand and moved closer. "I was mean and terrible. I'm sorry."

"I was rude. I'm the one who should apologize."

"You weren't. You were a gentleman."

"I was stupid. No matter how I feel, I shouldn't blow up like that."

"He deserved it." The anger flared in Giselle's eyes. "I was proud of you. I was proud to see that you'd stand up and speak your mind. Most people would have been afraid."

"I thought about what you said last night. You're right. I am stupid. I am a fool. I should learn to keep my big mouth shut. I know I've got a lot to learn."

The waiter approached and Pierre ordered coffee. For a long time they sat together in silence. But there was a feeling between them that was new. A tenderness and understanding was growing between them. It was as though the strange necessity of their being together was finally maturing into something more than it had been; as though the heat of circumstances that had been forging them together was cooling and the cast was beginning to harden.

"I've been lonely these past few weeks, Pierre. I know I haven't been much fun. I'm glad you've been around. You've been a big help."

"I wanted to help. I still want to help." Pierre said the words with meaning. His feelings for Giselle were suddenly intense. He not only liked and respected her, he loved her.

"I'd better phone," said Giselle looking at her watch. In a moment she was back. "The meeting has been cancelled. Isn't that wonderful? We can have the whole morning to ourselves." She picked up her purse, led Pierre from their rendezvous down the hallway, through the lobby and into the brilliant sunlight of the flawless, blue, September day. "It's so beautiful," she whispered, squeezing his hand.

Together they walked past Les Patineurs, where in only three short months the air would ring with happy crowds of ice skaters, then past the Glossier, where workmen were even now preparing for the winter fun. When they arrived at the Terrace, Giselle was exuberant. "This is my day," she sang. "A day like this was made for singing and dancing. But not working," she laughed.

They walked along the Terrace. "Those silly old statues,"

Giselle mocked as they passed the figure of Champlain. "They make the place look like a mausoleum."

Pierre frowned. "I thought you'd like them. Being in the Movement."

Giselle ignored the remark. Today was not to be spoiled by talking of such trivia. "Have you been here before?" she asked.

"I was here yesterday. I looked at the statues and read the inscriptions. Then I walked around the Terrace."

"Did you go to the Citadel?"

"No."

"Good! Then we'll see it together. Come on. You've got to see the Citadel." She took his hand again and led him to the end of the Terrace. Hundreds of feet below them and stretching as far as the eye could see in both directions, the mighty St. Lawrence swirled its way toward the sea. The town of Lévis glittered in the morning sun. A golden cross, crowning a massive church on the hillside above the town, reflected the sparkling rays. A white ship, flags flying from every mast, pointed downstream and approached the harbour. A policeboat, its sirens screaming, left the dock and circled the ship. A rope ladder was thrown to them as the police-boat approached. Pierre could see a man climbing up the ladder. Pierre thought of François' complaint about American ships not being inspected. "Aren't the police climbing up that ship's ladder?" he asked.

"Looks like it."

"Why do they search all the ships except the Americans?"

"What makes you ask that? The Americans don't get any special treatment."

"Nobody searches their gunboats."

Giselle laughed. "Who told you that?"

"I just heard."

She interrupted his thoughts. "Look," she pointed down the cliff. "Look at the seagulls trying to scrounge a meal."

Beneath them at the foot of the precipice was Lower Town. There was the Church of Notre Dame de Victoire, the dock with the ferry boat approaching, fighting the current on the way to its familiar berth.

"God, it's pretty!" Pierre whispered. Giselle looked at him and smiled. "There's more to see." She pointed to the height of land towering above them. And there perched high on top, as imposing as a Rhineland castle, stood the Citadel, the Fortress of Québec.

Pierre followed Giselle up the never-ending stairs. He looked first to the fortress, then down to the river. It was here, in this exact spot, where the course of history had been changed. He thought of the Fort de Musée and the story of the fall of Québec. The Citadel had stood there then, as surely as it stood there now. But in history, it had been something greater. It had been the symbol of French authority, the badge of French ownership to half a continent, from the mouth of the St. Lawrence through the Great Lakes and the Ohio river, then down the valley of the Mississippi. The French colony had flourished. The French fur-traders had tracked the endless wastes of the western plains. They had walked the timbered trails of the northland and the voyageurs had known intimately the rivers and lakes of the central watershed. Then, on that fateful day, a band of Englishmen had climbed up this very cliff, had dragged their cannons with them and then, having by-passed the Citadel, had drawn up their battle lines in a soft underbelly of the fort. In the bloody battle that followed, the British won and, from that moment, all the power had shifted from French to English hands. And the country, in most cases, had adopted the English language and English culture as its heritage.

What would have happened if the French had thrown the English back into the river, wondered Pierre, as his eyes searched the contours of the cliff, and his gaze dropped down the escarpment. What would have happened?

The white boat sounded three shrill blasts. It was an exciting promise of adventure on the high seas. The policeboat screamed its sirens in reply, and the vessel's propellers whipped the water.

"When I see the boats and hear the whistle," said Pierre, "I feel like a kid again. Did you know I grew up on this river? At Rivière du Loup. When I was a kid, I used to run down to the river and watch the boats. They weren't very big in those days, not like they are today. But we thought they were big and we liked to watch them. I used to have a friend. His name was René. He was my best friend and I liked him a lot. But he drowned."

"I'm sorry," said Giselle. "I know how it feels to lose somebody."

"I used to be mad at the river after that. I used to hate it. I felt the river owed me something. I wish I could have saved René."

"You shouldn't live in the past, Pierre. It's bad for you."

"I'm always living in the past," admitted Pierre, as he leaned against the railing. "I can't seem to shake off what was taught me, even when I think it was wrong." He stopped, his eyes following the path of the huge white ship as it slid silently down the river.

It appeared smaller now and its course was straight down the centre.

Giselle took Pierre's arm and leaned her head on his shoulder. "I wish I was on that boat, going to wherever it's headed. I'd like to run away. I'd like to get out of here. I'd just like to escape."

Why hadn't she said that yesterday? Why had he let himself get so mad last night? If only he hadn't phoned François. If only he hadn't made such definite arrangements. Maybe he should tell her, but his second instinct said no. She'd think he was crazy changing his mind every day.

"Would you go away with me?" he asked.

Her answer was a snuggle, and Pierre wondered how he could break his promise to François. Why couldn't he just pack up and leave, take Giselle with him on a ship just like that big, white one, and settle down somewhere — anywhere. But even as he thought, he knew it was only a dream. He couldn't go anywhere without money. Besides that, he couldn't let François down. Or Madame Hébert. On top of that, could he live with himself if he let Paul down again? The nightmares were getting worse. It seemed as though Paul was trying to climb out of the fire to get to him. He couldn't go on indefinitely like this. He'd have to make up for his guilt somehow. Maybe it would resolve itself if he continued Paul's work and, in doing so, he would be with Giselle most of the time anyway. "We'll be together here," he said. "François says from now on we'll be working together. He says you'll be leaving your job with the American and working full time for him."

Giselle was surprised, disagreeably surprised. This was the first time she'd heard about this turn of events. She hadn't even been consulted. Well, she'd see about that later.

"François says there's lots of work to be done in the Movement."

"Do you really believe in the Movement?"

"Of course."

"I don't."

"You don't?"

"No, I think this gang in the Movement are acting like a bunch of kids fighting over marbles. I don't consider myself French, I'm a Canadian, that's all. I think all this French-English ballyhoo is just a lot of political nonsense. Do you really believe the English or French came to Canada for any noble purpose? I don't. I believe they came for one reason, to see how many furs they could steal from the Indians, or how much gold they could send home. They were both foreigners, Pierre, the French and the English. All they wanted was to own this country. To sack it, to strip it clean. Neither one of them wanted to make something of it."

"It was the English who came to steal," Pierre said defiantly. Then he sighed and in a modest voice said, "I've got a lot to learn, Giselle. There's so much to learn, and I want to learn it. I want to learn it from you. But there's one thing I know, Giselle. I know it for certain."

"And what is that, my dear sir?" Giselle taunted, suddenly in a lighter mood.

"I know François is right about the river."

"In what way?"

"We own it. We own the river. François says that when we stand on this side of the river, we're in Québec. If we take the ferry to Lévis, we're still in Québec. This means the river's ours, because we own both sides."

"I think you're wrong about that. Paul used to talk about it. The river's an international waterway. It belongs to Canada and the United States."

"Not if we separate," said Pierre grimly. "I never told you, but Paul asked me to think about the river. Just before he died, he said how important it is. I don't remember exactly. We were just going into Montréal and I was scared. But he told me two or three times to think about it. Now, François tells me if we separate, we can claim the river. Paul was throwing me a challenge when he said that."

"A challenge?"

"Yes. A challenge to make me fight for the liberation of our people. For the return of honour, that's what François calls it. The river owes me something." He stopped abruptly, and stared at the white ship slowly melting into the landscape, as it propelled its way around a bend far off in the distance.

Giselle moved closer to him. "You're only fooling yourself," she said softly. "The river owes you nothing. Paul said lots of things. Most of the time, he just talked for the sake of talking, not because he had anything to say. You've got to kick those thoughts out of your head, Pierre."

"I can't. It keeps bugging me. I keep dreaming about it."

She touched his hand. "I know what it's like. It's terrible. I know how you must feel, but Pierre, you shouldn't. You mustn't." Suddenly, she remembered the terrible nightmares she herself had experienced when she had given her baby away. Her words came with difficulty. "You mustn't let a bad experience ruin your life," she said, and at that moment she felt closer to Pierre than to anyone she had ever known. She held his arm, leaning on his shoulder, and the presence was like a beautiful concerto, a rhapsody of feelings that Pierre could not define. He turned to her. They stood alone at the Lookout, halfway up the precipice. There was no one to be seen: there was no one on the steps leading down to the Terrace; there was no one on the path to the Citadel; they were all alone.

They had been alone before, but not like this. When they were at the apartment, there had always been the memory of Paul. At other places and times, there had always been François or Madame Hébert or somebody else. But now, there was no one, no one at all. Pierre gazed into Giselle's eyes and felt the music of her presence. The bells of a church in Lower Town began to ring the Angelus; the melodious tones echoing through the still, clear air and up the rocky cliffs where they mingled with the sounds of the other bells, wafting across the river from the church on the hill at Lévis. The music of the bells filled the air and Pierre could feel the irresistible magnetism of her body. She pushed closer to him. No words should break the spell. How many times had Pierre thought of holding her in his arms and how many times had she held him back? He had longed to touch her, to hold her, to feel her close to him. And now, standing here in the bright sunlight of this unforgettable September morning, he had reached out and she was his.

"Giselle, I've wanted to for so very long. But there was always Paul . . ."

Giselle silenced him with a kiss. Pierre understood. She didn't want to talk of Paul, she wanted to forget him. They kissed again, and the world seemed far away. He held her until the bells ceased their ringing, and the final reverberations echoed against the solid stones of the Citadel and rolled down the valley of the St. Lawrence. They stood there entranced, unable to draw their lips from one another, and not wanting to move ever again. Pierre wondered why he had never held Giselle like this before. He wondered why he had been so foolish, so backward, so passive. He knew that he wanted to so many times, but he had never dared. For Giselle, too, this was an awakening. She hadn't felt like this since Armand. But there was a closeness for Pierre that she had never experienced, even with Armand. It had been growing the past weeks. She had tried to expel the yearning. She had felt so many times that she was successful, that her feelings for Pierre were not real, just an idealistic dream. But she knew she was not being honest with herself. Pierre's presence had been the opiate that had kept her rational these past few weeks. Because of Pierre, she had not sunk into depression and self-pity. It was beautiful, her feelings for him. But there was a physical desire too. There was an excitement in his arms, a longing for his kiss and a yearning for his touch.

Giselle had felt like a fool with her first young love, Armand, who had left her with his child. Later, as a whore, she had felt base and rotten and the memory of it shamed her. With Paul, it had been only an adventure. But with this man, with Pierre, she felt secure because she felt needed, wanted. She felt like a woman.

She lifted her hands and cupping his face, kissed him tenderly. Then placing her hands on his chest, she pushed back. "We'll have to hurry," she said. "Or we'll not be able to see the Citadel."

Pierre grasped her hand as she tried to run away. "I don't care about the Citadel," he said. "I don't care about anything."

But Giselle broke away and ran up the steps, laughing as she went and Pierre, feeling like a schoolboy, ran after her.

13

Fear was the last thought in Giselle's mind as she waved goodnight to Pierre, walked into the lobby of her apartment and stepped briskly along the hallway. If she had been afraid it would have been a fear of what might have happened had she let Pierre come in, as he had suggested.

It had been a day above all days, a mark on the calendar that would never be erased. The lingering walk to the Citadel, the meeting of their lips so many times on the way, the cocktails in the Place de la Fontaine, the ride in the horse-drawn carriage over the Plains of Abraham. Giselle could never remember when the city looked as it had today, so rich, exciting, beautiful. They dined at the Chalet de Suisse, where the candlelight and wine garnished their appetite for one another. After dinner, they strolled down rue St. Jean to the Victoria Hotel, where the intimate darkness of the crowded lounge drew them together again. The smoke-filled air closed in from every side, as though encompassing them, shielding them from all intruders and inviting an intimacy that had to be.

They danced forever, their bodies touching in the tenderest ways, their passions rising with each motion.

Never! Never in her life had Giselle experienced the desire that held her tonight, a sacred desire; so beautiful it defied description. The love of a good man, an impossible dream, an unreachable goal. But at least she could pretend. In the protection of the misty smoke that surrounded them, she could believe that she was good enough. That she was not an ex-prostitute, a body-seller, an old woman in the form of a girl. Instead, she was innocent, a virgin experiencing the first awakenings of love, the first knowledge of passion, and the first desire for release.

It had all been so wonderful! She couldn't bear to destroy it. She couldn't let it sink into a sensuous game in the bedroom. Not tonight! There was more to Pierre's feelings than that. There had to be! There was. And there was more, much more to hers as well. She couldn't ask him in. It was too dangerous. She could trust Pierre, but could she trust herself?

She turned the key in the lock, opened the door, entered quickly and closed it. Before she could switch on the light in the hall, a strange indefinable feeling swept over her. She took her coat off as she pushed through the louvred door into the kitchen while the feeling persisted.

Coffee! She threw her coat on a chair in the alcove and plugged the kettle into the outlet on the stove.

It was then that she saw it. In the dim light, a form sat motionless and quietly on the sofa. Stunned, she was about to run for the door, when a familiar voice stopped her.

"Giselle."

It was François.

She stepped into the living room, switching the lights on as she went. It was François all right, and standing in the corner behind him was Roger. Giselle felt like screaming. They'd really frightened her, but instead, she waited momentarily for her feelings to cool. They were in her apartment like common criminals, waiting in the shadows like jackals stalking their prey. When she spoke, there was a noticeable quiver in her voice. "What in God's name are you doing here?"

François stood up quickly. "I was worried, Giselle. I've been worried all day." He was pleased with the reaction his visit had created. She was scared. Good and scared! It showed right through her cool.

"How touching." Giselle opened the cigarette box on the round, glass-topped table in front of the sofa. Composed now, she removed a cigarette and put it to her lips. François did exactly as expected. He took a lighter from his vest pocket, moved it with a flourish and flicked it expertly. "I phoned you this morning. They said you were at the Château. I checked there. Discreetly, of course, my dear," he added quickly, "very discreetly. But it didn't add up. You weren't at the Château. Your office didn't know where you'd gone. Then tonight, you didn't come home for dinner. It was then I called Roger."

Ignoring his obvious request for an explanation, she turned her back to him. What right did he have to check up on her, follow her movements, harass her? None! But he thought he had the right, and that was enough. She'd explain nothing. "How did you get in?" she demanded, turning fiercely.

François smiled, relieved to see her in such good form. It had been a trying day, his troubles starting with a simple phone call to her office. It hadn't been an important matter, but it had annoyed him when Giselle was not available. As the day wore on, black thoughts had plagued him. Had she been caught going through the secret files? Were they questioning her? What were her answers? Where was she? By ten in the evening, François was positive something drastic had happened. But he wouldn't let himself panic. He'd keep a vigil all night, if necessary. And the place would be her apartment. When he heard the key in the door, his heart almost stopped. But she was alone and her attitude clearly indicated she was no fugitive from any inquisitor. Probably was fed up, had a few drinks and got laid, he thought. His relief forced him to smile again. "Roger is an expert in these matters," he said in answer to her fiery question.

"Is he an expert in getting out as well?"

François wasn't anxious to continue the confrontation. Not now. Not in front of Roger. "You'd better go," he said, nodding to him. "Giselle isn't feeling herself tonight."

When Roger had gone, Giselle's anger flared again. "How dare you bring that goon here?"

"Roger is a very trusted employee," François replied smugly. "He's done an excellent job for the Movement. You should have more respect for him. Someday, you may need his help. He could be a valuable friend, Giselle. But he could also be a dangerous enemy."

"He's a psychopath. He gives me the creeps. I don't want him around."

"That's too bad." François laughed, enjoying the charade. "It's too bad about what you don't like. You'd better concentrate on the facts, my dear. You're working for the Movement, whether you like it or not."

Giselle sank into the sofa. François eyed her like a cat, trying hard to smile, but not quite making it. How long had she known him? And how long had she hated him? Almost from the beginning. She had tolerated him only because of Paul. Now there was no reason to give even lip service. With Paul gone, her connection with the Movement, with François, had no meaning for her. She'd done nothing but get information, useless information about American ships on the river. Beyond that, she wasn't involved. There was nothing to hold her. It was time to get out. She'd take this opportunity to make a clear break.

"I'm not interested in the Movement anymore, François. I'm tired of you and the Movement. I'm getting out."

François' expression changed abruptly, his Cheshire-cat smile fading abruptly, replaced by a thin-lipped contempt. Giselle's coldness toward him had been difficult to ignore, but strangely enough, he hadn't really cared. Sure, she's attractive, almost beautiful, he'd often thought. She'd be a fantastic lay. But not for me. I've got enough trouble without mixing business with pleasure. His decision had solidified some months before when he had made a passing remark to Paul about Giselle, referring to her as a whore. After all, he had a dossier on her, knew every morbid detail of her life, and assumed Paul was aware of it. But Paul's reaction was swift and betrayed his feelings. Feelings François had never suspected. He had bristled in anger at the word and François quickly changed the subject, never again mentioning her name in disparaging terms. But one day, shortly after Paul's death, he made his objectives clear to Roger. "One of these days, I'm going to make that bitch," he said, "just for the hell of it."

Circumstances, however, had prevented him from putting his thoughts into action. He'd been far too busy with affairs of the Movement. But the intriguing thought still persisted, that she could make the coming winter nights more interesting. That idea, however, fled his mind as she stood in front of him, repeating her demands. "I want out."

"Out! You can't leave. Not now!" François stood up, boiling with anger. But the warning signs in her eyes stopped him. Placing his hand behind his back, he clenched his fist, digging his fingernails into his palm, a trick he'd learned years ago while being interrogated. The pain forced the anger from him. Threats wouldn't work with this girl. Useless to try. She wasn't afraid. Not yet. "I mean," he continued, attempting to smile, "you can't leave now, because of Pierre. He needs you to help him."

Could François know about them? Impossible. She hadn't known for certain herself until today. Had they been followed? What did François know? There was only one way to find out. Bluff him out. "Since when do I have to worry about that kid?"

"Calm down, Giselle. I know it's no picnic for a girl like you working with that woodchopper. But after all, you promised . . ."

"What the hell's the use of talking to you, François? I've never promised you anything. I didn't get mixed up with the Movement because I agree with it. I couldn't care less about your plans. I came in for one reason — Paul." The words stopped her. Had she really come in for Paul? No! It hadn't been for Paul. It had been for a need, a desperate need within herself. A need to get out of Montréal, out of her filthy profession. A need to belong to somebody. Anybody! When she spoke again, her voice was subdued. "That's all there is to it, François. And now that Paul's gone, I want out."

"But look. Can't you see? We need you. You've been a big investment. We've set you up. Never asked anything from you. Now we need you. You can't leave. Not now."

"I can't?"

"I don't mean you can't." François began pacing the floor. "I mean we just can't replace you. That's all." He stopped in front of her. "We need you, honey. We need you very much." He put his hand on her shoulder. She stiffened.

He withdrew his hand, still speaking softly. "Just until the election," he pleaded. "Just help Pierre get started."

So that was it. The truth stared her in the face, or was it the truth? At least part of it was. She'd been sucked into the Movement by Paul, and now she was being asked to return the favour by drawing Pierre in. By the looks of it, Pierre didn't need much coaxing, but it seemed that François thought he did! And that's where the truth ended. How could François be so wrong? In spite of anything else Giselle might think of him, she didn't consider him stupid. Surely, he could see that Pierre was being swallowed up, overwhelmed by the activities of the Movement, caught in the current of the fast-moving events that surrounded him. François must be joking. He must know he has Pierre hooked. Look at the way Pierre talked, hardly a word that didn't have something to do with the Movement. François must have something up his sleeve, expecting me to be naive enough to believe he really needs my help. Sarcasm tinged her voice as she answered. "Pierre looks as though he's well and truly started."

"Not really. He lacks confidence. He's too immature. Too easily influenced. He needs a guiding hand." François was surprised at the reaction prompted by the statement. Her attitude softened abruptly as his words hit their mark. He had meant to use Pierre as an example of a good attitude. His criticism had come as a reaction to her statement, but at least it produced the desired effect. Christ! Who can understand a woman? Like a water faucet in a cheap hotel, too hot or too cold. But what the hell, who cares why she comes along, as long as she does?

It was true that François' answer had influenced Giselle. Pierre did give the impression of uncertainty, on the surface he seemed to waver. François was influenced by these outer attitudes, unaware of the proud spirit that lay beneath. Perhaps François, without realizing it, was giving her a golden opportunity, the chance to influence Pierre with François' approval. How she influenced him would be her secret. "What if I stay until the elections?" she asked.

"Then you can go with my blessing."

"And Pierre? How do you want me to influence him? What makes you think I can?"

François began pacing the floor again. "You can lead him. I can tell by the way he looks at you. By the way he follows you around."

"And if I fail? If I can't influence him your way? What then?"

"You can't fail, Giselle. You're a natural-born con artist. He'll believe you. I'm not afraid of that. My only concern is that I can't convince you to stay in the Movement. I can see great things for you. As a pivot. My right-hand man. My girl Friday."

"I told you, I'm not interested in any long-term project, François. I just want out. I don't know why you're making such a fuss. I know I haven't been much use to you. But I've done everything you've asked."

"We've been grooming you for the big job. The time is almost here. You owe it to us to finish what you started."

"And if I do?"

"Like I say. When the job's done, you get out, if that's what you want. Your debt will be paid."

"My debt?"

"Yes."

"What debt?"

"The money it cost me to get you out of the whore-house in Montréal. That debt! Or have you forgotten that's the deal?"

"You filthy bastard."

"Tut, tut, Giselle, can't you face the truth?"

"The truth is you're a stinking parasite, François. Can you face that? You're nothing but a maniac, who should be locked up in a nut-house. You're not interested in anything but blood-sucking. It doesn't matter to you who or what it is, me, Pierre, Québec. To hell with you, François. I'm getting out and never want to see your ugly puss again."

The words struck François like a slap on the face, and hate spilled out of him momentarily. "You'll get out! Yes, goddamn it, you'll get out! Just like Paul, you'll get out." He shrieked the words at her. "Why is it that fools want to quit when success is almost within their grasp? My plan will work. Why can't you see that?" He caught a glimpse of himself in the mirror on the far wall, and wished that he had maintained his composure. Silently, he cursed his greatest fault: his almost uncontrollable temper. He lowered his voice and sat down. "Giselle," he said as he went through his ritual with a cigarette, "if you only knew how I feel for you. I've such high hopes for you. How it hurts me that you want to quit. Giselle, please stay. I need your help. It can't be done without you."

She wasn't listening. Instead, François' words kept echoing in her mind, repeating over and over. "Get out? You'll get out! Just like Paul, you'll get out." And how had Paul left? In a raging death-dealing blast. A blast triggered by a faulty detonator. Or was it faulty? It had been François, himself, who had made the bomb. It had been François who set it, and it was François alone who had benefitted from Paul's demise. Paul had been the only real threat to François' ambitions. Competition! That's what had really frightened François the most. Giselle stared blankly at the creature before her. It was clear now. It made sense. François had murdered Paul. There was no doubt of that. And he had just threatened Giselle, exactly as he had threatened Paul in the workshop that night last spring. François was trying desperately to cover his mistake, but Giselle was not to be taken in.

Suddenly she decided. She wouldn't quit the Movement. She'd stay. She'd play François' game. She'd stay long enough to prove what she knew. She'd play along until she found out the plans this two-faced bastard had for Québec. And when she found out, she'd do everything she could to sabotage it. This was smarter than openly defying him. Yes! If she stayed, maybe she could convince Pierre that François had murdered Paul, and if she could do that she knew that Pierre would leave with her.

"Maybe you're right," she said quietly. "I suppose I did sound like a quitter. I'm sorry."

François was relieved. "You'll see, Giselle. You'll see that you're doing the right thing. Paul and I loved you very much. That's why we helped you. And now, by carrying on, you're showing your respect for Paul. Taking up where he left off, so to speak. If Paul was here now, I'm sure he'd be very proud of you."

He picked up his coat and left quickly. But as he walked down the hallway, through the lobby and out the front door into the cool autumn air, his thoughts were far from pleasant. Maybe I shouldn't have lost my temper, he said to himself. Maybe I shouldn't have talked so much. Maybe I should have shut up about Paul. But it doesn't matter anyway. It'll all be over in a couple of weeks. Then she'll see! When Roger gets through with that rotten bitch, she won't be a nuisance anymore.

14

François stepped jauntily into the room; his spirits very high indeed. Never had he been quite so smug about his powers of manipulation. What a master at that intellectual game of wits! He had each piece of his plan falling beautifully into place. Pierre was behaving beautifully, just like a trained seal. Even the difficult Giselle was co-operating in a most satisfactory manner. She had searched the files at her office, and come up with the schedule of American warships en route through the St. Lawrence. This was the most crucial piece of information for François. And Giselle had simply dropped it in his lap with no comment!

Now here he was tonight, holding court with that select group who had the power to make him president of the Sovereign State of Québec. These fools were about to make him one of the most influential men in North America, and they'd thank him for the honour of doing it!

Shaking hands with a pale Father Moreau, François thought the man looked worn out, defenceless. He'd be easy enough to handle. Then, accepting the quick, smothering embrace of Eloise Hébert, he felt he could even afford to indulge her tonight. *She's a goddamn fool, but she'll serve my purpose well for very little sacrifice on my part. What's a few more nights rolling in the hay with that fat bitch, compared to years of supreme authority over a nation?*

He nodded and beamed at the others. There was Inspector De Roche, almost unrecognizable out of uniform, really just a tatty, out-at-the-elbows cop. Henri Bédault, willing to go to any lengths to be Minister of Propaganda in the new world François was shaping for them. He made a special effort to exchange pleasantries with the three bearded youths from the University of Montréal. They were the flame-throwers of revolt, and François was aiming them just where he wanted. They were his shock troops, thoroughly brain-washed and ready to serve.

Madame Hébert linked her arm in his and led François to the punch bowl where she filled a cup and offered it to him. She was the young, gay Eloise tonight, the Eloise who had danced with and charmed the élite of international society so many years ago. Once again she felt the strength of her silver-spoon breeding. Tonight, she was mistress of the house that glowed once more with the vitality of human contact. This house had witnessed parties and salon gatherings for two hundred years. There had been a long sleep lately, but as soon as François had made her his first lady, there would be life again. Seeing François tonight, she could really believe it. It was no foolish dream.

Her eyes glowed with the echo of youth, and François impulsively accepted the cup she offered with a courtly bow and a delicate kiss on her hand. As she simpered, he felt a shiver of irritation run through him. Now, what made me do that? This old dame deserves nothing but contempt. A brainless fool I'll wipe my feet on soon enough! He looked curiously at her again, and for the first time François saw a person who had petty little dreams and desires, but who also had feelings and emotions that might complicate his plans. I must make no mistake: she has to believe in me completely, or she'll take vengeance if she finds I'm using her like any other tool. Fawn and flatter just a little longer, my good man; it'll pay off handsomely.

"Eloise, you are indeed the beautiful chatelaine this evening." She blushed a girlish rose and for once was lost for words. A sudden commotion at the door startled them, and saved François from continuing the tête-à-tête.

Jacques Ginette entered on the wave of extravagant welcome his very appearance seemed to evoke wherever he went. François watched it all with a growing sense of pleasure in his ability to manipulate even this paragon of personality. Wherever he went to spread the gospel according to François, the hoards followed mindlessly, bewitched by the charming smile, the glib speeches and the ready laugh. There was an inevitable twinge of envy as François looked at this handsome figure. He didn't have Jacques' kind of sway on people. He had to work much harder to make them come his way. Then he reminded himself quickly that he owned Ginette. Body and soul, Ginette was his and would always be ready to jump at his word. He didn't need the Ginette style, for it was his already, through Ginette.

Madame Hébert hurried off to welcome the newcomer, leaving François to reflect on her choice of punch. It was a revolting concoction, typical, he thought, of the counterfeit culture of these foolish people. This Québec was a poor imitation of the golden societies of Europe. Was it really worthy of his genius? His genius that would turn Québec mud into gold? It won't be long now until the world will see the result of my alchemy. The wealth of this country has hardly been scratched. And when it's mine, I'll strip it to the bones. And every one of these people here tonight will help me do it.

François forced his mind from these olympian musings back to the realities of the moment. The time for exultation was not quite here and, until it was, he must step carefully in his court. After all, he still needed this group to make it. Pierre, in the far corner of the room, caught his eye. Here was one he had to keep in tow. He strode across the room to greet him.

"Stick close, Pierre. I need your eyes and ears tonight. You must help me learn the desires of our people; help me analyze our current position. Come with me."

Pierre was not at all sure what this meant. But then the whole evening so far was a bewildering experience. He had just been listening to the students and was astonished by the eloquent expression of their views. How knowledgeable they were — and how dissatisfied! They ranted against the political establishment in Québec, they berated the Catholic church, and they were vehement against the federal government and all English-speaking Canadians. Those guys sure do know everything. This education thing must make them so smart. He had been joined by François, just at an interesting point in the conversation. One of the students had loudly declared, "No priest in skirts is going to tell me what to do. I'm glad the schools are getting rid of them and their pretty chants!" And Father Moreau had been not more than ten feet away. It had almost been a challenge aimed directly at him. Pierre would like to have heard the rest of it, but François claimed his attention. What could the fellow have meant?

Pierre's understanding of Québec's educational system was scant. He didn't know that all education in the province, for over two hundred years, had been under the direct supervision of the clergy, a situation that had resulted in a serious neglect of the technical education of the Québécois, to the point, actually, where economic control of the province had passed into the hands of the technically oriented English. He didn't know that Québec was the only province in Canada that didn't have so much as a Ministry of Education until the 1960's.

Pierre was dumbfounded at the anti-clerical attitude of the students, and wondered how they had come to feel this way. Such an attitude wasn't entirely new to him. Giselle had often made anti-religious statements, and François too was constantly criticizing the clerical establishment.

"There are many places in the world, Pierre," François had said not long ago, "where there are no churches. Where the buildings that were once so-called houses of God have been turned into museums. The thinking people in these countries laugh at the church-goers of the world and wonder at their infantile beliefs."

Pierre had been of mixed emotions on hearing this from François, whose opinions he truly admired. On one hand, his up-bringing made him resentful of the attack on the institution that offered him neat solutions for every situation. On the other hand, however, he felt a guilty sense of agreement with it. He had some-times felt himself that some of the things the Church had told him were rather silly. After all, look at the law that forbade eating meat on Fridays. He had been taught as a child that it was a mortal sin to break this rule, and he had been plagued with uneasiness whenever he ignored it. Then suddenly, there came an announce-ment that it was no longer a sin to eat meat on Fridays. Now, how could something be so wrong one day, and then be no sin at all the next? There were other things too, other sins. Not going to mass on Sunday, not going to confession, the sins of desire, and the sin of doubt in the Church's absolute righteousness. Oh yes, the thought of all these sins bothered him. They bothered him, most of all, when he thought of his carefree friend, René, who had drowned in the St. Lawrence, and who was still languishing in hell because he had sinned and not confessed before he died, and had not been blessed by a priest afterwards. Even Pierre's simple trust in the Church waivered when he thought of that happy, quick-witted boy suffering the tortures of hell. But when he thought like that, he knew he was committing the sin of doubt, and guilt would assail him. So he believed in the Church rather than suffer the guilt of not believing, but Pierre was highly intrigued by other people's opinions in church matters.

"Good evening, Father," François greeted the priest while Pierre almost blushed in his presence, wondering if the good Father could read his mind.

"François, I must leave early this evening," Father Moreau apologized. "It's been a very busy week for me and the drive back to the rectory is a long one. I'd like to talk to you for a few minutes before I go, however."

"We'll talk in the dining room. It will be more private there." François took Father Moreau's arm, signalling Pierre to follow.

Carefully closing the door behind them, François found a chair and settled down, nodding to the others to follow suit. Father Moreau shifted uncomfortably and, finally, sat next to François. Opening his mouth and then closing it again, he looked directly at Pierre, trying to find a diplomatic way of suggesting the meeting should be completely private. François sensed the priest's difficulty.

"I trust Pierre implicitly. You can say anything in front of him that you'd say to me." Father Moreau nervously removed a small box from his pants pocket, opened it carefully, and pinching a liberal quantity of snuff between his fingers injected the powdery substance into each nostril, inhaling deeply as he did.

"Have you made up your mind?" François took the initiative.

Finally it came, a solid "Yes."

It had been a difficult decision for Father Moreau. His conscience told him this was an evil man, perhaps one of Satan's soul-reapers, but he was the man that could give Québec what it had so long required, separation from the engulfing ways of the Americanizing hordes of English-speaking people. Father Moreau was a just man, but he could not and would not accept compromise within the frame-work of his beloved faith. He believed with a passion in the truth of the One Church. His Church was the only true expression of the word of God and was the only link on earth with Jesus Christ, who had been sent to save mankind. With this divine guidance, surely, the Church was the only instrument that could be trusted to control government without corruption. The idea of separation of Church and state was akin to heresy to Father Moreau; an idea that could only lead to decadence and downfall. The Church had to be the controlling force in all areas of life, or the people would be lost in their search for salvation. Only the Church could decide what was best for man in the winding road through life. Education and government were essential in the society man had structured for himself, but if they were necessary, it was equally necessary that these institutions be served only by the precepts of Christ himself as recognized by the Church.

Until a few years ago, the Church of Québec had faithfully maintained the leadership of the people in every area, but, recently, there had been a falling away from its guidance, particularly in education and government. Father Moreau's faith would not allow this straying of Christ's flock. Since he had taken his vows, he had led his people with a firmness and discipline tempered with compassion except when it came to those who questioned the absolute authority of the Church. He was quick to quell any such rumbles of dissension. But the rumble was becoming a roar these days. He was hearing it regularly in his own parish, that Church law was just one way to find the moral life leading to heaven. He soon discovered a small group in the parish, led by an English-speaking parishioner, who were raising just such questions in the community, and when he confronted them, they could neither repent nor keep their question to themselves. They had to be stopped. There was no other way to save the purity of the church. Obviously, the best way of stopping the English from spreading their heresy was to separate them from the French, to break the English influence in the province and to restore it to the glory of French tradition.

So Father Moreau became a separatist in mind, and it was just a short jump to becoming a separatist politically. His people had to be saved from the corroding effects of English ways and ideas. He would help them overcome the dangers of infiltration. He knew, of course, that there were evil acts committed in the name of separatism, but he viewed them as the desperate and misguided attempts by the oppressed to overthrow corruption. He would lead them back to the right ways. Hadn't Christ, himself, walked among sinners in order to save them?

"Yes," he said to François, with complete conviction. "I will support you."

François jumped delightedly to his feet, and grasped the priest's hand in a warm clasp. "Father, we are honoured by your faith in us. We will give the country back to the people, to whom it truly belongs." He had no love for the church and its ways, but François knew he had to have this man believe in him. He needed support from the clergy in his quest for supreme authority. With one honest clergyman to raise his voice for the Movement, François could count on the support of others and the support of their followers.

Here was an alliance of men whose moral convictions were in direct opposition. They both knew it, but both were sure of their ground, sure that the alliance would bring victory. Father Moreau knew he was backing the most radical of the separatist groups, but he felt it was the surest way to win the struggle against the waves of the English assault on Québec. François knew that with the support of a respected priest, he could only gain legitimacy and respect in his battle. He had just advanced his cause a hundredfold.

"You'll make a statement for the press?"

"A statement?" Father Moreau was suddenly confused.

"Why, yes, Father, the sooner more people understand that you are with us, the sooner they'll realize they too must support us. You are a leader of men and your men must know which way to follow."

"I see." There was a pause. The priest realized he had committed himself and there must be no waffling now. He must let his people know where they were to go for their salvation. But it could prove awkward.

"It does raise a few questions."

François looked up sharply. "Questions? Why?"

Father Moreau's pale face took on a tense expression. "They'll want to know . . . they're sure to ask, you see, why I have done this. What role I'll play in the Movement. What shall I answer them, François?"

Of course, Moreau was right. The clergy was traditionally synonymous with influence and power in Québec. The reporters were sure to ask what action the priest would take to help the cause and how the cause would help the Church. He asked the question aloud. "What do the clergy have to do with separatism?" François maintained an artificially sincere expression. He knew he had no use for the Church in his government, and he suspected that Moreau had no use for anything but the Church. Was the priest trying to play his game? Was he planning to use François to put the Church back in command? But this man of God was not suited to the game. In the months to come, he would be deeply troubled by the commitment he had made, and it was very likely that inner conflict would cause him to withdraw his support. That would be a move that could prove very embarrassing and possibly damaging.

"*Mon père*, I think you might say that you personally support our cause, but that you cannot talk for the whole Church which doesn't interest itself in political matters."

"But, François! You don't understand. Politics in Québec has been the Church for two hundred years! I cannot say that the Church isn't concerned."

"Ah, Father, the past two hundred years! That's history. People won't bother with what has been, only with what is to be. The people we speak to today will not listen to the past. They're sick of it. Why, the past two hundred years is the reason we must forge something better for the next two hundred!"

"François, you have missed my point. There is a moral question here!" Father Moreau drew himself up and spoke with quiet dignity. Here was ground he was sure of — moral right and wrong. "The Church is the true strength of Québec. Without the Church, there is no Québec. You must see, François, that because the Church has lost its grip with some of the people, corrupt ways have come into our country and they must be purged. Our people must be set back on the true path. Only the Church can guide them."

There was a strength to this man. François was not so blinded by his own ego as to realize that he must placate him to hold him.

"Father, the Church will triumph as it has for centuries. In our new land, our children will be educated in the ways of the Church. There will be special privileges. The Church will have rights." A sincere but meaningless speech, it clearly satisfied the priest for the moment. François glanced worriedly at his watch. "I must see to the other guests, Father. And I know you're anxious to get home. Henri will write the statement for you. No need to concern yourself about it." He shook the priest's hand and terminated the interview by walking determinedly out the door into the living room.

Father Moreau bowed his head. The doubts were beginning to assault him again. The Church had to be the voice of Québec and separatism would be the way to make sure of it. But only in the hands of the right man. "Have I chosen wisely, Lord? This François, he isn't a righteous man. He sounds sincere, and he looks sincere, but he has given no real assurance that our way is the way he will re-build our Québec. But, one must do something and in these times we have little choice but to ally ourselves with those who are strongest, and who will have the power to throw out our enemies."

The priest, deep in thought, walked slowly to the door, unaware of Pierre still sitting quietly in his corner. "I must believe it now," he muttered aloud. "I must believe that the end will justify the means."

15

While François was cloistered with Father Moreau and Pierre, Jacques Ginette had rounded up the university students and led them upstairs to Madame Hébert's study.

It was indeed a motley crew that entered that musty-smelling room. The bearded youths and giggling, long skirted girls seemed incongruous amidst the heavy veloured furniture and baroque decor. But they made the room theirs, the boys sprawling on the floor and on chairs. One particularly scruffy-looking fellow made a great show of examining the leather-covered volumes in the bookshelves lining one wall of the room. He snatched down a well-preserved copy of Proust and flipped through the pages, stopping to read aloud a passage here and there, disdain oozing with every gesture.

After a few minutes, François entered with Pierre tagging timidly along. The two found places for themselves in an inconspicuous corner. Jacques nodded to François and rapped sharply on the heavy oak desk, his voice rising above the din of the students as he called for their attention.

"My friends, we haven't a great deal of time. Perhaps we should get down to business."

Jacques waited patiently while the last whispers died down and he felt he had the full attention of the young people. "I'm sure you are all aware of the great honour being paid us tonight by the attendance of the man soon to become president of our new republic." He beamed his famous grin and gestured flamboyantly toward François, who bowed and tried to smile modestly as he felt the glances of the somewhat awed students.

Times had certainly changed since François had first set foot in Canada. It wasn't so very long ago that the introduction would have been considered seditious, treasonable, anything but the triumphant rally cry Ginette made it seem. "Well," mused François, "the average Canadian has slumped into apathy, his only interest is money-grubbing. We can say or do whatever we want and when he responds, a neatly dropped suggestion that he's a fascist, capitalist, imperialist, whatever, will silence him quickly enough. Oh, he's just a dull, self-satisfied fellow, without eyes or ears for anything outside his own tiny puddle of mud."

He looked round the room at the students, the cream-of-the-crop radicals recruited from across Québec, his eyes resting finally on Pierre, engrossed in every detail of the scene. "No, there's no doubt about it, circumstances are just right. Pierre makes a good barometer. I can see the desire for change, even in his ignorant eyes."

Jacques' speech continued. He held the group with his controlled emotionalism. His voice, trained as an actor's, ran through the entire scale: bitterness, challenge, hope and cajolery. His well-rounded tones filled the room. "The time for inactivity is over! The time for promises is over! The hour for victory is at hand. But," Ginette paused significantly, glancing at his audience. He lowered his voice and added in an almost confidential manner, "without your help that victory may elude our grasp. It's because we need you that we have asked you here tonight, to present the truth of our situation to you so that you will clearly understand where your loyalty must lie, in order to bring about the realization of the dream we have all held dearest for so long."

Ginette stopped again, his finger darted out, pointing dramatically at a young man slouched in front of him. "Claude, how long have you waited for action?"

The youth shifted uneasily in his seat. He glanced over at François, returned his attention to Jacques and shot out defiantly. "Too long, much too long!"

Jacques was pleased. This was the kind of response he needed; emotionalism, that could be bent their way, was the answer to all the problems that might still stand in his and François' road to international fame. He nodded triumphantly at the student and carried on with a new note of animation in his voice.

"Claude knows. He knows what I'm sure the rest of you also know. We have all been waiting much too long. And those of us who have been waiting with growing impatience must now realize that there is only one man who can give us victory. Only one man with a plan." Another dramatic pause, another exaggerated gesture toward François standing now almost at attention.

"François Lallemont! There is our man. If you are looking for action now, you must support François. You must give him your whole-hearted support. Half-hearted support won't do. Wishy-washy support won't do." Jacques was just getting into high gear. His arms waved, his eyes flashed, his voice demanded agreement.

"We expect sworn loyalty from every one of you here tonight. If you can't give it . . . resign!"

There were uncomfortable stirrings from the now self-con-
scious group. Jacques knew how to handle them. He paused,
seemed to compose himself and grinned broadly. "And I know
there is no one in this room who would resign!" At ease again,
they all smiled with him, nodding in unanimous agreement. François could see that these students were nestled in the palm of his
hand.

Of course, Ginette deserved some thanks for the way he
handled these people. He was, after all, an actor schooled in the
proven methods of persuasion. People were willing to follow him,
not just because of his charming manner, but because he was a
minor celebrity throughout the province. He was one of the top
television hosts on the French-language network and had had
plenty of opportunity to instill his point of view in the public's mind.
He often caused comment with his strong pro-French, anti-Ameri-
can attitudes and his outspoken criticisms of the English tongue.
He was clever though: he never let the true strength of his bitterness show through. He poked fun at the enemy and slowly tore
down the English prestige without appearing to be fanatical about
it. Ginette was beholden to no man, not on the surface in any
case. But François knew that Ginette was his man, not because of
his convictions, but because of his one weakness.

François had met Jacques in Paris in 1945 immediately after
the war. Young Ginette was a Quartermaster Sergeant in the
Canadian Army and, as such, had control over huge stores of
equipment. It was not long before François and Ginette had
worked out an extremely profitable arrangement. It was simple.
Jacques stole loads of equipment and François disposed of it on
the black market. They dealt in anything they could get their hands
on: food, cigarettes, gasoline, guns, ammunition, drugs and clothing. If Jacques could get it, François could sell it.

One of the most valuable commodities at that time was
cigarettes. The citizens were starved for a real cigarette, and if
they didn't smoke, the cigarettes could be used as cash in many
instances. Jacques and François had an opportunity to hijack a
load of them. Jacques had been assigned to bring a truck loaded
with tobacco from Calais to Lille. Jacques had with him a corporal
who had a certain weakness for alcohol. Together they left Calais
late in the afternoon with the cargo. They headed north-east, and
after passing through a small town outside Courtrai Jacques sug-

gested to his companion that they stop for a few drinks at the local café. The corporal was quick to take him up on the suggestion and Jacques was equally quick to inspire the corporal to reach oblivion on Calvados and beer.

On a pre-arranged signal from François, also in the café, Jacques half-carried the sodden corporal back to the truck. A short distance up the road he parked, and moments later was joined by François. The idea was to pretend that a robbery had taken place, so Jacques struck the corporal a vicious blow on the head with his revolver. François struck Jacques a mild blow and left the two men lying on the side of the road, driving off with the truck and its contents.

It worked beautifully! François disposed of the tobacco in short order, and then dismantled the truck and sold the parts for a handsome profit. After a respectable interval, he met Jacques in Paris to divide the spoils. François had been tempted to forget the meeting, but decided it might be smarter to play ball in the hope of bigger and better things for the future. After all, Jacques could put the finger on him if he wanted to. A show of fair play at this point was the best way, so François appeared at the café in Montmartre on the appointed day.

When Jacques arrived, he was in a state of real agitation. Something serious had obviously gone wrong. He seemed too anxious to get his money, discuss nothing and leave. But François was insistent, "What's the problem? Are we in trouble?"

"It's nothing, François. Nothing to upset you."

François still pressed him and after a few drinks Jacques told him bluntly that the corporal had died.

"He died from the crack I gave him. They've been questioning me for days. I gave a pretty good story but I think they smell something funny. I want my share, François, and I want it now. That's the end of it. I don't dare risk it again."

François paid up reluctantly. He never did tell Jacques how much he'd really gotten for the truck and tobacco. Why live up to a fifty-fifty split? Jacques was lucky to get twenty percent.

François went off to Russia and Jacques returned to Canada where he lived rather high with the help of his ill-gotten gains. His ostentatious style of living attracted the attention of some of Québec's theatrical types and they soon started grooming him for the life of a television personality.

Yes, François had the goods on Jacques, but he had a real admiration for him too. When he arrived in Canada, François had seen Jacques on a late-night talk programme and looked him up the next day. He had formed the nucleus of an idea. Jacques was going to be a big public figure in Québec one of these years and he couldn't afford to let his career get off the tracks through the hint of any personal scandal. He might be willing to pay quite handsomely for some insurance against ugly whispers.

Jacques had matured in the intervening years. His new-found self-confidence had François quite baffled. Jacques ignored the veiled threats of blackmail that François kept bringing into the conversation on their first meeting. It seemed that Jacques honestly didn't know what he was referring to, that he'd forgotten the whole incident and was only pleased to see François as an old drinking buddy.

"Maybe he's smart enough to know he needs me to succeed. Maybe that's why he works so faithfully for me." François pondered the enigma of the real Jacques, as he listened to him extol his virtues to the students. "Well, if he ever gets out of line, I've got an axe hanging over his head that'll come down on him with just a word from me."

Jacques had finished his set speech and it was easy to see the students were impressed. He opened the meeting up to discussion. "Does anyone have a question?"

There was a moment's silence and then Claude spoke up. "Bordeaux says we have to be careful. Non-violence is his line. What's your answer to that?"

Jacques laughed derisively. "My answer's a question. How long has Bordeaux been president of the Movement?"

"I'm not sure. Ever since I've been in anyway."

Jacques spat it out. "Ten years! Ten years he's been president and what's happened?" The students looked at one another but before anyone could answer, Jacques' voice rang out again. "Nothing! He hasn't accomplished one thing. He's just a lot of wind. Now with François it's different. Within six months of his election, the plan of our Movement will be complete and we'll win the next general election in Québec. According to our plan," he said, looking at François, "our independence is less than one year from today." He straightened up, thrust his chin forward in challenge and said, "Can Bordeaux match that? Can anyone match that?"

Dead silence greeted this demand for a moment. Then it came, a roar of voices: "No!"

Jacques glanced around the room anticipating another question. He didn't have long to wait. One sandal-shod youth sitting on the floor looked up. "Monsieur Ginette, the student association at our college has supported Bordeaux for the past four years. For the first two, we supported him because we thought he'd do something. For the last two, we've been supporting him because there was no one else. We don't really think he's accomplishing anything. He just talks a lot." He looked about the room and saw the nods of agreement encouraging him to go on. "However, we're concerned about getting too involved in anything really illegal, like tossing bombs around or something. If we back François, and he openly advocates violence, won't the rest of Canada be pushed too far? They've taken everything pretty calmly so far. Even when de Gaulle came to Expo and used our slogans, there wasn't that big a fuss. A few days and it was all over. How much will they take? If François gets elected, aren't they going to realize we're really serious and won't they try something to stop us from seceding? Are we going to end up with a real war of secession over your own river?"

Ginette looked at François with a raised eyebrow. Turning back to the student, he smiled broadly and reassured him. "No!" he said emphatically. "Definitely not! There won't be any civil war and I'll tell you why.

"Most Canadians don't give a damn about Québec. They don't care if we separate or not. First of all, they're enjoying luxury like they've never had before. They've made wealth and social position the most important things in their society. So, they can't be bothered to think about our situation. It's much easier to ignore things. Secondly, the Canadians that do think about it are not united in their ideas. Each one has an opinion, but the opinions vary to such a degree that no one can come to any conclusion. You're heard the phrase 'divide and conquer.' That's the philosophy here."

These students were able to understand this particular philosophy with regards to the rest of Canada. They were well-schooled in Canadian politics and policies. They knew that the face of Canada was changing. Not too many years ago, the country had consisted of the descendants of the original French and English populations. The immigration laws of the country had been structured so the English could gain strength with an overwhelming influx of British subjects. Anyone holding a British passport had been admitted to the country without question, for their loyalties were to the Commonwealth. But things had changed and laws had changed. So now Canada was a conglomeration of people from every country of the world. These new Canadians had no special loyalty to Britain, and no great love for the

Monarchy. They were searching for a new way of life in a new world. They wanted to have a voice in how this world would be organized. For economic reasons, most of the immigrants chose English as their second language. They gave no strength to the French cause. However, they soon became aware of the struggle for French equality. They decided that if the French, a minority group, were to have schools and the legal right to bolster their culture, then why shouldn't they, the new backbone of the country, also have schools and laws aimed at preserving their languages and cultures? So it was that the country was no longer divided between the English and the French. There were hundreds of different minority groups, each advancing a theory, each expecting a change to advance them in the new Canadian society. Added to the voices of the immigrant groups, there were also those who championed the rights of the only true Canadians, the Eskimos and Indians. If the French claimed equal rights as a founding group, surely the natives had as much right to lay a claim?

So now Canada was nicely divided. The English group had broken into many sub-groups and the French were still holding together. Of course, among the French, too, there was a wide variety of ideas and opinions as to how to gain equality but at least the aims were the same: more opportunity for the advancement of the French-speaking Canadian; better education, more job opportunities, better standards of living, and legislation designed to protect French culture.

As things developed, the Canadian parliament set up a royal commission to study the theory of bilingualism and biculturalism. There had been widespread discussion and theorizing by the best Canadian minds. Suddenly everyone in the country was on the B and B bandwagon. French-speaking schools sprang up, radio stations with exclusive French coverage went on the air and politicians across the country started promising French-English equality. Soon, Canadians were beginning to accept the idea that Canada was a "two-nation" country.

François and Jacques had discussed this particular concept many times. They both knew that it was just another way the English had of trying to soothe the French-speaking minority. It could not change anything. Complete separation was still the only true answer. But obviously, if the rest of Canada had accepted the idea of two nations, it was just a short hop to presenting them with the facts of two one-nation countries. It was on this idea that Jacques continued speaking.

"Every federal political party in Canada has adopted some

form of the two-nation theory in its national platform. We're going to make that work for us. Elements from across the country are meeting an impasse designed by fate to help us. We must move quickly! If we don't strike now while the iron is hot, we are lost! Waiting could only invite events that will make our position more difficult. We must move now, and the only way we can move is through François. He is the only one with a plan for action all laid out!''

"So you see, my friends," he continued, "you must take the responsibility right now for the fate of your children. If you refuse to stand up for François tonight, the opportunity for a free Québec may pass us by and it will be you who must answer for the consequences."

Jacques could see that he had these students' understanding perfectly now. They were a subdued, grave-faced group now. Each one seemed determined to take a personal responsibility for the future of Québec. Now was the time to wind up the meeting, get their commitments and leave no time for more thought to muddy up the waters of their minds.

"We need your support at the convention. We need your votes. François will win with you behind him. You will shout down any opposition. You'll help us show the world we mean business!"

Jacques seemed drained as he sank abruptly into the wing-backed chair behind him. The students broke into wild shouts of approval. They rose and clapped vigorously. They swarmed around Jacques and François, shaking hands with each in turn. They seemed jubilant at the thought that they were the makers of history tonight.

Pierre stood. He was overwhelmed by the proceedings. He couldn't fully understand what had happened, but he felt with certainty that he, too, was now one of those who stood in the wings and encouraged those who strutted on the stage of history.

François had completely forgotten the tiny doubts that had troubled him after his meeting with Father Moreau. He had recaptured the jubilant mood that had held him earlier in the evening. He looked sincerely into the eyes of each student as he shook their hands. These students, he thought, they'll do me more good than everyone else put together!

François motioned to Pierre to remain seated, then he tapped Jacques Ginette on the shoulder as the students left the room. Jacques understood and quickly broke into his familiar smile. It was easy for him to see that François was elated. And he should be. These students were sold. There'd be no more trouble with them. They'd hold down any opposition. They'd put every effort behind François. His dream of becoming president of the Movement was yet another step closer to reality. Jacques beamed at François who closed the door, took his hand and shook it vigorously. "Good work, Jacques," he said, "good work."

"Thanks," replied Jacques. "How do you think they took the new line?"

"Just as I expected," replied François. Then his gaze fell on Pierre.

"And what do you think, Pierre?"

Pierre licked his lips as he nervously contemplated what he would say. François always made him nervous with these sudden, unexpected questions. Jacques Ginette's quick smile, however, helped to raise his confidence. "I really think," said Pierre, "that they really want to help, that they'll really work hard for you."

"What do you think of their reactions, Pierre, their reactions to violence?" François slowly and deliberately went through the routine with his cigarette. Then he sat down and waited for Pierre's stumbling reply. Finally it came.

"I don't think they wanted any violence. No, they don't want violence," he said again as though to reassure himself.

"Do you know why?" François' gaze was intent.

"No."

"It's because of those stupid bastards in the FLQ. That's why. They almost ruined any chance we ever had with their bloody theatrics. Don't you remember, Pierre?"

"Sort of. But not everything."

François' reference was to a group of radicals known as the FLQ, a group organized in the mid-1960's to carry out a series of violent demonstrations demanding the secession of Québec, or else. Finally, after a series of confrontations with the authorities, a small hard-core group took matters into their own hands, and kidnapped a British diplomat and a Québec politician, who was ultimately murdered. Their exploits hit the front pages of newspapers in most parts of the world, and the resulting effect was a disastrous reaction on the part of Canadians. The government declared a state emergency, the army was placed on alert, drastic powers were given to the police, suspects were rounded up, and the War Measures Act, the legal document by which the army had taken control, was allowed to remain in force for some months. The result was the almost total annihilation of the FLQ and a great loss of prestige for all separatists.

It was almost total disaster, but not quite. Bordeaux had used the experience as a perfect example of his non-violent stand. His strategy had worked. It had helped him retain his control of the party against those who had advocated violence. But this was a long time ago, and things of this nature were easily forgotten by most people. But even so, François and Ginette were both convinced that a return to violence was not acceptable, not yet.

"Do you see why you must follow my plan to the letter?" questioned François. "It's the only way we can get anywhere without violence."

"But what we're going to do. Isn't that . . .?" Pierre looked puzzled as his eyes darted from François to Jacques, then back to François. He was surprised that François was making no attempt to hide his remarks from Ginette.

"It's all right," laughed Jacques. "I know all about the plan. François was only testing you." With that they both left the room.

There was still another fifteen minutes before the next meeting. Thoughtfully, Pierre stood there. Then, lighting a cigarette, he sat down in the same leather chair he had occupied during Jacques' address. The room was silent now, a marked contrast to the hubbub that had gone on only minutes before. He drew deeply on his cigarette.

Suddenly, the lights in the room blacked out. It shocked him mildly and he was about to jump to his feet when he heard a familiar voice outside the partially open door. "They've gone downstairs. They're finished with the meeting." Pierre relaxed again and settled back in the chair. It was just one of the servants talking to a companion. Without entering the room, they walked along the carpeted hallway and Pierre soon heard their footsteps on the stairs. In spite of the stale smoke permeating the air, there was a musty smell to the room. Probably from the books, thought Pierre. In the semi-darkness he sat, puffing on his cigarette, his thoughts wandering aimlessly through the happenings of the past few weeks.

They started with the vision of Jacques Ginette leaving the library only minutes ago, François' hand on his shoulder. Pierre thought Jacques looked like a little boy being given a lecture by his father. Jacques would fall apart at the seams if it wasn't for François, he mused. What a powerful man François is! What a leader! How he could make men do what he wanted. How he had changed things in the past few weeks. How many exciting changes; how many strange things? Pierre's thoughts drifted to Paul and wished that he had been here to see the result of his work. With Jacques Ginette at the lead and with François guiding his every move, the Movement was catching on like wildfire. Meetings had been held in almost every town and village across Québec during the last two months. Rallies had been staged in Montréal, Trois Rivières and Québec City, and although Pierre felt useless, having done nothing in the organizing of the rallies, François had promised that he would soon command an important role. "You're not quite ready, Pierre," François said repeatedly. "It would be foolish to give you a job before you're ready. It'd be like throwing a kid who can't swim into deep water. But remember, Pierre, I'm looking for big things from you after this little caper on the Sans Souci." The promises excited Pierre to the point that he was now looking forward to the day when François would give the go-ahead.

Voices in the hallway disturbed Pierre's thoughts. At first, they were vague and indistinguishable. They belonged to two people, a man and a woman, who walked along the hallway and stopped to talk very close to the door of the study. At first Pierre thought they'd enter the room, but they didn't. Then he recognized the voices. It was Madame Hébert and François. They talked quietly and confidentially. And Pierre listened.

"I assure you, Eloise" — it was François speaking — "there will be no danger. Giselle will be with you as well as Pierre."

"Of course, *cheri*, I'm completely convinced of that," replied Madame Hébert. "But this matter of the insurance bothers me. I simply can't afford to take the risk." There was a pause and then she continued. "I might as well confess, François. The house and the boat are the only two valuable pieces of property I have left. When my dear husband died, I thought he had left me well provided for, but there have been so many taxes, so many expenses. To be perfectly frank, François, I've been trying to sell the boat for some time."

"You know how dreadfully sorry I am to hear this, Eloise." François' voice was soft and condescending. "You know my sympathies lie with you. I want desperately to help you. To help you regain what is rightfully yours. To regain the position of influence your family name deserves. But the only way to accomplish this is to expedite the liberation of Québec. Then and only then can we take from our shoulders the insufferable yoke which has been on them for so long. Those miserable taxes put on us by the federalists; those miserable taxes that've robbed you of what's rightfully yours. They'll no longer be, Eloise, but I need your help before I can help you."

"You know I'll do anything for you, François. What is it?"

"How much is the boat worth?"

"I was told seventy thousand dollars by a boat dealer."

"Then we must insure it for a hundred thousand. Those boat dealers are always dishonest." Then, reconsidering his statement, he added, "Let me look after all the details, Eloise. You needn't worry about a thing. We must make absolutely certain that the insurance is in perfect order."

"Of course. It's the wise thing to do."

"And we must change the ownership of the vessel."

There was a slight pause, then Madame Hébert spoke. "Change the ownership? Why?"

"In case anything goes wrong." François' voice dropped to a whisper. "We must protect your name. We must protect it at all costs."

"I hadn't thought of that. Of course. But what could go wrong?"

"Nothing at all. Nothing at all. It's just a precaution."

"Oh. I see, François."

"Then you agree?"

"Yes. Yes, of course, *mon cher.*"

"I'll prepare the papers tomorrow. Pierre will bring them to you to sign." He hesitated. "Oh, there's one other thing."

"What is that, *cher?*"

"Remember, you must keep our little secret. Discuss it with no one."

"Of course not, François. I promise." Her voice was sincere and as Pierre listened, he thought she sounded like a little girl.

"We must go," said François abruptly. "I must attend a meeting downstairs."

Pierre sat very quietly in the chair. He was certain that Madame Hébert and François had gone, but he waited to hear their footsteps on the stairs before he stood up and walked to the door. He wouldn't want François to know he'd overheard the conversation, so he looked up and down the hallway from the darkness of the room before he ventured out.

Then he left the room. But when he reached the stairs a sudden thought made him look at his watch. It was 10:30. He had promised to phone Giselle by 10 o'clock.

16

When Pierre entered the drawing room, the meeting was in progress. François sat with Jacques and four others around a long table. In response to François' nod, Pierre sat down obediently without a word. The men at the table were the same group Pierre had met in the restaurant at Place d'Armes almost three months ago. None of them spoke or acknowledged his entry.

Pierre was late for the meeting because he had been on the telephone talking to Giselle for the past half hour, and their conversation had not been too pleasant. She had made him very unhappy. To him it seemed as though Giselle was trying to dampen his enthusiasm, to squelch his interest, in fact, to openly discourage him. It wasn't what she said, as much as the way she said it. Her remarks seemed hazy, almost incoherent at times and, at one point in their conversation, Pierre had accused her of being drunk. This had developed into a nasty argument between the pair which had lasted for some time. However, the tensions eased when Pierre promised that he would come to her apartment as soon as he could.

Now he tried to reject Giselle's arguments from his mind as he concentrated on the group. With François and Jacques were the lawyer, Charpentier, Jean Petrie, Henri Bédault and Roger Flynn. A flicker of bewilderment crossed Pierre's face as he thought of Roger's last name. Flynn, certainly not a French name; it was Irish. Why, he wondered, would a man with the name Flynn be interested in the cause of the French Canadian! It made no sense to him, but his thoughts soon changed as he became more and more absorbed.

"You have asked about the results of my study concerning the treaty which allows the passage of American ships through the St. Lawrence River," said Charpentier with authority. "I wish to report that my study is finished, but the conclusions of my committee are divided. There is a great deal of dissension concerning the legality of the moves which you propose."

Roger Flynn was quick to interrupt. "Nothing that can't be solved . . ." He looked at François, who nodded approvingly.

"I am referring only to the legal differences of opinion," continued Charpentier. Then looking directly at Roger he added, "Not the theatrical."

Without waiting for Roger to reply, Jacques Ginette broke in. "I'm positive," he declared, "that between us, we'll find the answers."

"Of course," said Charpentier, "that's all we're interested in. But we must be sensible, we mustn't be erratic. Otherwise, the only people we'll hurt will be our own." He looked coldly at Roger as he spoke.

"Of course," responded Jacques with a smile as everyone, except Roger, nodded in assent. "We must be sensible and practical."

François turned his head slowly and thought. Charpentier was too logical. Too businesslike. Too composed. He was a bloody stumbling block. But necessary. "And what were the dissensions and differences of opinion, Mr. Charpentier?" he asked, masking his thoughts with a smile.

"It would be difficult, or should I say impossible, to state them without looking into the background."

"We must be brief," warned François. "We haven't got all night."

"And we must also be explicit, Monsieur François," replied Charpentier with no change of emotion in his voice. "We can't be frivolous with a matter of such grave importance."

"Go on then," said François impatiently, "go on then."

Charpentier began to outline his proposition. "I will not refer to the past," said Charpentier. "I'm sure we're all familiar with the past. However, I will clarify the position at present." He stopped and looked slowly around the table. Then, after looking at all the men in turn, he placed his eyes squarely on François. "The present position regarding the St. Lawrence River is clearcut. If we were, at present, to interfere with the free passage of any ship along this system, we would be breaking an international agreement. We would be committing an act of war. We would, undoubtedly, end up in a serious situation with grave consequences." He waited for the impact of his statement to settle before he continued. The dead silence of the group told him he had made his point. "The treaty I refer to is the Treaty of Washington, signed in 1871, between Canada and the United States. This treaty clearly states that the St. Lawrence River is an international waterway with free access rights to American ships. There are no 'ifs, ands, or buts' in the treaty. It gives the United States right of access forever."

Jean thumped his fist on the table. "Not our agreement," he shouted. "Not our agreement at all. It was signed by the English."

"Sold out by a damned English Queen," Henri Bédault thundered in support of Petrie.

François smiled. He liked melodramatic displays of this kind. But Charpentier continued with no visible sign of emotion.

"The agreement was ratified by the Parliament of Canada, a duly constituted authority of which Québec was a part, and it was further ratified by the United States Senate." Charpentier's voice was firm and resolute. There was silence for a moment, then Charpentier continued, almost apologetically. "Gentlemen, you must realize that I am one of you. I am for you and I am with you. But you must also realize that as a lawyer, my legal mind demands that I work on principles founded on facts and law. Emotionalism in this case will not work."

Petrie lifted his head and nodded in approval. "I agree," he said. "I agree that we must be logical when we plan our strategy. But on the other hand, we must, definitely and positively, have dramatic arguments if we want people to follow us. I agree with François and Jacques on our need for an incident but, on the other hand, I agree with you. We cannot break an agreement of many years standing without a good reason."

"Precisely." Charpentier's voice was sincere and final. "So I repeat, gentlemen. The present situation is clearcut. Any action we might take to bar traffic on the St. Lawrence would be regarded as a criminal act."

Silence again descended on the room and, one by one, the eyes of the group turned to François who sat smiling. And as they looked, his smile broadened until, finally, it turned into a laugh. "Gentlemen, you are just now beginning to see the light," he said. "You are now beginning to realize what I have known all along."

Pierre sat, amazed and bewildered. Was there nothing François didn't know? He could see by the expressions of the men around the table that they were surprised at François' attitude. Obviously, they had been expecting a different reaction from him. Pierre sighed. Now he understood a little more about the river, his river. The mighty St. Lawrence which cut Québec in two and swept from Lake Ontario to the sea. The swift-moving passage for giant vessels from all parts of the world. At least he was learning something new. It was just too bad that he didn't like what he was learning: the river didn't legally belong to Québec. He listened as Charpentier responded to François' laughter. "Then we're all in agreement that the St. Lawrence belongs to the people of Canada.

It is federal property, protected by the Canadian army and the federal police. In addition to this, the Americans have a perfectly legal right to use it. As such, it seems rather secure, don't you think?"

François ignored the statements. "And what, Charpentier, was the next conclusion from your committee?"

Charpentier continued. "The next strategic problem we must deal with, gentlemen, is the timing of our negotiations. Since we cannot use force to gain our ends, then we must negotiate. If we must negotiate, we must agree on a strategy for negotiation."

"What is your advice in this matter?" asked Jacques.

Charpentier replied. "In our studies, we carefully examined the possibilities of a negotiated secession from Canada. Our conclusion is that this possibility is very unlikely. We don't believe the terms of separation would be acceptable to us. However, should we be forced to negotiate a separation, and," said Charpentier with a sigh, "outside the possibility of war, there are only three times at which negotiations could take place." He stopped and thought for a moment, then continued with more emphasis in his voice. "Remember, gentlemen, we are discussing the negotiations on a new treaty for the river in conjunction with negotiations for separation. But please keep in mind the fact that they are two completely different entities. For example, we may be able to negotiate a secession from Canada while, at the same time, we may have to forego our rights to a new treaty for the river."

"No! No!" Petrie led the chorus but Charpentier, determined not to be sidetracked, ignored their protests and continued.

"The most propitious time for us to negotiate a new treaty for the St. Lawrence would be after our secession. The next best time would be during the completion of the formalities. The worst time, and we all agree on this point, is before the move to secede begins. We should avoid any discussions on this point until final negotiations commence. We can act surprised and hurt if such a point is raised, but we must expect that it will be. For this will be a touchier point in our negotiations than even our claim to Labrador, Northern Ontario and parts of New Brunswick."

Jacques leaned forward on the table. "Do you believe, Monsieur Charpentier, that they will insist we honour the Treaty of Washington after our seceding?"

"Of course," said Charpentier. "We're not dealing with fools no matter how much some of us would like to believe we are." His eyes glanced at François but just as quickly retreated. "The men we are dealing with," he went on, "fully realize the significance of the passage to the sea through the St. Lawrence. They fully realize the economic damage to both Canada and the United States, should the St. Lawrence River be closed to navigation. They realize that their investment of billions of dollars in the lock systems on the upper St. Lawrence would be useless, if passage in the lower section were denied through blockade or heavy tolls."

"But we could be just as demanding. We could simply refuse to discuss the treaty until secession negotiations were taking place," said Jacques as he glanced at François. François didn't respond, being determined to let them talk themselves out.

Jean Petrie cut in. "Legally, we're stymied," he said emphatically. "I agree with Charpentier. Canada is in a very strong position, both in hindering our separation, as well as thwarting our sovereign rights to the St. Lawrence. But let's not forget our secret weapon, the youth. They don't give a damn about all this hocus pocus. They won't take no for an answer."

Charpentier appeared angry. "We have already discounted violence as the answer," he said sharply.

"You say Canada is in a strong position," Jacques Ginette interrupted, trying to stifle his antagonism. "What about the United States?"

Charpentier and Petrie began to speak at once, but Petrie stopped and nodded his head to Charpentier who continued. "Concerning our secession, the United States has no say whatsoever. It is simply none of their business what we do . . ."

Roger Flynn broke into the conversation. "You're right, it's none of their goddamn business and why should it be. . . .?"

Although Charpentier did not approve of Roger's attitude, he did not offer a rebuff. "May I continue?" he asked. Then, waiting for a moment, he went on. "Although the United States has no right to interfere with our plans to separate, we are certain that they would involve themselves deeply in our affairs, if their access rights to the St. Lawrence were in jeopardy. As far as the United States is concerned, they have an agreement with the government in Ottawa for international control of the St. Lawrence River and the Seaway."

"Only because we were sold out!" This time it was Henri Bédault who caused the interruption.

"Be that as it may, the position is still the same." Charpentier was beginning to show his aggravation at the constant interruptions. He tried to lighten the conversation by changing the subject. "It is not all bad," he said. "There is one condition that would change everything for us. The power we want and need would be in our hands if, by some miracle, we could find ourselves separated and be classified as a sovereign state." Charpentier looked at François whose face registered his dead seriousness. Charpentier went on. "If it were possible, and may I repeat . . . if it were possible to effect a separation without negotiation, we would be in a most powerful position as far as she United States is concerned. With our control of the St. Lawrence River, we could cut off all access to American ports. The inland facilities at Chicago, Milwaukee, Detroit, Toledo, Buffalo, Rochester . . . need I continue? All of these ports which represent the outlet for the huge export trade of the north-eastern United States would be at our mercy. They would be paralyzed each time we blockaded the river. And yet, they would be powerless to stop us without interfering with the rights of a sovereign state. If we could manoeuvre ourselves into this situation, it would place us in a most advantageous position. For being in these circumstances, we could use the river to bolster our own economic position which may be shaky as a result of our separation."

Without exception the faces of the group brightened at these words of optimism.

"We would make them dance to our tune for a change," Petrie laughed.

"It is only right that we should," responded Jacques.

"But I must repeat, gentlemen," Charpentier said sadly. "This would be our position only if we were able to secede from Canada without having first made an agreement. And I repeat again, it is our considered opinion that the federal government in Ottawa will not allow us to secede without making an agreement with them in respect to the St. Lawrence River."

"It looks rather hopeless then, doesn't it?" It was Jacques who spoke and Pierre was surprised that he could make such a statement and still remain smiling.

"Nothing is hopeless," replied Charpentier. "I'm merely stating the position as it exists today." He sighed and looked at the papers strewn on the table before him. "Perhaps," he said slowly, "the position will change."

"Can you get to the point more quickly, Charpentier?" It was François who broke the silence. His voice was abusive and as he spoke, he looked at his watch. "I, for one, would like to get away from this dreary pessimism."

The faintest flicker of anger showed in Charpentier's eyes. But it was only momentary and he composed himself quickly. "Of course," he said blandly. "I'll cover the third and final position which is based on our establishing a legally constituted party, gaining control of the provincial legislature and, by so doing, accepting it as a mandate for secession."

"What about the need for a referendum?" asked Jacques.

"We do not believe this would be necessary in the legal sense," Charpentier stated. "The fact that the political party was elected to power for the sole purpose of promoting separatism would, in itself, be a mandate from the people of Québec to secede by whatever means were available."

Pierre could not understand half of what was going on, although it was becoming obvious to him that the problems were greater than he had ever imagined. He sat quietly, listening intently, his head aching in an effort to comprehend the full meaning of the discussion. He had never imagined that anything could be so complicated; he had always thought that if Québec wished to separate, they merely had to do so. Now there was all this legal stuff. He shook his head. Then he bent forward in his seat and listened more intently. Jacques Ginette was the next to speak.

"Mr. Charpentier," he asked, "if our Movement were to form the legally constituted government of Québec, and as such proclaimed secession, would it be opposed? Say, for example, that we could back up our declaration with a show of force from the provincial police or, perhaps, some army units that might come to our aid or, maybe, just our own militia, would the United States or Canada use force to stop us?"

"We've considered that possibility," Charpentier went on, "and we're under the impression that the Canadian government would stumble around for some time before considering the use of force. We base our conclusions on the widespread opposition against the War Measures Act used when the FLQ took over. On the other hand, we feel we couldn't succeed with force against the federalists should they decide to fight us. Of course, you realize that a declaration of secession would be regarded by many people as a declaration of civil war and, as such, the federal troops stationed in Québec would be obliged to defend themselves immediately. There would probably be bloodshed on the first day or two. How soon, or under what conditions the federalists would enforce their position, is a matter of conjecture." Charpentier stopped for a moment to catch his breath. He had been speaking fast and small beads of perspiration showed on his forehead.

"The only fact that we can guarantee at the present time," he went on, "is that the people of Canada are well aware of our discontent. They are watching us closely and are waiting for us to do something. Many of these people expect us to take action and many of them, surprisingly enough, side with us."

"Do you really believe this?" asked Jacques Ginette in a voice full of surprise.

"Yes."

"On what basis do you come to this conclusion?" Jacques asked.

"On the basis that they are willing to make almost any concession in order to settle the present situation for which they feel responsible. They are convinced the English are to blame for our problem. Some of them appear to have a guilt complex. We believe that they are now on the defensive. The onus is on them to make the next move. Their guilt complex is working for us." They all laughed.

"They feel guilty because they are guilty," shouted Henri.

"Would you say we have them on the run?" asked Jacques as he looked at François, the implacable sphinx-like François, who seemed to be enjoying the performance.

"You could say that," Charpentier replied.

Pierre's ears strained to hear Charpentier, the top-notch lawyer who had studied the situation, for God knows how long, and he could make only one comparison. The lawyer and his committee and the years of study and the reams of facts had come to exactly the same conclusion that François had explained to Jacques and himself only hours before. François had said, "We've got them on the run." François was right. Pierre's admiration for François increased with every word that Charpentier spoke.

Charpentier continued. "The last point is this. If our Movement were elected into a governing position in Québec and as such we proclaimed our secession from Canada, the United States would be in an extremely weak position."

"That sounds good." Petrie laughed as he spoke. "But how weak would they be?"

"The United States would demand their rights under the Treaty of Washington," Charpentier continued, "but we could easily frustrate them by making our own demands. We would insist on our rights as a sovereign nation. To be specific, gentlemen, our right as a sovereign state would nullify all previous treaties. We would no longer be forced to honour a treaty made by a foreign power on our behalf. No longer would we honour treaties made by Canada or England or Washington. The St. Lawrence would revert to us. The river would again be ours!"

"But they wouldn't use force!" Henri's voice betrayed his amazement.

"How could they without taking illegal actions against us?" demanded Charpentier. "We prophesy that the American hawks will shout their threats at us, but we believe the doves will see the futility of aggressive action. If they attempt to use force against us, we would apply to the United Nations for aid. If they attempted to use economic sanctions against us, we would, at the same time, economically throttle them by bottling up their seaports on the Great Lakes. Yes, gentlemen, I must say that our position, under these final conditions, would be extremely strong. Our great problem, however, is to obtain a legal separation from Canada without ratifying the Treaty of Washington." Charpentier was silent for a moment and then he asked, "Are there any questions, gentlemen?"

François shook his head. The others followed suit, but Jacques lifted his finger and pointed it at Charpentier, asking, "Are there any convincing legal arguments which we could present to the Canadian government in order to obtain an agreement in respect to the St. Lawrence?"

Petrie cut in. "The only convincing argument we can give them is a bomb! I don't agree with Charpentier on his methods. Of course, we agree on one thing: we must secede. But how? I say to hell with the law, to hell with argument, to hell with pussyfooting around! I think we should pick a day to separate and, the next day, we should give an ultimatum to Canada. Either you make an agreement with us regarding the St. Lawrence or we won't allow you access through Québec to join east and west Canada." Petrie formed his fingers like scissors and snapped at the air. "We would cut Canada in two," he said and laughed loudly. "They'd soon come begging."

"This is a possibility," admitted Charpentier. "However, this does not solve our immediate problem. This problem consists of convincing the people in Canada, first, to let us separate and, second, to convince them that we do, in fact, own the river and that no arbitrary conditions be placed upon us in relation to this river."

Suddenly François came to life. He took his fist and slammed it hard on the table. So hard, in fact, that a glass of water that was sitting a foot from his hand was upset. Jacques jumped to his feet, pulled out a large handkerchief, mopped up the water and swept the rest onto the floor.

"Gentlemen," François said, "I have listened with great interest and patience and it is my opinion that I could listen with great patience for the next hundred years, unless we quit talking and begin taking decisive actions. I'm sick of legal technicalities. I'm sick of this bloody nonsense. For Christ's sake! We want to get out of Canada! We want to separate! Then, let's separate. I tell you, here and now, that we're going to retrieve our solemn and sovereign rights to the river. I ask you, by what right do American ships travel up our river without our permission or inspection?" He slammed his fist again on the table. "They have no more right, gentlemen, than we do on their goddamn Mississippi. No one anywhere in the world would agree with the monolithic United States, if it used force to steal our river. If they knew the danger that American ships inflict on Québec, the sympathy of every nation in the world would be on our side."

"Danger? What danger?" Charpentier's voice was shrill.

"A very grave danger," shouted François. "An extremely grave danger! When the Treaty of Washington was signed in 1871, it was signed only as a device by the British to keep the Americans from invading Canada again. In those days, the explosive that could be used was gunpowder. At that time Québec couldn't offer resistance because we were a conquered people. We were forced by the British Crown to follow the dictates of the Queen, and we didn't believe there'd be a great danger. But today, gentlemen," François again slammed the table, "Today, the situation is completely different. Today, the American warships ply the waters of our river with atomic bombs in their holds. They carry through our waters explosives so frightening that, should an accident occur, whole cities would be destroyed. That is the danger. That is our argument!"

Charpentier was quick to interrupt. "There have been no such reports of atomic bombs being carried up the St. Lawrence," he said. "This is not a believable argument. This is pure speculation."

Petrie, who had been quiet for some time but itching to speak, broke into the conversation. "How do you know the danger is only in François' imagination?" he demanded. "Are we allowed to inspect the inside of American destroyers? No! Are we allowed to even go aboard? No! Are we given a list of the armaments they carry? No!"

"Absolutely correct, Monsieur Petrie," interrupted François. "It is exactly and precisely my point. We, in the sovereign Republic of Québec, are not aware of what is being transported through our waters, directly in front of our homes, our shops, our churches and our children."

"We are not a republic yet," cautioned Charpentier, "nor will idle dreams help us become one. We must be calm, we must be methodical."

"On the contrary," countered François, "we must be bold and forceful. We must be angry when the occasion demands."

"I would then," said Charpentier, "make certain that the accusations are factual before expounding them. If American warships are carrying atomic weaponry through our waters, which I agree would be a danger to our citizens, then we should bring it out in the open."

"And that is precisely what I plan to do," stormed François. "Before many weeks are past, Jacques Ginette will make a statement that will charge the United States with just such an offence. And when the charge is made and then presented, we will demand the right to search every vessel on the St. Lawrence."

The group continued their discussion, sometimes on a reasonable basis, sometimes their emotions reaching such a pitch, that Pierre thought the talks would end in a brawl. They discussed the possibilities and dangers of an explosion on the river. Perhaps Montréal, perhaps Trois Rivières, perhaps Québec City would be devoured in the holocaust. Then, when the subject had been explored from every conceivable angle, François asked, "And now that we all agree that atomic weapons are being carried by American warships on our river, what must we do?" Charpentier looked closely at François as the group responded noisily to the question. Charpentier had dealt with many men in his lifetime; he could size most of them up very well. And, although he knew François was a liar and a fraud, he looked at him now and wondered what was in his mind. Charpentier knew that François was capable, willing and anxious to do anything to attain his ends, but Charpentier could not fathom the depths of François' connivance. Sadly, he thought about the years he had spent in his belief that Québec should break away from Canada. He thought of the years he had spent with Bordeaux building up the Movement and, as he looked at François and listened to him baiting the antagonists at the table, a feeling of hatred and disgust swept over him. And for Charpentier, the unemotional and knowledgeable aristocrat of the Movement, that was extremely unusual.

The meeting showed signs of breaking up. Everyone was tired. It had been a long evening and it was getting late. They had received the reports of the legal committee. They had discussed the reports in great detail but no motions had been adopted.

Jacques finally stood up. "Gentlemen, François and I would

like to express our appreciation for you having given your time this evening. We would also like to express our appreciation to Monsieur Charpentier and his committee for the production of his excellent report. May I sum up?" No one answered. He went on. "We all agree that whatever happens, we are in great need of public support. We need the sympathy of many more people to our cause. The second most important priority is the election of our members to the National Assembly. The third conclusion is that we must accept any victory at the polls as a mandate for immediate separation. No referendum will be necessary." Jacques deliberately stopped speaking for a moment and allowed dead silence to fill the room. The group looked at him wonderingly.

Then slowly, Jacques again began to speak, emotionally and forcibly. "But before we can do anything, gentlemen, before we can win and before we can take our rightful place as leaders, we must re-organize the Movement. For that we need François! This is our first task. To repudiate our present leader who has done nothing, and replace him with François who will lead us to victory. There is no time like the present to make up your minds. To make up our minds to fight and push for François. He must be elected president next month. There is no other solution. I can now assure you that we have the clergy behind us, supporting us; Madame Hébert, who represents the aristocracy of Québec, assures us of her support and that of her influential friends; the political arm of our Movement has a full slate, and the youth of Québec are solidly behind us. Now, gentlemen, we need only your support; I know we can count on it, but I would like to hear your affirmation. Can we count on your enthusiastic support to assure François the victory he deserves in next month's election?"

Jacques sat down abruptly, staring at the faces before him. He looked first at Roger Flynn who nodded his head and said, "You bet you can."

Jean Petrie, anxious to agree, responded quickly to Jacques' gaze. "You can count on me."

Without hesitation, Henri Bédault nodded his head in agreement. "I think Bordeaux has had more than a fair chance to prove what he can do," he said and then added quickly, "let's see what François can do."

Jacques' eyes finally came to rest on Charpentier. "And you?" he asked. "What is your decision?"

Charpentier moved slightly in his chair but, except for that barely noticeable gesture, he appeared calm and relaxed. "I must defer my decision, Monsieur Ginette," he said quietly. "I can see that François is not a man easily pushed aside; I can see that he is not a man to accept defeat easily; I can see that as leader of the Movement, he will indeed get things done. Yes," he said slowly and a little sadly, "I can see many sides ro Monsieur Lallemont. And because of that, gentlemen, I promise you that I will give great consideration to your question." He stood up gathering the papers in front of him as he did. As far as Charpentier was concerned, the meeting was over.

17

The small, cluttered living room in Giselle's apartment closed in on him as Pierre paced angrily back and forth. Disturbed and disappointed by her sudden change in attitude, he went on and on about the happenings at Madame Hébert's.

Following the meeting, he had hurried to her, anxious to tell her everything about the students, the support for François, the decision of Father Moreau and details of the other confusing events of the evening. But she was cold and full of hate. Every praising remark he made was countered by contempt. Her rebuttals were sharp, penetrating, hitting their mark unmercifully.

Her sudden attack on the Movement forced Pierre to think of something he had been pushing down each time the ugly thought came to mind. Why had Giselle joined the Movement? She certainly didn't seem as dedicated to its principles as even he, and yet, she'd been with them long before he had. He'd never asked her why she'd joined because he was afraid. Afraid of his suspicions that Paul was the real reason, the one and only reason. Paul had openly told him what it was like. Or had he? On the day he died, Paul had spoken of the fun he would have with Giselle that night. Pierre remembered asking him to get an extra girl for a foursome, but Paul hadn't seemed interested. Why? It was the answer that frightened Pierre.

He had believed that Paul and Giselle had only a mutual interest in the Movement. Paul had said that same day, "She's not that kind of girl, Pierre. She's a nice, clean-cut kid. We just work together, that's all." But now, Pierre knew this wasn't the whole truth, even if it were more comfortable to believe. The thought that Giselle might at one time have belonged to Paul made his stomach twinge. He could accept the relationship Paul had had with his mother. It had seemed good. It had made Paul just like a real father; made Pierre feel like the other kids whose fathers were around the house. Yes. That had been okay. But with Giselle!

Jesus, Mary and Joseph! Please don't let me think things like that! Their relationship was good and clean. He had to believe that or his memory of Paul would have been tarnished, turning into contempt for Giselle. The fear that that could happen stopped Pierre from asking any questions. But tonight he couldn't worry about the past, he had to convince her, give her some of the faith he had in François.

"François is smart," he said, trying hard to be convincing. "You should have seen him. They were all running after him like a bunch of kids. Even Jacques Ginette. You should've been there. You'd think he was a king or something. I saw the whole thing. If I hadn't, I wouldn't believe it. Everybody looks up to him." He paused. "There's only one thing I don't understand."

Silence.

"I don't know why he treats me so special. He really likes me. I can tell. You should see how he's trying to help me! He wants me to learn everything so I can be his right-hand man."

With mixed feelings, Giselle listened and watched as he strode restlessly about the room. She'd insisted Pierre come to her apartment after the meeting for one purpose only. She was going to level with him, tell him she wanted him out of the Movement now. Since the frightening experience with François and Roger three weeks ago she'd tried to find ways of telling Pierre of her suspicions. She had tried to find proof that Paul had been murdered. But it was useless, a dead-end street. She was just kidding herself. She'd never be able to prove anything. And in the meantime, she was getting in deeper. Her complicity with François' activities increased dramatically the day she turned copies of the secret files over to him. He had thanked her profusely with honey-sweet words, grinned his Cheshire-cat smile and excused himself. However he planned to use this information, it was clear that she had a share of the guilt. She wished desperately that she had run away when she had the courage, when she could have gone without Pierre. She might have escaped before it was too late.

It was too late now, far beyond the point of no return. She had done the bidding of François, getting the information he wanted; she had spent all her leisure time with Pierre, trying hard to chip away at his loyalty to François and the Movement, but it was all to no avail. Instead of destroying his faith, her too subtle hints only created a reaction in Pierre that destroyed the effect of her arguments. He countered with patience and understanding, always trying hard to convince her. And the results had been disastrous for Giselle, for his softness reached her and her love for him increased with each passing day until now, she could not bear the thought of leaving him at any cost.

"Is he really that clever?" she asked in desperation, "or is he just an opportunist? After all, François didn't dream up the idea of separatism. He's a Johnny-come-lately. Paul was in before he'd even heard of Québec. Bordeaux started the Movement!"

"Maybe so, Giselle. Maybe he didn't dream it up, but he's gonna make it work. Look! Why are you so damn hard to convince? If you'd come to the meeting tonight, you would've seen. If you'd seen how the priest wants to help François, how all the students in Québec are rooting for him, how a big man like Jacques Ginette is crazy about him, you wouldn't talk like that."

But Giselle had been to enough meetings in the past two years. She'd heard the same old story so many times, it sounded like a broken record. She hadn't gone to the meeting tonight, although she'd been invited to the cocktail party. She'd had just one reason, a tactical one. She had thought that if she didn't turn up it would mean something to Pierre. He'd see her motivations, and try to come her way; but the opposite effect had been produced. He was fighting her all the way. "For God's sake, Pierre, do you think I'm a child! Do you think I can't see what's going on? You think this is something new? Well, if you do, wake up. I was a separatist when I was ten years old just like every kid in Québec. I hated because I was scared, and I wished we could get rid of everybody that spoke English. And why did I hate them? Because I was taught to hate. Deliberately and maliciously I think. And this damn stinking fear was the seed of separatism. It was planted years ago, and do you know who planted it? François? Not on your life! There's been a steady stream of separatist agitators for two hundred years, and the most important one was the Catholic Church. Think, Pierre, think! Who's been bleeding us dry ever since the damned English turned the power over to them? Who educated us to fear and hate? Who controlled the politics? Sure, Pierre, we're backward in Québec because we've been living in a backward system. It's been the Church's advantage to run our politics for two hundred years."

Pierre remembered the university students. "Not any more, Giselle, not any more. I heard them tonight. They're not listening to priests any more. They're not gonna let priests in long dresses tell them what to do. I heard them."

"But they'll listen to a parasite like François!"

Stunned, Pierre stared at her. How could she, a member of the Movement, talk like this? And she continued:

"They used to bow to priests; now they turn to hypocrites who say, 'we want to help you,' but who really want the power that used to belong to the Church. Then there's the other hangers-on, like Madame Hébert, dreaming her stupid dreams of past glories and future honour. Christ! They make me sick. They think they'll be so important, big fish in a little pond!"

Pierre thought of Madame Hébert, of her kindness, her loyalty. A pinch of resentment twinged him. But Giselle wasn't finished, her fury seemed to have no end. "Then the politicians! Can't you see what separation means to them? International figures instead of provincial wardens. Today, the head man is a premier, just one of ten. But after separation, what then? A king? An emperor? At the very least, a president. Can't you see François as president? Or maybe Jacques with François in the back room pulling the strings? I could go on all night. There must be a hundred different kinds of separatists. The legal minds! Do you know what's in it for them? They'll have a field day, changing laws and playing international blackmail with the St. Lawrence. Oh yes, Pierre, separation will make a few of them very big. And we mustn't forget," Giselle tossed her head back and stood up, "We mustn't forget the college students. They're the ones that know everything. They're so damn smart! Dress in odd clothes, grow beards, smoke pot and pretend, pretend to speak for everyone. They know everything except that a little knowledge is a dangerous thing. They're the real pawns in this game. The big losers. Where will they go after they've boxed themselves into a prison of language? Where else can they study outside Québec? France? Who's going to pay the shot?"

Pierre angrily stubbed his cigarette. Giselle quickly lit another and passed it to him. He took it without a word.

"There are others," Giselle continued. "A few businessmen, a few idealists who can't see beyond the end of their noses. A few people who . . ."

Pierre's fist hitting the coffee table stopped her. "Shut up, Giselle, shut up! You're wrong. Completely wrong. You're twisting everything. We're all fighting for the same thing, the people of Québec!"

"Oh yes! Them!"

"We're going to make them rich. We're going to take the yoke of capitalism off their necks."

"Your words?"

"What do you mean?"

"I mean you sound like a parrot. Or maybe like a ventriloquist's dummy, François' dummy."

"Giselle. For Christ's sake!"

"Can't you see the only thing separatism will do for Québec

is to ruin us? Aren't we handicapped enough now? When that bastard François gets through with Québec, you won't recognize the place. He'll make the Québécois rich? He'll bleed us like a leech."

Strongly mixed feelings dizzied Pierre. How he loved this woman and yet, how he hated her at this moment. When he'd walked in the front door less than an hour ago, he'd never imagined he could feel this way. He didn't want to fight with her; he wanted to love her.

His groin ached with desire for the closeness she had denied him for so long. He'd tried so hard to impress her, to break down that invisible wall that kept her at arm's length. But this! What had happened to make her turn so viciously on all those people Pierre considered friends and compatriots? Without thinking, he blurted it out, the question he had so carefully avoided for so long. "If you feel like that, how the hell did you ever get into the Movement?"

The question stopped her and a vision of those terribly depressing days in Montréal flashed before her. She had hated every minute of the bare existence that had been her life. Like a caged animal, she wanted to escape and when Paul gave her the key, she'd grabbed it. She went Paul's way, anxious to please, to obey, to protect her new-found refuge. But could she tell Pierre the truth? It was too ugly. She knew his idealistic mind would cringe at the bare truth, and he'd be hurt, terribly hurt. So she softened the blow.

"I did believe in it at first," she lied, "that's why I joined. But lately, I've developed an allergy to the whole rotten idea. I suppose I could say I joined for the same reason as any of the others: François, Madame Hébert, Father Moreau, any and all of them. I joined because I was selfish. I had only one thought in my head when I joined. What it could do for me."

Relieved because she hadn't once mentioned Paul, yet disappointed at her answer, Pierre slumped into the chair. It cut him like a knife to hear Giselle admit she was selfish and thought nothing of her people. "Have you got a drink?" he asked. "I need a drink."

She went to the kitchen while he sat there. He rolled a cigarette, lit it and held it a few inches from his face, staring intently at the smoke as it slowly curled upwards. The fingers on his right hand were nicotine-stained almost to the knuckles. Why was he involved in the Movement? It certainly wasn't selfishness, his rewards to date had been paltry and the prospects didn't look diamond-studded. Then what was it? He used to think it was because of Paul, but he knew this had never really been the reason, not the real one. He'd wanted to be involved, really involved in something all his life, and this was it. An opportunity he couldn't turn down or turn his back on. He'd rubbed shoulders with the poverty of rural Québec too long to ignore it. He'd seen too many tar-paper shacks, too much hunger, too little money in his pay cheques not to notice. And the things he'd noticed first were the big houses of the priests, standing like palaces beside the castle-like churches with their enormous spires. At one point in his youth, he thought he'd like to be a priest, just to live in one of those big houses, but it was only a passing fancy that quickly left when he learned that to be a priest he would have to go back to school.

Then there were the American boats on the river, always big, always beautiful and always American. Once, with his friend René, he'd walked up the gangway of a palatial yacht docked near Rivière du Loup. They were peering in the cabin window when a stern voice surprised them from behind. The voice was English, the flag on the yacht was American and the hate, that was French Canadian, grew out of proportion with the passing years. So it hadn't been Paul, or anybody else, that had really persuaded him. Instead, the Movement was filling a need he had felt for years. This fact was becoming more lucid to Pierre with each new conversation with François. If he could only kick those nagging doubts from his mind, if only he didn't have to be plagued by gnawing contradictions deep inside him, if only Giselle would believe in him!

She returned with the drinks and gave him one. He set it on the coffee table.

"I thought you needed a drink."

"I've got something to say first."

"What?"

"I don't believe you when you say you're selfish. I know you too well. You're good and kind and you do care about people. And there's something else I want you to know. I'm not in this because I'm selfish. I used to wonder about Paul, but I know for myself. I'm in this only to get a fair deal for everybody in Québec, for you and me, yes; but for everybody else too, Emile and Yvonne, Madame Hébert, everybody." He picked up the drink, satisfied that he'd said what he wanted.

Giselle sat down beside him on the arm of the big chair and ruffled his hair. "Darling," she said, "I'd like to tell you a little story, but first I want to make a deal with you."

"A deal? What kind of deal?"

"Let me tell you the story and then let's not talk any more tonight. But I want you to think of my story and some day, I'd like to talk about it."

Pierre's eyes said yes.

"I guess I was about seventeen when it happened. I'd left the Abbey School and gone to live with my Aunt Rita in Montréal. I spoke very little English. The language at school was French, all my lessons were in French, we spoke French everywhere out of school and so it was only natural that I should speak constantly in French. However, my aunt spoke English and French."

"I understand exactly what it's like," said Pierre. "I grew up the same way."

"Well, anyway," continued Giselle, "here I was in Montréal where half the people spoke French and the others spoke English so I still got along okay, it wasn't too bad. But then, my aunt took me on a trip. We went to Toronto, and it was terrible. I felt like a foreigner, out of place, because nobody could speak a word of French and my English was pretty bad. They laughed at me when I made mistakes and it hurt. My aunt's business kept us in Toronto for a few weeks, and I hated it so much I used to cry myself to sleep at night. But finally we left and travelled across Canada to British Columbia, stopping at all the big cities on the way. My aunt was a consulting chef for a chain of hotels and we were on the road week after week. Everywhere we went I felt out of place, and this is supposed to be my country."

"Yes," said Pierre eagerly. "I understand. It makes me mad. They all speak English."

"By the time we got to Vancouver," continued Giselle, "I was a nervous wreck. Then we went to the States, first to San Francisco and then to Los Angeles. It was even worse there. They treated me as an oddity, something from outer space. It was worse than being alone. I was scared. I hated it. On the way back from California we passed through all kinds of cities, and I got more depressed as time went on. Everywhere I went, English was the only language spoken. Millions and millions of people everywhere spoke English; not one of them spoke French. I talked to my aunt about it. 'Of course,' she said, 'you must speak English to get along anywhere in North America except, of course, in some parts of Québec.' I couldn't wait to get home and, when I did, I vowed I would never travel again to visit these insolent people, these people who were so different from me. And then a strange thing happened, Pierre, as I got a little older, I began to resent the idea that I couldn't travel." She paused for a moment, searching for the right words. "Because of that I studied English."

"You shouldn't have given in. It's like being beaten."

"But that's not the point of the story, Pierre. The point is that my ideas changed. I realized that I was different from other people in only one respect. The difference was only in language. I liked the same things they did, the only difference was that we couldn't understand each other. At first I blamed everybody but myself. Then one day, I picked up a magazine and opened it at a page full of statistics. Do you know what they said? The statistics pointed out that there were two hundred million people in the United States and they all spoke English. On top of that, there were twenty million people in Canada, and over ninety per cent of them spoke English. I realized that I was a member of a group of people, so small in comparison to the others, that I represented less than one per cent of the population of the continent. I began to realize, Pierre, that the others were not out of step. It was me."

Giselle sipped her drink. "And then, Pierre, I asked myself why I was out of step. I asked myself why I didn't speak a language that was compatible with everybody else. And the answer was very simple. I was taught to speak a language that was foreign to most other people in my country."

"And why not?" asked Pierre. "Why shouldn't we speak our own language?"

"That was my first reaction," admitted Giselle, "but it didn't quite measure up. What did add up for me was that I was educated to be different. I was deliberately educated to speak a language that very few could understand. So I asked myself why and the answer disturbed me. Of course, I was given many, many reasons. But I was stuck with my answer. I felt that I was taught to speak a different language so that I could be controlled. They wanted me to be different so that I couldn't leave Québec. I felt I was part of a herd and they were putting their brand on me. It was as though they were saving me for future use. If they'd really wanted to help me, they'd have given me a fighting chance, they'd have let me assimilate.

"But that's as far as the story goes, Pierre. You're going to have to figure out your own answers. Maybe you'll see things my way eventually, I don't know. But one fact keeps hitting me in the face. We're surrounded by an awful lot of English-speaking people. We've got to rub shoulders with them, we can't play in our own backyard forever. We must do business with them. And to do business, we've got to communicate. Then, Pierre, I ask you, if that's true, wouldn't it be so much simpler if we all spoke the same language? But no! We can't be that realistic, that sensible."

"You've got it all mixed up, Giselle."

"Have I? Suppose the Dutchmen in the United States took our attitude? After all, their forefathers founded New York City. But today, suppose all the Dutchmen in the United States spoke Dutch because their forefathers founded the colony hundreds of years ago. Wouldn't that be stupid?"

"When we're separated, things will be different."

"If and when this ridiculous dream comes true," said Giselle, "it won't change geography. No matter how much you think you'd like to have it different, Québec will always be a part of the North American continent. And no matter how much you ignore it, the bulk of the people will always speak English. All separation will do for us will be to make our lives harder and more miserable."

Pierre sat hunched in the chair, his elbows resting on his knees, holding his drink in his right hand, his head bowed over it, a classic picture of dejection. Giselle moved closer, and touched her glass to his. He looked up. "Remember our deal?" she asked.

"Deal? What deal?"

"I was to tell you the story and then there'd be no more of it for tonight, don't you remember?" She lifted her glass to his and tinkled them together. "Now let's see you smile," she scolded. "You've got to learn to relax, Pierre. The world won't begin or end with your seriousness."

Pierre studied her. She was beautiful in the soft light and he wondered at his stupidity. Talking politics when he really wanted to make love. Her hazel eyes were inviting; her lips which so recently had taunted him with troubling questions, now tempted his desires. He raised his glass. "It's a deal," he said.

"Then drink it down," she said softly, turning to the record player and selecting a record. In a minute, the haunting music of the recording filled the room with romantic undertones. The lights, dimmed to a shadow, only accentuated the flickering candle which flashed behind the coloured glass in which it was encased. Before long, Pierre's mood had changed and with rising spirits he took her hand.

"May I have the pleasure of this dance, Mademoiselle?" he asked mockingly.

"Of course." Giselle bowed to him in return.

Together they danced and the music, the drinks and the soft shadows changed the room to a rendezvous in Paris, a carnival in

Venice, a café at the Mardi Gras. Gone were the thoughts of political gambits, the disturbing hatreds of the Movement, and in their place was a soft and tender feeling of desire. The magic of that day on the Terrace returned, the day they'd walked up the steps to the Citadel. That day and the evening that followed had been a promise of things, beautiful things to come. But they had never materialized. The dreams of making love to her had seemed remote, but now it was the same as it had been on that day. He felt welcome and wanted. And when they slowly danced across the room, he felt her closeness and his desire crowded out his anger. Her body and the sensuousness of her movements inflamed him. He danced with her, his passions mounting.

Giselle was quiet. She was full of remorse for what she'd said. She'd deliberately tried to dash his dreams to the ground and now she felt guilty, ashamed. He was not involved in the Movement for any selfish purposes. She knew that. He was like the average Québécois, so ruled by his emotions, his pride, that he could be too easily influenced, too easily used. The feelings of the French habitant of Québec are deeper than most people realize, she thought. Maybe it's our nature, maybe it's our culture. Or could it be our measurement of values? Is it a strength or is it a terrible weakness? Whatever it is, it's part of me and part of Pierre, and part of all of us.

How she envied those people who didn't have this intensity of feeling, this boiling hot or frigid cold temperament, with no in-between. Being like that was like living on a roller coaster, either right up on top or down in the depths with only brief flashes of the in-between. She had often asked herself, "Are we like this because we want to be, or are we victims of an unreasonable philosophy?"

She remembered a conversation she had once had in the lounge of the Mount Royal Hotel in Montréal with a man who had been a customer, one of the better kind. He was much older than she, and had been in the Air Force during the war. They drank together and the subject of French culture came up. The conversation drifted from one thing to another, generally concerning itself with the lack of understanding between the French and the English.

Suddenly the man, whose name she couldn't remember, became serious. "Something happened to me one time," he said, "that I've never forgotten. It was an experience I couldn't understand and probably never will, but it gave me a rare insight as a foreigner into the French personality. May I tell you about it? Perhaps you can explain it." Giselle had nodded in assent.

"It happened in Lille, a small city in the north of France," he went on. "I'd been flying fighter cover for a bombing raid on Hanover when I picked up some flack and couldn't get back to England, so I landed at the airport at Lille and, after being billeted in a local hotel, I found myself with the evening to spare. It wasn't long before I was at the bar of a huge beer hall on the Town Square.

"The Germans had retreated from the town less than twenty-four hours before and the people in general were still very excited at the arrival of the Allied forces. In this huge beer hall there was much evidence of the four-year German occupation. On the walls and ceilings were tapestries and murals emblazoned with the German coat of arms and the Swastika. The long bar was crowded with soldiers so I took a seat in the table area. As I sat sipping my drink my eyes caught sight of an attractive woman, about thirty-five years of age. A girl of about eighteen was with her. The older woman turned her head as though looking for someone. With her auburn hair glistening in the bright lights, she finally turned toward me. Our eyes met. I lifted my glass and smiled. She nodded, so I walked to her table. 'May I buy you a drink?' I asked her in my high-school French.

" 'Thank you very much,' she replied. So I ordered a round. And another. And another. It was fun. The conversation was stimulating, although limited by our lack of vocabularies in each other's language. She seemed to be a fine woman of good breeding and, remember, she was at least ten years older than I.

"But before an hour was up, she asked me the almost inevitable question, and it had a strange new twist to it. 'Would you do me the honour of coming to my home?' the older woman asked. I looked at the girl who was introduced to me as her daughter and only one thought entered my mind.

"I replied, 'It would be my pleasure.' They both smiled and then, without realizing why, a cold chill went through me. This was too easy, too pat. I thought of the German army not far from the outskirts. Or were some of them still in the city? The area around the centre of town was pock-marked with the remnants of the bombing and shelling and there were many damaged and bombed-out buildings. There could be Nazis hiding in the ruins, they could be anywhere. I felt the gun at my side. It was only a small side-arm. Certainly, if it were a trick, I would be an easy target. I looked at the men standing at the bar and noticed an Australian Air Force officer who looked friendly. 'Could my friend come along?' I asked.

"The woman looked at me steadily. 'Why, yes, of course,' she said with no hesitation.

"I left the table and approached the Australian officer. 'How would you like to join a little party?' I asked.

" 'Be delighted, old man,' he replied. 'Where is it?'

" 'I don't know,' I said. 'That's why I'd like to have some company. I don't know these broads and I don't know how far I can trust them.'

" 'Is it with those two lovely young ladies over there?' asked the Australian.

" 'Yes,' I said, and I felt like a damn fool.

" 'I'm sure we can trust them,' he said. 'Let's try.'

"Together, we left the beer hall and walked across the town square and up a side street. There was a quarter moon just rising and it sent eerie shadows down the cobblestone street. The Australian took the hand of the young girl, which I thought was odd, because he was much older than I. I took the hand of the older woman. She led us up the street and through the ruins of a group of houses, where a path cut its way across a corner, past another vacant lot and eventually to the doorway of a large, but old, house that had been sliced in two by some kind of blast.

"The door opened into a large kitchen and the woman promptly lit a kerosene lamp. There were two openings leading from the kitchen with curtains draped across them. I was curious to see what lay beyond them but I didn't want to offend my hostess and her daughter. 'Was there much damage to the house?' I asked.

" 'Come, let me show you.' The woman led me to the first doorway. You must understand that at this time of war, everyone, including me, was playing for keeps. I had a gun on my hip and the object of that gun was to kill anyone who might try to kill me. I was ending my fourth year of war and trusted nobody. Also, remember that in those days, it wasn't likely that a woman would walk so willingly or so unafraid into a lonely house with complete strangers, unless she either wished to seduce them or to kill them, and my hostess showed none of the signs of a whore. My Australian compatriot however, obviously didn't share my fears. He'd plunked himself on a couch right after we arrived, trying to make time with the daughter, who didn't show any more interest in amour than her mother. She simply sat beside him smiling.

"I kept my hand close to my gun as I cautiously stuck my head into the other room. There was a bed, a makeshift dresser, a rug and a mirror hanging on a wall. Nothing else. I backed out and walked immediately to the other room. I didn't want to leave the job half done. But my fears were unfounded, there was no one there. I offered a cigarette to the woman. She accepted it. I lit one for myself and sat down on a high-backed wooden chair at the kitchen table.

" 'You have done me a great honour,' said our hostess.

"The statement puzzled me. I concluded that since there was no danger, we were going to be seduced. Expectation began to rise in me. However, there was to be another surprise. The woman got up and, walking to the outer door, locked it.

" 'Will you move the table and couch, please?' she asked as she returned. Puzzled, I looked at the Australian, but, without any argument, we did as we were asked. She went into one of the side rooms and returned a moment later with a hammer. Handing it to me, she instructed me to remove the nails from the baseboard along one side of the kitchen wall. I did so and, again following her instructions, removed tacks which held the linoleum to the wooden floor. The Australian helped me and together, we rolled back the linoleum. There in the centre of the floor was a trap door. I looked at the woman and her daughter.

" 'What now?' I asked. 'What do you want us to do?'

" 'Open it,' she said simply.

" 'What's in there?' I demanded, as my instinctive suspicions arose in me.

" 'A dream,' she said wistfully. 'Just a dream. It is not a trap.'

"I looked at the Australian, then at the hammer which I held in my hand and began to work on the trap door. It had been nailed tight and the nails were rusted from the long years. Finally, the door loosened and we lifted it. There was something about three feet down but I couldn't see what it was. The woman advanced with the lantern, and looking down I could see that it was a case, yes, a box of something. I reached in, grabbed the edge and tried to lift. The Australian helped and together we lifted it up to the kitchen table. It was nothing more or less than a case of champagne, vintage 1939. That's all there was in the cave. We closed the door and rolled back the linoleum.

" 'Won't you please open a bottle?' asked the woman. I removed a bottle from the case and wiggled at the rusted wires which held the cork. The woman must have read the expression on my face and known what I was thinking. I wanted to know the reason for this strange midnight ceremony.

" 'In 1939,' said the woman, 'my husband was called into the army. He was on duty at the German frontier. On his last visit home, he predicted the disaster which was soon to envelop France.' He had a premonition, he confided to his wife, that he would soon die. Unshakable, relentless, the fear held him in its grasp.

" 'It is all because of the Nazis,' he had said, 'there will be no peace in the world until they are defeated. But I don't see how we can stop them. We have waited too long to prepare.' The woman's face became sad and, in the flickering light of the lamp, I noticed a drawn expression around her eyes.

" 'On his last visit,' she said wistfully, 'he bought this case of champagne and made me promise that I would share it with him when the Nazis were driven from our land. I promised him, but he was not satisfied. He had one more condition. 'If I die, as I think I will,' he had said, 'you must promise to fight the Bosche until you are dead or until they are defeated. Then, and only then, must you drink this toast to me and you must drink it only with a member of the Allies who enter Lille.'

" 'I promised him that. I gave him my word,' she whispered. The woman lowered her eyes and looked pale. 'He was killed a week later.'

"We drank five bottles of champagne that night and we talked and we laughed and the woman cried a little. I even felt like crying myself. And when the first grey light of dawn streaked across the war-ravaged skeletons of the houses on that dismal street, we were still talking and we were pretty drunk.

"But I was not so drunk that I didn't realize that this poor woman needed money, so I offered her some. 'Not for the drinks,' I emphasized. 'Just for yourself and your daughter.' But she was hurt and my youthful mind could not understand the reason. I hastened to explain to her that the money meant nothing to me, that I could afford it. But the more I explained, the more proud and hurt she became. Finally, I desisted, apologized profusely, and the two of us left the house.

"I learned a lesson that night but it was not a lesson in the art of making love. We had nothing sexually to do with either of the two women. But I did learn a little bit about the French that night. Or maybe it was something more universal, something about human nature in general. But whether it was a French characteristic or not, I did learn a little bit about the feelings of people.

"You see, I have always thought of myself as a practical man and I thought that, if it had been my case of champagne, and if I had been in the same position as that woman and her daughter, I would have done something more practical than fulfilling a useless promise, and if someone had offered me help with no strings attached, I would have accepted it. I would have taken it because my mind would have told me that this was the sensible thing to do. But this woman thought with her heart; she acted in response to her feelings alone. Her feelings were not governed by her mind. Instead, her mind was controlled by her feelings. Anyway, that's the way it looked to me, and I've always thought of the French as having a culture which encourages them to think with their hearts rather than with their heads."

With that, the man's story had finished and although Giselle had never seen him again, she never forgot the story. Like the memory of a first ride on a merry-go-round for a child, or the first tender feelings of love for a schoolboy, or that of the first kiss for a blossoming woman, this story had remained with Giselle as her first experience in philosophy. And although she had slept with this man and performed her arts for him, she could not remember his face or anything else about him. Only his story.

And she remembered his story because she believed it to be true. For most of her life, she, herself, had thought with her heart and ignored the protests of her mind. Almost everyone about her placed high values on their pride in being French, on their having strong emotional feelings and deep ties with their history and culture, yet she rarely heard anyone reconciling these feelings with logic or reason.

And now, here she was with Pierre, who felt exactly the same way. With his heart, he held a love which reason would have destroyed. He thought with his heart just like the woman in the story. There was no reason in his love; there was no understanding. He did not love her for what she truly was. Instead, he loved her for what his feelings told him she was. And Giselle was caught in the middle, for, on the one hand, she was glad he loved her this way and yet, on the other, it frightened her, for surely some day he would find out the truth about her and it would all be finished. She shuddered as the thought crossed her mind and Pierre, feeling the quiver in her body, held her closer as they danced.

Why shouldn't Pierre feel the way he does, she asked herself. Why shouldn't she, herself, have the same right to think with her heart? In fact, why shouldn't all the French people? After all, isn't that what had been taught to them in their schools, in their churches, in their homes? Wasn't that the main difference between the French and the English culture? Of course it was! The basic philosophy of their Catholic religion was faith, not reason. If that was true, thought Giselle, as she laid her head on Pierre's shoulder, then it must be right and good to think this way. After all, the people with open emotions are the most lovable, the most inspiring and the most easily inspired.

The conflict in Giselle's mind came into focus. Wasn't it this method of thinking that had led her into her most disastrous mistakes? If she had thought first and used her emotions later, she would never have experienced such a disaster with Armand. She would never have become a prostitute, she would have been spared the tortures of the past five years. And if she had been spared, she would not have learned. And if she had not learned, she would be exactly like the man who held her in his arms. Innocent, naive, trusting. And as she thought, the feelings welled up in her, and she knew she loved Pierre. Somehow, she had to find a way to help him without destroying his faith.

She felt his kiss on her neck and her thoughts reached out for reality.

"I love you, Giselle," Pierre whispered. "I love you with all my heart." They stopped dancing as the record changed, and he held her close, waiting for her to answer. She looked up at him and hesitated momentarily, before she spoke.

"You don't know enough about me to know that you love me," she said, and the words caught in her throat.

"I know all I need to know," he whispered. "I know all I want to know."

There was nothing in the world that Giselle could wish for, beyond the sound of those words. Yet, how could she accept them? Pierre did not know the ugly truth, and in Giselle's heart, she did not want him to know. How could she let him love her if he did not know? She shuddered and Pierre, feeling it, thought it a response. He held her closer.

"Pierre, there are some things I must . . ." Pierre kissed her lips and muffled her vain attempt to be honest.

"I don't want to hear anything," he said firmly. She kissed him quickly and then withdrew, but Pierre was not to be denied this time. Again, he drew her to him and kissed her until she felt enveloped, overpowered and mastered. The passion of love rose within her. She could feel warmth and love for Pierre that she had never before experienced. Now was not the time to confess her inner thoughts. Tonight was too beautiful to destroy. She would tell him tomorrow. She pulled away from him quickly and, grasping his hand, she led him out of the living room and down the hall to the bedroom.

18

François raised the goblet to his lips, finished the drink and set the glass on the coffee table. Everyone had left the house and he was alone, except for Eloise Hébert, and he was in no mood for her. The elation which had accompanied his brain-twisting exercises in the earlier part of the evening had left him, and the anticlimax produced a depressive melancholy. He was sick and tired of talking to this old woman and yet, he knew it was necessary. In the past two hours, he had convinced her to go along completely with him. She was to have the insurance papers changed within the next two days, and the fifty-foot cruiser, which was to figure so prominently in François' plans, would be available to him.

"I must go now, *cheri*," François said, looking at his watch. He had said this on three previous occasions but Madame Hébert had insisted that he stay.

"Just one more drink, *cheri*," she said pleadingly. "I know there are more interesting things we should discuss."

"But the hour is late," François insisted, as he wound his watch. "It is after three o'clock, Eloise, and I worry so much about your health."

"Oh, François! My health is perfect. Sit down," she demanded, as she picked up his goblet and filled it to the brim.

François sighed. He could not refuse nor could he let his real feelings be known. "Thank you so much, Eloise," he sighed. "You know how I love to be with you."

He sat on the chesterfield near the fireplace and tried to smile convincingly. After all, he thought, the whole plan depends on this deplorable idiot. Madame Hébert, after pouring the drink, plunked herself down beside him. She sat so close to François, he could feel her bulging hip pressed against his. Disgusted, he tried to move away, but the side of the chesterfield prevented him.

"And I love to be with you," she cooed as she turned her face to his.

François looked at her puckered lips and thought to himself: she is the only possible source of a power yacht. My plan depends on her yacht and on her too. Without this woman, I could not even begin to operate. He kissed her on the lips and then drew back.

"Eloise," he said, "I have such plans, such great plans for

you and me. You will never regret your decision to go along with me. I know what you want, my darling, and I will see to it that you will get it. Soon this house will echo to the sounds you long to hear. It will be filled again with the glories of Old France. And then, Eloise, you will no longer be a second-rate citizen of this foolish country, which should never have existed in the first place. But instead, my dear lady, you will be a Duchess, a Queen, a figure-head, for these poor, unfortunate people of Québec to follow, a reincarnation of all the beautiful things which this land of the French really implies. All the wonderful, all the beautiful things of life which you truly deserve." He stopped and looking at his drink, marvelled at his own powers of persuasion and of his logic.

"François, oh François! I can see it all now," Madame Hébert murmured. "We shall have such wonderful experiences, you and I. We shall make up for the past, we shall have such fun, the two of us."

Yes, thought François, but I am afraid that my fun will be more scintillating than yours, my dear. For you will be dead. As dead as an Acadian lobster in the boiling pot. As dead as the foolish dreams of history which you, in your backward way, wish to create. His thoughts raced forward to that day which was not so far away. To that day when the searing explosion would tear the limbs and entrails of this supercilious ass and would silence her prattling tongue forever. He smiled at the thought.

"I am convinced that your plan will work, *cheri*. I know it will work," she said solemnly.

His plan would work. François was sure of that. How could it fail? First of all, the papers would be signed so that the insurance for the yacht would go to François through Pierre. In order to allay any suspicions, Pierre was to be the beneficiary, but he would sign papers in advance, giving the entire estate to François. What a deviously clever plan! It was so simple that at first François had thought of discarding it. It couldn't possibly work. But the more he mused over it, the more feasible it became. With one fell swoop he would rid himself of Madame Hébert and become beneficiary of her estate which, including the boat and the house, would be well in excess of a quarter of a million dollars, a tidy sum for a man who had nothing.

In addition to this, he would establish the most important fact. The fact that the presence of American ships on the St. Lawrence posed a danger to Québec. This would not only insure his election to the presidency of the Movement, but it would plant the seeds from which the revolution in Québec would bear fruit.

There was only one small detail he had not yet decided. There must be two shattered bodies found after the explosion. One was to be Madame Hébert's, there was no doubt about that. But the other one François had not yet chosen. It could not be Pierre for, without him, the beneficiary plan would not work. It could not be Roger. He was needed for other important work. He didn't want it to be Giselle; François had other plans for her too, which included a bed, wine and soft music. He licked his lips at the prospects of her firm, young body, and then with a grimace, compared her with the creature that sat beside him. He finished his drink and, eluding another attempt by Madame Hébert to keep him, he freed himself and left the house.

He drove quickly back to the deserted streets of Québec City and a strange loneliness followed him. The thoughts of his basement apartment depressed him. He needed something. He needed someone. He needed release. He needed a woman. Giselle! Maybe she had gotten over her high-hatted attitude. Maybe tonight, she would be the kind of woman François wanted. Uninhibited, savage. Maybe she'd had a change of mind. There would be nothing wrong with finding out.

He changed direction and drove directly to her apartment, parking in an empty space directly in front. He entered the outer door with his key and walked quickly along the hallway. He was about to knock on the door when he heard whispering voices inside. He listened intently. The voices were almost inaudible, but he could tell that it was a man and a woman. Hate and anger rose in him as he forced himself to stop breathing. He listened for a long time and then he heard them more clearly. It was Giselle and Pierre. He stood like a department store dummy as the truth pounded in his head. It was Pierre. There was no doubt about that. And there was no question about what was going on, either. That dumb bastard, Pierre. That simple-minded, backwoods stud! He stemmed the desire to smash down the door and, instead, clenched his fist and walked down the hall to the entrance and his car.

On his way home, he made the decision. The second body which would be found floating in the St. Lawrence after the explosion would be Giselle's.

19

Although he wasn't fully awake, the warmth of her body next to him filled Pierre with a glorious sense of wonder. The height of emotion he had experienced the night before came rushing back. He moved closer, his heartbeat quickening as she stirred. He found her mouth and kissed it. "I love you," he whispered to ears that didn't hear. "I want to marry you." As he said it, he wondered if he would have the courage to repeat it when she was awake.

She breathed so lightly that he could scarcely hear her. Her face was a picture of contentment. She's so innocent, so pure and perfect. He was fully awake now, his mind filling with thoughts of last night. He knew now it had really happened. He had made love to his beautiful Giselle. She was his now. She was no longer a person apart. Until last night, she had been a million miles from him, as untouchable as the stars. But now, in the unfamiliar ecstasy of her bed, she was his ideal; precious, beautiful, dreamlike, and yet, wondrously real!

He kissed her again and she snuggled close. She seemed so comfortable in his arms, as though she had always belonged there. She was home. How could he be so lucky! Giselle belonged to him and to him alone. He was sure that she had never belonged to anyone else! Even as he thought this, something deep in him stirred and questioned. Could she have ever been with anyone else like this? He was repulsed by the idea. Impossible! It was wrong to even consider the possibility. She could only be with him now because she loved him. She was the perfect woman. Like the Blessed Virgin Mary he had worshipped and prayed to in his early life. He knew the woman he loved could never have been defiled by another man.

But why did thoughts of Paul insist on creeping into his mind, whispering ugly things; destroying the beauty of these moments? Pierre suddenly felt sick.

"I can hardly wait to get back," Paul had said moments before he died. "Back to my Giselle."

And now, as Pierre lay close to her, the words kept ringing in his ears. He shook his head to cast out the thought. It was impossible. Giselle could never have been like this with anyone before.

His agitated movements had awakened Giselle. She opened her eyes slowly and reached her hand out to find him.

"Good morning, darling," she whispered. As he kissed her, his quickly rising passion swept the disturbing thoughts from his mind. At first their caresses were gentle, loving and affectionate. They felt a genuine desire to share, a need for each other that couldn't be denied. Their passions grew, and like a thundering avalanche, their desire carried everything in its wake until, finally, they lay entwined in each other's arms, breathless and exhausted.

They remained that way until the peaceful silence of the room was disturbed by the raucous jangle of the telephone. It rang twice before Giselle moved reluctantly to answer it. She left the bed, and grabbing her dressing gown from a chair, ran to the living room to stop the incessant ring. It was François.

"Giselle, I have something for you to do today."

Giselle was furious but couldn't think of any excuse for not co-operating with him. "What is it, François?"

"I want you and Pierre to take some papers to Madame Hébert to sign. I need you to witness her signature. Pierre will pick up the papers here and then pick you up and take you to the boat. I'm going to call him now." François carefully kept every trace of irony out of his voice. He waited while she fumbled to cover up.

Giselle's thoughts raced. She didn't want François to call Pierre's rooming house. The landlord would say that Pierre had been away all night. That would make François curious and Giselle knew that when François was curious, he wouldn't be satisfied until he found out where he had spent the night.

"I'll call him," she said.

François was thrilled with the hint of panic in her voice. "Oh, no, I'll have to explain a few things to him anyway. Don't bother, Giselle."

"Really, François. I can call him now and he can pick me up before he gets the papers. Then he won't have to go out of the way to pick me up." She held her breath hoping she had said it convincingly.

François waited a moment, enjoying the pain he was obviously inflicting on her. "Well, all right," he said finally. "I guess that would save time. Meet me in the workshop in about an hour." He was satisfied. It was obvious she didn't want him to know of her involvement with Pierre. He wondered momentarily, why a woman like her would care who knew with whom she slept. But the question was quickly forgotten as he was struck with the pleasant realization of the power this would give him over her. With

Pierre for bait, he thought, Giselle will be easier to twist.

When the conversation was finished, Giselle stood beside the phone for a moment before calling to Pierre to get up. Then she made some toast and coffee.

They drove to the workshop in silence, an unspoken secret shared between them. When they arrived, Pierre went in alone and returned with Roger Flynn moments later.

"We're going in François' car," Roger said as he flung open the door of Pierre's car and took Giselle's arm to hurry her. She shivered at his touch. There was something about this man that repulsed her, frightened her. She pulled away from him and walked close to Pierre until they came to François' Peugeot, parked around the corner. Pierre opened the door and pushed the front seat forward for her to get into the back. Roger, already behind the wheel, glared at him. Pierre climbed into the back beside Giselle without a word.

It was a beautiful day. The sky was a brilliant blue and the changing leaves of autumn stood out crimson and gold against it. High in the sky, a formation of Canada geese, like an arrow pointing south, soared through the crisp air evacuating their homeland before the harsh winter arrived. The car headed into the outskirts and along a narrow gravel road through the gently rolling countryside. Past a grove of maple trees, their leaves red in the dazzling sun; past a massive stone church whose proud spire split the sky; past a small farming community where a horse-drawn plough still turned the soil of summer fallow.

Finally they came to the yacht basin, a small white frame building shielding the harbour. Madame Hébert's yacht was moored outside it. She stood on the forward deck, waving as they approached. The picture was an elegant one, the yacht so bright and sparkling in the morning sun.

Giselle and Pierre left the car and Roger stayed behind the wheel. "I'll wait here. Don't screw around. Just get the papers signed. I'm in a hurry."

Pierre followed Giselle along the wooden planks leading to the door of the boathouse. They passed through the boathouse to the gangplank on the other side. Madame Hébert greeted them gaily as she welcomed them on board. "You're just in time for coffee." She led them into the salon.

"I think we'd better finish our business as quickly as possible, Madame," said Pierre. "Roger is waiting in the car for us. He's in a hurry to go somewhere."

"Oh, Roger! He can wait." Madame Hébert ignored the protest and proceeded to pour coffee for the three of them.

"François asked me to tell you how sorry he was that he couldn't come. He said to tell you first thing."

"My poor, dear François!" exclaimed Madame Hébert. "He works himself so hard! He called me this morning and told me he wouldn't be able to make it. Something dreadfully important just came up! Well, I'll see him later and make him relax." Her mouth curved in a happy smile that made her pudgy face almost pretty.

Pierre offered her the envelope François had given him. "Here are the papers. François said to tell you that all you have to do is sign them. He said he needs them this afternoon. He'll explain later." Pierre handed her the envelope and stepped back.

"Oh, I'm sure everything's just fine. François would make certain that my interests are looked after properly. He's so understanding and thoughtful!" This last was aimed at Giselle, who smiled in response but said nothing. She was sure that if François was a thoughtful person, it was only because he was thinking of himself.

Madame Hébert motioned the two to sit down and join her as she poured the coffee. "I have a wonderful idea. Why don't I just sign these papers, you give them to Roger and then the three of us will spend a lovely morning on deck. I spend so little time here now that my husband is gone." She sighed. "My dear Alphonse and I used to have such good times on the Sans Souci. We used to spend a lot of time cruising up and down the river. Sometimes we'd even go up the Gulf to the Atlantic. I was never very sure just where we were but Alphonse always knew, he was a marvellous seaman. One summer he took me to New Brunswick where we fished in the big river there. The Remigouche, I think, or something like that."

Restigouche, thought Pierre, but before he could correct her, memories flooded his mind. That was the river he had looked across so often as a youth. He had envied the people who owned the big yachts that cruised up the river. Now as he listened, he remembered that Paul had told him the yachts were all owned by Americans, and it came as a surprise to hear that, at least one of them had belonged to a French Canadian. How many others had . . . ?

"Well, what do you think about it?" Madame Hébert broke into his thoughts, demanding an answer to her invitation.

Pierre, startled back to the present by her voice, looked to Giselle. "Do you think it would be all right?"

Giselle grinned broadly, looking more carefree and lovely by the minute. "Why not?" she said. "It'd be fun." She had often dreamed of spending her life like that; one of the idle rich, cruising the world's waterways in splendid yachts with servants at her beck and call, ready to do her bidding. "Why not?" she asked again. "Roger can take the papers back when we're through with them. It'll be a good way to get rid of him."

Madame Hébert opened the large envelope and took the papers out, spreading them on the coffee table in front of her. The heading on the document startled her. "I didn't realize it was a will!" The heavy, black scroll at the top of the first page was unmistakable, "*Last Will and Testament.*"

Giselle was surprised too. She hesitated a moment, but then felt bold enough to question. "What did you think it would be?"

"Why, I was expecting a bill of sale." Her expression changed into one of apology. "I never could understand this kind of thing. Alphonse used to tease me about my foolishness when it came to legal matters."

"Perhaps I can help. I've worked with legal documents." Giselle held out her hand.

Madame Hébert handed them over with a definite hesitation. What would François say, if he found out that she asked for Giselle's advice?

Giselle hastily glanced through the sheets of paper. There was no doubt about it. This was Madame Hébert's will. All of her property was listed: the boat, the house, her furniture, insurance policies, securities, jewellery. Everything. At the top of the third page, the most amazing thing struck her. Pierre's name. She looked again to be sure. Yes, there it was. Pierre LaPointe was the sole beneficiary. He clearly inherited the entire estate except for a very small amount which went to a trust fund that had been set up a couple of years ago for the Movement.

She was totally confused. Giselle knew that Madame Hébert liked Pierre and that she encouraged the growing interdependence of François and Pierre, but she had never thought for a moment that Madame Hébert would leave her entire estate to Pierre and not a single memento to François. Why, in God's name, did François want her to sign this document? It would do nothing for him.

Madame Hébert put out her hand to take the papers back. She suddenly realized her imprudence in allowing Giselle, a junior in the Movement, to get involved in François' business. He probably didn't want Giselle studying these documents and, besides, what did she know of such matters? She would instead discuss the matter with François later. "Just show me where I sign. I'm sure that's all it needs. I doubt if there's anything at all to change."

"Don't you think you should see your lawyer before you sign that piece of paper? I'm sure that'd be the best way to do it." Giselle had no particular feelings for this silly woman, but couldn't resist asking the question. After all, something was terribly wrong. This had to be some kind of a trick.

"Lawyer? Oh, no, there's no need to call him about this. François explained it all very carefully. I'm just very backward when it comes to understanding. He assured me that it was a simple matter, a formality. He says it's a very small, but very, very important part of his plan. I must sign." Madame Hébert wanted to get this dreary business over with, and get on with the pleasure of the day.

Giselle's suggestion did cause her a moment's wonder, however. She thought of how patient and gentle François had been to her the night before when he had explained it all. He'd said it was an agreement and she hadn't asked any questions. But he'd been so concerned about her, worried about her health and especially complimentary about her appearance and her charms as a hostess. Oh, he loved her, she could see that very clearly. She felt guilty questioning anything he said. She trusted him implicitly.

"I'd better sign it. Roger is waiting," she said. Then she added solemnly, "François needs it to get on with his business. He depends on me." She looked at the papers again to pick out the space to be signed.

"Wait!" Giselle leaned forward in her chair. The silly old woman. It was obvious she was infatuated with François. And the way she threw herself and her money into the Movement. Giselle was sure that François was the only reason for that too. Madame Hébert was just too selfish a person to be really interested in anything beyond herself. She'd probably never given a thought to political matters in her life until François came along. But now it was obvious he had a tight hold on her, as he did on the others: Jacques Ginette, Pierre, Roger, Father Moreau, Jean Petrie. Those were just a few! What was it about the man that he could demand the loyalty of so many different people? Was it really loyalty or just greed for something they believed François could give them? Well, he held them no matter how.

Madame Hébert was startled at Giselle's sudden gesture. "Wait? For what?"

"Nothing. It was nothing," Giselle replied quickly. Then, in order to cover up her feelings, she pointed out the spot where Madame Hébert was to sign.

She signed it quickly, then handed the papers to Giselle for her signature. "Is there anything else?" She turned to Pierre.

"Yes, that's why we all had to come," replied Pierre. "I mean Roger too. François said there had to be two witnesses, and that Giselle and Roger would have to sign."

"Then fetch him quickly." Madame Hébert was becoming annoyed. "I'm tiring of this sordid business." Pierre quickly left the salon and found his way to the car and Roger.

"It's going to be such fun." Madame Hébert poured more coffee.

"What's that?" asked Giselle absent-mindedly.

"Our trip." Madame Hébert eyed Giselle, wondering how any girl could forget that she was going on a cruise, especially with her young man.

"The trip?"

"Didn't François tell you?"

That son-of-a-bitch, thought Giselle. What a hell of a lot of nerve, making plans for me behind my back. What kind of a surprise is this supposed to be? But she didn't show her surprise. Instead, she looked squarely at the older woman and said blandly, "Yes, François said you'd explain the details."

Madame Hébert was delighted. It was flattering to know that François had such confidence in her. "Well, we'll be going down the St. Lawrence on the Sans Souci, the four of us, you and I and Pierre and Roger." She stopped and made a face at Roger's name.

Giselle waited for her to continue.

"François has a plan. A magnificent plan I assure you. Very sophisticated. Psychological. Not like those foolish FLQ. Not like Paul's post office bombs. This will prove that we really mean business." There was a twinkle in her eyes. "At first he wouldn't let me get involved, you know. But then I convinced him that he must. He's always so protective with me, doesn't let me take any of the risks. He's such a dear."

"What are we supposed to do?" interrupted Giselle.

"Top secret. François says that silence is imperative. But you shall find out, my dear. Very soon." Then she changed the subject abruptly. "François is gentle and good to me, just like Pierre is with you." Her eyes were suddenly very penetrating and Giselle felt uncomfortable. This old girl had a way of looking right through her. Giselle changed the subject as abruptly as the older woman had only seconds before.

"When do we go on this little trip?"

"Next week."

"And where?"

Madame Hébert was dying to discuss it, but François had made her swear to keep her silence. "I can't say. But you shall find out in good time." Madame Hébert was enjoying her Mata Hari role. "We'll be like the 'Three Musketeers.' You and me and Pierre. I'll be D'Artagnan. We'll go ahead fearlessly on our mission, no thought of the consequences." Madame Hébert romanticized. "It'll be a lovely trip. It's so beautiful this time of year on the river. We'll combine business with pleasure, get the job done, but have fun at the same time. You and I and your young man."

"My young man?"

"Why yes, my dear. Surely you know how much he loves you. He worships you. He is living for you. He'd die for you, if you asked." Madame Hébert's voice was soft, full of emotion.

Giselle felt a sudden anger for Pierre. Why did he let this old fool know of their affair? "Did Pierre tell you this?" she demanded.

Madame Hébert's answer was soft as she smiled broadly. "Only with his eyes, my dear, only with his eyes."

The sound of footsteps on the deck reached their ears. Pierre entered with Roger who signed the papers and pushed them into an inside pocket as he left the cabin without a word.

20

Giselle walked with a determined step down rue Belvédère. Her anger echoed round her as her heels clicked sharply on the pavement. Although the time on the Sans Souci had been pleasant, anger was rising within her as she thought of how Madame Hébert had casually let her in on the plans François had made for her. It was obvious that the whole thing was meant to be secret. It was almost like a conspiracy. Even Pierre obeyed François to the letter and hadn't said a word about it! Did he know that she was to be involved?

She had excused herself from Pierre immediately after their drive back to town and, heading in the direction of François' workshop, she was determined to settle the thing, once and for all. She had to stop as the traffic light turned red. She felt like bulldozing her way right through the oncoming cars, but rush-hour was in full swing and there wasn't an inch between cars. She turned with an exasperated gesture, and bumped sharply into a small boy of about ten. He looked up and smiled at her. "In a hurry, lady?" She glared down at him and his smile quickly evaporated. She suddenly realized that her anger showed. She couldn't confront François this way. She had to play it cool, get the upper hand with him.

"I guess I am." She smiled sweetly at the boy. He grinned back at her, then ran ahead as the light changed to green. Giselle shook her head. It had taken a small boy to show her her mistake. François could be a formidable opponent under the circumstances and, if she barged in on him in a flaming temper, he'd figuratively rip her to pieces. She forced herself to slow down.

François answered her knock cautiously. When he saw Giselle on the doorstep, he threw the door wide open and greeted her with a ridiculously exaggerated smile of welcome. "What a pleasure, Giselle! Come in. Let me take your coat."

"No. I'll be just a few minutes."

"No time for a drink?" He was wiping his hands on the front of a greasy smock that had once been white. Obviously, she'd interrupted some handiwork.

"No, thanks."

"Cigarette then?" He dug into the pocket of his smock and

produced his familiar silver case, snapped it open and offered it to her. She took a cigarette without a word and waited while he lit it for her.

"Well, sit down, my dear. I wasn't expecting to see you. How's everything going?" François obviously meant to treat this as a social call.

"Just fine." She was determined to maintain her composure, but face to face with this scum, she didn't trust herself to say more just yet.

François was amused. He could see quite clearly that she was agitated and he was going to enjoy toying with her. Good. "I'm always so interested in your welfare, Giselle."

"Why's that, do you suppose?"

"Because I'm so very fond of you, I guess. But I've told you that before, and you never seem to believe me." His hurt expression was a masterpiece. "But that's life. Like all true Frenchmen, I continue to try." He paused for a moment. She showed no sign of response. "Is that a new hairdo? It looks lovely on you. In fact, I detect a special radiance about you today." There was just the slightest hint of sarcasm.

Giselle was getting angrier with each word and fighting harder to control it. She looked straight ahead of her. She knew if she dared look at him, she'd be lost. The very sight of him made her feel violent. Perhaps it was because he was so clever and he made her feel inadequate. "I didn't come to talk about hairdos, François. I want to know all about the little plan you've made for me on Madame Hébert's boat!" In spite of her desire to control it, the anger was clear in her voice.

"Plan?" François inquired pleasantly.

She felt like screaming at him. Instead, she drew roughly on the cigarette in an attempt to control herself. "You know exactly what plan I mean, François. After all, since everyone else seems to be in on the secret, I just thought you might like to tell me about it, since I'm supposed to be dragged into it."

François turned to his work bench, littered with a variety of electronic gadgets. He picked up a fork-shaped piece of metal about two feet long and fondled it thoughtfully. There was a bright gleam in the depths of his eyes. "Of course, Giselle. Of course, you're curious. I'm sorry I didn't get around to telling you all about it sooner. Simply an oversight on my part. I'm so involved with petty details these days. You must forgive me for forgetting just one."

No reply. François continued. "There are so many irritating

details, Giselle, so many frustrating delays and so much incompetence around me. I quite often tend to forget niceties." He paused and looked at her for some reaction. There was none. "Come over here," he beckoned. Giselle moved to the makeshift bench which occupied one full side of the room. "Do you know what this is?" He held out a complex piece of metal and wire.

"I've no idea," she said sharply. Then, curiosity got the better of her. "What is it?"

"It's a simple homing device. Basically wire and transistors and photoelectric cells. It adds up to one thing, Giselle. A beautiful, beautiful idea." François started in on another lecture. "Ideas are what really count in this world, Giselle. There are so few people with real ideas. Most people are sheep, looking for a shepherd to lead them around. They have to be told what to do and how to do it. Always, they're looking for a leader. Well, I'm Québec's leader. I'll lead the Québécois where they wouldn't dare go without me. Just like Moses with the Jews. I'll show Québec the Promised Land."

But Giselle wasn't interested in analogy. "What's all that got to do with your contraption?"

François looked at her, irritated. He didn't like being interrupted when he was just getting his wind. "This apparatus, Giselle, is my guidance system. It'll take us on a short-cut to our goal. It is the only tool we need for final liberation. Here, let me show you just how it works. See this small antenna here in front?" Giselle nodded, interested in spite of herself. "When it's directed toward a certain spot, metal, say the side of a ship, perhaps a warship," François smiled craftily, "Maybe even the side of an American warship like the Apache, Giselle. You told me yourself that the Apache will be on the St. Lawrence in a few days. When this guidance system is programmed properly, it will steer the Sans Souci directly into the side of the ship." François laughed out loud. "You do see, don't you, Giselle? How simple it is? Just imagine you're on the Sans Souci, steaming up the St. Lawrence. In the distance is the Apache, easily visible in the moonlight. In the bow of the Sans Souci there is a small bomb." François again laughed with delight. "When I say small, Giselle, I mean small compared to the hydrogen bomb! The bow of the Sans Souci will be packed with enough explosives to split the destroyer in two!"

Giselle quivered with fear and anger. François was dead serious. His eyes were glassy as he pictured the whole scene. His picture of it was so vivid that it seemed real and she, too, could almost see it all.

"Imagine yourself, Giselle, setting this apparatus to guide the Sans Souci directly to the centre of the Apache. The boats collide! And when they do . . ." François' maniacal laughter echoed round the room. "That will be the end of Confederation in Canada. We will have proven, beyond doubt, that the St. Lawrence River, our river, has been made untenable for the people of Québec. The whole world will believe us when we say that the American aggressor has made our shores dangerous for our people, the simple, trusting people of Québec. The world's ready to believe anything against the States. It's the times we live in. Maybe I'm clairvoyant. I sometimes see things before they happen. But I know now, as if it had already happened, that the world is just waiting for the United States to collapse. Not just the Communist world, Giselle. Sure, they stand to gain a great deal. But there are many others in the world who will laugh at the downfall of the States. We're approaching a climax, a turning point in history. My clairvoyant mind tells me that it will be the greatest thing the world has even seen. And your little caper will help make it happen.

"We're living now with the confrontation of two great ideals, both of them absolutely impossible ideas to live by. Unrestricted capitalism in the United States. Socialist dictatorship in the Communist world. I don't know which will win in the final analysis. But right now the Communists are winning at psychological warfare, and that's why I'm so sure the world will believe our bluff."

Giselle looked at him, totally stunned by the sheer arrogance of this man who was preparing to play with the world as if it were a child's beach ball. He was insane. She had no doubt about it now. He would use any method to achieve his goal. Everything for personal power and to satisfy his stinking greed.

"I promised you, I'd stay until the conference. No longer!" she said flatly. "I felt I owed you something, François. But you promised me that you'd let me out then, no strings. I still expect that. I will not be a part of any of this idiocy." She stopped for a breath and examined François' face. It was ominous, but nothing would stop her now. "I will not have any part of it, François," she repeated with finality.

François hadn't moved. If he could just convince her to go along with this part of his plan, he'd be rid of her. She was like a fly on a horse's back, a simple, little irritation he could just swat away. "Of course, Giselle. You promised to stay until the conference. I haven't forgotten that. That's still it, but this has to be done before the conference ends or it would be a wasted effort. I counted on you. I still do. I simply expect you to be there to follow my orders as you promised." She didn't show any signs of giving in. "You don't understand, perhaps, why I want you on board? You're a woman with a great deal of common sense, and you're considerate of other people. I can see things in people, things they sometimes don't even see themselves. I see these things in you and that's why I'm sure you'll go along with the plan. Let me tell you why I need you on board."

Giselle stood, stone-faced.

"I need you to protect Madame Hébert. I'm sure you know how very fond I am of her. I want you there to comfort her, be a true friend for her. I don't want anything to happen to her, Giselle. I couldn't live if she were to be upset in any way. Please, Giselle. I ask you as a friend, a compatriot, won't you reconsider?"

Giselle looked through him. She knew him for what he was. An actor! And a lousy one at that, she thought. He had about as much use for Madame Hébert as he had for her! "I will not do it, François. I will *not!*" Her voice was emphatic.

François was not defeated yet. He turned his back and walked to a closet on the other side of the room. Without a word, he opened the door, removed his filthy smock and replaced it with his suit coat. He moved to a small mirror hanging on the wall and combed his hair meticulously. He then adjusted his coat and walked back to Giselle.

"I don't give a good goddamn what you say you'll do or not do, Giselle! I say you will do it. And you will!" He was emphatic.

Giselle was surprised. She had somehow expected that François would back down, maybe compromise, make a deal with her. He removed some papers from his inside pocket. "Just let me read a bit of this to you," he said casually. "It may help you change your mind. I think you'd better sit down. This may come as a bit of a shock."

Suddenly mesmerized, Giselle sat.

"This is a dossier on a person known as Marie LaClaire. Born in Québec, twenty-two years ago. Educated at the Abbey School in Ste. Rose." François glanced at Giselle and saw the rising concern in her eyes. "At seventeen she moved to Montréal to reside with an aunt. She became involved with a young man by the name of Armand. She had a child by Armand which she gave away. Gave away like an unwanted kitten! No thought of whether it might live or die. She didn't care at all. But why would she, a whore!" He spat out the last words and they filled the air with their ugliness. François went on, unmercifully. "She didn't care about the child, about herself, nothing!" François sneered at her. "You know, of course, Giselle, who Marie LaClaire really is? Well, so do I. Here are all the records." He waved the sheaf of papers under her nose.

Giselle was unable to move or speak. All along she thought that only Paul had known. Only Paul! He would never have told! But here it was in front of her. No use denying any of it.

"Need I go on?" He stood over her threateningly.

No reply.

He threw the papers in her lap contemptuously. "Look at it," he ordered. "Just look at it and then tell me you won't do as I say!"

Giselle weakly brushed the papers from her and they fluttered to the floor. There was no fight left in her. How strange it seemed that she had almost forgotten that part of her life. It all sounded like another person now. But she couldn't completely cut three years out of her life and pretend it had never been. She should have known that some pig like François would find out and use it to blackmail her!

"There are some people, I think," François taunted, "who would be very interested in that document. What do you suppose they might say or do, Giselle? You'll find out if you don't do exactly as I tell you." She sat, eyes fixed on the floor. She was drained of all feeling.

"It can easily be overcome." His tone softened now. "There's no need for anyone to ever know. Just do as I say." She should be on her knees to him now, he thought. But there was no reaction at all.

He strode across the room and slammed his fist on the bench until everything on it was set in motion. The noise forced Giselle to pay attention. "Why be a damned fool? Stop being so stubborn! Just go on the boat, that's all. You'll just be a passenger. I want a witness there. Someone to say exactly what happened. You're a friend of Eloise's. It's natural for you to be there with her." Giselle still said nothing and François went on in exasperation. "I want you to ride the escape boat with Pierre and Roger and Eloise. I need you to watch out for them, Giselle." Still nothing. "I want you to protect Eloise." Suddenly he was finished. He had nothing more he could say.

"No! The answer is still no!" Giselle clenched her fist and looked up at François with hatred. "I won't do another thing for you. There's no use begging!"

François was amazed at her defiance. "I am not begging. I'm ordering you to do it! You see, I know all about you and your lover-boy. I am not stupid. He is ignorant of what you really are, and he's too idealistic ever to accept the fact that he's fallen in love with a slut. If he finds out, he'll kill you. He thinks you're a goddess and when you fall off that pedestal he's got you on, the shock will drive him crazy. You know it too, Giselle. And you know that you couldn't stand the torture of having him call you everything that's dirty and rotten either. He'll spit on you, and that will be more than you can take!"

"I don't care! I don't care what happens to me." Giselle buried her head in her hands to hide her sudden tears. François was delighted. He'd won. Now he just had to put her emotions back in place.

He went on more gently. "Of course you care, Giselle. That's why you'll do what I ask. You're as deeply involved in this business as any of us. After all, you sheltered Pierre, you spied for us. In fact, you obtained the most vital piece of information for making this mission a success. You know, you're technically as guilty as any of us. If we fail, you will go to jail. If we succeed, you'll be a heroine of the revolution! The new world's Jeanne D'Arc! Come on, Giselle, look at it that way. See what you have to win."

Giselle composed herself somewhat. There was nothing left to do. She had nowhere to turn. She had to follow François' orders, and hope she could live with herself afterwards. She stood up and started for the door. François quickly opened it for her. Then he put a hand on her arm to stop her. "You've made a wise choice, Giselle. You won't regret it, I promise you."

He closed the door after her. What a goddamn nuisance! What a pain in the ass! Then a smile crossed his face as he thought ahead. "Patience, François," he said to himself as he studied his image in the mirror. "Patience, my friend. You won't have to put up with this kind of garbage-can people much longer."

21

"Is that you, Pierre?"

"Yes."

"I told you I'd call when it was time."

"Yes."

"It's time. The stuff's ready, isn't it?"

"Yes."

"Then get it."

"Yes."

"Tomorrow?"

"Yes. Okay. Tomorrow."

"Bring it to the boat."

"Yes."

"That's all." The phone went dead.

"Who was that, Pierre?"

"François."

"How did he know you were here?"

"I told him."

"What did he want?"

"I've got to pick up the dynamite from Emile."

Pierre was so thrilled with the prospects of finally getting into the action that he didn't notice the deep concern in Giselle's eyes.

"I don't care! I don't give a damn if François finds out. I couldn't care less what he thinks. You're coming with me. As far as I'm concerned you can throw your job in the river. Come on, Giselle, let's tell the whole world to go to hell. We'll have a ball. I've gotta go, but we'll make it fun." Exuberant, excited, Pierre was far from his normal self. "It'll be great driving through the country up the Matapedia Valley. It's the best time of year. Honey, it's beautiful! We'll go dancing; we'll see my friends, Emile and Yvonne; we'll dance the quadrille together. Come on, Giselle, please say you'll come."

In a sheer negligée, Giselle sat on the edge of the bed, quietly listening to Pierre's convincing arguments. But her ears seemed deaf to his pleas, for her fear that François would find out stilled her voice. Suddenly, Pierre's attitude changed and he became submissive. "You do want to, don't you? You do want to go with me?"

She waited for a minute before she replied. "Of course, *cheri*," she said. "I really want to go. But . . ."

"To hell with the buts. Just say you'll come. We don't need to bother with anybody else. Just you and me. Come on," he said as he saw her weakening. "Say you'll come."

The answer had to be yes. Giselle would go because she couldn't say no. Being with Pierre was the only thing that really made her happy anymore. Her job, or François' attitude if he found out, meant nothing when compared with being with her love.

The St. Lawrence glistened in the sunshine as they made their way across the bridge and up the highway toward Rivière du Loup. The long, thin farms stretched back from the river and up the gently sloping hills, unchanged since the dawn of the nation's history.

The magnificence of the village churches contrasted dramatically with the squalid frame buildings clustered around them. On one hand, the magnificence of the churches shouted out to the world the religious faith of the French Canadian. On the other, the obvious poverty in which they lived documented the proof that their faith was not so nobly rewarded, at least in this life. But these thoughts were not Giselle's, or Pierre's, on this happy morning. The church bells pealed and their pleasing sounds added depth to the peace and contentment already in their hearts. Pierre wanted her with him; Giselle knew that for certain now. And even more beautiful than that, it seemed as though Pierre's life was surrounding hers, encompassing her, and she knew too that this was what she wanted, what she needed.

The sound of the bells across the meadows reminded Giselle of those beautiful days in the Abbey School so long ago. Life had been so beautiful then, so full of hope and promise, so vital, pure and purposeful. The bells seemed to speak to her, to tell her that the way back to this peaceful state was through her love for Pierre. Filled to overflowing with emotion, they drove eastward along the south shore of the St. Lawrence. Giselle opened the window of the car and the stinging freshness of late autumn filled her nostrils, blowing away the cobwebs of doubt and fear that had lingered there too long.

Pierre felt it too. A unique bond existed between them. The common loves of their childhoods were moulding them into one. The faith, the Catholic faith, into which they had been born, had somehow formed the cornerstone on which their understanding grew. The magnetic quality of their faith was like the warmth of a fire drawing two strangers together on a cold, dark night. The purity, the beauty of their feelings for each other made them as one. And in this country, this big country, this clean, wholesome country of the North, they were together, body and soul. For ever and ever, hoped Giselle, as she snuggled close to Pierre. They drove away from the river and, on a rougher road, headed straight into the heart of the wild highlands of the Gaspé.

"You'll love my friend Emile. He's as solid as a rock. No phony! He's as good a friend as God ever made. We've done a lot of things. When we were kids, we played together." Pierre laughed. "Did we have fun! Well, most of the time we did. Emile was my best friend, except for René. I told you about him, didn't I?" Giselle was silent. Pierre continued. "One day, Emile and René and me went down to the river. We weren't supposed to play on the ice, but we did and René drowned. I've never forgotten that, Giselle. Do you know what Emile and I did? We went for a walk down by the river after they buried René, after Father DesMarche wouldn't tell us René went to heaven. Do you know what we did?"

"No."

"We cried. We cried for René, because we didn't want him to be in hell. He was no worse than us, Giselle. He was no different than us. He'd done exactly the same things we did. He'd stolen some candies from LaCourte's grocery store, and Father Des-Marche said it was a sin. And he didn't go to confession before he drowned. Father DesMarche said that if you didn't go to confession, you'd go to hell. I've often wondered about that. God, it's unfair. Poor René burning in hell all these years. Just over a few lousy candies. But that's what Father DesMarche said. He said that only confession could make up for sin. Confession could have stopped him from going to hell."

"You don't believe that, do you?"

"I don't know for sure. I think I really do. It bothers me a lot. You see, the way I look at it is, if it's right, I mean, if some things are sins and you have to be punished for them, then I guess maybe René should be in hell. But so should I, and that's what scares me. I've done lots worse than René ever did."

"They only told you that to scare you. You were only a kid. They wanted to make you obey them."

"Is that what you think?"

"Of course. They only told you that to keep you in line."

"But if that's true it would mean the priest lied to me when I was a kid. Why should he do that?"

Giselle was silent.

"I'd hate them all, if I believed they were only scaring me.

178

They'd all be a pack of liars. If they'd scare me like that when I was a kid, scare me so much that I'd never forget it . . . God! And I found out it was a lie, I'd never believe anything they said."

"I think they tell you all that stuff just to make you do what they want," replied Giselle, blandly. "I used to be scared silly when I thought I might die, because I knew I had committed some silly little sin. Then, one day, I just gave up. There were so many sins, I couldn't open my mouth to speak without committing one, so I just gave up. I just don't think about it any more."

"But how would you feel if you did think about it?"

Giselle drew herself away from Pierre and shuddered. She knew that deep in her heart she still believed. Deep down, there still lingered a belief of the power of a Catholic priest to forgive sins through confession. She knew her whole life had been a sin. Her life as a prostitute, her life with Paul and now her life with Pierre. What was it? This life with Pierre. Was it the beautiful thing she felt in her heart, or was it a sinful desire? The thought disturbed her. "I don't want to talk about it," was all she said.

Pierre was silent for a long time as they drove into the hinterland. The Gaspé is as rough and rugged as its inhabitants, in some areas so primitive that, in the whole of North America, there is no counterpart. The animals of the forest, the bear, the wolf, the lynx and deer run wild. Except for the coastal areas, the population is sparse and in the interior, there is nothing but the rough-shod woodsman.

They drove until the sun, a great ball of reddish fire, fell low in the sky. Suddenly, they came to a tiny village nestling between two mountains. About a mile beyond the village, Pierre turned into a driveway and stopped at a frame building, half-hidden in the scarlet-leaved trees. He went quickly to the door and without knocking, walked in. Giselle waited in the car for a moment until he re-appeared with a tall, heavy-set man who was thumping Pierre on the back and talking excitedly with him. They approached the car, both laughing.

"Giselle," said Pierre, "here he is, just like I said. The greatest guy in the world. My best friend, Emile."

Giselle, caught up in the mood, laughed as they walked into the house where Yvonne, a plump, red-faced, happy-looking woman, was waiting.

Within minutes, Giselle felt completely at home and, when Pierre and Emile disappeared through the back door of the kitchen into the woodshed for a private conversation, she sat and chatted happily with Yvonne over a cup of hot coffee.

When the men returned, they were both smiling and Giselle knew that Pierre had accomplished his business.

Emile and Yvonne had welcomed Pierre as a long lost brother, and their reception for Giselle was equally warm. As Pierre had promised, they went to a dance at the village church that night. The local band, a group of fiddlers, played an ancient tune and the couples danced the quadrille in groups of four, as they had done since the dance was introduced in Louis XIVth's France. The safety and security of the environment encompassed Giselle. Although she had never been here before, a homey feeling of familiarity seemed to emanate from the heavy stone walls of the church. How long had it been since her last visit to church? Paul's funeral? No! That didn't count. She thought as she danced of that day so long ago when she had walked with Sister Thérèse in the beautiful garden of the Abbey School. They had been so close then, it was almost as though Sister Thérèse had been her guardian angel. "I feel so good when I'm with you, Sister Thérèse," Giselle had laughed.

"That is because you are such a good girl," replied Sister Thérèse, always anxious to guide her wards into a life of strong principles. Principles so strong they would condone no compromise. Right is right and wrong is wrong. Right was rewarded and wrong was punished. This was Sister Thérèse. This was her belief and this is what she taught Giselle. She knew Giselle was innocent and therefore good, and so her sympathies and love were directed toward her. Not like it was afterwards, thought Giselle, when the same garden of contentment had turned into a place of ugliness and despair when Sister Thérèse had turned on her, the sinner. Tonight, as she danced with Pierre, she felt the unreal emotions of her childhood flooding through her and forcing the hurt she had harboured for so long from her mind. The spirit of the eternal God, who rested in the tabernacle above, overwhelmed her. She danced as though she were on a cloud, alone with Pierre in a mythical garden in heaven. The other couples who flashed past, smiling and bowing, were only symbols that told her she belonged in this place and must come back. The music slowed, they danced close, molded together as one. "I love you," whispered Pierre. There were no words after that. But the silence spoke as no words could ever speak and they knew that, from that moment on, they were destined to be as one. Together, forever.

When the music stopped, Pierre led her through the church doors into the ethereal light outside. The whitish moon beamed down and silhouetted the mountains against a pale, blue sky. A million stars sparkled in the endless void above and the faintest streaks of the Northern Lights danced across the horizon. With their arms embracing one another, they found themselves at a vantage point where the moon cast the shadows of the cross from the church spire directly in front of them. They stopped. Frozen in their movement, an inexplicable feeling gripped them both. Pierre turned to Giselle and pulled her to him. She lifted her mouth to his and he kissed her. "I love you, Giselle." He held her as though he would never let her go.

In all her life, Giselle had never felt so wanted. She had experienced passion and desire and physical satisfaction, but she had never once experienced this need to belong. This fervor that made all the others dull by comparison. This eagerness to belong, to be needed. Was it real? Was it what she deserved? The shadow of the cross on the ground before her had a disturbing effect. This symbol of compassion, love and forgiveness derided her. You do not deserve this love, you are not a good woman. But what was good? A girl with no feelings at all? A girl who sins and then suffers remorse until she confesses? A girl like Giselle, who after having experienced almost every evil, had made a choice. A deliberate and wilful choice for love. A choice to share her love with a man, with Pierre. But confusion was the result of her inner conflict and she could not think. She turned her eyes from the image of the cross and lost herself in Pierre's arms.

"I want to marry you, *cherie*," she heard him say. "I want you as my wife. I want you to marry me in this church. Will you, Giselle?"

She wanted so much to say yes, but the word caught in her throat. She thought of their journey to this lonely settlement. Then she thought of the purpose of the trip. Explosives! To cram between the decks of the Sans Souci. Did Pierre fully comprehend the consequences of his actions? Did he realize, as she did, the danger that was involved? On top of that, did he realize what kind of person she had once been? Of course not! If he knew that, he would never marry her. And yet, with all these forbidding thoughts torturing her, she thought in the simple terms of a woman. She thought of a home, of love, and of children.

"Yes, Pierre," she said finally. "I love you. I love you and I want to marry you."

"Hey, what's going on out here?" It was Emile's voice and he was alone.

Pierre turned to greet him. "Nothing," said Pierre sheepishly. "Nothing, except that I just found myself a wife."

"You've what?"

"I've just asked Giselle to marry me and she said yes."

"By God!" shouted Emile. "It's about time." He stepped between the pair and linked his arms through theirs. "By God, we'll have a time tonight." He ushered them toward the entrance. Then he stopped. "*Magnifique!*" he shouted. "How many times have I told you, get married. Be happy like me and Yvonne. And what did he say? He said he'd wait for the right girl. That's what he said. And now he's found her." He put his arms around Giselle. "This is the greatest night in history." He laughed. "Hey!" Emile's voice took on a different tone. "Isn't there something in the books that says I can kiss her, Pierre?"

"There probably is."

"Then, by God, I'll take care of it." Emile picked Giselle up as though she was a little girl and held her above his head. When he lowered her, he kissed her first on one cheek and then the other.

A shiver passed through Giselle. Foreboding, almost prophetic, the disquiet that filled her was far from what she had expected. It was a kind of fear. But why should she feel it from this jolly man, from Pierre's best friend? Was it because of the explosives he was procuring for Pierre? Was Pierre so lucky to have a friend in Emile, or was Emile the instrument that would destroy him?

She shook her head to force the thoughts from it. Emile was a good man. And Pierre knew how to handle the explosives. Everything would be all right.

Emile hugged her again and kissed her. "I envy you, Pierre," he said. "She is so beautiful. We must keep her here forever."

"I wish we could," Pierre replied smiling, "But we've got to get back to Québec City first thing in the morning."

22

Back in the city, Giselle tossed and turned in bed. The endless hours of the night dragged on; the sound of falling rain and the occasional honking of a car horn in the distance, her only companions. She was alone. Alone with her thoughts and fears. Outside, the dark, unfriendly sky offered no balm to ease her thoughts. The dim light from a street lamp reflecting on a neighbour's window was her only protection against the pitch blackness of the night.

At first, she thought it was the rain that kept her awake. But it wasn't. Perhaps she was hungry. She went to the kitchen and nibbled on some crackers and warmed a glass of milk. It was still no good. The room was too hot. She opened a window wide, but the cool night air soon chilled her and she closed it. Going back to her bedroom, she realized it was her thoughts, the turmoil in her mind that kept her from her sleep. Why had Pierre asked her to marry him now?

She wanted so desperately to marry him, but how could she? Her relationship with him was a lie from the very beginning. It could be no other way now. François was right in that respect. If Pierre ever found out the truth about her now, there was no telling what he would do. It would surely destroy his love for her. It would hurt him deeply. Just how deeply, Giselle could not imagine.

How different was her love for Pierre! When she compared it with her previous experiences, when she compared it with her feelings for Paul, it was like comparing a flickering candle to the light of the sun. It would have been different, if it had been Paul who had asked her to marry him. He wouldn't have given a damn about anybody else. He wouldn't have cared how many others there had been. But what's the use? What good does it do to compare and think and wish? It wasn't Paul who asked her. It was Pierre. Pierre was so different. He asked so sincerely. So humbly.

Why couldn't she just say "Pierre, I love you and I want to marry you." Why couldn't she just go away with him? Anywhere. Just the two of them. Away, where nobody knew them. Where they could just be in love.

But there were other things she would have to do first. She would have to move out of the apartment, quit her job. She'd never be free of François if she didn't. Her job linked her with the Move-ment. If she wanted to make a clean break, the job would have to go. She'd get another. But it would have to be away from Québec City. Anywhere, as long as it wasn't here.

Why was it such a damn chore trying to start a new life for herself? The answer, of course, was François. If it weren't for that bastard, there wouldn't be a problem. But as long as he was around, it was hopeless. With a sob of despair, she pushed her face into the pillow.

Would François live up to his bargain? Would he let her go when the job was finished? Would he keep her secret from Pierre? The answer was obvious. Of course not! François was a filthy liar who'd stoop to anything. His promises were just a ruse, a trick to keep her where he wanted her. How much more would he demand? When this was over, would he make another demand and another and another? And because of her fear, would she go along? Of course she would! There was no other alternative, was there? As long as François held this over her head, he had the perfect black-mail that would always work. As long as a statement by him could destroy her relationship with Pierre, François had Giselle exactly where he wanted her. She was at his mercy. The only other solution would be to tell Pierre the truth herself. God! What a stupid idea! That would never work. Or would it? Giselle tossed and turned, wondering and worrying. Maybe that was it. There was no way of destroying François' power, unless she told Pierre first. But what would that accomplish? Even if she told him, then what?

How could she get Pierre away from François? Pierre's loyalty to the Movement was too strong, his loyalty to François undivided. But why? Why has he become so inflamed with the idea of sepa-ratism? Is there any future in it? No! Is there any money in it for him? No! There is nothing in it, except false pride. He's François' patsy, that's all.

Giselle threw the covers from her body in disgust. Naked, she went again to the kitchen and opened the refrigerator. Nothing enticed her. Nothing would, until she found her way out of this maze. As she started to push the door closed, the light caught a newspaper lying on a chair. She had thrown it there soon after Pierre had brought her home from the Gaspé. Reluctant to leave, he had stayed for three cups of coffee until, finally, Giselle had told him she would prefer to be alone. Disappointed, he had left, but only after a promise to see Giselle the next afternoon. Now she scanned the headlines and, becoming interested in a by-line, switched on the light. A report of a bomb explosion in Montréal startled her. The newspaper reported it as being of unknown origin, but went on to say that the police had strong suspicions that it was the work of the separatists.

A shudder passed over her. Who else did François have on his payroll? Was it Roger? Or was this the action of a rival separatist gang?

As she read the account, the full significance of her own role in François' plot flashed into focus. As though someone had just come up to her and said, "Giselle, you're in this thing pretty deep," the report of the incident and its reactions by the public, the police and the government told her the full truth of her implication. She was no longer the distant spectator she had been when Paul was around; she was no longer the innocent, uninvolved typist in the employ of an obscure American government office.

Now, she was a full-fledged informer, an integral part of a conspiracy. Exactly the same as those misguided youths who murdered Pierre Laporte not so long ago. Exactly the same as those other members of the now disbanded FLQ. The only difference now was the stiffer attitude of the government.

The realization helped her to decide. She had to get out! There was no other way. She'd try to convince Pierre to leave. Another day, maybe two. It had to be done now. It was less than a week to the conference. And there was the explosion. It was scheduled during the conference! There was nothing else to do. If Pierre wouldn't listen, she'd leave him. *Finis. Au revoir.* Goodbye!

The thought gave her a strange feeling of relief.

She thumbed through the pages of the paper again until she came across the "Help Wanted" section. There was a secretary wanted in Lévis. She'd apply for the job in the morning.

Now was the time to start making a clean break with the past. Now was the time to stop worrying and take decisive action.

Tomorrow, she'd get a new job. Tomorrow, she'd tell Pierre the truth about herself. Tomorrow, she'd put an ultimatum to Pierre. Get out of the Movement or goodbye.

23

At Québec City, the St. Lawrence is almost a mile wide. On the opposite bank, Lévis is connected to Québec City by a car ferry which runs the year round. The current, the shifting river bed and the width made it necessary to construct the closest bridge about seven miles upstream at Ste. Foy.

The air was crisp and fresh as Giselle rode the bus to the Château Frontenac. Skirting the hotel entrance, she walked along the Terrace to the elevator which hangs on the edge of the cliff, separating Upper and Lower Town.

With only a quick glance at the Château, glittering regally in the morning sun, Giselle jauntily passed through the heavy iron doors into the Ascenseur. It descended noisily and slowly, until she found herself on the winding, narrow streets of Lower Town. A short distance beyond was the ferry dock to Lévis. She was lucky. A boat was there almost ready to go. Full of new purpose and energy, she quickened her pace and got on board in time.

The water swirled in response to the heavy engines, boat and shore parted company, and soon the current fought the turbines for control of the blunt-nosed carrier. Giselle leaned against the rail, her face pointing defiantly against the raw wind. She was partially relieved, for despite the long and lonely night of thought, she thought of the coming interview. She would surely get the job.

How nice it was to feel free. And just as suddenly as she thought of her freedom, she thought of Pierre's imprisonment. Yes! Pierre was in François' prison.

He had been sold a bill of goods and like a robot, trained to do his master's bidding, was blindly following the orders given to him. But what about this bill of goods? Was it an invention of François'?

Giselle thought of Pierre's background. What on earth could have happened in Pierre's life that would make him fall for such a line? It wasn't as though he had been born completely different than most other Canadians. His skin was white; he could not plead discrimination because of a natural colour difference as could the American blacks. His Roman Catholic religion was common to millions of other people in the country; he could not claim persecution in this area.

Québec was not much different from any other part of Canada. The house he lived in, the music he danced to, the clothes he wore, the food he ate and the car he drove. Everything! Everything he was involved in was North American. But, somewhere along the line, he had been sold the idea that he was different. Was he a member of a different social structure? No! He had counterparts in all parts of Canada and the United States. Did he have different political beliefs? Definitely not. He believed in freedom and he lived in a free country.

Then what, in the name of Jesus Christ, made him so different? The bill of goods said it was his language and his culture.

Giselle inhaled a great breath of the cold air. They were half way to Lévis.

Language and culture! How sick Giselle was of hearing these stupid words. How sick she was of the connotation that had been placed on them. Language! As though language was something sacred; as though it was a precious jewel that must be treasured; as though it was an inheritance of great value.

She watched the water as it was forced away from the onrushing steel sides of the boat. With deep thoughtfulness in her eyes, she remembered Pierre's words: "Je t'aime, ma cherie." What difference did it make whether he'd said it in French, English, Dutch, Spanish, or whatever else? It meant the same thing in any language.

To hear that he loved her was all she cared about; the language meant nothing. "Isn't language just a method of communication?" she asked herself aloud.

What a flimsy, rotten excuse for hate. To take an innocent child and to teach him deliberately an impractical language to create mistrust, misunderstanding, and then, to compound the meanness of the trick, do everything possible to stop him from learning the language of trade and common usage in North America. Why wouldn't they try to simplify language problems instead of complicating them? But, thought Giselle, as she moved into the warmer enclosed area of the ferry and looked through the glass at the approaching cliffs of Lévis, that wouldn't be the thing to do. They would lose their control over people. It would be like a jailer opening the doors of a prison.

Giselle thought of the trips she had taken with her Aunt Rita as a young girl. One voyage, in particular, stood out in her mind. They had been in Amsterdam, and, suddenly, her aunt had said, "We're going to Cologne in Germany."

They boarded a bus in Amsterdam and proceeded south

through Holland. Everybody had spoken Dutch and Giselle couldn't understand a word of it. It was like being alone in the world. She couldn't understand one thing these people said, although they seemed very nice. In the late morning, they arrived in Belgium. "What a funny language they're speaking," Giselle remembered saying.

"It's Flemish, dear," her aunt said. "It's another language they speak in this small section of the country." A few moments later, the bus had started and they were on their way. Within an hour, the bus stopped again. This time is was Walloon.

The bus started rolling through the countryside within moments and soon they arrived in Brussels, where a strange French was spoken. Now Giselle could understand what they were saying, but as the bus rolled along the narrow highway and entered Germany, she was lost again, unable to communicate, unable to comprehend.

"Isn't this ridiculous," Giselle had laughed. "They can't talk to each other. They're all strangers. Why do they have so many languages?"

"When you grow up, you'll understand, my child," her aunt had said. "It's all mixed up with history and religion."

"History and religion?" Giselle had been fascinated. "What do you mean? Tell me now. I don't want to wait until I grow up."

"Well," said her aunt resignedly, knowing Giselle's love of detailed history too well, "in ancient days before there were planes and cars, even before there were trains and stage coaches, away back in the old, old days, people very seldom travelled."

"You mean they never went anywhere?"

"Only a very few," replied her aunt, "a very chosen few."

"That must have been awful. I love to travel!" She thought that over for a moment, then amended her enthusiasm. "Well, I'd love it more, of course, if people in all foreign places spoke some language I could understand!"

"Everybody is a foreigner," said her aunt wisely.

"Everybody is a foreigner! How can everybody be a foreigner?" The child's natural egoism wouldn't admit such a thought.

"As soon as you travel out of your own country, Giselle, you become a foreigner. You must know that."

The idea had puzzled Giselle at first, then wearying of it, she shrugged and listened as her aunt continued. "In those olden days, Giselle, when the people couldn't travel and had no communication with letters, they naturally spoke differently."

"Why would they do that?"

"Well, Giselle, think of it like this. If you lived in a little village and everybody called a house 'la maison,' you would always think of the house as being 'la maison,' wouldn't you?"

"Of course I would. A house is 'la maison.' "

"That's right, my child," continued her aunt, "but if you had moved to another village and they had called a house a 'hus' or a 'hoyz,' you would have thought it was strange, wouldn't you?" Giselle was thoughtful.

"And then, if you moved to another country and they had called a house a 'casa' or a 'haus,' you'd think that was funny too." Giselle laughed delightedly at this word game.

"Of course."

"Well, that's the way languages started. It's only a habit of history. When people began travelling to neighbouring villages, they compared notes and used similar words, and soon, many local languages sprang up. Then, whole countries adopted a similar set of words and they called it a national language. But now, Giselle, now that transportation has become so fast and people have to communicate in order to live decently, it's better if they all speak the same language or, at least, try to learn each other's language."

Giselle's mind whirled. She pictured people going from village to village making up languages and was enthralled by it all. But a religious education had been so seriously impressed on her that it was natural for her to ask, "What has religion got to do with language?"

"Because the so-called holy men of the tribe or village wanted it to work for them," snorted her aunt. "Because religion added an aura of mysticism to language." There was a note of cynicism in her voice. "Did you ever hear the story of the Tower of Babel?"

"No."

"It's a Bible story about a group of Jews who wanted to build a tower up to heaven," said her aunt. "But their God objected, so the story goes, and the punishment was that they would all speak a different way." Aunt Rita's voice softened from her usual harsh pitch for a moment. "Don't believe those kinds of stories, Giselle, they're not true. As long as the world believes that poppycock, there will be trouble.

"There is only one way to unite people," Giselle's aunt said solemnly. "And that is through common understanding, and the shortest route to common understanding," she added emphatically, "is a common tongue."

And now, as Giselle watched the approaching wharves of Lévis, she knew her aunt was right. To divide was to destroy and the beautiful French language was being used to divide and destroy the very roots of Canada.

The vessel bumped against the jetty and Giselle's thoughts abruptly returned to the coming interview. Quickly she walked to the gangplank, through the exit doors and up the ancient road to apply for the job that would give her a new start in life.

24

The trip back to Québec City from Lévis contrasted sharply with Giselle's morning crossing. The weather was no better, no worse. The sun still shone above in a glorious, technicoloured sky, but Giselle's feelings were completely changed. Gone was the hope she had held in her heart on her journey to Lévis. Gone was the confidence that had been such a part of her this morning. She hadn't gotten the job.

It wouldn't have mattered as much if the position had been filled, but it wasn't. She could have understood if she hadn't had the qualifications. She might have accepted the rebuttal with less hurt if the woman, who interviewed her, had seemed sympathetic. But she hadn't.

Instead, the woman had been like a cold fish and had dampened Giselle's spirits from the moment she walked into the office.

Speaking English in a manner that confirmed it to be her one and only tongue, she appeared to Giselle to have made up her mind not to hire her from the first minute of the interview. Giselle's quick reactions told her that it was a decision based on this woman's dislike of the French. Nothing the woman had to say could convince Giselle that this was not the case. Every reason the woman gave for not hiring her sounded like an excuse, and when Giselle left the office, she was disappointed and angry.

With fallen hopes, she leaned against the steel bulkhead inside the huge elliptical cabin and looked wistfully through a porthole. In front of her, the cold, fast expanse of water swirled and eddied, and in the distance, the high cliffs reached up like a barrier between herself and Québec City. Much like the barrier between herself and the illusive and obscure goal she was seeking.

Maybe Father Moreau was right. "We are a conquered people," he had said dismally one day to Giselle. "We are a conquered people forced to live outside our own environment, forced to speak a foreign language, forced to live in a culture that is not ours."

Giselle had disagreed emphatically with him at the time. The idea seemed ridiculous. Could an educated man like a priest really believe this nonsense? What did he think she was, a child that would swallow anything? What country in the world had never been defeated? Almost every people in history had lost a battle or two. England, the ruler of the seas, was defeated by the French in 1066; Spain was taken by Hannibal; Germany was conquered by Napoleon; the Greeks had defeated the Romans and the Romans had defeated the Greeks. The Italians had beaten the Hungarians; the Hungarians had beaten the Polish; the Polish had defeated the Russians; and the Russians had defeated the Latvians and the whole stupid charade went on and on and on. And this foolish priest was crying because Québec was a conquered nation and the Québécois, a defeated people. Couldn't he forgive and forget after three hundred years?

Giselle knew she wasn't subservient to anyone, nor any more subdued than other Canadians. She was proud of Canada. She had travelled the whole of the country and was proud to be a part of it. Proud of its history, proud of her involvement in its homogeneous culture, proud of its record of sharing the continent of North America peacefully with its neighbour, the United States.

No! Giselle was not a conquered peasant! Not a "white nigger" as some pseudo-intellect had said. Not a member of a defeated race as Father Moreau would have her believe. There was no gun at her back forcing her to speak English. There was no propaganda on the radio or television urging her to speak English. On the contrary, there were those who forced her to speak French.

She knew it was only sensible to speak English so that she could do better. So that she could progress further in life. So that she could gain a greater understanding of other people in her country. She could travel more extensively and understand and talk to more people and she could make more money. Life in English Canada would be so much fuller for her than it could ever be in the isolation which François, and his group of gangsters, wished for Québec.

But if this is the way I really think, Giselle asked herself gloomily, why do I feel so bad right now? Did I really lose this job because I speak English with a French accent? Why do I get mad at English-speaking people every time something goes wrong? Why do I blame others for my own misfortunes? Is it because I'm like Pierre? Maybe, even a little bit, like François? Just because it's an easy way out. Whatever it is, I do resent them! I can't help it, it's what I feel. I've lived with it all my life.

I might as well be honest with myself. I've felt like this ever since I was a kid. But I really couldn't give a good reason for it. Except that maybe hating English-speaking people was taught to me, but I don't know who taught me or how. I just know that somehow, I mistrust them. I'm afraid of them. I don't like them. It's all tied up in early experiences, I suppose. Fear what you don't understand and hate what you fear. How can anybody understand when you're told you are a conquered people?

Why can't we all forget that idiotic, childish fight our great-great-grandfathers had? You'd think it all happened yesterday, instead of two hundred years ago. Why has the church in Québec kept harping on that theme for all these years? Why do politicians still natter on and on, in an endless drone, about our plight? For what purpose? Only to attain their own ends? Only to hold power? There can be no other reason.

Oh, God, thought Giselle wearily, why can't people think? Why can't people see when they're being taken in? What good does it do to remember ancient feuds? If all people thought of past battles lost and won, everyone in the world would be killing one another. Vengeance would be the rule. There would be no mercy. There would be no compassion.

Giselle looked at her watch. In another few minutes the boat would dock; in another five minutes she would be on the Ascenseur to the Terrace, where Pierre would be waiting. Funny, for the first time, she was not looking forward to seeing him. She wished she could change her plans and not see him today, but it was too late.

I wonder, she asked herself, why people can't use history to make themselves understand the folly of hate? Why can't they learn the lessons history teaches? Why do they have to make the same mistakes over and over again? It would take too much effort, she mused, because people are basically lazy. History is used by the instigators to sow hatred and mistrust. Their motives are to inflame the people by creating differences and when the hatred bursts into an uncontrollable force, they use the resulting chaos to gain their own ends.

The motors of the ferry growled as they were thrown into reverse. After a slight jolt, the motors stopped and the boat was docked in Québec City.

If the instigators of trouble and discontent can use history, she asked herself as she walked through the turnstiles, why can't the innocent people in the world use it for their own purposes?

The answer came to her suddenly. The innocent do not realize they are being duped! Pierre did not realize that he was being taken in by François. But was he really innocent, or was "ignorant" a better word? He did not question François' motives because his entire education had instilled faith in him. Faith in his superiors. Faith in his church. Faith without knowledge, question or reason.

That's what happened to Pierre. His misplaced faith was now in François. François, who was using it to a flagrant degree. And Pierre, having been trained to believe that faith was a great virtue, considered himself innocent in giving it to François. Perhaps he was ignorant in doing it, mused Giselle, as she walked up the narrow, winding streets towards the Ascenseur. But who can blame him?

He is only the product of his heredity and his environment. His image has been cast in an almost unbreakable mold. He believes he must protect his language and culture at any cost. This he has been told. But at what cost? And at whose gain? To the gain of people like François who are building great fences of hate around this beautiful country. Walls of hatred built with bricks of language and culture and the mortar of history. We are going backwards, thought Giselle. We are groping backwards to the seventeenth century.

What, in God's name, has perverted the French Canadians in Québec that they could accept a dogma like separatism? Was it just plain stubbornness? An inability to change? Or have they really been mistreated? Have they been exploited by outsiders? Or, wondered Giselle, as she stepped into the Ascenseur, have they just been brainwashed? Have they been told, just once too often, that language is all important and their culture worth more than bread on the table and the comforts of a well-furnished home? Is hate really stronger than love? Are lies stronger than the truth? Is this what is destroying the French Canadian? The Ascenseur rattled on its journey up the cliff to the Terrace.

Giselle suddenly realized that this was what was wrong with herself. Wasn't she being just as dishonest in her own little world? Wasn't she refusing to be honest?

The only weapon that François held over her head was the truth. Her only weakness was her dishonesty. The only weapon the separatist element had over Québec was its lies. Québec's only weakness was its apathy. If they were to stand up and shout, if they were to cry out the truth, they would say, "We are not a defeated people. We are not French. We are not enslaved. We are the same. We have the same rights as all the other people in this great country. If we choose to speak a language which is not common, then we, ourselves, must take the consequences. If the consequences are lack of opportunity, lack of monetary gain, then we will accept it without criticism, without remorse. With no regrets. We do not believe that because our forefathers fought two hundred years ago, that we must continue to fight. We believe that we should co-operate, that we should get along, that we should be Canadians and, if we must change, we will change because it is for our own good." The Ascenseur stopped and Giselle walked through the turnstiles.

She had, in this strange journey of thoughts, found the answer to her own perplexing problem. Like the people of Québec, she must be honest too. She must first of all be honest with herself. She must realize that she had made a mistake in her life. She must realize that this mistake was not indelible. Although she had taken the wrong road once, it did not mean that she had to grovel in its dirty mud all her life.

Her two years of prostitution had been an ugly experience, an escape. Her involvement with Paul had been one of weakness. But her love for Pierre! Was it a mistake too? Was it also a weakness, a sick need? There was only one way to find out. She must tell Pierre exactly what she had been and what she wanted to be now. There was no use in trying to pretend that she didn't have to tell him. And when she did, François' power over her would be dead. She could not deny her own history, but her history was dead. The same as it was dead for Québec. Why should she ruin her life today, for something that had happened in the past, as Québec and her own people were doing? There was no use giving in to threats either.

Giselle reaffirmed the decision she had made the previous night. She would tell Pierre everything and, if he could not accept it, then it would be the end. If he didn't believe in her, then he didn't love her. And if Pierre didn't love her, then nothing François could say would harm her.

She walked along the Terrace in front of the Château. Pierre should be waiting near the Glossier. She hurried. Then she stopped suddenly, and looked up at the Citadel, high on the hill alone. If only those great stone walls could speak the truth, they would say, "Yes, this land was once a French colony, and while we were a French colony, our ancestors fought with the English and, through a freak of history, they were defeated. Two foreign nations fighting one another for the fur-bearing creatures they could kill.

"Yes, in those ancient days, this was the truth. But today, it is no longer the truth. We are no longer a colonial subject of a French king. We are no longer a subservient underling in a British empire. We are free citizens in a free country. We are the proud members of a multi-cultural country. If we want to speak French, we can speak French; if we want to speak English, we can speak

English. If we want to speak German, Chinese, Japanese, Gaelic or Italian, there is no one who will stop us. But we prefer to speak a language that everyone can understand because we wish to be understood. We wish to grow together rather than apart. We like to look at our history with pride in our hearts, not with revenge. We look at it as an experience of our ancestors. It was not an experience which we, ourselves, endured, so we do not know what it was really like.

"In our lifetime, there has been no civil war. We should be proud of that. But there has been too much hate, and that hatred is dividing us. We have inherited only the hatreds, they do not belong to us. For when the hatreds were sown, we did not even exist. What an unfortunate inheritance. This hatred. But we do not have to preserve it. This country does not belong to our ancestors. It does not belong to those people who have long since left this world. It belongs to us, the living people who inhabit it today. It belongs to the living Canadians and we can do with it what we wish. Let us inherit the good from the past, let us damn the instigators of destruction into hell where they belong!"

Giselle took a deep breath of the frosty air. I'd better stop thinking or I'll go crazy, she mused, as she looked at the Glossier, almost ready for the winter frolic which was to come. And there was Pierre, talking with a group of workmen who were putting the finishing touches to the most spectacular ice ride in North America.

25

Giselle and Pierre walked, hand in hand, up the long deserted steps from the Terrace to the Citadel, the same walk they had taken only a few short months ago, the day they had heard the bells and experienced the first feelings of love. It was summer then, but now the warm and opalescent days were gone; even Indian summer had given way and now the semi-naked trees predicted the arrival of the first wintry blasts of snow.

They stopped at the Lookout and silence remained between them. Pierre looked at the river and the roofs of the old town far below them. He thought of the white ship they'd seen sailing down the river on that beautiful day so long ago. "I'd love to be on that ship," Giselle had said. "I'd love to go away, to travel to strange lands and romantic places." And how glad he was that she hadn't gone; how glad he was that she was here beside him. Here in this place that was so private. No tourists now, the walkway to the Citadel was deserted and the Terrace, far below, was deserted too, except for the workmen on the Glossier.

But while Pierre's mind was filled with thoughts of love, Giselle's mind was racing, conflicting, torturing. She had to talk to him. She had to talk seriously, frankly, even bluntly today. Now. There was to be no change of mind. She was determined. Why then, did she have this sick feeling in her stomach?

It had been there ever since she'd suggested they walk to the Lookout. "It's such a beautiful day," she had said, "and I'd like to be alone with you." Pierre had agreed readily.

And now they were here and she knew that this was the moment, the moment of truth and, perhaps, of doom. She held his hand tightly for a moment, then suddenly let go. "Pierre," she said in a voice that betrayed her feelings, "I want to talk to you seriously about something that is very important to me."

Pierre looked at her. Her expression, her voice, her manner reiterated her words. Seriously? Everything she did was serious as far as he was concerned.

"I want to talk to you about my past," she said blankly. "About what happened before I met you."

Before she knew him? That was when she had known Paul. She wanted to talk to him about Paul. It seemed a lifetime since he'd thought about him. Paul was dead and buried. How could she still be thinking of him? An unreal feeling of jealousy and fear swept over him. She wanted to tell him of her love for Paul! He couldn't listen. He didn't want to know. Sure, Paul had told Pierre of the times he'd been with Giselle, how they drank together, how they'd done so many things, but, somehow, Pierre couldn't remember Paul having said that he'd been in bed with Giselle. Or had he? Pierre couldn't think of it. To hell with it. I won't think of it. Christ! That thought's like a knife in the guts.

He remembered that day when they planted the bomb in Montréal. Paul had said he could hardly wait to get back to Giselle. He'd said he would get drunk with her, that they'd have a wild party. Yes, Pierre had remembered this one day, and the thought had hurt him so deeply that he'd said to himself that he didn't want to remember; he didn't want to hear about it. He still didn't want to know that Giselle had been with another man. He was afraid. Could he love her as much with the knowledge that she'd belonged to someone else?

"I don't want to talk about Paul."

"Neither do I."

Suddenly, he was relieved. "I'm glad," he said. "I don't want to talk about Paul. It hurts me to think of him. I'm glad you don't want to talk about him," he repeated.

"It was before Paul that I wanted to talk about." Giselle's voice was hard and robot-like.

"Before Paul? That was a long time ago, Giselle."

"I know, but I have to tell you about it, Pierre," she said with a seriousness in her voice that Pierre had never known before.

"Sure, Giselle, it's fun to talk about the past. It's fun to talk about when we were kids, especially the nice parts. About the good times, about the fun. Everybody has fun when they're kids. I did. Me and René and Emile. Everytime I think of when I was a kid, I feel good, except when I think of René getting killed. But it's best to forget the bad parts." He turned and faced Giselle. "Tell me about some of the fun you had, chérie."

"I didn't want to talk about the fun, Pierre. I wanted to tell you of some of the bad things I've done."

Pierre laughed. "Bad things, Giselle! You couldn't have done any bad things. Not like me, or Emile, or even René. Before you knew Paul, you were only a kid. Nothing you could have done was bad." He laughed. "I used to do bad things too. Like steal candies from LaCourte's store or playing hookey from school, or jumping on the back of freight trains when they moved out of Rivière du

Loup towards Rimouski. I suppose we all do bad things when we're kids, Giselle. But when we grow up, they don't seem so bad. They're just nice memories."

"I went to Montréal," cut in Giselle. "I went to Montréal right after leaving the Abbey School. I was not very happy at first and I was very lonely.

"I met a man. I suppose you would say he was a boy, Pierre. His name was Armand." She looked at Pierre and stopped when she saw the look in his eyes. There was excitement in them as he touched her hand and then pointed toward the river.

"Look," he said, "Look, isn't that the same one we saw before?"

Down the river steamed a great white vessel glistening in the sun. "It looks just like the one we saw in the summer," shouted Pierre. "I wonder if it's the same one. I wonder where she's going?" Pierre sensed the lack of interest in Giselle. He had diverted her thoughts only as a ruse. He knew it was not the same ship. It had a different shape. It didn't look at all like the one they had seen before. But he wanted to change the subject. He knew what she was going to tell him. She was going to tell him about love. Puppy love, childish infatuation. A passing fancy. She wanted to be honest about something that needed no explanation. He too had thought, more than once, that he'd been in love. He knew that her love must have been pure. *Mon Dieu*, he thought, how decent she was to tell him about it. He wouldn't let her hurt herself. She didn't have to ask for his forgiveness.

"I understand, Giselle," he said. "I understand, but I'd rather not talk about it."

"But I want to tell you," she protested.

"No! I don't want to discuss it, Giselle." Then, in the same breath, his voice was filled with tenderness. He remembered where he was. In the very place where their love had been born. This almost sacred sanctum. The arbor of love where he had first tasted the sweetness of her kiss. The first kiss had told him all he wanted to know. That fervor, that warmth he had never known before. That ecstasy of love. And as long as Giselle loved him, that was all that mattered. He did not want to spoil it. "No," he said again, "I do not want to discuss Armand."

"But there were others . . ."

"There was never anyone else," Pierre shouted defiantly. "There was never anyone else for me, and there was never anyone else for you."

Giselle looked down the cliff and a foreboding gripped her

as she stared at the rocks and the prickly shrubs that clung to them.

"I must tell you. You must listen. I was a . . ." She felt Pierre's hand clasp over her mouth and silence was forced on her. She was trying so hard to be honest, but he wouldn't listen. He removed his hand, but now, her voice was still. She was trapped. Imprisoned. And behind it all was this vague, restless fear. She could almost see her lifeless body lying on these jagged rocks below. She could see herself as dead as Pierre's love for her would be, if he were to know the truth.

Her courage was gone. She couldn't tell him. Why did it have to be so different now? Everything was spoiled. Why couldn't it have been the same as last time? Instead of the bells, the wind whistled through the naked trees, foretelling the cold and bitter days that lay ahead. She wished she could cuddle in Pierre's arms; she wished he would hold her tight and kiss her again, as he had in the warmth of the August sun. But when she looked at him, she realized their love could never be real. It would have to be a charade. A lie. He could never face the truth. He could never love her for what she really was. His love for her was based only on his dream of her. He had to think of her as pure as the Blessed Virgin Mary. And to destroy this image, to destroy this false sense of purity he had placed on Giselle, would be to destroy his love, perhaps even destroy him.

She couldn't do this to him. There must be another way. There must be another place. But not today! She couldn't tell him now.

"I love you, Pierre," she said finally. "And I've made my decision. If you don't want to talk about it, then we won't. Not if that's what you really want."

"Then we'll get married right away?"

The question startled her. Almost as though she had forgotten her promise. It was a long time before she spoke. "Yes," she said finally. "We'll get married right away."

For Pierre, the world turned into a gay, ecstatic paradise. A warm glow hung over this place, this magic rendezvous where his dreams were being answered. He would never forget the Lookout. He moved toward her with outstretched arms and, bending, kissed her tenderly. He could hear the bells ringing across the waters and up the sides of the cliff as he had heard them the first time.

But for Giselle, there were no bells. There was only a numbness.

26

The two-ton truck looked innocent enough. There was nothing about it to attract attention. It had Emile's name on the side in big letters, the licence plates were current, all his signals worked and it was driven well within the speed limits. There was a very good reason for all these precautions. Explosives! Filled to capacity with high explosives. Enough to rip out the side of a mountain. Enough to blow tree stumps from ten acres of ground. Enough to blast a road through twenty miles of rock. Enough explosives, thought Pierre as he sat beside Emile on their way to Québec City, to blow the Sans Souci into a million pieces.

Hardly a word had passed between Emile and Pierre on the long trip which had started in the blackness of night. They had loaded the cargo Emile had so carefully cached not far from Rivière du Loup. He was supplying the explosives for two reasons. One was simple. He needed the big money he was getting for it and the explosives had been easy to come by. The other reason was more complicated. Pierre was his lifelong friend. Pierre needed the explosives, and Emile wanted to help him. His mind passed reluctantly to the reasons for Pierre's need. Certainly, it was not for anything within the law. Emile knew this and he knew, too, that Pierre had been a friend of Paul's. And he knew what Paul had been connected with. But his thoughts remained hidden behind his laughing face. *Mon Dieu*, he didn't mind supplying the explosives. Pierre knew enough not to get hurt. And Emile wouldn't ask questions. Whatever happened, he would keep his mouth shut.

Pierre sat quietly immersed in thought. What a hell of a good friend. What fun it was just to be with Emile! It had always been like this. As boys, they had gone to school together. Emile had always befriended him and, he thought with pride, how many times he had helped Emile. Yes, Pierre knew that he could trust Emile completely.

Pierre directed Emile across the river to Ste. Foy, then to Québec, and finally east along the river to the Sans Souci at its slip, half hidden in the morning mist. The truck was parked and the gangplank was lowered. A space was prepared in the forward section of the craft and, together, Pierre and Emile carried the explosives, box by box, from the truck. Finally, it was all stowed neatly aboard the Sans Souci's bow. Pierre looked at his watch; it was 11:45 and, although the day was chilly, he was bathed in perspiration from the exertions of the morning.

"I'd give a day's pay for a beer," Emile said good-naturedly.

"Let's look in the galley," Pierre volunteered. "Maybe there's something to drink there."

Together, they searched through the refrigerator, but there was nothing. A further search revealed high up on a shelf, a bottle of cognac. Pierre mixed his with water while Emile drank it straight.

"She's a beautiful tub," laughed Emile, looking around. "I wonder how much she's worth."

"A lot of money," said Pierre. "I heard somebody say she's worth about four hundred thousand."

"*Mon Dieu!*"

Pierre was in the midst of pouring another drink when he heard a noise outside. He looked quickly through a porthole. It was Madame Hébert crossing the gangplank, preparing to board.

"Who's she?" Emile asked.

"She's Madame Hébert," said Pierre, pushing the cognac bottle back into the cupboard and trying to hide his glass. "She owns the boat."

Emile gulped his drink and pushed the glass onto the counter as Eloise Hébert entered the salon. She stopped for a moment, startled at the sight of the two men.

"I thought you were here alone, Pierre," she said. "Who is this?"

"A friend of mine," answered Pierre. "Emile."

"What is he doing on board the ship?" demanded Madame Hébert.

"He was helping me," said Pierre. "He was helping me load the boxes of . . ."

Madame Hébert looked coldly at Pierre, then her eyes moved to Emile, but she did not speak to him. "Is the job done?" she asked, turning her eyes back to Pierre.

Pierre's answer was interrupted momentarily as Roger entered the salon.

"Yes," he said. "Yes it is." He nodded to Roger in recognition.

Roger looked at Emile. "Who's he?" he demanded.

"A friend," said Pierre. "He got the explosives for me."

"A friend? We don't have friends." Roger's hate showed noticeably. He welcomed the chance to become abusive. "You'd better tell him to get the hell off the boat if the job is finished."

Pierre's eyes flashed. "I would never tell my friend Emile what to do," he said. "If anything, I would ask him." He looked at Madame Hébert for her reaction.

"You mustn't be so rude, Roger. Emile looks like a very fine young man and he has helped his friend, Pierre. We can't be rude. Here! Let's have a drink together," she suggested amiably as she moved into the galley. Then, seeing the bottle of cognac almost empty, she fumbled in a locker and produced another full bottle. Pierre walked into the galley behind her.

"I'm sorry, Madame Hébert," he said. "We'd worked so hard and we were so warm, we helped ourselves to a drink. I'm sorry. I know we shouldn't have done it."

Madame Hébert's face beamed out in a happy smile. "Pierre," she said, "Think nothing of it. You are welcome to a drink. Here, give me a hand. Get some glasses."

Soon they were drinking together in the salon, the four of them. Madame Hébert was enjoying herself. "This had been a happy boat," she said. "It was a happy boat when my husband bought it. He bought it for me, you know." Her eyes glistened as she spoke. "I want you all to drink with me," she said. "Drink with me to the memories of the Sans Souci and to my husband, Alphonse. Sometimes Alphonse and I would go cruising, just the two of us, anywhere, everywhere. On the Sans Souci, we always had lots of fun." She lifted her glass and tinkled it against Pierre's. They all tipped their glasses. Then she poured another and another.

The nostalgic memories of the ship's cruises poured from Madame Hébert's lips. For long moments she was ecstatically happy, then without warning, her voice would change as her spirits dropped, and she became morose and sad.

They drank until all the cognac was gone. "It is such a sad thing that this beautiful boat must go," she sighed. "It is a terrible thing that my beautiful yacht will be destroyed. Sunk into the river like an old barge. How terrible! It is a sin, a mortal sin."

The drinks had affected Eloise Hébert to a greater extent than the other three. Roger had been silent as usual, but now with no preliminaries, he pushed himself from his chair and, without a word, went into the galley.

"What are you doing in there?" It was Madame Hébert who called out.

Roger grunted, but did not reply. Madame Hébert heaved herself from her seat and, unsteadily, entered the galley. Roger was opening the drawers and cupboards, removing the contents and throwing them about. "What are you doing?" she demanded.

Roger turned on her and his eyes were cold. "I want a drink," he said. "Do you have any objections?"

"There is none left," said Madame Hébert. "We drank it all. Besides, you're breaking my beautiful china. Stop it! Stop it immediately!"

Contemptuously, Roger ignored her and continued looking.

"Get out! Get out!" Madame Hébert grabbed Roger by the arm and tried to pull him from the galley. He turned swiftly on her and swinging his arm, slapped her squarely across the face. Madame Hébert ran screaming into the salon. "Get him off my ship," she demanded of Pierre. "Throw him overboard. He struck me!"

"It must have been an accident," Pierre protested.

"It was no accident. He struck me like a beast. Get him out of here."

Pierre walked to the galley. "Roger, let's get out of here," he said quietly. "We don't want any trouble."

Roger turned on him. "Are you going to throw me out of here, little boy?" he laughed.

Pierre hesitated for a moment. "If I have to," he said finally, "I will."

Roger roared with laughter. "You'd better go and get your big brother. It'll take a hell of a lot more than you to get me off this barge."

"Come on," said Pierre, thinking Roger had had too much to drink. "Why don't you be sensible? We don't want any trouble with Madame Hébert."

Roger was not drunk. It was only natural that he would turn ugly. He had nothing to lose. With Madame Hébert's boat crammed with explosives, she couldn't phone the police. That was for sure. And, Roger laughed to himself, in a few days she won't be phoning anybody. I'd better have my fun while I can. And fun to Roger was to taunt, to insult, to deride, to mock.

"Why shouldn't I smash up a few things?" he asked casually, as he removed a heavy, glass serving bowl from a cupboard and deliberately dropped it at Pierre's feet. It broke on the floor as Roger laughed. "It's all gonna be blown to hell next week anyway."

"That's different," protested Pierre as he felt the anger rising in him. "The Sans Souci is being used as a weapon of war. We're sinking her for a good reason."

"That's only your stupid, backwoods logic," scoffed Roger, as he pushed a series of glasses from a counter and sent them crashing to the galley floor.

"Stop him! Stop him!" It was the hysterical screams of Madame Hébert who stood behind Pierre.

"Sure," said Roger with contempt. "Stop me." He picked up the empty cognac bottle by the neck and then, with an expert movement of his wrist, knocked the bottom from it, exposing the jagged edges which he pointed at Pierre. "Stop me," he taunted, as he made a sudden menacing movement toward him.

Pierre quickly backed into the salon with Roger in close pursuit. But once through the door, he side-stepped and, in the same movement, grasped Roger's wrist. Then, twisting hard, Pierre spun him to the opposite wall while the bottle fell to the floor and rolled under a chair. Dazed for a moment, Roger sat on the floor, shaking his head. Then he rose to his feet and, advancing on Pierre in the small confines of the salon, he lashed him across the face with his fist.

Madame Hébert screamed as blood spurted out the side of Pierre's mouth. "Stop it! Stop it!" she screamed. "You are ruining my boat. Look at the mess." But Roger would not stop and the two men pummelled each other. In a few minutes, it was over and Roger was on the floor gasping for breath while Pierre, with blood pouring from his nose and mouth, stood over him.

Madame Hébert screamed at the two. "Get off my boat! Get that dynamite out of my beloved Sans Souci! Get everything that belongs to you out of here. All of you. Do you hear me? Get out! Get out! Get out!" Her screams were so loud that Pierre was worried someone would hear and send for the police. Then the trouble would really start.

He motioned to Emile. "Try and keep her quiet," he whispered. "I'll be back in a few minutes."

Quickly he went ashore and soon was on the telephone to François. "We've got trouble," he explained. "You'd better hurry down."

After returning to the boat, Pierre attempted to calm Madame Hébert, but she was beyond any reconciliation. "I want to have absolutely nothing to do with any of you. You are nothing but common thugs."

It seemed an eternity before François arrived. "What has happened to you, my dear?" François was at his theatrical best as he hurried straight to Madame Hébert. "Oh, my poor darling, what has happened to you?"

Madame Hébert, her eyes gushing teardrops, looked at him, blew her nose, wailed and began crying again.

"If anything has happened to you," continued François, "I'll never forgive myself. Who was the ruffian who started this?"

"It was him." Madame Hébert pointed at Roger who still lay sprawled on the floor, caressing his wounds. "It was that terrible man," she repeated, her eyes drying quickly. "That beast! That ogre!"

It was only then that François noticed Emile, and his face clouded. What was this stranger doing in the midst of this?

"Get off the boat immediately," he commanded, and without a word, Emile and Pierre half-carried and half-dragged Roger from the salon. Madame Hébert slumped into a heavy, leather chair.

"How can you ever forgive me?" asked François, in a show of self-abasement. "It is all my fault. I am the one to blame. I should never have left you alone. But it won't happen again, I assure you, Eloise, when we are married." He turned into the galley, moistened a towel and returning, caressed her forehead.

There was an immediate and distinct change in Madame Hébert. How wonderful it was to have a man's attention again. Especially François. She turned her face to kiss him. François, holding his breath, kissed her tenderly.

How he'd like to wring her ugly, thick neck! Wasn't he having enough trouble without this stupid bitch making more? Why did he have to be constantly surrounded by bungling idiots? He thought of the proverb: "If you take on idiots as partners, you are run by idiots."

Madame Hébert interrupted his thoughts by suddenly throwing her arms about him and, pulling him on top of her, kissed him passionately. In a reflex action, François pulled back. "You are exhausted," he protested, as he applied the towel to her face.

Maudit! he thought to himself. Why do I have to have so much trouble? On top of this, the conference! What had been shaping up as a pat affair was now becoming awkward. Bordeaux had again taken the initiative. He had personally visited every important member of the Movement and begged them for support. He had seen Father Moreau, Charpentier and even Jacques Ginette. Who else? God only knew! And there was no way of telling how maliciously he was attacking François, or how successful he had been. Only Jacques had told François of his visit. The others had kept silent. Maybe they didn't place much importance on his remarks, or maybe Bordeaux had convinced them that François should not become president as he had tried to convince Jacques. Soon it will be over, he thought as he continued to apply the cooling towel. Soon the Sans Souci will start on her mission and with a little luck, all my opposition will be crushed. In the meantime . . .

"Are you feeling better, darling?" he asked in the softest voice he could muster.

"Yes," she cooed.

27

François threw the duster into the wastebasket with a curse. He had seen himself in the mirror dusting the furniture and his reaction was one of disgust. He despised living the life of a pauper. But what else could he do? In his own right, he was nothing. Penniless, he lived off the contributions of friends and separatist supporters. But it won't be long, he dreamed, it won't be long before I will have twenty servants to do my bidding. A house, Madame Hébert's house, he laughed, will be mine. Then I won't be holed up in this stinking workshop, cleaning up my own garbage. Instead, I'll get what is justly mine, the very best. Dignity and pride will be mine. My time will be spent only on those things that please me. No more trivialities! Only the matters of great importance will be handled by myself. Matters such as bargaining with France on special grants to sustain our culture. Selling the rights for military bases to the highest bidder. Fortifying the boundaries of Québec. Organization of a national police force. And then, François laughed aloud, for his thoughts turned to his leftist dream. Bargaining with international powers, especially the United States, for the rights to use the St. Lawrence River.

He surveyed the room. It was tidy enough. Certainly clean enough for the visitor he expected soon. Certainly, good enough for Bordeaux. François looked at his watch. Although Bordeaux had set the appointment for 10:30 a.m. François knew that he would be late. It was one of Bordeaux's habits. Maybe it was a habit of self-esteem, maybe it was a device Bordeaux used to create tension, or maybe, François mused, maybe it was just a lazy habit. Whatever it was, Bordeaux was always late. Indeed, it had been a surprise to François that Bordeaux had called him. It was the last thing in the world he expected. He hadn't been thinking of Bordeaux lately.

So François' first reaction to Bordeaux's call was one of condescending niceties. At first, Bordeaux had been haughty, almost demanding. After all, he was the president and founder of the Movement; François had almost forgotten that. In fact, he didn't care who he was or what he had done. The only thing that mattered was that François was going to defeat Bordeaux in the race for presidency of the Movement. On that point, François was determined. And Bordeaux's telephone call was somewhat of an admission that he, himself, was concerned about François' chances. But Bordeaux's initial demands soon moderated when François showed little interest in what he said, and as the conversation progressed, Bordeaux's attitude became constantly more conciliatory.

His initial request was that François withdraw from the race and place his support behind him. "I have great things in mind for the Movement," he had told François, "and I feel that during the next three years, we shall accomplish a great deal." François had almost laughed. With his plan, Québec would be separated within a year, two years at the very outside. And here was this simpleton talking about three years as though he had a hundred to work with.

Bordeaux crumpled beneath François' response and soon his voice had changed into a plea that they meet. "I'm sorry," François had said, "I can't come to Montréal to see you. I'm far too busy. Perhaps you could come to Québec . . .?" Bordeaux had agreed, too readily. He showed his anxiety by his too-eager response. François knew that he had him on the run.

The clock had barely crossed the mark at 10:30 when a knock sounded at the door. It was Bordeaux. He's more worried than I thought, François mused, as he opened the door. After the formalities of meeting were finished, Bordeaux's mannerisms unmasked his inner feelings. He was nervous, upset and obviously concerned about many things. François enjoyed the charade.

"May I pour you a drink?" he asked.

"Never in the morning, thank you. I never drink before three in the afternoon. It's bad for the liver, you know."

"Of course," replied François. "Please sit down. Are you having a pleasant time in Québec City?"

Bordeaux was silent for a moment, but looked quizzically at François.

"Have you been here long?" François asked, knowing full well that Bordeaux had come especially to Québec City to see him.

Bordeaux grunted. "Oh, yes, of course," he coughed. "I'm enjoying myself."

"I was very pleased that you could come to see me," said François pretentiously. "It is always a pleasure to see our president."

"Really?" Bordeaux was anxious to get to the point of his visit. He didn't like François' hedging. But he had to try. So he did.

"I haven't heard from you for so long, François," he said. "And I wondered how things were progressing. After all, our annual conference is only a few days from now, but I wasn't sure in which way you were going to support me."

François laughed to himself but his face was straight. Maybe this fool did not even know what was going on. "I am hard at work," said François. "I am hard at work with the business of the Movement. I am spending my complete time with the organizational structure, the political necessities and the mountains of monotonous details." François waved his hands around the apartment. "It is for this reason that I am living so humbly. I hope you can understand and excuse the surroundings."

"Of course," said Bordeaux. "It's an admirable quality. Sacrificing yourself for the Movement. Perhaps I appreciate it more deeply because I myself have given so much to the party. I appreciate the loyal support and the hard work of my executive council. Most of all I appreciate and respect their loyalty." He half smiled. "Do you know what I mean?"

"I would prefer to word it another way," replied François. "I would prefer to say that loyalty to a plan is more to be expected and admired than loyalty to a person." François stopped, waiting for the words to make their meaning clear. They did.

Bordeaux's lips quivered slightly before he spoke and, when he did, there was a tell-tale quiver in his voice. "An idea," he said, "is only as good as the man behind it, François. And let me tell you this. The idea of separatism is mine. I am the president of the Movement. I am the founder of the Movement. I am and always have been the prime mover behind this Movement, François. While the rest of this country was hiding behind their fears and hatreds, I spoke out. I risked everything. I risked imprisonment and public abuse. I was chastized by the press and called a traitor by the English. Even some of my own people turned on me, François. This I shall never forget." He stopped momentarily and took a deep breath.

"But I took all these abuses," he continued. "Took everything that was thrown at me and I continued step by step, speech by speech, to convince the people of Québec that they were different from the others. You might say it was easy, but let me tell you, it wasn't. I have travelled every road in this land. I have visited every city, town and parish and I have spoken to anyone who would listen to me. I told them my story when it was an unpopular story. I gave my speech so many times that many school boys now know it off by heart. Do you know how I did it, François? I did it by being a beggar. I wouldn't have eaten, if kindly people hadn't taken me into their homes and fed me. How many times I've slept on a couch in one of my countrymen's living rooms, I cannot say. Do you know how long I've done this, François? I've done it for years. I've worked and I've talked and I've denied my-self for twenty years. Can you match that?'' Bordeaux stopped abruptly. He had been pacing the floor, but now he walked to a chair and sat down. He looked tired, worried, exhausted.

François was delighted to see it. The man was showing him-self up for exactly what he was. A worn-out huckster. Something like a vacuum cleaner salesman trying to sell an inferior product. An inferior product that every housewife in the country knew was no good. Defeated, thought François with pleasure. He is going to give up. Soon, he'll be crawling to me.

"Of course, Bordeaux,'' François stood up, "You have done a magnificent job. I am perhaps the one man in the whole of Québec who knows the magnitude of your contribution.'' François thought he noticed a curl on the end of Bordeaux's lip. "If ever there was one man in Québec who feels that a statue should be erected in your honour, Bordeaux, it is me.''

Anger flashed in Bordeaux's eyes. "If you have such a high regard for me, François, why do you try to cut me down?''

"Cut you down! How can you say that?''

The quiver was gone from Bordeaux's voice. He had brought the conflict into the open and it eased him. "Let us speak frankly, François. There is no one else in this room. There is no one else to hear us. So let us speak the truth. I know all about your meet-ings. I know all about your treachery.''

François, with a curse in his heart, smiled at Bordeaux as though the words did not affect him. How much did this imbecile know? And who was the informer? He thought of the individuals who had been at the meetings, and his mind by-passed all the others and went straight to Charpentier. That's who it was. It had to be. He was the only one in the group that had any loyalty to Bordeaux. But François' outer appearance did not betray his thoughts. "Of course I wish to speak frankly, Bordeaux. Haven't we always spoken frankly?''

"That is a matter for debate,'' Bordeaux replied angrily. "But since you agree, perhaps we could start first by being frank about your so-called plan.''

"My plan?''

"You know exactly what I mean."

"What do you want to know?"

"I don't want to know anything. I want you to know, it won't work. It's just a cheap gimmick. It was only intended to be that from the very beginning. We used it to get the college students going. It accomplished its purpose but now it's best to forget it."

"Suppose I don't agree with you."

"It doesn't really matter," said Bordeaux, with renewed confidence. "Anyone in his right mind knows we can't turn back history. We can't lay claim to the St. Lawrence. We can't use it as a bargaining agent and we can't live off it."

"So?"

"So it's all a lie, François. There's no truth in it at all. It's a wonderful dream, but that's all there is to it. There are two convincing reasons why it won't work."

"And what are they?"

"The first reason is the Dominion of Canada," said Bordeaux emphatically. "The idea that the Canadians would let us take over the control of the St. Lawrence is preposterous."

The statement did not have the effect on François that Bordeaux had hoped for. François lit a cigarette.

"And the other reason?" he asked.

Undaunted, Bordeaux went on. "The United States," he ventured, hoping to convince François. "The United States will not waive their rights. They would use force. They would send in the marines. Then what would we do? Would we go into the woods and fight a guerrilla war? Would we bottle ourselves up in the Citadel and fight a last-ditch stand like we did in 1759? There is no use pretending to ourselves, François. It's a fantasy, and the sooner you realize that, the sooner you'll stop your propaganda about this insane plan of yours."

François jumped to his feet. "Insane?" he demanded. He walked to the table and in his typically theatrical manner, slammed his fist hard on it. With no apparent concern, Bordeaux sat down and listened.

"You're wrong on both counts," shouted François. "On the one hand, the people of Canada don't give a damn about the river. As a matter of fact, Easterners look on it as a nuisance. It takes money away from them. Every time the St. Lawrence River is used, the ports in New Brunswick and Nova Scotia lose business. They'd love to see the St. Lawrence Seaway blocked off. To any of the provinces west of Ontario, they'd just as soon ship their goods through the ports of British Columbia or Hudson Bay. That leaves only Ontario to contend with in Canada."

"A formidable antagonist I would say, wouldn't you?"

"It would be, if they cared. But the politicians would have more trouble than they could count if they took a hard line on French Canadians. Or have you forgotten the enormous French population in that province? No! I don't think they would act."

"And what about Ottawa?"

"Oh, Christ, Bordeaux! Don't make me laugh."

Bordeaux did not believe him. He knew Canada and he knew Canadians. When the chips were down, they were not as docile as they appeared. They would not sit idly by and watch the disintegration of their country. At least, Bordeaux did not believe they would. Was François a fool, believing what he chose to believe instead of the facts? Perhaps, it would be a man like François who would push too far to find out if the English-speaking Canadians would act as a unit in a single purpose, and if this were to happen, a bloody civil war would erupt.

"Your second point," François went on, "about the United States is ridiculous. You say that if we were to seize the St. Lawrence River, which is rightfully ours, the United States would come running with guns and bombs. Bosh! That is the theory of the chicken! Have you never considered that the United Nations could defend our position of sovereignty? Have you forgotten that sovereignty would entitle us to discard old treaties? Have you forgotten Cuba? Did the United States dare go into that country? Do you think for one moment, Bordeaux, that the United States, with world opinion as it is today, would dare to attack a small, insignificant sovereign state like Québec? Why, they would be chastized by every country in the world."

With a flourish, François was finished and, standing erect, he strode to a position directly in front of Bordeaux who still sat in the chair. François pointed his finger down at him. "Do you know where the difference is between us, Bordeaux? There is a difference, you know. You say I try to cut you down. You think I want to take your place. I could never take your place. I could never take your place any more than I could turn back the hands of the clock or turn back the pages of history. You have done your job and you have done it well. You took a situation which existed twenty years ago, and you built the foundations for something which must happen today. You are like the architect, Bordeaux, the architect who makes the plans and then, when they are completed, turns them over to the construction engineer who turns the plan into reality. That doesn't mean the architect is not important, Bordeaux. It only means that the plan has passed from one phase to another."

Bordeaux looked at François. He knew what he was saying. It was clear that François was telling him that he was finished.

"Maybe I can put it like this," said François. "The architect needs certain tools, you know, like paper and drawing boards and rulers and things like that. But when you get to the building stage, you need bricks and mortar and so on. Do you agree?"

Bordeaux agreed wearily. He had decided that to argue with François was futile.

"Well, the same theory applies to the Movement. In the beginning the Movement needed what you had. Idealism. It was only a dream, Bordeaux. You had a dream and the only tool you had to use was the old hatred between the French and the English. But compare that with the situation as it is today." François broke into a smile. He loved the deflated expression on Bordeaux's face. "Today, it is different. Instead of your idealistic dream, we are dealing with realistic facts. Today, it is a power play." François watched for a reaction. There was none. "The power play will win for us when all the other methods have failed."

He turned his back on Bordeaux and walked to the liquor cabinet. "I hope you will excuse me, Bordeaux, I would like to have a drink. Won't you please join me?"

"No! I cannot drink to treachery," said Bordeaux, rising from his chair.

François turned. The expression on his face spoke violence. "Treachery!" he demanded. "How dare you say treachery! I have been as frank and honest with you as any man could ever be. I am only a flower blooming from the seed that you planted long ago. I am simply one of your disciples. And you call that treachery!

"If you think it's treachery then you're alone. Alone! The others do not believe it is treachery Bordeaux. They look to me for leadership. The clergy is with me." François slammed his fist again on the table. "The legal profession is with me. The politicians are with me. The businessmen are with me. The students are with me."

François was pleased at the reaction in Bordeaux. He sank again, like a lead weight, into the chair. François walked to the liquor cabinet and picking up a glass, filled it with Grand Marnier. He walked back to Bordeaux. "And if you were not so stubborn, Bordeaux, you would give up. You would see how futile it is to fight me." He reached out his hand and offered the drink to Bordeaux.

Bordeaux stood up and looked steadily at François for a moment. Then, pushing him to one side with such force that the liqueur sprayed across the room, he walked to the door and, picking up his hat, left without a word.

28

As the Sans Souci pushed its way against the relentless current of the St. Lawrence toward its fateful rendezvous, Pierre stood by a window in the salon, mesmerized by the monotonous hum of the motors and the changing patterns of the passing landscape. He had thought at first the vessel was travelling at a fast rate of speed, but as he studied the river bank, he realized he was wrong. They were not making as much headway as the rushing waters indicated, for the current was strong and the Sans Souci was heading dead against it. During the past hour, he had become accustomed to the motion of the boat and the smell of the diesel fuel that occasionally drifted into the cabin.

Even now, the grim consequences of the voyage had not formed a clear picture in his mind. He knew the explosives that he and Emile had stashed in the forward section of the Sans Souci were enough to blow a huge hole in the bow of this excellent boat. The craft would surely sink, especially with the boxes Roger had loaded up front with the ballast. What a queer bugger, that Roger! Wouldn't even let me help move the boxes. Must've been a hundred, heavy too, marked "cement." Well, to hell with him. I didn't really want to help anyway.

His thoughts wandered to Giselle and Madame Hébert who were on the aft deck, enjoying the noonday sun. Protected from the biting cold by a canvas windbreak, Giselle, obviously annoyed with Pierre, had completely ignored him and entered into a woman-to-woman conversation with Madame Hébert. How could Madame Hébert be so happy, he had asked himself. After what she'd said the other day! She's been real nice to me and she even talks to Roger. God! I'll never understand women! I thought she'd spit in Roger's eye the next time she saw him. His thoughts shifted back to Giselle. How glad he was that she was with him! But how he wished she was not so cold with him.

He watched a small village appear on the river bank: a big, stone church dwarfing the houses around it. He'd seen a thousand such villages but, until lately, he'd never noticed how big the churches were. François had pointed it out to him. "Those priests have lived pretty high on the hog for too long," François had grumbled as they drove through a small village on the way to

Madame Hébert's. "One of these days, you'll have that big house instead of a priest. Wouldn't you like that?" He laughed as he pointed to a stone mansion beside the cathedral-like church.

Pierre was surprised at the remark. He'd never even imagined himself living in such a house. "You'll have one like that if you do as I say," François had continued. But his attempt to inflame Pierre's unswerving loyalty still further with his promises of wealth and power fell on deaf ears. The only impression left in Pierre's mind was the size of the house and the church.

His thoughts switched again as he turned from the window and lit a cigarette. That lousy, little suitcase, full of dynamite, that Paul had taken to Montréal, was nothing when matched with the floating bomb on which he stood. And yet that simple little bag, the briefcase they had so carefully taken to Central Station, had blown Paul to Kingdom Come. What would happen, he wondered, if something were to go wrong on board this ship? A false setting of the triggering device, a short circuit, a sudden jolt, a miscalculation?

Nervously, he licked his lips. That same fear that had been with him all his life immobilized him. When René drowned, when Paul got killed, when François told him what he wanted, and now. Now! It was beginning to appear again. The fear made him want to turn and run, anywhere, any way, as long as he could get out. The fear had always begun the same way, a queasiness in the stomach, his mouth would dry up, his heart would thump a little harder. He'd remembered the feeling as long ago as René's death when he went through the ice.

Panic stopped him from helping his friend. When René was dead and in his coffin, the panic returned and he had run away, as though some of the fallen demons in hell were after him. The same pattern had always persisted.

On their trip to Montréal, the fear had told him to stop and consider what he was doing. To get out while there was still time. But no, he thought, I can't chicken out in front of Paul. His bravado kept him going again. But when he saw the consequences, Paul battered and bleeding to death in the front seat of the car, he had panicked again and run to Henri's place in St. Hyacinthe.

Now, here he was again. Another situation, but the same miserable fear. And after what he'd been saying to Giselle, about his loyalty to the Movement, his hopes for Québec and all the other bragging statements, he knew he'd have to stay to the bitter end.

He shook his head. He mustn't think like that. He must have

confidence, like François. A transistor radio sat on a shelf. He turned it on. There was music. He looked at his watch. It'd only be five minutes until the 12 o'clock news. He might as well listen. Nothing else to do.

While he waited, he pondered Giselle's mood. What the hell's wrong with her today? God, you'd think she'd know by now. I've told myself so many goddamn times! I've told her about what I promised François. But she doesn't care. He thought of what she'd said yesterday. "After this is done," she had insisted, "you've got to quit the Movement. There's no future in it for you, Pierre. François only wants to use you. He's a murderer, a coward, a traitor. Everything that's rotten!"

Christ! If she thought François was such a rat, why did she work for him in the first place? If she thought the Movement was so bad, why was she here now? Why was she part of something she hated? Pierre thought of the day, the beautiful afternoon, on the Terrace when she had wanted to talk to him, heart to heart. She wanted to tell me about some puppy love affair she'd had, he said to himself. Why the hell didn't she tell me why she was in the Movement?

He glanced at his watch again. It was 12:00. Noon, Angelus! It was somehow funny for Pierre when he thought of noonday and Angelus. They were synonymous. Even now, noonday was Angelus.

The thought carried him back across the years to when he was a boy on this river. He remembered the noon prayers. "The angel of the Lord appeared unto Mary," the teacher used to say when she began the prayer. Then he wondered what the reply had been. The teacher always said the first part and the students had responded. What were the words? It seemed so long ago. He remembered part of it. "And the Word was made flesh and dwelt amongst us." God, he thought, how stupid! No wonder I hated it. The words didn't make any sense.

He remembered one time when he was only six or seven years old. Anyway, it was his first year at school. When noon had come and they were ready to recite the Angelus, he had asked the teacher if he could go to the washroom. "You will stay for the Angelus," she replied.

"But I have to go," he said through tears. "I have to go." But she refused and he stood beside his desk. When it was half over, he could hold it no longer.

All the other kids laughed at him and the teacher was furious. "You'll wipe it up yourself," she screamed. Pierre sat in the corner all afternoon looking at a statue of Saint Joseph, and ever since that time, he had felt resentment and had made fun of the words. They are stupid and monotonous, he had often said to René.

Pierre's recollections were disturbed by the radio announcer's voice. "This afternoon," said the voice, "Jacques Ginette, well-known member of the separatist movement, will open the leadership convention for the party at Trois Rivières. Mr. Ginette, known particularly in the Montréal area for his radical views, is expected to announce the initiation of a political wing for the party. According to reliable sources, Mr. Ginette is confident that his party will be the next government of Québec."

Pierre looked again out the porthole and across the water. Before he met Giselle, before his baptism into the party, he had been unthinking, unquestioning, uninterested, but now, the questions came from every direction and he could not ignore them. Why did the newsman ignore François? He was the big man. Jacques was just his helper. Why had François planned this expedition of the Sans Souci to coincide with the leadership conference? Why was it necessary to bring Madame Hébert along to witness the destruction of her most cherished possession? "Of course," he answered himself aloud, "It's her boat. She's supposed to be on board. Or is she? It'll break her heart when she sees this thing sink."

His mood lightened as he remembered François' promise. "When this is over, I'll need you for bigger things. No more bombs. No more rough stuff. You'll be my most trusted assistant. There's a big future with me, you know that don't you?" Pierre had agreed.

His efforts, however, to convert Giselle were frustrating. Instead of changing her mind, she was the one determined to change his. She had been at him for the past week with no let-up, no respite, day after day, until Pierre had felt like hitting her. They had been fighting about it constantly and the fights had always ended the same way. Pierre defended François and Giselle damned him to the pits of hell. But she was here. That meant he was winning.

That miserable bastard, Roger, was here too, thought Pierre angrily. He'd locked himself in the wheelhouse and commanded the craft as though it were his own. If he were to be blown sky-high in the explosion, it wouldn't bother anybody, thought Pierre, but he expelled the thought as quickly as he could. He wanted no one to get hurt. Not even Roger! There would be, without doubt, a fantastic explosion on impact, and a shudder passed through him as he thought of it. What if there was a sailor near the point of impact? What if someone got hurt in the explosion? What if someone got killed? François had assured him that it would hardly dent the destroyer, but how could a destroyer be so strong?

He shuddered again and shook his head as he tried to shake the worries away, but they would not go and the questions kept pouring at him. He turned off the radio and walked through the salon and down the narrow corridor to the aft deck. He had to talk to someone and he would talk to Giselle, even if she was mad at him.

Jacques Ginette strode across the floor of the old church hall followed by two of the student leaders. They carried a makeshift sign, "François for President." The hall was buzzing; people rushed busily about; small groups assembled in every corner discussed the future of the Movement. There was shuffling and yelling in the main section of the hall where a group of young men were arranging chairs.

Jean Petrie moved from one group to another, drawing each youth leader to one side and talking to him privately. "François has asked for a special meeting," he said to each one in turn. "You are invited. Won't you please come? He has some important announcements to make."

"All the important matters will be discussed during the conference," protested one youth. "François will have his chance to speak."

But Jean Petrie was a persistent man and hammered away until, finally, they all agreed. Soon they were assembled in an adjoining room. François walked back and forth in front of them.

"Close the door," he commanded, when the last one had entered. Jacques Ginette quickly obeyed.

"No doubt," François finally began, "you are wondering why I have called this special meeting, but I, for one, feel that it was necessary to have an open caucus." The group, puzzled by the unscheduled meeting, remained silent, anxious to hear.

François waited, sensing their interest. When he felt the precise moment had arrived for the most dramatic impact, he spoke. "We have been betrayed," he said lustily.

"Betrayed?" The delegates looked at each other while François remained silent. Finally, one of the men spoke. "Betrayed by whom?" he demanded.

"Bordeaux!" shouted François without hesitation.

"How has he betrayed us?" There was anger in the voice.

"By lies. Deceit. Connivance!"

François felt he had the group in his command now. He could talk squarely to them and they would listen. There was enough anger, enough curiosity now. They had to listen. Cautiously, he chose his words.

"We have been betrayed," he continued melodramatically. "Bordeaux's betrayal is his attempt to enslave us in the limbo of the past ten years. His inactivity, his back-pedalling, his hopeless lethargy has led us nowhere. And yet, he is forcing his platform on us again. And do you know how he is forcing us? I'll tell you how, my friends. He has rigged the conference. He has rigged the elections. He is gagging the expression of anyone who opposes him. Look about you. Do you see anything that resembles a democratic election? Everywhere you see the plea for non-violence: Bordeaux's plea! Compromise, he asks you. Be patient, he cries. He has spent more time in denouncing me than he has in obtaining the facts. Compare his philosophy with mine. I say to you, do not compromise. I say to you, be violent. I say to you, be impatient and take what is ours today. Now!" François stopped for the reactions. There was nothing but a dull mumbling as the group quietly exchanged views.

François began to speak again, in a loud and commanding voice. "You have not heard me out," he shouted. "I have not made my point." The mumbling stopped and François, lowering his voice, continued. "Bordeaux has betrayed us because he has refused to acknowledge the danger we are in. And we are in terrible danger, my friends. All of us who live along the banks of the St. Lawrence. Our river! Our beautiful river. Our river that someday soon will spell death for us."

A couple of young men in the back row snickered at the remark. The laughter was taken up by a number of others and the resulting relief gave another youth the courage to ask, "It sounds extremely bad, François, but what is this terrible danger you speak of?"

"I have information," François began slowly in order to get the best effect, "I have secret information that the United States is carrying nuclear bombs through our river." He stopped to survey the impact of his statement. It was immediate and intense.

"That is impossible," shouted a youth. And then he added in a more subdued voice, "But if it is possible, we must stop it!"

"Of course," replied François smugly, "but how?"

"Search the ships," came the chorus of replies.

"We can't," replied François simply.

"Can't? Why not?"

"Because of the treaty. Because of the treaty made in our name by the English and the government in Ottawa, the Americans can pass through our river at will. We cannot stop them. We cannot search them. We cannot even go aboard their warships."

"We must stop them," screamed a redhaired lad with freckles. "We must stop them! We can't allow that!"

"How?" François threw his arms out in a gesture of futility. "How are you going to change something that has been an institution for almost a hundred years?"

"A hundred years?"

"Yes. One hundred years. And I ask you again. How will you stop it by using Bordeaux's tactics? Bordeaux's non-violence, Bordeaux's nothingness? You must get rid of him. You must trust me. Listen closely to what I have to say and you'll understand."

The reactions were perfect. The room became as quiet as a library. François spoke again in a confidential voice. "There is an American warship proceeding down our river," he said. "It has come from Rochester. It will soon be leaving Montréal. Tomorrow night, it will pass Trois Rivières within five miles of where we stand at this moment. My information further states that this American destroyer is carrying atomic weapons. My claim, gentlemen, is that the presence of American warships on our river constitutes a great danger to us. We must put a stop to it immediately. I am in favour of blockading passage to this ship until we can inspect its cargo and expose the danger to our people." He stopped abruptly as the surprised and unbelieving faces looked up at him.

François noted their expressions and was delighted. What a shock they would get tomorrow. It would be all he needed to gain total support.

Jacques Ginette winced. What kind of a fool was François? He was spelling out his plan; he was prophesying tomorrow's events so vividly that no one could forget that he had said it. He was telling them everything; everything, except that he, himself, was masterminding it. How could they fail to see through the rest? And yet, as Jacques looked about the room, he realized that not one of the group suspected the truth.

"Bordeaux is short-sighted. He has lost his usefulness to the Movement. He's been terrified to speak out ever since the FLQ screwed things up for us. He can't see the dangers of procrastination. He can't see that our Movement has lost its viability. He doesn't understand that we must take bold action or die. This year. This month. This week. Today. Now? Will you support me?"

A hush fell over the room. Finally, one young man spoke. "You said earlier that Bordeaux has betrayed the Movement. I don't understand what you mean. You didn't explain it to my satisfaction."

"Bordeaux's betrayal is his insistence on withholding the truth from us. If he were truly leading us, would he not warn us of the danger we're in, instead of trying to whitewash it?"

The youth did not reply, but another one asked, "You want us to board the American warship? Are you really so naive as to believe they would let us?"

"No."

"Then what is the purpose in trying?"

"To get public support," explained François. "In order to succeed in our plans for separatism, we must obtain public support. We will need that support whether we separate by peaceful means or by a coup. We will need it after a coup, should we take our case to the United Nations."

"But how will this get us public support?" protested the youth.

"By creating an incident," replied François in a solemn voice, "that will become international news. It will focus public attention on our problem. It will surely invoke public sympathy."

The full force of François' request was now felt by the group. He wanted them to blockade the river, storm the ship and search it. Ridiculous! Impossible! There was not one of the audience that believed he was serious. His request was incredible. The army would be brought in again. The action would be more disastrous to the Movement than anything since the FLQ. François could see the thoughts on their faces. "When you have voted for me, when I am your new president tomorrow night, then I will tell you more. Then I will tell you how we shall do it. As for now, there are more important things to be done." Abruptly, he turned and left the room.

He had barely closed the door when the hoots and shouts began. They were laughing at him, making fun of what he had said. Even Jacques Ginette couldn't understand what François was doing.

Jacques considered the meeting a total flop, thought François, as he moved into the main section of the hall. The same with that stupid ass, Jean Petrie. Petrie and his big mouth. Christ! The way he'd been talking lately, you'd think he had every student group tied up. What a dumb bastard! Half of these kids are obviously sold on Bordeaux. At least tonight they are. But, thought François, smiling at everyone as he pushed his way through the crowds to the front door, whose side will they be on tomorrow night?

Darkness had fallen and the cold night air bit at him. He stepped outside, took a deep breath and looked up at the pitch blackness. It's funny, he thought, it's always darkest just before the dawn, or just before the moon comes up.

He laughed to himself. It's just like success and failure. Those punks in there think I'm a failure tonight. They think I'm a madman. But the important thing is that I know I'm not. It's all strategy. My own personal kind of strategy. I know that within the next half-hour, everybody at the conference will know what I said, and they'll laugh. But, thought François as he smiled inwardly, they won't laugh tomorrow night when it really counts. When the explosion lights up the sky tomorrow night, I'll turn from a fool to a prophet. I'll be their saviour. They'll vote for me *en bloc* and I wouldn't give a franc for Bordeaux's chances.

The cold began to chill him through and he turned back into the hall. As he did, he noticed that the sky was beginning to take on a lighter shade from the reflection of the rising moon. It's early, he said to himself, just perfect. It couldn't be better if I'd ordered it. It should provide the perfect silhouette tomorrow night when the Sans Souci searches out her target.

"Why are we stopping?"

Madame Hébert moved to a window of the salon and looked out into the pitch darkness.

"We're going to moor here for the night," Giselle replied softly. "Pierre is helping Roger with the anchor."

"But why here?" protested Madame Hébert. "Why can't we tie up at a marina? Why are we mooring out here in the middle of the river?" She looked out the porthole. "It's so dark out there, Giselle. I feel so frightened and lonely. I'm glad you are here with me."

Roger tipped the bottle of cognac to his lips and drank from it lustily. He would sleep on the floor of the wheelhouse tonight. It would be fun to go aft and scare hell out of those two broads, and maybe, thought Roger, as he patted the .38 Colt he had neatly tucked in his shoulder holster, put a couple of slugs into that wood-chopper, Pierre. Right in the nuts, he laughed to himself. When that bastard gets it from me, the first two are going to be right in the nuts.

Then he remembered François' warning and promise. "Roger," he had said after last week's episode on the boat, "if you pull off another fool move like that, you're finished." Roger had been about to tell François to stick his job when the magic words stopped him.

"On the other hand," François had said, "if you do a good job for me, if you do exactly what I say, I'll see that you get a nice bonus and a trip to Cuba when this is all over."

François had often promised Roger that he would send him to

Cuba to get a real first-hand look at Castro's guerrillas. But up to now, it had only been promises. "Is it for real this time?" he asked.

"For real."

"Right after this? No waiting?"

"Within twenty-four hours." François would be glad to get him out of the country.

"Okay. It's a deal. No more fooling around."

Roger put the bottle to his lips again. The Sans Souci was safely moored, out of any possible danger in this backwash bay. No one would bother them. He would get drunk tonight and save all the fun and excitement for tomorrow. "I'd sure like to see how those Cubans operate," he laughed, as he sprawled out on a canvas and propped himself up in a corner of the cabin.

It was 3 p.m. the following day when François walked belligerently to the speaker's podium. He had succeeded. He had done what everyone had said was impossible. He had forced Bordeaux's hand and Bordeaux had finally agreed to an open debate.

It had not been easy. All morning in a frantic surge of meetings, accusations and harangues, he had been able to raise the atmosphere to fever pitch. "Suppose it was you," he had asked an informal group put together by Jacques, "supposing it was you who had a revolutionary idea, an ambitious plan for the party, and suppose he would not let it be expressed. Suppose he stifled your plan, your idea for success. What then?"

By noon, he had convinced a number of people that he should be heard. By 1 o'clock, a majority of the delegates decided they wished to hear him. By 1:30, the delegates had convinced Bordeaux that an open debate in a plenary session would solve the problem, once and for all.

"You will surely win, Bordeaux," a friend confided. "We are all with you. We have confidence in you. But you must let this man speak openly, otherwise, you will do a lot of harm to yourself, especially among our younger members."

Bordeaux grudgingly agreed, and the meeting was set for 3 o'clock. A chairman was selected and the rules of conduct were spelled out. No man could speak for more than three minutes at a time. The antagonist must not interrupt. The chairman was to decide whose turn it was to speak. François made sure there was no time lost in formalities. He was the first to speak.

"Let us clarify our motives," he said. "We are attempting to decide the future of our Movement. We must decide against the stagnation, the inactivity of the past" — his voice rose — "the decadence of our present leadership."

The chairman tapped his gavel on the table and turned to François. "I must insist, François, that you limit your remarks to the matters of fact and resist the temptation to indulge in personalities."

"I'm sorry," François lowered his head in mock penitence. "I'm sorry. May I continue?" he asked humbly. The chairman nodded.

"Today we must decide whether we are going fast enough.

We must ask ourselves the question: 'Do we have a hundred years to accomplish our aims?' Then we must answer that question with a fact: it *will* take a hundred years with our present tactics. We must then ask ourselves: why don't we change our tactics? There is a momentum in Québec now — yes, I give credit to Bordeaux for that — but this momentum is dying. It is being wasted. It is being expended in useless actions which are not taking us one step toward our goal. Gentlemen, we cannot, we will not stifle that momentum.

"How long ago was it that de Gaulle came to Québec? And when he came, what did he say? Let me tell you, 'to these peasants,' he said, and he referred to you as 'the little people who cultivate the soil,' and that's what you are. He complimented you. He said that he knew for generations you have multiplied magnificently to keep your heads above the rising flood of the invaders. That's what he said, gentlemen, and that's the truth. Our ancestors fought and fought well, but they were defeated. Defeated! Beaten! And ever since that defeat, our people have been mistreated. Shamelessly abused.

"Now, we have made the decision. We must separate. We must establish strong ties between Paris and Québec. It is the only chance of survival for French-speaking people in North America. We are overwhelmed by the masses of homogeneous English people who surround us. We must separate now, for in ten or fifteen years, we will be bled dry. We will be absorbed by the Americanizing forces which strike at our very heart. We must re-establish our connections with France immediately, in order to protect ourselves. And the time must be now. Now! Now!"

The chairman struck his gavel. François ignored it. "My plan will produce an early separation. There will be no shilly-shallying. There will be few delays, but you must have faith in me, for I know what I am doing. I know where I am going." François lowered his voice, almost to a whisper. "And I want to lead you."

The chairman banged his gavel on the table again. "Your time is up, François," he said, and turning to Bordeaux, he nodded.

"But I am not finished," protested François.

"You will have your turn again," said the chairman, hitting his gavel on the table once more. Bordeaux rose to speak.

"My friends," he said, with all the sincerity of a practised politician, "I plead with you to maintain control of your reason." Bordeaux was obviously nervous and kept wiping his hands, wet with perspiration, on the seams of his trousers.

"We must be careful or all our work to date will be wasted.

A sovereign Québec can only be possible with a well thought-out set of policies. It takes time to institute the policies and more time to put them into effect. It is true what General de Gaulle said so long ago. It is true that we must establish strong links with France, but who has done more than I to establish these links?" There was a ripple of applause. Bordeaux continued.

"I have travelled to France on many occasions and I have established close links with important people there. I have raised money for our cause. No one can say that I have been slow or backward in this respect. But there is nothing particularly intriguing about again becoming a colony of France.

"We are a small compact family group called French Canadians. We must help ourselves because no one else will help us, but this does not mean that we are against everyone. We cannot cut ourselves off from the rest of North America. We are part of it. We cannot do what François says. We cannot build a wall around our Québec. We cannot seal off the St. Lawrence River. If we do what François wants, we will find ourselves, in no time at all, crawling back and begging for re-admission to Canada." A rumbling of discontent arose from the assemblage. A few stomped their feet in a show of protest and Bordeaux stopped for a moment.

A man stood up and yelled. "How could it be any worse? We've been skinned alive for so long we could get used to anything."

The chairman slammed his gavel on the table. "Quiet," he called. Bordeaux began to speak once more.

But François jumped to his feet. "Bordeaux's time is up," he shouted. "I have been watching the clock. He has already spoken for three minutes."

"But he has been interrupted," ruled the chairman.

"This is unfair," shouted François. "You are rigging the discussion."

"Sit down," commanded the chairman. François complied grudgingly.

"We are not a self-centred race of people," said Bordeaux, his voice rising. "We are not racists, we are not anarchists, and we do not want war. But let me tell you what we are. We are deeply and passionately interested in what we can do for ourselves. That's normal, isn't it? That's healthy, isn't it? But it's a shameful thing when a man like François, who has just come to our country, tries to make us out for something we are not. He treats us like colonials. He is as bad as those out-of-touch Québécois in the federal establishment in Ottawa. They are the ones to blame. Like people in exile, they are out of touch with the real Québec. They are intellectually dead.

"We are a tolerant people who respect others. We want in our sovereign Québec the most open of societies. We will respect all immigrants; they can come from any and all lands as long as we have enough schools to teach them French. But we will not tolerate an immigration policy that interferes with French culture. We will have only one language. Two languages are ridiculous. Foolish! Insane! It leads only to bitterness and lack of understanding. Yes, we must have only French in our new Québec."

The chairman hit the table with the gavel. "It is now time for François," he said.

"I will correct you," said François emphatically. "It is far past my time. You have given Bordeaux far too much time to ramble on. To thrash about in vague circles." A light twitter passed through the audience. François grinned.

He looked at Jacques Ginette who sat in the sidelines. Even he was smiling. François was gaining ground. He could feel it. "Yes," he went on with renewed confidence, "while Bordeaux is pussyfooting around and confusing himself, as well as everyone else, I will tell you some facts. One fact is that we must act. Talking is great. Like little old ladies do at their bridge clubs. Little boys do it to impress one another. Salesmen do it to plug their products. But, my friends, we do not have any more time to talk."

He pointed to a large, round, old-fashioned clock hanging on the rear wall. "Look at that," he said and all heads turned. "The clock," he shouted, "the clock. Each tick of that clock measures another moment when we could have acted. And when it is too late to act? What then? Will we say, as Bordeaux has said, it will take time to work out the details. It will take time to establish priorities. Will we take time for everything but action? Look! It's twenty after three in the afternoon. Do you know that by 8 o'clock tonight when the voting begins, the situation will not have changed? We do not know, my friends. We do not know when our time will run out. But one thing I can tell you," François slammed his fist so hard on the table, it almost cracked beneath his weight, "some day and in the not-too-distant future, an event will take place that will set us all back on our heels and, when it happens, remember that I've told you. Remember, that when I wanted to act, it was Bordeaux who wanted to talk."

As far as François was concerned, the debate was finished. He had made his point, loud and clear. Now he must wait. He looked at the big clock. It was almost 4 o'clock. Just another three hours, four at the very latest. The news would not be long in coming. Jacques would leave the meeting shortly. He would check the escape boat and the position of the destroyer. Then he would relay the information to Roger. Minutes after the explosion, he would telephone the hall. Then all hell would break loose.

François smiled as he listened to Bordeaux drone on in his dull monotone. "Sovereignty for Québec is not an end in itself," he said, "it is a tool. It is a tool to help us help ourselves. If we must sacrifice something for this tool, it is a worthwhile sacrifice. For, by our sacrifice, we will gain something for ourselves. It will be a lot better for all of us," he said. "But we must do it right."

François closed his eyes and leaned back in the chair as he listened to Bordeaux's ramblings. He was talking himself right out of business, thought François mirthfully. He looked at the audience. Many were stifling yawns.

"The history of Québec," Bordeaux continued, "has always been a history of struggle. A struggle for survival. First, it was a struggle against the Indians and the cold, then the hardships and disease took their toll. After that, it was the struggle against the British. Then later, the Americans. But we have always kept our heads held high. We took strength from our church, from our spirits."

"*Maudit!*" cursed François under his breath. "He is telling the story of the whole human race."

Bordeaux continued. "We have always been a reluctant partner in an impossible union instead of being masters in our own house." He spoke as though he were reading a Bible lesson to a group of children. "In 1867, when Cartier, Macdonald and the other self-seeking politicians sold us out into the federal union known as Canada, we still did not give up. Sure, we can speak French in Québec, but it's like being on a reserve. Once we get out of the reserve, we can no longer speak French. We must conform to the status quo, to the establishment of the English-speaking majority. But we have fought and struggled. The same old struggle. And we will have that struggle no longer when we become a sovereign state. But," Bordeaux pointed his finger across the audience, "we must begin our sovereignty on solid ground. We must do it step by step. We must do it sensibly and reasonably." He stopped for a moment and the chairman took the opportunity of switching the argument to François.

François opened his eyes and wearily leaned forward over the table. He yawned and shook his head. The audience laughed. He yawned again. "Is it my turn to speak again?" he asked. The chairman nodded. "It is so difficult to keep awake," François said in a mockingly weary voice, "when I listen to drivel." The audience welcomed the jocularity. A raucous laughter filled the room.

François changed abruptly. "Common sense and reasonableness be damned," he shouted. "Since when is a true Frenchman so full of English virtues? Look! Listen to me! To hell with common sense! Let's be frank. Let's be ourselves." He pointed at a student leader to whom he had spoken the previous night. "Why are you a separatist?" he demanded.

"I am a separatist," the boy answered quickly, "because I'm sick and tired of speaking English when I go to work."

"And what will separatism do for you?" prompted François.

"It will change everything," replied the youth fanatically. "Then things will be different. Instead of us speaking like the Americans, they will have to speak like us."

François slammed his fist on the table. The boy stopped. "You have hit the nail squarely on the head," François bellowed. "You speak like a true Frenchman, and you are right. After our separation, everybody, yes everybody, will speak French. The Americans will have no say in our affairs unless they do as we say. They are running our affairs now, but not for long. After our separation, they will pay for what they now steal. Today, they use our river and compensate us nothing for it. They clear our forests and pay us a pittance. They scrape the ore from our ground and, after taking the lion's share, leave us with barely the crumbs from their table." There was silence. Then, there was wild excitement and applause. François had told them what they wanted to hear. He sat down.

It took some time before Bordeaux could be heard. "You speak eloquently, François," he began, "but you speak in the circles you accuse me of using. You say we should take what is ours and use it as a weapon. Let me ask you, François, what is ours that we could take and use?"

François waited for complete silence. "We can take our river," he said slowly and softly. "We can demand control of the St. Lawrence River."

"How can we do that?" scoffed Bordeaux. "It is an international waterway. We would be laughed out of the country if we made such a demand publicly."

"Sooner or later," replied François, "we must meet this challenge. We must get off this fence you're sitting on and say what we're really thinking. The river is ours. It traverses our country from end to end. World leaders understand our problem and world opinion sympathizes with us. Look at the Suez Canal affair, the Gulf of Agaba, the Canal Zone, Pakistan, Cuba and Biafra. Need I go on? You say the St. Lawrence is an international waterway. I say it is the property of the Sovereign State of Québec."

A wild flurry of claps, hollers and thumping followed François' statement. When it died down, he screamed at the audience so frantically that his voice broke. "And I say again, the passing of uninspected American warships through our river is a crime against our people."

Bordeaux interrupted. "There's no danger," he scoffed. "In all our history, there has never been anything but a minor collision on the St. Lawrence. You are placing far too much importance on your notion that we are in a position of grave danger, François. This is a tactical error on your part. I agree with you that it would be of tremendous value to us were we able to control the exits and entrances to the St. Lawrence. It would be worth billions of dollars to us. In fact, it could easily make us self-sufficient as a sovereign state. We could establish tolls sufficiently high to maintain our economy. If our demands were not met by the United States, we could bottle up every one of their Great Lakes ports. They could never handle the freight by railroad and, even if they could, it would cost them more than the tolls. On top of that, it would take ten years to widen their only other access, the Erie Canal. Yes, it would be the perfect answer for us." Bordeaux heaved a sigh. "But I am afraid, my friends, that the annexation of the St. Lawrence River is a pipe dream, a fairy tale for children. Not a workable plan."

Bordeaux was finished. Without a word, he turned from the table and, walking to the sidelines, was quickly met by one supporter after another. As François stood up to leave, he watched Bordeaux out of the corner of his eye. It was obvious now, they were not all fools; a few of them perhaps, but not all. They were dreamers. They wanted their dreams fulfilled, but they did not want to make a nightmare out of what had started as a pleasant dream. François' supporters began to stream toward him.

Later on as Jacques Ginette was preparing to leave for his final rendezvous with Pierre and the Sans Souci, François motioned him to one side.

"How does it look to you, Jacques?" he asked. "I mean beating Bordeaux for the presidency."

"About fifty-fifty," answered Jacques.

"Then it's lucky we have our little insurance policy. Don't you think?"

"There's nothing like being sure," said Jacques with a wink. With that, he walked out the door into the blackness of the early night.

François looked at the clock. It was 5:45.

30

The sun had fallen from the sky in a glorious burst of colour and darkness had quickly followed, before Pierre had crawled from the forward compartments of the Sans Souci. All the detonators were attached, all the fusing devices were rigged and the ship was now a floating mine. The impact detonator protruded from the bow like a lance and was the only mechanism yet to be attached. And when it was, the slightest jar against it would blow the craft and its occupants to bits.

Roger was still at the wheel. He had stood there, seemingly without feeling, during the whole trip and had barely spoken a word to anyone. Now he was heading toward shore, to a complex system of piers, part of a huge marina. They docked without incident and Roger explained to the attendant: "We want mooring space for the night and we'd like to register now." Then, as an afterthought, he added: "We're planning to cruise to Trois Rivières before we dock. But we'll be back before 9."

Soon the formalities were completed. The Sans Souci's name and number were recorded in the registration book. Madame Hébert was listed as the skipper. There were no other questions. "There are only three of us on board with Madame Hébert," volunteered Roger as the attendant gave docking instructions.

The night was made bitterly cold by the wind which swept down the river and cut through Pierre's heavy clothing as he stood on deck. He had been plagued by a thought for hours and he was determined to do something about it. Why should Giselle's and Madame Hébert's lives be further risked by keeping them on this floating bomb? According to the plan, they would both be transferred to the get-away boat at the last minute. It's stupid! A ridiculous chance to take, thought Pierre. If they ever fell overboard . . . ?

Muttering to himself, he turned and made his way quickly to Roger who had reboarded the vessel. Pierre, Giselle and Madame Hébert had remained on board, moving about so that they could be seen, while Roger had tied the Sans Souci's lines and made the arrangements with the attendant.

"I think it would be very wise to take the girls off the boat now," said Pierre, hoping that Roger would agree.

"Take them off the boat? Are you crazy? The whole idea of

the plan is that everyone will think that they have been blown up by the explosion."

"No one will know," said Pierre. "The dock is very dark and they could get off with me when I meet Ginette."

Roger had not considered any such request. The idea of complying was impossible. "Don't be a damn fool," he said, "the attendant in this place has got eyes like a hawk. You'll be lucky if we can get by without him seeing you."

"We've got to get them off," Pierre persisted with rising anger. "They could walk up into town and get a cab, go somewhere until after it's all over."

"No." Roger's voice was firm.

"It doesn't make any sense that you should take this attitude," said Pierre. "What good will they be with you? What can they do to help? Everything is all set."

"They're coming with me. François said that's the way it had to be, and that's the way it will be."

"What's the matter? Are you afraid of being alone?" There was a challenge in Pierre's voice.

"You son-of-a-bitch. I'll fix you for saying that. But you're not going to get me mad now. I'll settle that score with you when this is over. In the meantime, the two of them come with me. Maybe I need them with me so you won't chicken out." Roger sneered. "There's always that danger. I've seen pricks like you who rat out at the last minute. Giselle's my insurance policy. With her on board, I've got confidence. So make sure you're at the right place at the right time, lover boy. Do you know where to meet Ginette?"

"Yes."

"Well then, get going. We haven't got any more time." Roger began to unfasten the stern lines. Pierre quickly disappeared into the darkness.

With running lights ablaze and klaxon sounding fiercely, the Sans Souci left its berth and slid from the protection of the marina. Looking out of the corner of his eye, Roger saw that the attendant was watching. The unwilling witness who would play such an important part at a later time.

Within ten minutes of their departure, Roger spied the American destroyer. It was less than three miles from them and perfectly silhouetted against the dim light of the rising moon. Even at this distance, it seemed enormous.

Roger looked at his watch. It was just past 6:30. The job had to be done and there was no time to waste. He reduced the speed to a crawl, then climbing on the foredeck, attached the fusing device. Then, slipping back to the wheel, he connected the automatic pilot and took a fix on the warship. The mechanism worked perfectly. Then he called out to Madame Hébert and, in a moment, both she and Giselle appeared.

"Not the two of you," he said abruptly. "I only want Madame Hébert."

"But she's very upset," protested Giselle. "Look at her." The older woman's eyes were red-rimmed and tears streamed down her face. "Let me help you. What is it you want done?"

"I need Madame Hébert to help me here!" replied Roger gruffly. "And I need you to help me outside. Take this," he said pointing to Madame Hébert. "Take the wheel and hold it tight."

"I can't," Madame Hébert wailed. "I can't let you hurt my beautiful ship."

"For Christ's sake," shrieked Roger. "At a time like this! It's too late to stop. Now, shut up and take the wheel." Madame Hébert dumbly followed his dictates, but continued to cry. "Hold it tight," commanded Roger again, as he seized Giselle's arm and pulled her down the steps into the salon. "I want you to stand watch on the aft deck," he half shouted as he continued to force Giselle through the passage. "I want you to watch for Pierre and signal him with this flashlight. Everything depends on him getting to us. Do you understand?"

"Yes."

"Then do it. I'm having enough trouble with the old woman." Roger let go of her arm. "I'll be turning out the lights in a minute," said Roger. "And I don't want you to leave this deck. Do you understand?" Giselle was silent. "Not for anything."

With that, he was gone and Giselle was alone. Alone with her thoughts. Alone with her knowledge of what she was doing. Alone with her fears and her doubts.

It had been easy for Pierre to find Jacques Ginette. He had slipped off the side of the dock as Roger had instructed him. He had found the path and followed it to the street and Jacques was there, waiting.

Wordlessly, they drove a short distance to a boathouse in a small bay. A high powered inboard lay there. In minutes the motor was started and Pierre was at the wheel. Jacques leaned over the gunwale from his kneeling position on the floor of the boathouse. Cupping his hands around his mouth, he spoke directly into Pierre's ear.

"When it's over, come directly back here. Don't wait for anything. There are three lights on the boathouse. I'll flash them for you. If anything goes wrong, come back here alone. Now hurry. You haven't much time."

With that, Ginette pushed the boat from its shelter and Pierre was soon sliding across the black, foreboding waters.

But he didn't have time to be lonely for the Sans Souci was moving slowly through the current with every light ablaze. Suddenly, all the lights blacked out and the Sans Souci became invisible in the poor light. He aimed the inboard directly toward the spot where he had last seen it and opened the throttle. *Mon Dieu*, he thought, there's no turning back now.

Frightened and alone, Giselle looked into the blackness of the night. In the distance were the lights of Trois Rivières and, on either side, the black silhouette of the river's banks, dotted with the dim lights of widely separated dwellings. The river flowed swift and black between the Sans Souci and its quarry, while behind it, the rising moon cast its shadowy spell.

Giselle's fears choked her, strangled and contracted her to the point of collapse. What was she doing here? How could she be involved to this point? It had all seemed so impossible at first. It had almost been a laugh, an April fool's joke. Even the last few days when the explosives were on board, it had not seemed real.

But now the truth came crashing about her. She felt like a swimmer who had foolishly bathed in the gentle waters far above a dangerous waterfall. She had seen the ripples that betrayed the current, but she had not heeded the warnings.

Now, she was caught in the current, over her head in the forces that were dragging her to her doom. She had made a lousy, mixed-up job of her life. Why had she always become involved with the riff-raff? The flotsam of society that always hurt her? It's always been my own stinking selfishness! I've always wanted something I couldn't get. And what was it this time? Pierre? That was the filthy truth. That was the weakness that had led her to this. She cursed herself. This time her stupidity would hurt someone other than herself.

And what of Eloise Hébert? That sobbing, broken woman, now being sadistically treated by Roger. What of her? Would she still be here in her precious yacht, if Giselle had refused to come? Probably, thought Giselle, and she felt a little better.

Her eyes strained into the blackness for the lights of Pierre's boat. She looked around the canvas canopy and along the gangway of the upper deck. The Sans Souci's lights switched off suddenly and, for a moment, she could see nothing.

Then a piercing scream echoed down the corridor. It was

Madame Hébert. Giselle was about to run up the passage when it sounded again. Panic filled her mind and she stopped. What could she do against Roger? If only Pierre were here to help! But he wasn't. But look! There he is now.

Way back in the blackness, the tiny red and green running lights bounced up and down in the waves. Another scream, fainter this time, sounded over the relentless rumble of the engines.

Reacting more from intuition than from reason, she climbed onto the gangway of the upper deck. Grasping the wire supports, she edged her way up to the bow. Past the portholes of the sleeping cabins, past the salon she inched, until she stood opposite the wheelhouse. She looked through the window and the sight made her feel sick.

The room was lit up with a small flashlight which lay on the console. Madame Hébert lay on the floor, blood streaming from her mouth. Roger stood over her with a wild look of pleasure in his eyes and slashed her with a heavy wrench. Again and again he hit her. Then, throwing the same tarpaulin over her that had been his bed the night before, he picked up his weapon and hurried from the cabin.

Giselle stifled the scream which forced its way to the back of her throat. She could vaguely hear Roger calling to her. "Giselle. Giselle! Where are you?"

She dropped to her haunches and crawled across the deck. "Giselle! For God's sake, where are you?" Roger screamed repeatedly. But Giselle dug her face into the deck, barely breathing. Every thought had left her mind, except that of self-survival.

"Giselle!" The voice came from another quarter and this time, she welcomed it. Pierre! He was calling her from the escape boat. She looked up. Roger was making his way along the upper deck. Giselle sprang to her feet and quickly, retracing her steps, jumped recklessly into the boat close to Pierre.

The distance between the Sans Souci and its target was closing fast. The destroyer lay less than half a mile away, anchored well off the channel, its light clearly visible.

"Let's get out of here," she said. "Let's go!"

"We can't," replied Pierre, "until Madame Hébert and Roger get here."

"But Madame Hébert . . . !"

Roger appeared at the railing and, without a word, jumped into the smaller craft. "Go," he commanded as he pushed the boat away.

"Where's Madame Hébert?"

Roger was quick to reply. "She's gone," he said. "She's gone!"

"What do you mean, she's gone? Go get her. There's no time to waste."

"She jumped overboard," said Roger as he pushed himself into the front seat.

"What the hell do you mean?" Pierre kept the launch as close as he could to the side of the Sans Souci whose path was still dead-on its target.

"I mean she jumped overboard." Roger crossed his arms and pushed his .38 into Giselle's side. She got the message.

Self-preservation clutched Giselle. Not only for herself, but for Pierre. She must think for them both.

"Madame Hébert jumped overboard," she said, pointing into the blackness behind them.

"Mon Dieu," groaned Pierre. Then he gunned the inboard, turning it as though on a pivot and raced back into the darkness.

"Where . . . ?" he yelled over the roar of the engine. "Where did she jump? We must save her."

"It's a long way back," Roger replied. "Go in a straight line toward the other shore. I'll show you."

Pierre pushed the craft to its maximum, and as he did, Giselle looked over her shoulder. In the distance the Sans Souci, guided by its electronic helmsman, continued its bulls-eye course toward the very centre of the American ship. Giselle wanted to speak. She wanted to cry out to Pierre. Turn this thing around. Go back to the Sans Souci. Disconnect its lethal cargo. Stop its motors. Help Madame Hébert if she's still alive. Give respect to her body if she's dead. And above all, help to put the right hand of justice on Roger's shoulder. Put this scum where he belongs. But no! She could say or do nothing. For she knew that Roger would as soon kill her as look at her. Pierre as well as herself. The only thing that puzzled her was that he had not already done so. She remained silent.

Pierre stood up, scanning the waters as he drove. "Turn on that flashlight," he commanded. "We must find her. Did she have a life jacket on?" His questions were a stacatto-like burst. Giselle could not reply. Roger did.

"Keep going," he said. "We're not back to the spot yet."

"But we're almost back to where I started. There are the lights of the boathouse. Surely to Christ, you know where she went in."

The answer never came for the darkness of the November sky lit with a blinding flash as though someone had suddenly turned on a bright light in a pitch black cellar. There was no sound, just the brilliant flash. But the roar of the explosion was not long in coming. It was accompanied by another flash of white light, even brighter than the first.

"We've hit the jackpot," screamed Roger jubilantly. "We got the bastard right in the guts."

The shock waves fought the wind. And won. Although the trio were over three miles from the inferno, the blast hurt their ears. Explosion after explosion ripped the warship. Roger was right. The Sans Souci, like a fire-spitting dragon, had torpedoed itself right into the very bowels of the destroyer, breathing death and destruction as it ignited the dumps of ammunition aboard its unsuspecting victim.

Pierre stopped the motor and the inboard wind-cocked. They looked in awe as the flames and smoke roared skyward. "Oh, my God," cried Pierre as though he were praying. "She's smashed to smithereens."

Giselle could think of only one thing. One stark and gruesome thought. It was Madame Hébert she saw being blown to bits. And her filthy murderer was sitting here, gloating over his triumph. Pierre, stunned by the fierceness of the holocaust he had created, kept repeating over and over, "Jesus Christ! I never thought it would be like this. François said it wouldn't sink the American ship. Jesus! I never thought it would be like this." Finally, the smell of gunpowder, driven by the wind, reached them. There were still minor explosions, but now the white light had given way to rich, red flames.

Roger was the first to shake off the hypnotic effect of the odious sight. "Let's get the hell out of here," he dictated.

Pierre hardly understood what he said at first. When it sunk in, he said, "But Madame Hébert?"

Giselle could feel Pierre's reaction. She must stop him. "Madame Hébert is dead. She's gone. She's drowned. There's no possible chance of saving her, Pierre. The only chance we have is to save ourselves. We must get out of here. Hurry, Pierre, start the motor. Get us out of here. If we are found . . . !"

Obediently, Pierre started the motor and racing as though he was being chased by a demon, headed straight for the boathouse.

Jacques was there. They scrambled from the small craft, moved hurriedly to a waiting car and sped away, with Jacques at the wheel.

A short while later, the car stopped. Jacques handed a suitcase and package to Roger. "This is your ticket," he said. "Don't miss your plane."

With that, Roger was gone, leaving Pierre and Giselle alone in the back seat while Jacques disappeared momentarily into a phone booth.

When he returned to the car, he swung it around and, in a wild burst of speed, headed due north.

31

The news was not long in reaching the conference. The explosion was first heard as a low rumble in the distance, a flurry of excitement, an announcement by the secretary and, finally, a statement by François.

"It has happened!" he said dramatically. "It has happened far sooner than even I expected, but it has happened! A disaster! How many lives have been lost? No one knows. There is no use racing to the banks of the river," he said. "There is no use raising a cry of alarm. It is all over. Those who are dead are dead. And those who are maimed are maimed. All the shouting and screaming we can do is of no use now."

A hush fell over the audience. François stood on the stage determined to make the best of it. "I have warned you of this danger for years," he sobbed. "I have pleaded with every authority, every government and church leader in the country to do something about it. But no one would listen. My warnings have fallen on deaf ears. Everyone except you, my dear friends, have repudiated me. You alone have seen this danger. You proved it today. You proved it when you asked me to debate with Bordeaux. You proved it in your eyes when you sided with me. I could see it. You agreed with me. I could see that you had decided to vote for me."

François sensed their minds and he was right. There was a danger. The explosion proved it. Bordeaux was short-sighted, stupid and lethargic. He was all the things François had called him. François had seen the danger and had warned them. Bordeaux, on the other hand, had laughed it off.

"I am only the instrument," François shouted above the rising hubbub. "I am only the instrument of truth," he said in a voice filled with humility.

And so, the seed of François' lies fell on fertile ground. His audience believed him. They had all heard him spell out what was to come. All the delegates had heard him tell Bordeaux such a thing was possible. Now that it had happened, they were filled with a new respect for him.

It was as though Bordeaux had vanished like a wisp of smoke. He proposed that the meeting be adjourned and that the voting take place the following day. But he was shouted down without even a word from François. Then the ballots were distributed.

François stared as the delegates completed their election procedures. As though in a dream, he had taken a giant stride toward his goal. To everyone else, François was becoming the new president of the Movement. To François, he was now well on his way to becoming the first president of the Sovereign State of Québec within the next six months.

"François!" said the chairman finally, "is the new president by an overwhelming majority."

The applause was spontaneous. François bowed humbly and his face was wreathed in smiles. But the thoughts he had were not as pleasant. "You stupid bunch of bastards," he said to himself, "you stupid bunch of bastards, I've tricked you. I've had to eat crap to do it, but now it's done. Now, you'll follow me. And, if necessary, you'll follow me to the very pits of hell!"

32

Pierre swung his axe with one last paralyzing blow against the sturdy base of the pine tree. The shock rustled the needles and the powdery snow filtered through the branches to the ground. The tree shuddered momentarily, but Pierre caught it easily in his left hand before it toppled over. Then, with a few well-placed slashes, he cleared off the lower branches and threw it over his shoulder.

Across the snow-covered meadow, he could see the cabin hidden in the dense woods. The sun, its blinding rays reflecting on the snow, made the sky seem more blue than ever. A clear blue that presented such a beautiful contrast to the white landscape that Pierre couldn't resist the urge to stop. It was the kind of day that made him feel happy just to be alive. He stood the tree, their Christmas tree, on the ground, pushed his toque back on his head, and then drawing a package of cigarettes from his parka, lit one. "Holy smokes," he said aloud, "just three more days 'til Christmas." It hardly seemed possible.

But since Giselle's attitude had changed, how time had flown! At first it had been pathetic; then, as though a miracle had taken place, wonderful things began to happen. Giselle had stopped insisting the door be barricaded at night. She had started to talk about things again. Light, foolish, little things, like they used to. Even her crying spells were becoming less and less frequent.

It was almost like it had been before. Why? Pierre took a deep drag on his cigarette. What made her change? Let's see now. It started about the time I suggested we take off for Montmorency. No! It was before that. I remember, because that's why I asked her to go. Because she was starting to be nice again. Let's see. I remember now. I was mad at François because he wouldn't let us come back to the city. Yeah, that's it. I was bitching about it something awful when she sat down beside me.

I went on and on about it. What I wasn't going to do! I was going to quit the Movement. I was going to tell François to go to hell. I was going to push Roger's teeth down his throat when he got back from Havana. Hey! That's when she picked up. That's when she started to talk. Christ! She must hate that creep!

She seemed so interested in where Roger was and when he was coming back. She's real funny about him. Hates his guts, that's for sure. So do I. Who wouldn't? Especially after letting poor Madame Hébert fall overboard and not even trying to save her. Jesus, that was awful. Every time I think of it, I get mad. If he'd done what I wanted, she would have got off at the marina. Then she'd still be alive. Damn it! Every time I think of it, I can't help wondering if that bastard wanted her dead. I could almost believe he pushed her overboard. She told me. Some day though, I'm gonna have a talk with François about that guy. He's no good for the Movement. He's too mean.

Pierre threw away his cigarette and picked up the tree again. Walking steadily across the meadow, he couldn't help remembering. The days of December had slipped quickly toward the mid-equinox and grew shorter so that it was scarcely 4 o'clock in the afternoon when darkness crept over the land. But now, the darkness brought love and they cuddled together on the great bear rug in front of the fire. It was cozy now, and even the howling wolves and the screaming wind did not bother them.

During the daytime, there was still the uncertainty of Giselle's feelings, especially when François or Jacques Ginette were interviewed on the radio or their names were mentioned in a news item.

The party was making fantastic gains, but instead of being happy, the news depressed Giselle. "Sacré!" Pierre would say to himself. Then he would think of his good friend Emile. "Never try to understand a woman," he had often told Pierre, and now Pierre was beginning to realize that Emile was right.

"A woman is beyond understanding," he said to himself.

And so it had gone. Bewildered, not knowing which direction her pendulous emotions would draw her, Pierre concentrated his efforts on doing what was possible. He had taken her ice fishing on Lac St. Jean. He took her for walks through the woods on snowshoes. Through the wonderland of the Québec winter, where the snow piles so deep that a telephone pole can be almost submerged. They sometimes fought each other, but now it was with snowballs, or at other times they compared giant icicles they found in their travels, while yet at other times they just walked side by side in silence.

One day Pierre drove Giselle to Montmorency in a car borrowed from a friend they had met ice-fishing. At the base of the falls, where the ice formed cathedral-like cones, they stood together. The silence between them now was not the muteness of hate. Instead, it was the sonorous hush of a love that lived between them. Strong and good. A love that had taken the test and had passed with honours.

Giselle cuddled close while Pierre held her in his arms. Around them, the frozen waters of the river formed gargantuan figures as the crystal spray from the falls, in the first stages of the winter freeze-up, had grasped the rocks and trees in a tenacious grip. Then with the relentless cold forming a cohesive mass of crystalline solidification, the ice figures had grown to massive proportions. Alone in this ice cathedral, the two clung to each other. It was again what it had always been for Pierre. A love so deep that he could scarcely fathom it.

Standing close, they gazed at the ice formation that surrounded them. Pierre remembered his feelings on that first day, the day on the Terrace when he had first kissed her. With the bells echoing against the cliffs and the hot sun of the August day warming them. Now it was the depth of winter, but the feeling was the same.

Giselle turned, and in doing so, her cold nose rubbed against his cheek and made him laugh. The sound echoed through the ice caverns and the stillness was broken. He kissed her.

"We'll get married soon," she said simply. "We'll get married and then we'll go away."

Pierre had been quiet on their way back to the car. That gnawing conflict had begun again. He wanted Giselle so much, but how could he pick up and walk out on François and the Movement just when things were starting to go so well?

That was over a week ago and Giselle hadn't said anything more about it. "Holy Jesus," whistled Pierre to himself, as he swung the Christmas tree onto his other shoulder. "Emile is right. There ain't a man in the world who can understand a woman."

Giselle scratched a peep hole through the frosty etchings on the window pane and smiled as Pierre approached with the tree. She felt good. It had been so wonderful this past week, or was it two? It had almost been like heaven compared to their first weeks in the cabin. To her, it seemed as though Pierre's fanaticism for the Movement had diminished while his attentions to her had increased.

On top of that, she was feeling better. Gone was the depression that had been gnawing at her. Gone was the fear that had made her bones feel as cold as the icicles that now hung from the eaves. Even the morning sickness she had experienced for so many weeks didn't really bother her any more. Instead, a deep feeling of warmth engulfed her when she thought of the event that the sickness predicted. How wonderful it will be! That is, and the thought stuck in her throat, if only . . . if only she could get him away, anywhere. A cabin in the woods like this, a home in a city far away.

And there . . . And there to have his baby!

The door opened and in a bluster of snow and scratching pine needles Pierre hauled the tree through the narrow portal. "You like it?" he laughed as he stood it up in the centre of the room.

"It's beautiful! It's lovely! Oh, Pierre, where did you find it?"

"In the woods across the meadow. There's a million of them there." Then he laughed again. "You better get some towels," he said, as the snow quickly melted from the branches and ran down the trunk to the floor.

"Don't worry about it," Giselle replied good-naturedly. "I'll mop it up later."

Together they trimmed the tree. Giselle made ornaments from coloured paper and cardboard while Pierre fashioned a stand from two pieces of wood. Then he spliced some wires together to which he fitted the bulbs acquired from the general store. When they were finished, the tree was a rare combination of rustic atmosphere and Christmas feeling.

After dinner, when the pitch black of the arctic night had enfolded the cabin in its bosom and the biting cold north wind whistled like a demon through the trees, they huddled together on the rug in front of the fire. Giselle cuddled in Pierre's arm and the two gazed at the flames while they talked.

"I was thinking," said Pierre after a long silence, "how much fun it would be if we could see Emile and Yvonne." He stopped and waited for a response. "I always see them at Christmas," he continued, when there was no answer.

Giselle wondered how she could face Emile. Surely he knew what had happened to the Sans Souci and, just as surely, he could not have misunderstood the part played by herself and Pierre. If there was anyone in the world who knew how the explosion occurred, beyond those directly involved, it was Emile. "Do you think it would be wise?" she asked. "Don't you think he would ask questions?"

"Emile? Questions? Hell, no." Pierre laughed. "He'd never ask any questions about anything. Not from me, anyway. He's my friend and that's all he cares about and that's all I care about, ma chérie. We've done so many things together in our lives, Emile and me, that we'd never try to be guardian angels over one another now. I've helped him out plenty. More than just getting a few sticks of dynamite." He laughed knowingly. "I could tell you a lot, but I won't. I wouldn't even tell you, Giselle, because Emile is my friend and I am loyal to my friends. But I will tell you one thing for sure. You don't have to worry about Emile."

"But how could we get to their place? They live so far away. There's so much snow. It's so cold. The roads are bad and, besides, we have no car. And even if you could borrow a car, it would cost too much for gas."

"Just excuses," scoffed Pierre. "I can get the car and I can afford the gas. We could go to their place, or on second thought, we could meet them in Québec City. Say, that would be fun. Let's meet them in the city."

Giselle shuddered. "Québec City?" she asked. "We can't go there."

"Why not?"

"Because of François. I thought you promised him that you'd stay here."

"He's not my keeper."

An immediate flush of pride swept over Giselle. Surprised and elated, she realized that this was the first time Pierre had shown the slightest bit of contempt for François. She must not stifle this feeling. Instead, she must encourage it, in spite of the danger. The danger of being discovered in their disobedience was not too high a gamble if it would inspire Pierre to defy François.

"I think it's a wonderful idea," she agreed. "We must make arrangements as soon as we can."

Pierre jumped to his feet and danced about. Then he lifted the lid of the ancient victrola that stood in the corner and, winding it up, placed a record on the turntable. The needle scratched an old French-Canadian folk song from the pitted record, blasting a garbled sound across the room, but the music was recognizable. Even the scratching could not dispel its enchantment. Pierre bent over Giselle and lifting her face to his, kissed her. "I love you. I love you," he whispered.

He had been stirred by her expression of delight. She wanted, like himself, to see Emile and Yvonne. This is what she wanted and this is what she would have. No matter what the consequences, they would spend Christmas in Québec City. They would have a wonderful time with Emile and Yvonne!

33

Pierre lifted the telephone receiver and began to dial. "Darling," he said, "come here." Giselle responded and sat beside him on the comfortable chesterfield. It was good to be back home. He kissed her on the cheek. "Be very quiet," he said, "and don't ask any questions, and for God's sake, don't make any noise."

"What are you going to do?" She was curious.

"Never mind." Pierre tapped her nose with his finger and then dialed a number. The phone buzzed six times before it was answered. Then, smiling at Giselle, Pierre directed the earpiece so that Giselle could plainly hear the voice on the other end. It was François!

"It's me," said Pierre. "I almost didn't call you today. It's so cold here." He winked at Giselle. "It must be twenty below."

"Never mind," François replied sternly. "Never mind. You're a young man and you can take it. It's better to check in. Then I know where you are and I can give you your instructions."

"When are we going to get out of here?" Pierre stifled a laugh. "We're both sick of sitting around looking at the four walls." He grasped Giselle's hand and squeezed it. Then, putting his finger to his lips in a gesture for her to be quiet, he continued, "I'd like to come to Québec City. I'd sure like to get some more action. Besides that, I need some money."

"I'll send you some." François seemed agitated. "You shouldn't need much."

"Why can't I drive in and pick it up?"

Silence followed. Then François' voice boomed. "Don't come to Québec City."

"But François!" Pierre protested.

"I don't want to talk about it," snapped François. "Just stay where you are. Don't come to Québec City. Listen to me, this is an order. Roger will soon be back. Giselle must be kept there. Do you understand?"

Anger rose in Pierre. "No, I don't understand," he said. "I don't understand at all. What has Roger to do with Giselle staying at Lac St. Jean?"

François' voice switched abruptly. "I am only thinking of her well-being. I am thinking of the danger." There was a note of apology in his voice. Pierre had changed. His wits had sharpened in the last few months. There was no doubt about that. And François was well aware of it. When he had first come to the Movement, Pierre was still wet behind the ears. Everything that François told him was swallowed, hook, line and sinker. After all, wasn't that the reason he had been used? But now his attitude was altered. He was becoming a smart aleck. Beginning to question, beginning to doubt. I won't take this bullshit for long, thought François.

"What I wanted to say," he went on, "is that I have another big job waiting for you both as soon as Roger gets back. Stay where you are and enjoy yourself. Have a good time, but don't forget to call me tomorrow." With that, François hung up and Pierre sat there, the buzzing phone still held to his ear. For a moment he was angry, then the irony of the situation tickled him. He had completely fooled François and it had been so easy. Here was François, with all his brilliance and supposed knowledge, who didn't even suspect that Pierre was only a few blocks away.

"Did you hear him?" Pierre laughed raucously. "Did you hear him when he said, 'this is an order'? I almost howled. He sounded like an old school-teacher of mine." Then his voice lowered and the happy expression left his face momentarily. "But he's got the wrong boy," said Pierre. "I've been doing too much listening lately. Especially to the radio." He stood up. "I've been doing a lot of thinking and a lot of wondering, too. I've been wondering if there isn't a better way to settle our problems." He began pacing back and forth in front of Giselle. "I've been wondering what is right. What is sensible? What's the best thing in the long run? What this whole goddamn problem is all about? I mean really, Giselle."

He looked at her and felt embarrassed. Wasn't it she who had started these questions in his mind? Wasn't it she who had first prompted him to think? Pierre realized this as he spoke and the thought vexed him, but something inside would not allow him to admit it. His instincts as a man demanded that what he did was the product of his own thinking. But had it ever really been so? As a child, he was dominated by his mother. As a boy, he was dominated by a combination of his school-teacher and the priest. As a youth, it had always been Paul. Now as a young man, it was François. Lately, there were the roots of discontent. A growing need inside him for freedom to think for himself. A desire to solve his own problems and come to his own conclusions.

Now he had taken the first step. He had defied François. Not openly, but maybe that wasn't the way to defy François anyway.

It was not the way François would defy him and Pierre was beginning to realize it.

It was cold but exhilarating when they left Giselle's apartment early in the afternoon. First they made their way up rue St. Jean, window shopping, then when each was satisfied with his choice, they parted. It was in their minds to surprise each other with their gifts. Fascinated by the Christmas decorations in the shops, Giselle pointed, oohed and aahed, while Pierre whistled. "What's that?" He pointed to a group of workmen erecting a scaffold.

"They're building the Ice Palace."

"The Ice Palace? What's that?"

"It's for the Carnival. Have you never been to the Carnival?"

"Never." Pierre was curious. "But I've heard of it. What's the Ice Palace for?"

"It's just a fun house." She sounded like a little girl as she went on. "People walk in and out. They have fun, they laugh and everybody is happy. There's music and behind the Palace, they dance in the street."

"In the middle of winter?"

"At ten below zero," laughed Giselle. "Come on, I'll show you." Together they walked across the street to where the men were building the scaffold. "Here's where they dance," Giselle pointed to the street. "They block it off."

Pierre bowed to Giselle. "May I have the first dance?" he asked capriciously.

"Not now, silly! We'll have to wait 'til Carnival time."

"And when is that, my darling?" joked Pierre.

"In a couple of months. No, less than that. In about a month and a half, I think," replied Giselle thoughtfully. "It's in the middle of February."

"Well, then, I want you to promise me," Pierre took Giselle's shoulder in his hands and turned her toward him. "I want you to promise me, no, I want you to give me your sacred vow, that you will dance with me at Carnival time. Here, at the Ice Palace."

"With pleasure," Giselle laughed as she bent in a mock curtsey. But as she raised her eyes to his, her breath caught in fear. He stood there, his heavy parka fastened tightly, his heavy scarf bulging around his neck, his red tassled toque sitting jauntily on his head and a big smile on his face. And yet as she looked, a weird, uncanny feeling crept over her. This man standing in front of her was not her lover, not her husband to be. He was an apparition, a phantom. Her smile vanished as she looked at the face before her. Gone were the laugh wrinkles around his eyes, his mouth seemed open in surprise. Worry lines pulled his face into a spectral mask and his eyes were slitted in hate.

"What's the matter, darling?" she heard him say. "What's the matter?"

As suddenly as the premonition had come, it left. Giselle shook her head and looked at him. He was still smiling. "Nothing. Nothing is wrong, darling!" She forced a smile.

The Ice Palace came back into focus. The laughing sounds of people milling about pleased her ears and the jolly spirit of Christmas again filled the air. "There's nothing wrong, darling. I just felt funny for a moment, that's all."

"Let's go and get a drink," urged Pierre. "That's what we need, a drink."

Without a word of dissent, Giselle placed her mittened hand in his and he led her down the busy street.

Together they sat in the lounge of the Victoria Hotel. There was a nostalgia here for both of them. It was here they had danced that night so long ago. The night they had first known of their love. They drank dry martinis and talked of other Christmas eves.

"When will Yvonne and Emile arrive?"

"About noon."

"Then we'll be with them all afternoon and evening. Won't that be nice?" Giselle's voice betrayed her fears. The last few weeks at the lake had given her a peace of mind that she had never known. Now they were back in the city again, and the contentment and security she had felt in the solitude of the forest was replaced by a gnawing fear which she could not understand or explain. Suddenly, she changed the subject and turned to Pierre.

"Would you take me to Midnight Mass tonight?" she asked.

"Midnight Mass? I never thought you'd . . ."

"I haven't been for so long. I just feel like it. It's just a whim. I don't know. Maybe I won't want to go later and maybe, when I get there, I won't want to stay. But will you take me anyway?"

Solemnly and lovingly he studied her. "Christmas has never been real to me without Midnight Mass," he said after a long pause.

Horse-drawn sleighs jingled in the frosty air. Bells tolled from every church. Brilliant coloured lights sparkled from every light standard. And people, dressed in their finest winter regalia, walked in happy groups toward the Basilica de Notre Dame de Québec.

The cathedral, a masterpiece of beauty, was crowded and

the organ thundering out a "Joyeux Noel" sent shivers of gladness through the two.

Giselle was mesmerized by the altar and the statues of the Archangels, plated in gold. To the left was a statue of Our Lady of Lourdes. Great banks of votive candles, lights glittering in their red and white holders, blazed away. How many hours had Giselle spent as a young girl, visiting her God in the solemn beauty of such a place of worship? It had been her second home while at the Abbey. It had been as much a part of her life as the clothes she wore and the food she ate.

What had driven her away? Was it her own base desires? Or was it the possible demands of the church? The demands that defied her very reason and frustrated her every desire. Or was it the hypocrisy of placing a sinful connotation on every natural and normal feeling and then, repetitiously confessing these pseudo-sins, knowing full well that they would be repeated because there was no logical reason why they should not?

Yes, it had been a place of beauty and consolation for Giselle, but somehow she had lost it. Was it because she was evil and wrong and did not belong in that beautiful place? Or was it because the Church was wrong?

Tonight was not the time and this was not the place to search for the answer. It was enough to know that the feelings, invading her soul this Christmas Eve as she stood beside the man she loved, were real. She knew as she walked up the aisle and genuflected toward the altar, that her faith was not dead. She knew that she could recover her lost convictions. The doctrine she had left so very long ago. These principles of beauty, of tranquility, of peace, of harmony with everything in the world could, once again, be hers if she were only to reach out and grasp for them. And as she sat there listening to the carols, to psalms and chants of the mass, the sermon which followed and, finally, the roaring of the organ as the faithful filed from the church, tears formed in her eyes and trickled down her cheeks. She quickly daubed them with a handkerchief. Pierre turned to her. "We'd better go," he whispered, "almost everyone has left."

Giselle turned to him. "Come with me first for just a minute." She left the pew and led him to the altar where they knelt before the statue of the Lady of Lourdes. Giselle moved closer to Pierre. "She was my mother when I was a little girl," she whispered. "I would pray to her every day. She watched over me. She knew when I told the truth, and she knows now. Now, when I tell you that I love you, Pierre. And by the Virgin, I swear . . . I swear to you that I will make you a good wife. If you still want me."

"If I still want you?" For how long had he wanted to marry her? He could not remember. It must have been from the very first moment of their meeting. But what of her? She had consistently put off the wedding date, except for that night at Emile's when she had promised to marry him. But now as she knelt before the statue of the Virgin, he knew that she wanted to belong to him.

Giselle lifted a taper and lit a votive light. "I'm lighting this for us," she said. Pierre, using the same flame, lit another candle. "And I light this for you, chérie, as a symbol of my love."

"And why shouldn't we go out and have a good time?" Emile's voice boomed across the living room. "It's Christmas Day, isn't it? And I'm with my old friend." He lifted his glass to Pierre. "And I hope my new friend, too." He winked at Yvonne who sat on the chesterfield. She smiled. "Why shouldn't we go out and have some fun?" Emile repeated.

"I didn't say we shouldn't. I just said . . . I just . . . well, I thought . . . What I really meant, Emile, my good friend," Pierre moved toward him, "is that we should definitely go out and have a good time." Emile laughed, Giselle nodded in assent, Yvonne smiled, and before long, the four were in Emile's car happily rolling down rue St. Jean.

Giselle laughed and sang with the rest despite an increasing uneasiness she could not escape, a disquiet even Pierre's arms could not soothe as they huddled together in the back of the car. She had been glad when Pierre had agreed to go; she interpreted it as a refusal to bow to François' dictates. On the other hand, François' specific orders of yesterday afternoon still rang in her ears. "Don't come to Québec City," he had commanded Pierre. "Giselle must be kept at the lake."

These words had awakened her fears, the same anxieties which had overwhelmed her at the cabin. She must fight hard or they would get the better of her again. Thoughts of the exploding ship, the bludgeoning of Madame Hébert, and the threat of Roger still haunted her. But this new and ominous uncertainty was even worse.

As they passed the place where only yesterday the workmen were building the Ice Palace, the same strange premonition swept over her as she thought of Pierre's words. "Giselle, I want you to promise, no, I want you to give me your sacred vow, that you will dance with me at Carnival time. Here, at the Ice Palace."

"Look!" It was Yvonne's voice. Though usually a very quiet

girl, she was now as excited as the rest, especially after Emile's description of the toboggan slide at the Château Frontenac. The Glossier! She had heard of it for years. Today, she was to see it, perhaps if she had enough nerve, to ride on it. "Look," she repeated, "look at the lights on that big tree. Isn't it beautiful?"

They passed the Basilica, then drove down a narrow street, scarcely wide enough for the car, past the Restaurant de la Paix, and finally, to Place d'Armes in front of the Château. Wheeling the car into a parking space, they scrambled from it and hurried around the Château to the Terrace.

There it was! The Glossier. Like a gargantuan ski jump, it soared high above the Terrace, so high it almost levelled the flag-topped stone walls of the Citadel. The tobogganers, in a steady stream, hauled their sleds up a long incline. Then when they reached the top, they would descend, three toboggans at a time, racing one another wildly at unbelievable speeds down the icy drop, with the only thing holding them on their course being the deep ruts in which the sleds were imprisoned. Faster and faster the toboggans flew until, finally, the Glossier flattened out and they whizzed along the Terrace almost to the end.

Yvonne looked over the edge of the Terrace to the roofs of the lower town far below. She gasped. "If those things hadn't stopped, they'd have gone over the cliff."

"That could never happen." Emile took her hand. "Let me show you. Look!"

Three more toboggans appeared on the slide, racing wildly in their plunge to the bottom. Although they were almost a quarter of a mile from the end of the slide, their cries and screams could be heard as they raced one another to the finish. With toques swirling and scarves flying, they raced toward Pierre, Emile and the two girls. Then, as if the toboggans were equipped with brakes, they came to a dead stop exactly where they were supposed to do so. Emile pointed to the surface of the ice. "Look at the pumice they've spread on the ice," he said jovially. "It stops the toboggans easily. There's no danger."

"There may be no danger," Yvonne said, "but you won't catch me on that thing. Look. That's what I want." She pointed toward a skating rink which flanked the Terrace. Laughing gaily, they followed her and made their way around the edge of the toboggan run to the rink.

"Hey! We can rent skates!" And it wasn't long before she had convinced the others that they should go skating.

The Skater's Waltz filled the clear air. The ice statues, looking friendly and happy, smiled down from a dozen vantage points around the ice and added to the atmosphere. The deep red sun falling into the western sky made beautiful images on the snow and the four walked shakily but playfully to the ice.

"I haven't done this for years," laughed Emile, "but I bet you I can still do it. Watch." He pushed himself from the rubber matting at the entrance to the precarious footing of the slippery, smooth sheet of ice. They laughed as he made a desperate attempt to put on a show and ended up sprawling ungracefully. Yvonne skated over to help him, followed by Giselle and Pierre. But Emile was not hurt. Not even his pride. And he laughed and joked and soon they were skating around to the music. With rosy cheeks and exhilarated feelings, they enjoyed themselves playing chasing games.

Pierre spied a group of teenagers forming a human whip. A group, holding hands, was swung in circles. An anchor man stood in the centre controlling their speed and direction.

"Let's join them. It looks like fun." And so Pierre and Giselle were the last two skaters on the whip. Faster and faster the anchor man swirled them. Stronger and stronger became the momentum. The wind whistled by Giselle's ears and burned her face, but she hung on desperately to Pierre. Around and around they went, faster and faster, until, finally, the pressure became too great and, with a scream, someone let go and the chain was broken. Pierre and Giselle were thrown toward the edge of the rink and an ice statue which stood there smiling down at them.

"Let me go," shouted Giselle. "I can stop all right."

Realizing that the two of them together would not be able to control themselves, Pierre let go. Instinctively, he swung in one direction while she went in the other. They both continued at breakneck speeds in opposite directions. Finally, Giselle turned her skates and skidded to a stop. But not quite fast enough. She tumbled, head over heels, into a fluffy pile of snow, but she was not hurt. Not even scratched.

She wiggled about for a moment trying to stand up but the momentum had pushed her so deeply into the snow that she could hardly move. It was then that a man, dressed in a heavy parka, a red toque and a knitted face mask, appeared above her. Without a word, he reached his hand to her, offering to help. A crawly sensation followed his touch and as he pulled her from the snow bank, still without a word, the same irrational fear seized her. She stood there before him momentarily, mesmerized by his piercing brown eyes. "Thank you," she said. Then, again without a word, he turned abruptly and walked away. Giselle stood and watched. Something about the way he walked made him seem familiar. She stared at him and the goose pimples climbed up her back.

"Are you all right, darling?" Pierre had skated off the ice and stubbing his skates into the snow approached her. He put his arm around her.

"Yes, I'm all right," she said.

Pierre helped her back on the ice. "Let's get a cup of coffee."

"Okay." They skated to the exit.

The coffee was hot and strong and it felt good. Before Giselle was finished, Emile and Yvonne came in and joined them.

"By Lord, that was fun." Emile took off his toque and using it as a brush, whisked the snow from his clothing.

"You didn't hurt yourself?" Yvonne was genuinely concerned.

"No, not a bit," answered Giselle. "It was fun. It was the best fun I've had in years. Are we going to do some more?"

"Emile says he's determined to go on that toboggan ride." Yvonne looked at her husband and shook her head. "I think he just wants to show off. He won't admit that he's afraid."

"There's nothing to be afraid of," Emile said stoutly. "It's all in your head. Fear is one of those things that you build up in yourself. Come on, let's get these skates off. Then we can go and have some real fun on the Glossier."

"It's okay by me." Pierre turned to Giselle. "How about you?"

"I won't promise, I'm a bit of a chicken. I'll take a look, but I'll probably end up waiting for you at the bottom."

"Me, too," echoed Yvonne. "You couldn't drag me up that thing with a pack of huskies."

"Okay." Emile winked at Pierre. "You can be a stick-in-the-mud if you want to, but I'm going on the toboggan ride, even if I have to go by myself. You three chickens can wait at the bottom." He left to rent a toboggan. "Wait for me here," he called as he left.

The lights of the Glossier sparkled like those of a circus against the clear night sky. A lively French song telling of the fun of the Carnival filled the air. Toboggans flashed by as the trio stood beside the railing. Giselle gasped. "I don't think I could stand that. I'd better stay here with Yvonne."

"Okay, if that's what you want." Pierre wished Giselle would change her mind.

The next three toboggans were preparing for take-off and, for no reason at all, Giselle could feel the goose pimples rising on her flesh. She had decided not to go down the slide, so it couldn't be that. It was not the temperature, she was too well dressed. No, it was something else. The same strange chill passed through her again. She snuggled close to Pierre for comfort and then, turning her head, she noticed him.

There was no mistake. It was the same man who had helped her at the ice rink and his touch had made her skin crawl. Now he was standing beside her and he gave her the creeps. But why? Why was he standing so close? There were very few people lining the fence. Maybe he was only stupidly rude, thought Giselle. This man frightened her. She could not stay beside him.

Emile appeared with a toboggan. "Let's go," he said. "I can hardly wait."

"Okay." Pierre gave Giselle a loving hug. "We won't be long," he said.

"Wait. I'll come."

"But you don't have to."

"I want to."

"Don't come if you're nervous, Giselle. That's the time a thing like this becomes dangerous. When you're nervous. When you don't do the right thing. That's when something can go wrong. You've got to keep control of yourself. Please, don't come, Giselle, you look too scared."

"I'm not! Let's go." Pierre realized that there was no use trying to stop her. She would go. Nothing would dissuade her.

"Okay," he laughed, "come on."

Giselle wasted no time in joining the parade up the long incline.

"Emile," she said. "I'll help you pull the toboggan."

"Don't be ridiculous, there is only room for one to pull it on this narrow walkway." He pushed her in front of him. "You walk ahead of me, little one," he said. "I will pull the toboggan."

Soon they were at the top and Giselle could feel her heart pumping as she looked down from the dizzying heights. The control house at the pinnacle was staffed by an attendant who did not care to mince words.

"Ready!" he shouted to the riders of the three toboggans preceding theirs. Then, with a snap, the holding hooks were released and the laughing, screaming, happy groups began their plunge. Within seconds, they were out of sight. Emile pushed his toboggan into the outside slot. The other two runs were quickly filled. The holding hooks clicked into position.

"I'll sit up front. Then if we hit something, nobody will get hurt," he laughed. Giselle forced a smile as she tensed. The shouts and screams from the other riders had faded in the distance. Pierre jumped on the toboggan behind Emile.

"Climb on behind me as quickly as you can," he said, looking over his shoulder at Giselle. With quivering knees, she responded, sitting behind and straddling him with her legs. He grasped her boots and lifted her legs high enough to protect them from the ice ruts at each side. "Put your arms around my neck and hold on tight." The attendant gave the ready signal.

"*Aller!*" everyone shouted.

Hanging on to Pierre, with a scream ready in the back of her throat, she felt someone jump on the toboggan behind her and kneel down. She turned and caught a glimpse of a red knitted toque and a matching face mask.

"Oh, God, no! It can't be him!"

"What's that, *chérie*?"

"Oh, Pierre, I'm afraid!" The figure behind her moved close and touched her back. "I'm afraid."

She felt a pair of hands on her shoulders at the exact moment the click of the release mechanism sounded, and Giselle's screams were lost in the wild sounds which followed. First, there was a sudden lurching movement as the toboggans, weighed down by almost half a ton of human cargo, dropped into an almost perpendicular void. The wind burned her face and forced her to close her eyes. Then, as though in a nightmare, she felt the hands behind her creeping higher and higher on her shoulders. Its speed increasing, the toboggan dropped over the second ledge.

But Giselle was conscious of only one thing. This man, this man who had been following her. This man who knelt behind her, was leaning hard against her. His fingers clutched her shoulders in a forceful grip and his weight, pushing her sideways, affected her balance.

"Pierre!" she screamed. "Help me. Help me!"

"Hang on," Pierre yelled back. "Hang on, Giselle. For God's sake, hang on."

"I can't. I'm slipping."

Giselle's arms, weakened by the relentless pressure of the heavy weight against them, loosened their grip on Pierre's shoulders. The pressure became more pronounced. It was too much for her. As the toboggan bounced over the third and final ledge, her grip was broken. Her arms flew up. Her body yielded to the force and she fell backwards. But Pierre's grip on her legs was like that of a vise. Even the full weight exerted on her now could not push her sideways. The drop was over. Their speed decreased as they flew along the Terrace. The grip on her back was released abruptly, and seconds later, the toboggan ground to a halt. Hysterically,

Giselle grasped Pierre around the neck.

"We've got to get off." Pierre turned his head. "We've got to get off before the next toboggan starts coming. We can't just sit here!" He jumped to his feet and, while Emile grasped the rope to pull the toboggan from the runway, he helped Giselle. He could see that she was crying.

"That man," she said. "That man. He tried to kill me. He tried to throw me off."

"What man?"

"Him!" She swung her arm and pointed to a man disappearing in the crowd. "That man," she screamed again, "the one that's running away."

Pierre took her hand. "Your imagination is getting the best of you, Giselle. There was no one else on the toboggan. There was just the three of us. You were nervous. You panicked."

"That man was behind me." Giselle spat out the words.

Pierre was embarrassed. Her screams were attracting attention. He took her arm and led her away to a quieter spot. "I'm sorry, darling," he said. "I didn't see anyone on the toboggan with us."

Giselle began to cry. "It was that man. It was that man with the face mask. He's been following us around ever since he saw us skating . . ." She rubbed her mitts across her eyes to brush away the tears. "Do you know who I think it was?" She didn't wait for Pierre to answer. "I think it was Roger." There was a wildness in her eyes that Pierre could not ignore.

"Roger?"

"Yes. I'm sure it was Roger. He's back. He's back and he's going to kill me."

"Giselle, my darling. No one is going to hurt you. No one is going to kill you."

She clung to him like a frightened child. "Roger is going to kill me. François wants him to. Don't you believe me?"

Pierre turned his head. There was something he could not understand. He did not want to understand it. He had known of people being crazy, people who imagined things that were not real.

It was like the little girl who said she had seen the Virgin in a grotto at Québec. There had been headlines in the paper. Pierre had been impressed by it. Even the priests had said she was a sainted child, but then, after a lot of questioning, the girl had denied it all. The child had been put in a hospital. Everybody said she was crazy.

That was the closest that Pierre had ever come to anything like this, and now Giselle was telling him that she had seen someone who wasn't there. François was right. How many times had he told Pierre that the experiences had affected her mind. That she should be looked after. "I will look after her," he had said to Pierre one day on the phone. "I can have her cured. The only problem is that you will have to leave her with me for a few weeks." He wished he could cry.

Emile approached, still pulling the toboggan. He had gone to see Yvonne.

"Are you ready for another one, *mes amis*?"

Pierre shook his head and Emile, understanding that something was wrong, nodded and went away.

"We'd better go home, Giselle," said Pierre sadly. "We'd better go home."

François' anger was clear and unmistakable. He repeatedly tapped his fingers on the big mahogany table in the late Madame Hébert's drawing room. His face was criss-crossed with lines of hate and his eyes gleamed with fury.

"You're positive it was them?" he demanded of Roger, who sat nonchalantly in a chair halfway across the room.

Roger puffed his Havana cigar until it glowed. Then he took a mouthful of smoke and blew a ring toward the ceiling. "I lifted her out of the snow. I stood close enough to touch them. I rode on the same toboggan. That's how I know."

"But you could be mistaken?"

Roger stood up in defiance. "Are you calling me a liar?" he yelled. "I said I saw them. If you don't goddamn believe me, then you can go to hell. But I saw the bastards." He stopped as he recollected the toboggan ride. Then a grin came slowly over his face. "I scared the shit right out of that little whore," he laughed. "She was so goddamn scared, she probably pissed her pants."

"And what good did that little charade do?" demanded François disgustedly. "Do you know what you almost did? You could have let the cat right out of the bag. Let them know we're up to their tricks. Maybe you did."

"Impossible. Not with that face mask."

"How can you be so sure? There's more ways to recognize somebody than by their face. Why was she so frightened?"

"Wouldn't you be scared if somebody tried to push you off the Glossier?"

"Yes," said François, thinking. "Yes, I suppose I would." But Roger's answer had not pleased him. He added up in his mind the variety of experiences he had of Giselle. Hysteria was not a part of her nature. Not without reason. Not because of a ride on the Glossier.

He thought of his talks with Pierre on the telephone. "She's worried sick," Pierre had said repeatedly. "But she won't talk."

He remembered too, Giselle's stinging remarks of only a few weeks ago. Before the incident. "I want out!" she had screamed at him. Her screams were not hysterical then. They were screams of anger. She had turned from an angry, defiant rebel into a whimpering mental case. Why? Something had happened to change her. Was she sick because of her involvement in the explosion? Or had she learned something? If she was frightened to the degree expressed by Roger, then she must be aware of something, something dangerous. She must be disposed of immediately. There must be a way.

"Yes," François repeated. "I think I understand. But there's one thing that puzzles me, Roger. How did you happen to be there?"

"The superintendent at her apartment phoned me. I have a deal with him. I followed them."

"Very good." Sometimes Roger is more clever than I give him credit for, thought François.

"I thought you had her tucked away in that little shack in the woods." There was an element of contempt in Roger's voice.

François tried to hide his anger. "So did I," he said briskly. "Go on, tell me everything."

François listened as Roger went on. So Pierre would dare to pull a trick like this? To pretend that he was following orders. To disobey deliberately. For how long had he done this? If he betrayed once, he would betray again.

When Roger had finished, he stood directly over François. "Why don't you just kill both of the bastards?" His eyes glistened with expectation.

François tapped the table as he stared into Roger's eyes. Finally, he said, "I can't."

"You can't!" Roger had never heard François admit that he could not do anything.

François didn't like Roger crowding him. "Sit down," he said, pointing to a chair. "I'll tell you why Pierre must be kept alive." Roger sat down.

"Pierre must appear alive and well at the settling of Madame Hébert's estate. There is a bonus for you to keep him alive. Our deal is still on. The bonus is extra."

"I get a bonus for keeping him alive?" Roger laughed. "Then I get the contract to tuck him away?"

"Exactly."

"How long will the game last?"

"A month, two at the very most. You see, I groomed Pierre to fill the role of the beneficiary. You know what kind of a dumb slob he is?" Roger nodded. "You know how gullible he is?" Roger nodded again. "Well, now do you see why he must be looked after properly?"

"It smells," said Roger. "Suppose he pulls out? He'd end up with the house, the money and everything."

"You must know me better than that. I had Pierre sign everything over to me."

"He signed everything over to you? Then why the hell keep him alive? Why would he have to appear anywhere? Just show them the papers. Tell him he's out of town."

"That may not be possible," said François rising. "He has to be available in case. Just in case. Now that would be difficult if he were dead, wouldn't it?" Roger was silent. "It'd be one hell of an expensive mistake for me if you were to fill your contract now."

"I should have stayed in Havana," Roger grumbled. "Why didn't you tell me before? I wouldn't have come back."

"I didn't expect you back, Roger. I didn't expect you back for another week or two."

"I guess I got anxious." Roger almost sounded apologetic. "I guess I don't forget that easily. I can't forget the way those two bastards ganged up on me."

François bit off the end of a cigar. "That brings up another point of interest. Have we forgotten about that backwoodsman and his wife? They know all about the explosion. They know all about Pierre's involvement." He spat out the end of the cigar into the fire. "I think we should plan a little surprise party for them."

Roger's face lifted. "A good idea!"

"I'll leave the details to you. But now I must get back to the problem at hand." François lit up with a splinter which he doused in the flames. "Did you ever play cat and mouse, Roger?" he asked slowly, after drawing in heavily.

"As long as I can play the cat, I'll play the game."

"You will be the cat."

"And who will be the mouse?"

"Giselle."

"Why not Pierre?"

"Patience, Roger, patience. There are better ways of hurting him than to kill. The hurt can be greater if you don't kill. You should know that. Tell me, Roger, would you really like to hurt Pierre?"

Roger nodded.

"Then do it my way. I can show you how to hurt him. Hurt him to the soul. Torture him. Twist his insides like you were twisting his arms off or cutting him up with a knife. Do it my way, Roger. You'll enjoy it." He puffed the cigar until the tip shone. Then, removing it from his mouth with an exaggerated gesture, he blew a huge puff of smoke to the ceiling. Roger waited for him to continue.

"It's pretty obvious what's going on. Pierre has fallen in love with Giselle. He's been up in the woods, screwing her ass off for the last couple of months. He was doing the same thing here before they left. But now, the stupid bastard has fallen in love."

Roger laughed. "Can't get enough, eh?"

"That's not the point. Giselle's game is not so playful. She's setting him up to betray us."

The smile left Roger's face. "So you want me to kill her?"

"Not yet, you fool," François snapped. "Don't jump to conclusions. Just do as I say. I'll show you. I'll get them back into town tomorrow. We'll start from there."

"But they are in town," Roger laughed. "They're at Giselle's place.

François' anger showed. He could see that Roger's laugh was not entirely without contempt. "As far as you and I are concerned," François paced back and forth, "they are not in town." He stopped directly in front of Roger and pointed the cigar into his face. "Just remember, you're playing my game, and the first rule is, 'don't ever let them know we're aware of their treachery.' "

34

Giselle was in her bedroom when she heard the key in the door. She slipped into her skirt.

"Darling!" There was no answer. She pulled her blouse on over her head. "Pierre!" Still, there was no answer. She walked, "Pierre," she said again softly as she moved down the hallway. This was not like him. Something was wrong.

"Giselle." It was François. His voice came from the living room.

"What the hell are you doing here?" Giselle was furious and she showed it. He was alone and he just sat there on the chesterfield, smiling. That damned key, thought Giselle. I should have changed the lock.

"You don't seem very happy to see me."

"Why should I?" demanded Giselle. "Walking in here as if you owned the place."

"But I do in a way don't I?" François shrugged his shoulders. "I suppose you could say I own a little bit of you too. Can you deny that?" He stood up. "But that isn't what I came here to talk about, Giselle. Not about our differences. May I take off my coat? It's very warm in here after the bitter cold outside."

"Pierre will be back in a few minutes."

"No, I don't think he will." He removed his coat and threw it on a chair. "Pierre is doing a little job for me. I told him I'd tell you about it. He won't be in until quite late. I thought it would be a good time to have a heart-to-heart talk with you. Just you and I. Alone. With no interference from anyone else."

"We have nothing to talk about, François. Nothing at all." Her hand shook noticeably as she lit a cigarette.

François gloated. He was going to enjoy this. Her fear was so obvious.

"Giselle, we have plenty to talk about and you know it."

Maybe he was right. She sat down, remembering the promise he had made to her the last time they talked. The promise that had not materialized. She had done her job. She had gone along with Pierre and Roger and Madame Hébert. She had done exactly as François had dictated. And now, as though she were awakened from a dream, she remembered that François had made her a solemn promise. A promise that he would release both herself and Pierre from the Movement as soon as the job was finished.

"Maybe we do have something to discuss," she said flatly. "We should talk about the deal we made."

François snickered. This girl was strangely like himself. She could hit the nail right on the head. She could come to the point immediately. No beating around the bush. Then his face hardened as he thought of her as an enemy. He would be just as straightforward. "I had every intention of living up to my word. I had no intention of breaking my promise. But after all . . . !"

"After all, what?"

"It's simple," replied François smugly. "Very simple. Pierre's attitude! His attitude has changed. He questions my authority. It seems as though he is becoming disillusioned. An attitude like that could be dangerous."

"You know as well as I do what's wrong with Pierre," she said fiercely. "He only wants out. Out of the Movement! That's all."

Slowly and deliberately, François chose his words. "Him, or you? Is it Pierre who wants out of the Movement? Or is it you who wants him out?"

A long silence followed, so deep that Giselle was sure François could hear her heart beating. How much did he know for sure? How much did he suspect?

François watched. She's scared, he thought. Scared clean through. Just like a mouse! She was playing her part beautifully. "You can't win, you know," he said softly.

"Win!" There was hysteria in Giselle's voice. "Win what?"

"Anything! You can't have anything that I'm not willing to give you."

"What can you give me?"

"Your freedom. Your life. Pierre. Those are just a few."

"What makes you think I can't . . . ?"

"Go ahead," François settled back in his chair, enjoying the charade. "Go ahead and finish what you were going to say."

Giselle reddened.

"Then I'll finish it for you." He rose. "I'll tell you what's in that pretty little head of yours." He paced back and forth. "I can fix François, I can hurt him more than he can hurt me." He pointed his finger at her. "That's what you're thinking, isn't it?" She was silent. "Well, let me tell you something, young lady. You could cause me a bit of inconvenience. You could even give me some trouble. And that's the reason for this little heart-to-heart talk, but it's time you learned a few facts of life. Sit down." She did so.

"You know a lot, Giselle." He studied her face. She was terribly frightened and it showed. There was no doubt about that. "You know too much. But let me make one point very clear. Your knowledge will not hurt me. Be sure of that, Giselle. You think if you were to open your mouth and tell what you know, that I would be ruined. The fact of the matter is, my dear, that you are entirely wrong. You are the major culprit, together with Pierre. Not me! I was miles away and really knew nothing of the affair. I have a thousand witnesses. You and Pierre and Roger are the murderers. Not me. You were all on the boat. Pierre is the beneficiary of the will. Madame Hébert was murdered for her money. Pierre is the prime suspect and you are the accomplice." He stopped, pulled one of Roger's Havana cigars from his pocket, bit off the end and spat it on the rug. Giselle hardly noticed. François was free and clear. What he said was right and she knew it. Pierre was the real criminal according to the law. She was lost so deeply in her thoughts that she scarcely heard François as he continued.

"You could cause me some trouble, Giselle. I know it. Unless, of course, Roger could get to you first." He was pleased to note an intensification of her fear at the sound of Roger's name. "You see, my dear, I have no intention of becoming involved in a scandal. I have ways to protect myself. To prove my point, I will strike first, if necessary. If you intend going to the news media, let me tell you that many of our most important members work in this field. If you go to the police, perhaps you will recall your last interview with them. But above everything, Giselle, remember that Pierre will be the scapegoat. Oh! Oh, yes. I almost forgot. Another thing, it's the matter of Emile and Yvonne. Of course, you realize that they will have to be sacrificed should you talk."

The words numbed Giselle. They were like bonds that tied her hands and feet. Gagged her. Fettered her. She could do nothing without destroying herself and everyone who meant anything to her. Shivers of fear went through her body, thoughts whirled about in her head like a tornado and, finally, confusion overwhelmed her.

"You have an option," he said. "There is a way out, you know."

Pleadingly, Giselle raised her head and looked at him.

"You see, I am an honourable man," said François. "When I make a promise, I live up to it. I made a deal with you, Giselle. I promised to let you and Pierre out of the Movement. In spite of your treachery, I intend to live up to that deal." He stopped and watched the reaction taking place in the girl before him. Every thought was mirrored in her face. Now she was like the mouse that was escaping into the crevice where the cat could not follow. Hope lit up her face. François continued.

"But you see, I can't let you go without some change in our conditions now, can I? You can see that I'm afraid of you, Giselle. I'm afraid of you because I think you hate me. Now, if there was just some way that you could prove that you don't hate me. Something you could do that would prove that you like me. If only this could happen, Giselle, then I could live up to my promise."

Giselle lit another cigarette. Then, taking a deep breath, she spoke almost in a whisper. "What do you want me to do?"

"You know I've always liked you, Giselle. You know how I've always wanted you. I've told you. Now haven't I?"

"Yes, you have."

"Then the answer is simple," said François, moving closer to her. "Very simple. You can prove how much you like me by going to bed with me."

Her response was instantaneous. "You filthy bastard!" Her eyes spit fire. "I'll see you in hell first."

"Come, come, my dear. Be reasonable. Would you rather die with all the others just to prove your virtue? Look! I am not a fool like Pierre. I know that you're not a helpless, little virgin. I know what you were before you met Paul. I know all about you. Why do you try to pretend with me?"

Stupefying, unbelieving silence. Unable to speak, she just sat there. The effect pleased him.

"All this worry, Giselle! All this worry is beginning to tell on you. It shows in your eyes. Even Pierre's beginning to notice it. He doesn't know what to do about it. He keeps asking for advice. He tells me everything, you know. He tells me you're quite a little bundle in bed. He tells me he wished he could spend another couple of months in the woods with you."

The words were like a knife cutting out Giselle's heart. A terrible sadness came over her. Was François saying these things to force her to betray Pierre? Or had Pierre really spoken to him? Had Pierre openly discussed their personal, secret relationship? No, Pierre couldn't do this to her! Not when they meant so much to each other. Anything, but this!

"He thinks your nerves are getting bad, Giselle. This frightens him and he comes to me for advice. What can I say to him, Giselle? Can I tell him what you really are? Can I tell him what you have been? Why, only this morning he told me that you made him come to the city at Christmas. He said you didn't want him to tell me."

Violent anger quickly took the place of Giselle's sorrow. "That's a lie! That's a dirty lie! He never said anything of the sort, and you know it! Roger told you. Roger was the one that reported to you. Not Pierre! You had that psychopath trailing us. I know it. And now you're trying to use your tricks to break us up. Well, it won't work." Her anger gave her strength. She stood up. "It won't work, François. You'd better tell that crazy friend of yours, I saw him kill Madame Hébert." The words choked in her throat. She stopped. The forbidden words had been spoken. Nothing could erase their impact.

François shook his head slowly. "You surprise me, Giselle," he said. "You surprise me. How could it have been Roger? He's been in Havana for the last month. He won't be back in town until tomorrow."

What an actor he was! His voice, his expression, his actions. They were perfect. She was convinced. He knew this by the way she backed up and flopped into the chair. Confusion swept over her. Was she really going mad? She must be. It was becoming more difficult, almost impossible, to distinguish between reality and fantasy. Compared to the nightmares she had experienced at the cabin, the reality of today ran a close parallel. With quivering lips she looked up at François until finally it came. Like a gushing waterspout, like a torrent of emotion draining from her, the tears flowed down her cheeks in endless rivulets. There was only a whimper behind them; a whimper of confusion and fear and helplessness.

François pulled a cheque from a book in his pocket and filled it out. "Look." He held it in front of her face. "This is a cheque for five thousand dollars. It is my gift to you and Pierre for what you have done. But you can't have it until you have proven that you like me."

"I can't, François. I can't. It's impossible. I love him. I'm carrying his baby."

François tore the cheque into little pieces and put them in the ash tray. "I'll give you twenty-four hours to think it over." He looked at his watch. "After twenty-four hours, the offer no longer stands. Think it over carefully. A few hours with me and your whole life will be changed. Pierre will be out of the Movement. I promise you that. The cheque will be yours. It's the chance of a lifetime, Giselle. For just a lousy few hours."

"I can't! I can't!" Giselle lay her head on her knees and sobbed bitterly.

François picked up his hat and coat. "Roger will be back tomorrow. He has better ways of solving these irksome little problems. In the meantime, you will be watched. Don't leave the apartment." He picked up the telephone. "I'd better remove this temptation," he said as he pulled the cord and broke it from the wall. "If you want to contact me, get the superintendent to call."

He walked to the door. Then, turning, he looked back at her, still sitting there, sobbing uncontrollably. "For Christ's sake, Giselle, why don't you wake up? Look at the bright side. Think of the fix you'd be in if you didn't have the kind of stuff that turns me on."

35

The heater in his car didn't work and it was bitterly cold. Pierre cursed as the windshield frosted and he constantly rubbed it with his gloved hand so that he could see the road. Giselle sat beside him, her hands in the pockets of her coat and her collar muffled around her ears. It was almost dark when they entered the driveway of the late Madame Hébert's mansion.

The lights in the coach house were on and Roger's car was parked outside. They trudged through the snow to the front door and, moments later, François answered their knock.

"Come in. Come in," he said affably as he reached out, grasped Pierre's hand and shook it vigorously. "Come in, Giselle," he said. "It's cold and you must be freezing."

He directed them into the drawing room and, without asking, poured them a drink. The place was warm and cheery. The fire crackled.

François is outdoing himself, thought Giselle.

Soon the three were seated around the fireplace, sipping their drinks.

Giselle knew exactly what was supposed to happen. What François was supposed to say and do. But would he do as he had promised? Not likely. The sly bastard looked like the fox he was.

After an interminable amount of small talk, François finally opened up. "You are probably both wondering," he said slowly, "why I asked you to come here tonight." He stared into the fire as though contemplating the future of the universe. "I brought you here," he went on," because I want you both to know how pleased I am. I also want you to know that I think you did a magnificent job. On the Sans Souci, I mean." His expression saddened. "Despite what happened to poor Eloise." He paused. "I can only say that no one could have done a better job. I'm extremely pleased with you."

He's repeating himself, thought Giselle. When the hell will he get to the point?

"But now it's over," François continued, "now that it's finished and the job is done, I'm afraid for you. I'm afraid for both of you. It's dangerous for you to stay in the Movement." He stopped and waited.

"Dangerous?" It was Pierre who spoke.

"Yes," replied François. "Dangerous. I'm afraid that somehow, someplace, sometime, someone will start asking questions. Someone will connect you with Madame Hébert and the Sans Souci. Someone will ask an innocent question." François waited to assess their reactions, then he continued. "God knows what could happen. All I know is that I couldn't bear to see the two of you persecuted for something you've done out of loyalty to Québec."

"But no one has connected us with the accident," protested Pierre.

"Only because you've been out of circulation," said François as he turned his glass in his hand. "Only because I insisted that you stay hidden in the forest. But you must understand this, Pierre. The incident is not yet closed. There is a board of inquiry which will last for months, maybe years. They will look into every detail of the case and somewhere along the line, they will be sure to seek you out."

"But no one would know. Nobody knows we were on the boat. Who could connect us with the explosion except yourself and Roger?" Then he added, "And Roger's in as deep as we are."

"Nevertheless," said François with authority. "I see a great danger for you and I want you and Giselle to quit the Movement."

Giselle listened in amazement as Pierre spoke.

"Quit the Movement! Why, François, I'm just getting . . . we're just getting started. Why would you want us to quit?"

"Pierre, please don't talk like that. You sound as though I were throwing you out, as though you were being court-martialed when, in fact, you're being given an honourable discharge. You see, Pierre, the Movement is going into a new phase. Our new operations preclude the use of force. The Movement doesn't need this type of activity any more. I want you to quit. I want you to quit with great honour, the pair of you, I mean." François went to the liquor cabinet, produced a bottle of Grand Marnier, and returning, filled their glasses.

"I want you both to go away," he said. "There will be money for you. You can keep the car I gave you, Pierre. And you, Giselle." He put his hand on hers. She drew back. "I want you to know especially that without your assistance none of it would have been possible. We owe you a debt we can never repay."

"How can you do this?" It was Pierre. "How can you make us leave the Movement when you know how we feel? We've been looking forward to working with you. Didn't you promise us that we could go places with you? Now you tell us we're not wanted. We're not needed. We're finished."

With unbelieving ears, Giselle listened. She had made a bargain with François, a bargain she was sure he would not honour.

"You're not being thrown out. For God's sake, don't say that. You're only being asked to leave for your own safety."

"But! I don't want . . . Please, François, don't throw us out. I want to be loyal to you. I want to be loyal to the Movement. Please, don't make us quit."

François lifted a poker from the rack and shifted the burning embers. They sparkled and crackled and gave small hisses as the fire ate into the inner crevices of the logs. "I'm sorry, Pierre. I'm sorry, but this is final. I can't listen. I can't give consideration. My mind is made up. You must leave the Movement. Immediately. Tomorrow morning, I will give you a cheque. It will be a substantial amount. We'll not leave you wanting. The only condition is that you and Giselle leave the city. I don't care where you go. That's no business of mine. My only request is that you let me know where you are in case I need you."

He threw a log on the fire. "Life is like this wood," he said. "When I first put it into the fire, it burns with usefulness. It has the ability to light and heat the room. But when it is burned through, it's no longer any use. It has nothing to offer. No matter how much we may wish it to keep burning, only the embers remain."

He looked at Giselle. Christ, what a dumb bitch! This was something she hadn't counted on. Let's see how she can wiggle out of this one.

"It's getting late and I have an appointment. I hope you don't mind my rushing you, but I do have some very important business waiting for me."

"But it can't end like this," protested Pierre.

"It has ended," said François. "Let me get your coat. You'll be hearing from me tomorrow," he said to Pierre. "I will send the cheque. I'm certain you'll be pleased." Then he turned to Giselle. "And you shall be hearing from me too, my dear."

"Of course," said Giselle. "I'll be expecting you."

François closed the door behind the two. Then, looking through the curtained window, he watched them make their way along the path flanked by high mounds of deep white snow to the car. He heard the door slam and the car motor start. He switched off the lights and walked slowly back to the drawing room and the warmth of the fireplace.

When the telephone rang, François let it ring five times before he answered it.

"Hello."

"It's Pierre."

"How did she take it?"

"She was very happy." There was a catch in his voice.

"And she didn't try to talk you out of it?"

"No. She said it was for the best."

"Well, don't feel badly," said François. "We found out what we wanted to, didn't we?"

"I suppose so. She really wants to get out."

"You say that as though you think she's selfish," François scolded. "Don't think of it that way, my boy. She's not selfish. She's sick. You must realize she's not responsible for her actions. Why don't you look on the bright side?"

"The bright side?"

"Now that we know what's bothering her, we can help her. Isn't that what we wanted to find out? What was bothering her. Now that we know, we'll be able to help her."

There was no reply.

"You really don't want to get out of the Movement, do you?"

"No! No! Definitely not!"

"Good," said François. "Good. Now don't worry about her. Now look, Pierre, I know it's late but I've got an important job I want you to do for me. Okay?"

"Sure."

"I'll send Roger around in a couple of hours. Be ready."

36

"What did you tell him?" François helped Giselle with her coat.

"I told him I wanted to be alone. I asked him not to come in."

"He didn't suspect?"

"No. He went home."

"Good."

A feeling of revulsion crawled over her as she felt his breath on the back of her neck. "Let me help you with your shoes," he said, following her.

"I can manage."

But François insisted. He sat on a small bench beside the coat rack while he pulled the heel of her snowboots with one hand and grasped her leg with the other. Pulling away in a reflex action, her foot hit him.

François slipped backwards. His temper flared. "You seem to have forgotten why you're here," he snapped.

"I'm sorry, but I'm nervous. Surely, you must know how I hate to do this."

"There are lots of things I hate to do myself, but I do them anyway. I thought you'd made up your mind."

"I have."

"Okay, my pet. Be as rough on me as you like. I'll test your ferocity a little later. Where it really counts!"

She made her way into the drawing room and stood before the fire. François opened the door of the liquor cabinet.

"Drink?"

"Why not?"

"I filled my part of the bargain," he said, as he poured. "And in doing so, I think I've proven myself as a man." He lifted his glass to her. "And now I want you to fill your part. I want you to prove to me that you're a woman."

"There's more to being a man," said Giselle slowly, "than to force a rotten deal." She raised the drink to her lips, gulping it. "And there's more to being a woman than jumping into bed," she added.

François laughed. He was enjoying this already. Even the rapport was good. How much better it would be later. He put his arms around her clumsily, trying to kiss her. She turned her head.

When he persisted, she pushed her glass at him. "I've finished my drink. Get me another one."

He took the glass and refilled it. There she stood before the fire, her curvaceous body silhouetted against the flames. What a piece! This was going to be one hell of a lot more fun than he had anticipated. He felt a sharp ecstasy in his groin. This was the perfect way to mix business and pleasure.

"Sit over here," he said, pointing to the chesterfield. "We'll lie down here." He was trying desperately to make his voice appealing. "We'll get to know one another better."

"Not until we've finished our business." Giselle's voice was cold.

"Business? I've done my part."

"Only half of it," stated Giselle flatly. "You seem to have forgotten the part about the five thousand dollars."

"That will come later." François was obviously annoyed.

"It will come first!"

"Or . . . ?"

"Or there's no deal."

"You're pushing too hard, Giselle. I don't like it."

"Well, don't like it. You say I'm pushing you. Well, what do you think you're doing to me? Let me tell you this. You're getting a bargain." She gulped the rest of her drink. "Get me another."

Why couldn't she follow through as she knew she must? Hadn't she wrestled with her conscience and her reason for long enough? All last night, she had lain awake, tossing and turning; gone into the kitchen to make more coffee; stared at the clock. Good God, yes! She had thought it over enough. This was her only way out. François had kept his promise. He had told Pierre he was through. He had made no bones about it. He was, apparently, willing to live up to his bargain. After all, how many times had she gone to bed with a man, some of whom were even more repulsive than François? She had gone to bed with them willingly. There had been no guilt. No depression. But now it was different. Completely different.

Only two years ago, one man, more or less, would have meant nothing to her. But now, today, it was as though she was giving away the most precious gift that she had: her pride, her self-esteem, her love. Was it the only thing she could do? Roger was back. That meant things would start happening again. Dirty rotten things like murder. But if she could only get that money. If she could only get out of town. Now that Pierre was out, there should be nothing to hold either of them here! Everyone would soon forget and she and

Pierre could settle down. She could have his baby and they could begin living again.

François returned with the drink. He'd let her have her cheap victory, let her treat him like a valet. What a stupid female she is. She really thinks she's getting away with it. Just for one piece of ass. He stifled a laugh. The stupid bitch must think it's a gold mine. But the cheque! Now she wanted the cheque. He looked at his watch. He'd better have her in bed in another half hour or he'd miss a lot of fun and the whole deal would blow up. What difference does it make? He chuckled inwardly. Hell, why not go through with the whole bloody thing? Pretend to give in all the way. He let his feelings flow and his face broke into a smile.

"Giselle, you little vixen. You've outwitted me again. I had every intention of giving you the cheque tomorrow. But if it's so important to you, well . . ." He produced his cheque book and with a flourish, filled out a cheque for five thousand dollars and handed it to her.

This was it. She knew that there was no going back. She had to give herself. No stalling. It was here and now. She put the cheque in her purse.

"Now, let's go upstairs."

Docilely, she followed him up the stairs, along the hallway, past the library and into the master bedroom with its huge canopied bed. The lights were bright, the fire crackled on the hearth. François prodded the embers with the poker. Then, using it as a prop, he added another log.

"Can we turn the lights down?" she asked. She could feel François' nervous fingers on the back of her dress, unzipping it. Then he slid the dress from her shoulders and kissed her neck. Dropping her hands, she allowed it to fall to her waist. François' breathing quickened and his hands swarmed over her. Gripping her dress, he forced it to the floor. With uncontrollable desire, he held her as he bit her neck hard. She whimpered and tried to pull away, but it was impossible. Then he swung her around and ripped her slip from her body. "Beautiful!" He pulled her toward the bed, and threw her on it. He tore off his clothes and, standing naked over her, he ripped her panties and brassiere from her body.

"François said he had a job for us. He said it was important. We'd better not drink too much."

Roger looked at his watch. They still had a half hour to kill. "Have another one for the road. We've still got plenty of time."

"Okay."

The bar was almost empty. They sat at the far end.

"How did you like Cuba?"

"It was great. They've got the right idea down there. We should use some of their methods."

"Some day," said Pierre, "I'd like to go there. But first, I'd like to see Paris."

"So would I," Roger smiled when he thought of François' deal. His bonus for taking care of the two. He couldn't resist the urge to revel in the thought. "Maybe, if we work together, we can help each other get there."

"I hope so," said Pierre naively.

Roger laughed heartily, but the joke was one-sided.

"I hear you were in the city at Christmas," Pierre said.

"Here? At Christmas? Who said that?"

"I just heard."

"Well, you heard wrong," Roger lied. "Let's see now. On Christmas Day, I was drinking tequila in the Hotel de Rio in Havana. Man, you should see the broads down there. Jet black hair. Brown eyes. And hot! Christ, are they hot! By the way, who was it that thought they saw me?" Roger studied Pierre's expression.

"Nobody you know," replied Pierre thoughtfully. "I didn't believe the story anyway."

Roger looked at his watch again. "Better gulp it down, boy. We've got to get going. We don't want to be late."

She lay there, her eyes closed and her head half turned from him as though trying to pretend that it was only a dream, a nightmare. At least, not real.

She felt his hands on her breasts, her hips, her legs. He mauled her every niche and crevice. But he could not arouse her. She lay there, her hands by her side, thinking. How bloody unfair! The one man in my life who deserves my fidelity is the one I've cheated. Armand deserted me. Paul took me for granted, and the others were nothing. She felt François' lips on her breasts. Like a half-starved animal, he chewed at her body. Rough, vicious and crude, he explored every tissue and mound. But still she just lay there, as though in a coma.

How could fate force a situation like this on me? Why has my life been filled with such evil things? Why is it that the carnivorous, exploiting pigs have played on me? The innocent like Pierre! The people of the world who like to believe what is told to them. Who like to follow blindly, who like to be a sheep, always looking for a kindly shepherd.

She could feel François climbing on top of her. She could feel him pushing her legs apart. Tears welled up behind her eyes. But still she said nothing. No matter, she thought, he can do no harm to me. Inside my womb is Pierre's baby, wrapped in a cocoon and protected by nature as though enveloped in a sealed-off enclosure. How could this filth enjoy what he was doing? Even an animal's instincts would not allow it to do what this creature was relishing.

"You're beautiful! My darling!" His sweaty body plunged at her. Finally, he was finished and he lay gasping and moaning on top of her. She pushed him off and he fell beside her, breathing hard in ecstasy.

She tried to sit up but he flung his arm over her waist. "I want a cigarette," she protested.

"Later," he ordered as he restrained her. She fell back on the pillow. Eventually, his breathing returned to normal and half sitting up, he looked at his watch, holding it up to catch the flickering light.

"I'll get you a cigarette," he said. "Do you want one of mine or would you prefer your own?" She didn't answer. He gave her one of his.

She was scarcely half through her cigarette when he started again. His hand inched slowly up her legs and she could once again feel that crawly, evil feeling that he inspired. She knew she couldn't stop him, so she took one last drag on the cigarette and stumped it out in the ashtray. François, reaching for the light at the head of the bed, switched it on.

"Turn it off."

"No," François stated flatly. "I want to watch you while we make love. You're so beautiful, I must look at you." He kissed her breast and navel. "You're delicious. I must watch you make love." He looked again at his watch. It wouldn't be long now, he thought, and he didn't know which he enjoyed most. What he was doing now, or what would happen shortly.

He went for her again, and for Giselle, it was worse than the first time. The strange, familiar, unreal fear began to creep over her. It was the same sensation that had followed her from that night on the boat, the vigil at the cabin and the ride on the Glossier. That indelible impression of horror and despair and hopelessness. It was the same morbidity that had pursued her, had haunted her, ever since the first time she had laid eyes on Roger. And now, here she was lying in bed, this plunging madman fornicating her, and the same horrible fear engulfed her. It became more uncontrollable with each passing moment. She opened her eyes and looked wildly about. There was no one in the room, only she and François. It was easy to see now that the light was on. She listened intently, but the sickening sounds of François muffled any other noise.

"Ah! I have awakened you. I knew you couldn't pretend all night." He kissed her on the lips. In response, she grabbed his hair and tried to force his mouth from hers.

"You wolverine! Scratch me, you bitch!" He bit into her neck and the pain was unbearable. She stifled a scream, trying desperately to push him away. Forcefully, relentlessly, savagely, he pushed himself on her until she could fight no longer. Her head fell back on the pillow and she stared blankly across the room.

Was she imagining it or was the door handle turning? She gaped intently at it. Good God, it was turning! It turned a full cycle and then it began to open. Slowly at first and then swinging in its full arc, the door opened. François stopped. Disengaging himself from her, he knelt up and looked toward the door.

It was the end. The requiem to everything Giselle had done in her life. Standing in the door was Roger, and in the shadows behind him was the unmistakable figure of Pierre. He stood there, an unbelieving mask hiding his face. But it was he. There was no doubt about it.

François bounded from the bed and strode naked to the two. "How dare you bust in here like this?" he shouted angrily at Roger. "And you, Pierre. I thought you'd know better than this. Get out! Get out! Can't a man have a little fun and not be bothered by the likes of you two? Out!" he shouted again and slammed the door in their faces.

Giselle watched the door, sure it would be forcefully pushed open and Pierre would rush in, kill Roger and François and carry her away. But it did not open. Only silence for a moment. Then the slam of a door, the roar of an engine and the screech of tires from a car racing off, crashing into something as it went. "Oh, no! God! No!" She ran across the room and scratching a hole in the frost of the window, looked out. The car careened up the road and its screaming tires said more to her than a volume of words. "Oh, no!" she cried again.

"Oh, yes!" It was François' voice behind her. "Oh, yes, my little whore. It's exactly as it seems. Your lover boy knows all about you now. You're nothing more than a cheap ten-dollar trollop now. He saw it all." François laughed. "You little pig." He spat on the floor as he said it. "You and your two-bit plans. You and your stupidity! Did you really think you were going to get away with it?" He held the cheque up in front of her. He'd taken it from her purse as she looked out the window. "And as far as this is concerned," he waved the cheque to her, "five thousand bucks would be paying you too much for a thousand times, let alone for once." He tore it into bits.

"You stinking rat! You filthy piece of garbage," Giselle screamed at him across the room. "I'll kill you for this."

François laughed. "You, kill me? The shoe is on the other foot, baby. You're the one that's going to get it! Roger!" He called loudly.

A blinding torrent of hate tore through Giselle. With no thought but escape, she grabbed the fork which François so recently used to stir the fire, and, racing across the room, lunged straight at François' naked body. He was almost too slow. One second more and he would have been lanced like a pig on a spit. But he spun around and the fork, instead of piercing his chest as had been her intent, cut deeply into his left arm. Giselle pulled back and the fork ripped out of the wound. François screamed in pain and Giselle, swinging again, slammed him across the chest. But the fork hit sideways and, although it stunned François, it did not pierce him.

With blood spurting from his arm, he ran to the door and up the hallway with Giselle in close pursuit. Lunging through the open door of the study, he slammed it, knocking Giselle down as he did. On the inside, François turned the key. Regaining her wits, Giselle repeatedly swung at the door with the fork but it was useless. It was solid oak. She screamed. "I'll kill you!" But only silence answered her.

She stopped and listened. There were noises from inside now. François was trying to move something. She listened, the fear rising in her. In a moment, the noises stopped and then came the resounding crash of breaking glass. The window! François had smashed the window in the study and it was only seconds later that Giselle learned the reason. She could hear him shouting. "Roger! Roger, come here. Come here."

Roger was undoubtedly in the coach house. If he didn't have the radio on or the television, he'd hear François and then . . . Giselle raced into the bedroom, grabbing her clothes and pulling them on as quickly as she could. The car! François' car. Where were the keys? She fumbled through the pockets of his trousers which still lay on the floor. She ran downstairs and, furiously searching his coat, found them. Then, without thinking, she opened the door. The twenty below zero blast brought her to her senses. She grabbed her heavy coat and struggled into it as she ran for the car.

Breathlessly, she jumped into the car and turned on the ignition. It turned over slowly because of the cold. But it turned. The motor coughed and then caught. She rammed it into reverse and it spun around on the ice. In fear, she looked back at the house. Roger appeared at the door of the coach house. She could hear François yelling to him. The wheels found traction and the car moved onto the road. She headed in the direction of the city.

Terror chased Giselle and would not let her go. On the roads leading into the city, every car behind her was Roger, every light was a flash from a gun.

Once in the city, the buildings and narrow streets closed in on her. Could she return to her apartment? No! That was for certain. She thought for a fleeting moment of the police. Impossible! Which ones could she trust? When she thought of Pierre and the solace she could find in his arms, a tear welled in her eyes and flickered down her cheek. Never again. It was finished. There could be nothing any more.

Without really knowing why, she passed through the city, through the town of Ste. Foy, crossed the St. Lawrence on the suspension bridge and headed east along the south bank of the river. Toward what? It didn't really matter as long as it was away from the terror she had just left.

She passed through Lévis and realized where she was when she saw the lights of the Château just across the river. She had gone down the river, crossed it and doubled back. It was only when she saw the sign, "*Rivière du Loup — 125 milles,*" that she knew where she was going.

Emile and Yvonne!

The sun was erasing the blackness from the night sky when she passed through Rivière du Loup and, when she arrived at Emile and Yvonne's, the sun was high, reflecting off the snow, luminous, vivid, resplendent.

Emile was at work, but Yvonne was sympathetic, didn't ask questions and in her quiet way listened to Giselle's semi-hysterical outbursts. She helped her to remove her torn and dishevelled clothing and then put her to bed.

When she awoke, Emile was back and, over a dozen coffees, she told them the whole story, omitting nothing. She warned them of the danger that both of them were in. "I have brought it on you," she said. "It is my fault. I had to warn you."

Emile laughed. "A few weeks up here with us," he said, "and it will all seem like a dream. We are in no danger, I tell you that for sure." He laughed again and, for the first time in so very long, Giselle began to feel unafraid.

37

Roger walked up the narrow staircase to Pierre's room and knocked on the door. Not bothering to wait for an answer, he entered and bent over the unconscious form. He shook it vigorously. Pierre grunted in disapproval, but Roger was insistent.

Three days had passed and Pierre was still in a drunken stupor. Now it was time for coffee and the sobering up. François had spoken and Roger was there to do his bidding. He had a container of black coffee and soon Pierre was sitting on the edge of the bed, bent over like an old man sniffing at the paper cup.

"François is broken up about this, Pierre. He hasn't eaten or slept since the bloody thing happened."

Pierre gulped his coffee and rubbed his forehead. "Christ, I feel awful. I feel sick."

"François will do anything to make it up to you. He wants you to know that," Roger kept on. "I want you to know I never had anything to do with Giselle," explained Roger. "I never looked at her like that. I only looked at her as a member of the Movement. But hell, Pierre, you can't blame François. She's been throwing herself at him for months. Hell, I've seen them together at least a dozen times and I know François was getting sick of her. Christ, man, I never thought of it. I always thought she was one hell of a nice girl. I never knew she was your girlfriend. Man, you really kept it a secret, didn't you?" He laughed and watched Pierre's reaction.

"I'm not blaming you, Roger." Then he added slowly. "I'm not blaming François either. You can tell him that." He forced a laugh. "She wasn't really my girlfriend. Hell, anybody could have seen that. She was just convenient." His voice caught. "She was just a good piece of ass."

"What about her?" Roger eyed Pierre closely. "Where is she?"

"I don't know."

"Haven't you any idea?"

"I don't know where she is," said Pierre, "and I don't give a good goddamn. I hate her guts." But when Pierre spoke, the words were a lie. They almost choked him.

"Why can't you find her?" François asked Roger.

"I've looked everywhere. I've hung around outside her house

for the last week. I offered the superintendent fifty bucks to call me if she came in. Not a word. I've followed Pierre. It's cost me a fortune buying him drinks. I've been up to the lake. She's not there. I've got at least a dozen buddies of mine looking for her in Montréal. I think that's the best bet. Where else can a whore pick up a buck the easy way? That's where I think she is, François. I think she's in Montréal. Maybe I'd better go there for a while."

"Have you looked for her at those friends? What's their name? The guy with the dynamite?"

"Emile? Christ, no! Why should I go there? They're not her friends. They're friends of Pierre's."

"You never know, Roger. You never know."

"Why don't you report the car stolen? When it shows up, so will she."

"The stakes are too high, Roger. I can't risk it. We've got to do this silently and alone and when we get her, it's got to happen quickly. Remember that, Roger. Quick!"

"No more cat and mouse game, eh?"

"No." Roger smiled. He was glad to hear the waiting was over. "Which reminds me," he said, excitement in his voice. "We had a contract on that bastard Emile. Remember?"

"When he goes, his wife goes too. You know that?"

"I know it." A look of distinct pleasure formed on Roger's face. "I also remember the bonus."

"I haven't forgotten."

"Maybe there'll be a double bonus in this one."

"What do you mean?" asked François, setting down his drink.

"The noise might flush out the quail."

"Giselle?"

"Who else?"

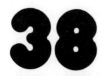

38

Giselle was feeling happy and relaxed as she drove François' car from the village to Emile's house. She had even lost her fear of driving the car in the past week. Emile had changed the licence plates. Life with him and Yvonne had been so tranquil and quiet that Giselle's nerves were now beginning to relax.

Yvonne was a fantastic example of inner strength. Quiet and yet secure with her feelings, she was always willing to compromise. Admiring her qualities, Giselle wished she could be like her. Emile, of course, was always his friendly self and it was he who had persuaded Giselle to get out of the house. "Get into town," he had said. "Do some shopping. Make yourself useful."

Giselle had done as he suggested and for the last week had run errands for the two. It had done her a lot of good. She was resigned now to the fact that Pierre and she were finished. She still loved him. She missed him and the movements of his baby within her made it worse. But she knew it was finished.

Approaching the laneway that led to Emile's house, half hidden in the woods, she was about to turn when that old familiar awesome feeling crept over her. It was a premonition, the same uncanny obsession that had been her companion since she had first met Roger. There was a car parked behind Emile's, blocking its exit. There was something familiar about the car and, as she stopped and took a better look, she could see. Roger's. It was Roger's car!

Without thinking, she continued up the road and turning around at the first opportunity, raced back toward town.

It was less than a ten-minute drive back into town. She found a dime in her purse and inserted it in the pay telephone outside a gas station. The number rang incessantly. But no one answered. She tried it again. And again. But still no answer.

The shadows of the Gaspé hills brought early dusk to the valley. She returned to the car and headed back to Emile's. When she arrived at the house, Roger's car was gone. Heaving a sigh of relief, she wheeled her vehicle into the lane, pulled it to a stop behind Emile's and ran to the side entrance.

"Yvonne," she called out.

There was no answer. "Yvonne," she cried again, louder.

Still no answer. And the strange, creepy, crawly feeling passed up and down her spine. She grasped the door handle and turned it, but it wouldn't open. She pounded on the door as loud as she could and screamed, "Yvonne! Emile!" Still, there was no answer.

She ran to the front door, onto the porch, turned the handle and pushed. It was open.

"Yvonne." There was a quiver in her voice. "Yvonne! Yvonne!" She ran up the hallway toward the kitchen.

What she saw made her freeze like a pillar of stone. Her stomach heaved into her throat. Her jaw dropped and her hands raised in a helpless gesture.

The bodies of her two friends lay there on the floor. Their eyes stared in death. Emile's shotgun lay by his side.

She screamed hysterically, backed down the hall and stumbled out of the house.

"I saw her running up the road," a young man said to the policeman. "When I asked her what was wrong, she just screamed."

"They were her friends," said the policeman slowly and sorrowfuly. "Emile and Yvonne. I've known them for years. Whatever possessed them to do it is beyond me. Suicide! My God! She went home and found them on the kitchen floor, shot dead. God, what a shock!"

"Suicide?"

"It's hard to believe," said the officer. "But that's what is says on this piece of paper we found on the kitchen table."

The dazed policeman handed the note to the youth who read it. "There's no way out. My problems are too great. I had to do it."

39

Pierre parked the car in the driveway, jammed the keys into his pocket and walked up the steps. His rooming house looked as ugly as ever. He wished he had never seen it. He hated to be back in Québec City. He hated it and yet he was glad. The last three weeks in Montréal had been full of activity. Roger had made sure of it. François had insisted that he go. So he'd gone and now he was back.

He turned the key in the front door and took off his rubbers in the vestibule. He was halfway up the stairs when the landlord came out of the kitchen and called to him. "Some dame's been calling you."

"Who was it?"

"She wouldn't say. Kept saying she'd phone back."

It must be Giselle. Mixed emotions of hatred and satisfaction collided within him. She wouldn't find him as easy to get along with as before. That was for goddamn sure! "Didn't she leave her phone number?" he asked.

"Nothing! Nothing at all. But she sounded anxious. Kept asking when you'd be back. Said she'd call back again about one."

Pierre said nothing but continued up the stairs. He looked at his watch. It was almost on the dot of noon. It had been a long drive up the slippery road from Montréal and he was bushed. So he lay down on the bed, but he couldn't sleep. He lit a cigarette and blew the smoke rings toward the dirty ceiling. Thoughts of hate and revenge raced through his mind, but he still kept looking at his watch. When it was 12:55, he became restless, stood up and walked about the room impatiently. The telephone rang on schedule. It was Giselle. There was panic in her voice.

"I must see you, Pierre."

"I don't want to see you."

"I've been phoning every day."

"I don't give a damn if you've been phoning for the last three years. I've been away and I wish to hell I'd stayed away."

"Please. Please . . ." There was a plaintive wail in her voice like that of a child who has lost its parents. A whimpering, sobbing plea, one so pathetic that Pierre could hardly resist.

But then he thought of the last time he had seen Giselle. There could have been no misunderstanding. It had been a black and white picture. He shook his head. He couldn't stand to think of it. But, Christ, it was good at least to see that she was remorseful.

"No," he said, "I don't want to see you. François told me what you are! You're a ten-dollar whore. I'll tell you what I'll do. I'll call you when I'm hard up. But right now, I'm a little short of change, and I can't afford a ten spot. Would you go for five?"

The hatred, contempt and scorn in his voice pierced Giselle.

"Pierre, I want to talk."

"Maybe next week, baby. Maybe next week I'll have ten bucks. Then I'll call you."

"I don't blame you, Pierre. I don't blame you."

"Blame me! Blame a simple, backwoods bastard like me? Blame me for what? The only thing you can blame me for is being stupid. But let me tell you something, baby. I'm not as stupid as you think."

"Oh, Pierre! If you only knew."

"I'm busy. I've got lots of things to do. I can't waste my time with a cheap whore."

"You made me promise, Pierre. You made me promise I'd meet you at the Carnival. You made me give you my sacred vow. I gave you my promise, Pierre. I promised to meet you at the Ice Palace."

"To hell with your promises." Pierre's voice rose in fury. "To hell with your stinking lies."

"You call me a whore, Pierre. You call me a whore today but you don't remember that I tried to tell you what I was before. I did try to tell you, Pierre, but you didn't listen. You wouldn't listen to me when I wanted to be honest with you. There was a time when all I wanted to do was tell you. All I wanted to do was tell you what I had been. I wanted to tell you all about myself but you wouldn't listen."

"So now I know." There was a melodramatic note in his statement but it was betrayed by a catch in his voice.

"I didn't want to tell you on the telephone, Pierre," she said, her voice cooling. "I wanted to tell you to your face. I wanted to be with you." Her voice broke. "Honest, Pierre, I didn't want to do it this way."

"Tell me? Tell me what?"

"Pierre . . . I can't . . ." she sobbed. "Pierre, I can't tell you like this. It's too cruel. Pierre, remember the first night I ever met you."

"I'll never forget."

"Don't you remember, Pierre? Don't you remember what you had to tell me?"

There was silence. "Pierre, you had to tell me about Paul. Now the situation is reversed. Now, I have to tell you about Emile and Yvonne."

"What about them?"

"You don't know?"

"Know what? What should I know?"

"Pierre. Pierre, they're dead. Both of them are dead. I know who did it."

At first, he was dumbfounded. Then his voice boomed. "Is this another one of your goddamn dreams?" Fury rose in his voice. "Is there nothing sacred to you? Will you stoop to anything? Don't say things like that about my friends."

"It's no dream, Pierre. It's no dream!" Her voice sobbed hysterically. "Believe me. They were buried yesterday."

"It's one of your stinking tricks. It's a trick so that you can see me."

"No!"

"You liar! How did they die?"

"I'm afraid. I'm afraid, Pierre. Please come to see me."

Pierre's heart pounded unmercifully. Nothing had happened to Emile or Yvonne. It was impossible. Emile was as strong as an ox. No sickness could knock him from his feet. It must be a trick. Of course it was. But would Giselle sink to such a trick just to see him? Then he thought again of that night and he knew that she was capable of anything. "I'll see you," he lied. "Where will you be?"

"At the Basilica de Notre Dame."

For a moment his anger took possession of him. "In church? Meet you in church?"

"Where else?"

"At the Château. In the bar."

"I don't dare. My life is in danger. Yours too, Pierre. Try to believe me," she sobbed. "Why can't I make you believe me?"

There was no use arguing. Pierre knew what he had to do. He looked at his watch. It was ten after one. He would phone Emile. Make sure that nothing was wrong, that it was only one of Giselle's lies. One of her sick dreams. Then he would leave her waiting at the church. It would be a good place for the little bitch to repent her sins. When she'd had a damn good wait, maybe he'd call François and tell him where she was. From what Roger had said, François was mad at her for what she did. "She's been lying her head off to him about you, Pierre. Saying she was finished with you. Saying neither of you cared for each other. That's the only reason he had anything to do with her. But now he'd like to tell her what he thinks of her."

Maybe I'll tell him, thought Pierre. But he said. "Okay, I'll see you at two. At the church."

When Pierre entered the Basilica de Notre Dame, his face was flushed. He was greatly disturbed and he breathed hard from running the last block. Instinctively, he put his finger in the holy water font at the entrance and blessed himself. Then crossing to the opposite side, he genuflected.

With his eyes searching the deserted cathedral for Giselle, he hurried down the side aisle, his feet echoing noisily through the vast chambers. He passed the pulpit, which clung to a supporting pillar halfway up the aisle before he could see the altar of Our Lady.

Giselle was kneeling at the railing in front of the statue of the Virgin. But he had too many tormenting thoughts on his mind, too many horrible questions to ask, to let this sight of hypocrisy remain with him. How many things had happened since Giselle's phone call? How many unbelievable facts had made themselves known? He had phoned Emile. The number was disconnected.

In a panic he had phoned the police in the neighbouring village and had learned the awful truth. This time Giselle had not lied to him. The police told Pierre that at first it had appeared to be a murder-suicide, but that investigation had proven it to be a double murder. Pierre had to talk to someone about it. He had tried to call François but there was no answer. Roger had been hanging around but he didn't want to talk. Instead, he had excused himself almost immediately. Who else could Pierre turn to? There was no one else. Painful as it was to him, he had made the decision to see her.

He had run through the crowded streets. Carnival in Québec is the high point of the winter season. It is marked with many exciting winter events. There is the crowning of the queen, the building of ice statues and the ice palace, revelry day and night, auto races in the snow, dog sled races on the outskirts of town. It lasts for two weeks and during this time, the exuberant visitors swell the city's population to almost double. The festivities come to a climax on the last day when teams of canoeists, reminiscent of the ancient voyageurs, race each other across the St. Lawrence River, dragging themselves from ice floe to ice floe. The tradition of the voyageurs, the famous French explorers of the Northwest, still lives on in the spirit of the enthusiastic French Canadians who swarm along the river banks to watch.

Pierre had pushed his way through the crowds. He had to walk from his rooming house because the streets were blocked.

Giselle turned her head and watched as he approached. She waited until he was beside her before she stood up. There were tears in her eyes as she faced him.

"We can't talk here," said Giselle. "Come with me." She led him into an alcove off the side. "Do you believe me now?"

Pierre looked at her for a moment, his eyes red with unshed tears. "The policeman said it was murder. Why should anyone murder Emile and Yvonne?"

"It was Roger, Pierre. Please believe me. Roger killed them both."

Here it comes again, thought Pierre. How can I believe her? This maniacal sickness of hers. This crazy, out of proportion hate she has for François and Roger. "How do you know?" he demanded.

"I was there."

"Where?"

"At Emile's."

"Did you see it?"

"No, I just saw Roger's car."

"When?"

"Five days ago."

Pierre thought back. Five days ago, Roger was in Montréal. He had been there for the last two weeks and had seen Roger almost every day. Not every day to be sure but Roger had always made a point of explaining to Pierre where he had been.

He couldn't believe her. No matter what she said or did, he couldn't believe her. Not any more. His hurt, his anger, his hate. How they confused him. He wanted to run. He wanted to cry. He wanted to talk. He wanted to pray. Anything! He had to do something. But he could do nothing. He stood beside her like a little boy and listened.

Giselle explained in whispers how she had gone to Emile's, how she had been welcomed and how they had helped her. Then, when she was finished, when she had told him everything, she stood there, tears streaming down her face. "They were so happy. I envied them so much. They were the most wonderful people in the world and now they are dead."

A priest tending the altar noticed them. He nodded, passing them on his way to the vestry. Giselle wondered what Pierre was thinking. He had been so quiet, he hadn't said a word during her explanation. He was terribly hurt. She could almost feel his pain.

And yet she could do nothing. How she wished she could tell him the truth about her futile efforts to stop François, about her feelings, about her plans and especially about their baby. But this she could never do. It could never be the same. The hurt was too deep.

"Come on," she said sadly. "We must get out of here."

Pierre followed dumbly as she led him into the street. The clouds were black and heavy with snow. The wind whistled in gusts between the buildings and whipped the snow in eddying swirls. For moments they could scarcely see. But then the wind would decrease and the whirlwinds would stop, the snow would fall to the ground, and the air would be still once again.

They found a table in the corner of a restaurant and ordered coffee. They sat in silence together for a long time, neither one daring to speak. It had always been silence that had bonded them together. The silence of the Terrace on that summer day so long ago. The silence at Lac St. Jean which had cemented them together and made them one, and now it was the silence of parting. For there was no other answer. No ties could bind them again. There was a wall between them, too high and impregnable for either of them to scale.

"I'm going away, Pierre." The words came simply and abruptly. Pierre did not seem to heed them. "I'm going away and I will never see you again. But I want you to do something for me before I go." She looked at him but there was no sign of acknowledgement in his face and he said nothing. It was as if he were hypnotized. She continued. "I'm asking only because, at one time, I really believe we meant something to each other." She searched his face for an acknowledgement. There was none.

"When I was a little girl," she said, "I used to travel a lot with my aunt. We used to go to Europe. I've told you about it. Well, one time we were in France. The place isn't important. All I remember is that we were staying with some friends and one night I couldn't sleep, so I walked down the stairway which led directly to the living room. I was in my stocking feet and my aunt and a man were talking. I stopped at the bottom of the stairs and listened. I was only about ten years old and things made an impression on me."

"The man said, 'You don't believe me, Rita. Well, I'll prove to you that I'm not lying.' My aunt asked how he could possibly prove it and he said, 'We'll split a bottle of wine together and we'll both vow to tell the truth over that wine. We'll tell the truth as we see it and we'll both swear to each other that nothing will be hidden.'

"I never forgot that experience and I make that vow with you, here and now, because I've got something to say to you before I go." She looked at him pleadingly. His face was a mask. He seemed to be made of stone.

She ordered a bottle of wine. The waiter poured the first glass. "I swear to tell the truth. God's truth." His eyes met hers and held them for a fleeting second. Wordlessly, they drank the wine. It was only when the last drops of the bottle were drained and Giselle had signalled to the waiter for another, that she began to speak.

"I believe that François, Ginette and Roger are a gang of murderers whose only interest in Québec is for their own selfish aims. For power." Giselle said it as though she were reciting a litany. "I believe they'll do anything to gain control. And they think that now is the time to act. Their best ally is the language difference. The Church used it for so long to maintain their control. Now it's passed over to this gang of would-be dictators.

The waiter arrived with another bottle. Pierre seemed to neither accept nor reject the statements. So she continued.

"But why have we always followed these instigators in Québec? Why have we always hated the outside, especially the Americans, and even other Canadians? Because we were taught to hate. The Catholic Church in Québec never really wanted to help us. They wanted to use us. If they had wanted to help, they would have let us assimilate. They would have educated us. People like you and me and Emile and Yvonne and the other millions. If we could converse freely with the other North Americans, who can deny that our lot would be better? After all, what do we all want? We want a share, a fair share, of what we can produce. They can't blame us for that. And then there's the natural restlessness of people like us. If we didn't have dreams, we wouldn't have any spirit, any heart, any soul. But where can we play out our dreams? In Canada? Not unless we want to change the habits of a lifetime. We almost feel like traitors when we speak English, and yet English is our only link with the rest. So, what do we do? We turn to a far-off country and call it Mother. And why? Because we are looking for a way out. But haven't we done everything to lock ourselves in?

"Remember the story you told me about the American who stopped you on the side of the road? He had a big car. Do you remember how you felt when he drove away? You were mad. You told me you were mad at him because he was different. There's something I can't understand. Why were you mad at him? Why weren't you mad at those people who made you different? They are the seeds that produced most of your problems."

Pierre reddened and opened his mouth as though he was going to speak, but he closed it again and said nothing. Giselle continued.

"The people of Québec are not stupid, Pierre. They've just been badly led, that's all. Or should I say, badly misled. They've never been able to make the same kind of money that other North Americans make and they're mad about it. I've been mad about it myself. And I've asked myself why the hell should I take twenty-five per cent less wages than anybody else in the country? But we'll never make it as long as we're different. I've known that for a long time.

"But when I think a little further, I ask myself, why are we different? And do you know what the answer is? The differences are artificial and inflicted on us. We're part of the North American continent. We're part of the economics of the North American continent and yet, we refuse to acknowledge it.

"How have we been educated in the past? We've been educated to speak a language that nobody understands. Our education has been limited because we demand this difference. But who wanted us to be different? Who was it that insisted we speak French? Look at the roots of our Church to find the answer. For centuries, they've held us back. They've wanted to keep us isolated so they could control us. They taught us hate and suspicion, but more than anything else they taught us to be different. We're different because we want to be different. It's like a wheel that keeps turning around."

Pierre fidgeted. The wine seemed to have no effect. Why does she go on like this? Why won't she talk about Emile and Yvonne? But there was no fight left in him, so he asked, "And where do François and Roger and Father Moreau and the rest of this gang of murderers, as you call them, fit into the picture?"

She was quiet for a few moments, thinking. At least trying to think objectively, while all the time tormented by her own conflicting thoughts, about Pierre, herself, about the futility of everything. She was talking in the hope that she could help him. Yes, but more than that, she was talking to be near him.

When she did speak, there was more sadness than anger in her voice. "The instigators," she said slowly, "they are the instigators, using a manufactured problem to serve their own purposes. While Father Moreau and his group maintained a division of two hundred years ago in order to satisfy the ambition of the clergy, the politicians of today are using their divisions to satisfy their own greed for power. They will ruin Québec by clinging to a philosophy of the middle ages. But they don't care. As long as they get their dreams of power. They are the worst enemies of the people of Québec and they are the greatest hurdles over which the people of Québec must jump, in order to get what they want. But these instigators have done great damage. Their smoke screens, their deceptions, their hates have confused, almost destroyed our country. This danger must be eliminated to be understood by our people. And if it isn't? If people like you and me keep on working to destroy our country, what then? It can only end in a civil war. Not a war over separatism. But a war over economics. A war over who owns a river traversing a sovereign state. You'll have to figure that out for yourself. But you asked me what is François? Can't you see? He's only taking advantage of a situation born of past follies.

" 'La revanche de berceau.' The revenge of birth! Imagine that! The very Church that condemns revenge has used our people to breed like rabbits in a vain attempt to maintain power and control. Families of fifteen and twenty children, then blaming the resulting poverty on the outsider. Then look at the hatred fired up by inflaming kids with the idea that they are a defeated people! How stupidly cruel! How self-destructive! What a horrible legacy to pass on to a child.

"The only defeat our generation has had is in our minds. This country doesn't belong to the pillagers of two hundred years ago, the English and French armies who were here to rob the land of its furs. This country belongs to the living Canadians of today. Those Canadians who are loyal and true and abide by the law and work toward making it a better place to live. Not to the promoters of destruction! Not to them, Pierre. That's all I'm asking you. Don't work for them. Don't be drawn any further into their trap. Don't let them imprison you with their lies. Don't allow them to build a wall around you and say 'you are mine; you belong to me; you cannot leave because out there they are all foreigners.' Pierre, the other North Americans are not our enemies. You have no enemies in North America. In Canada and the United States, there are millions of people of French extraction. They get along fine with other people of all races."

She stopped and felt sad. The wine was finished but she couldn't feel it at all. She looked at her watch. It was almost six o'clock. "We must go," she said suddenly. "I don't want any more wine and I'm not hungry." She moved, but Pierre reached his hand across the table and almost touched her.

"Sit down," he said. "I want to ask you one question." She remained motionless in her chair.

"After what you did to me," he said slowly, "after what you did to us, how can I believe you give a good goddamn about whether or not I stay in the Movement?" There was a pathetic passion in his voice.

Giselle looked around the restaurant. The place was crowded with customers. No seats were available and the waiter was paying more than an ordinary amount of attention to them. "I want to tell you, but first we must go. Come with me." She stood and he followed her out of the restaurant.

It was dark and the street lights showed dimly through the snow which swirled around in ever-increasing gusts. Like a playful child, the vagrant wind would pick up the fine snow and swirl it up the narrow streets and into the faces of the Carnival crowds which swarmed through them. "This way," said Giselle as she grasped Pierre's hand. She felt no response from him, but he followed.

Suddenly, the air stilled and the wind-blown snow fell quickly to the ground. Where seconds before it was impossible to see an arm's length ahead, it was now easy to see the Place d'Armes and the Château Frontenac opposite it. Giselle looked into the doorway of a store across the narrow street. A man stood there, huddled against the building. It was Roger. Her eye caught his. Quickly, Roger tried to hide by pulling his coat around his face and tipping his nose down so that his face was almost invisible. But it was Roger. Clear and unmistakable.

"Look," she moaned. But just as suddenly as it had stopped, the vagrant breeze began again, picking up the snow and Roger was no longer there.

"What's the matter?"

She was about to tell him when she thought of the other times. Of the times when he had looked at her unbelievingly and thought she was sick. If she told him now that she was afraid for her life and for his, he would think she was sick again and wouldn't believe a word she said. "Nothing," she said. "It was just the snow."

They walked across the Place d'Armes to the Terrace and directly to the Ascenseur which descended to Lower Town. "Hurry," she said. "We'll go this way. It's warmer." She looked over her shoulder but could not distinguish Roger from the many vague forms which followed them like ghosts through the wind-swept snow.

Roger's anger with himself was only momentary. Then he began to realize the significance of the happening. When he had considered it, he was glad she had seen him. It'd be more fun now.

Now she was on her guard, the terror would rise higher. After all, Pierre hadn't seen him.

This had been a good plan. Keep Pierre in Montréal long enough so that he wouldn't know of Emile and Yvonne. Sooner or later, Giselle would contact him and, sooner or later, Pierre would seek her out. How right can I be? I'm batting a thousand. I suppose it's been worth it. Worth freezing in that goddamn alley for the last two hours.

40

The elevator grunted to a stop in Lower Town. The doors opened noisily into the small anteroom and they soon found themselves in the frightful cold outside where the biting wind nipped at their faces and the snow, still whipped by the gusting wind, lashed at them. A snowplough crawled up the street, slithering from one side to the other, as it lunged at the drifts. Another vehicle, with caterpillar tracks, had preceded it, breaking the snow with a sharp attachment on its front.

Pierre's heart was as cold as the ice floating in the river before them and he felt distaste at Giselle's touch. Even when they walked over a mound of snow left by the plough, he almost had to force himself to touch her arm so that she wouldn't fall. And yet, he was drawn to her and dreaded the words of good-bye. He walked beside her down the narrow streets, struggling with his conflicting emotions.

While he couldn't resist the gnawing feelings of hate toward her for what she had done, his heart softened as he listened to her relate the experiences with Emile and Yvonne during the last weeks. After being caught as she was, why did she run away to their place anyway? It was like François had said so often. She was sick.

Giselle's feelings were less complicated. She had suggested coming to Lower Town to get away from Roger. He hadn't followed them into the Ascenseur, so they must have lost him.

Besides Roger, there was only one other reason why she was here. She was still so much in love with Pierre that his presence made her content and happy. But she knew that no matter what she said or did, she would not reach him. She had to resign herself to this fate; the fate that would take her from his side and leave her alone and uncomforted through the trying months of pregnancy ahead. But she had to try. She had to make her confession to Pierre so that someday, somewhere, somehow, he would believe her. He would know that she had not betrayed him.

They found themselves in the waiting room of the Lévis ferry, a large building fronting the river. The room was crowded with people, all of them waiting to board the boat which was just now approaching the dock. Without discussion, Giselle led him through the turnstiles and waited. She looked desperately through the swelling crowd for any sign of Roger. "Oh, God," she prayed. "Please say we've lost him."

The turnstiles opened, the passengers filed on board, the cars rolled through the cavernous mouth into its lower deck and soon Pierre and Giselle were in the circular salon on the main deck. It was warm there and the hundreds of people sitting on the rows of seats were, for the most part, in a holiday mood. Carnival was in full swing and spirits were high. Together, and yet alone, the two stood in a corner as far as they could from anyone else and leaned against a window.

Outside, black eddying currents flowed swiftly between the huge chunks of ice. Giselle looked at the broken ice-pack through which the ferry had so recently cut to reach the dock. How quickly the new ice was beginning to form! Already a sheet, as thick as window glass, had knitted itself across the opening which the steel-bowed ferry had broken. If only the rift between herself and Pierre could be so easily bridged.

The motors came alive and shook the two from their morbid thoughts. When Giselle spoke, she seemed to be talking to the window and the river. But she knew he could hear.

"I must tell you why I hesitated when you asked me to marry you." She felt him move nervously, as though he were to walk away. "No, don't go." She grasped his arm.

"I'm not good enough for you, Pierre. I've wanted to tell you ever since that day on the Terrace. I thought I could change. I thought my values could become like yours, like mine used to be. But I've done too much and I can't be anything different." She told him about her early life in the convent. About her love affair with Armand, about her pregnancy and the baby. She told him about Sister Thérèse, how she had become disillusioned and full of self-pity and how, in her weakness, she had turned to prostitution.

He stood there beside her like a man of stone, with no feelings, no emotions. As though he was impervious to pain, as though none of this mattered. Whatever she said was no more than what he had already seen. He was like a priest hearing a confession, strangely distant from her freely admitted sins.

"The worst thing I ever did was to leave my baby, Pierre. I had conceived him in love, or at least what I thought was love, and it was this one thing that has haunted me ever since. Where is he? What is he like? Is he all right? I could ask no one. I could talk to no one about him. Paul? He didn't understand. When I was down in the dumps, depressed and lonely and tried to talk to him, he would laugh. 'You're just stupid, Giselle,' he would say. 'Nobody in their right mind would worry about some kid.' But I did worry, Pierre, and I vowed to myself, that I would never, ever, do it again. I would never give up my baby. I would give up anything before I'd do that. I'd wash floors, take all the abuse and criticism anyone could throw at me, but I'd never give up my baby again." She looked at him for understanding, but there was none; only the detached, staring eyes, looking out across the frigid waters. The noises of the boat smashing hard against the giant cakes of ice sent shudders through the ship. Giselle grasped the window sill to steady herself.

"I lived with Paul. I did everything he asked. I belonged to him. But I never loved him. To me, he was like an anchor that would hold me against the current. He stopped me from going on the rocks and for that, I was grateful. He was a guiding influence to me and I cared for him, but I did not love him, Pierre. And when I met you, it was the same. Nothing. It was as though I was incapable of love; like I was old and worn out and had nothing left to offer. But I was glad of your company, Pierre. I was glad to have you to talk to. I admired your idealism and, as we got to know each other, I began to give you something that I have never given another human being for too long. I began to respect you, Pierre. I began to believe you and I began to realize that you meant exactly what you said. I wondered what an honest man like you was doing in this den of thieves. This bunch of liars that included me."

The boat hit hard. It stopped suddenly and violently, the motors roared in reverse and it backed off. Then they roared again and the boat lurched ahead, this time crashing against the frozen obstruction, and forcing giant chunks of broken ice to swirl in the black waters, their grotesque forms standing out vividly in the bright lights of the vessel.

In the excitement, Pierre grasped Giselle to hold her against the force of the impact. When it was over, their eyes met but they quickly turned away.

"I don't know when it first happened. I think it was that first day on the Terrace," said Giselle simply. "It happened when you kissed me. After that, I couldn't help myself. After that, there was only one thought in my mind. Get you out of the Movement! Go away! Be together. But all the time, I knew. I knew you and I were in danger and then, Pierre, when we were on the Sans Souci, just before the explosion, I saw Roger kill Madame Hébert. He killed her deliberately. I watched through the window. Then I knew! I knew we were in worse danger than what I had thought and yet, we were trapped. Like lobsters in a trap and François, the fisherman."

There was an uneasiness in Pierre again and Giselle sensed it. "Don't stop me! Please, don't stop me, Pierre, and I'll make you a promise. When I'm finished, I'll say good-bye to you. I'll turn my back. I'll walk up the street. You'll never see me again. I won't bother you. I won't ask for anything. But please, Pierre, listen to me now and try to remember what I tell you." He consented in silence and she went on.

"After the explosion, I spoke to François. He made no secret of the fact. You and I were marked for death. When I told François that he must live up to his bargain, he was furious." Suddenly, as though awakened from a dream, Pierre turned his eyes from their steady gaze through the window.

"What bargain?" he demanded.

"I told him that I would go along with you and Madame Hébert on the Sans Souci, if he would agree to release us both when we'd done our job. I did it because I loved you, Pierre, and because I wanted you out of the Movement. That was the only reason. But when I asked him to live up to his bargain, he threatened me. He threatened to have Roger kill me. That was why I was so worried."

The motors reversed and the vessel bumped heavily against the sides of the dock. They had arrived in Lévis. The passengers by foot and in automobiles streamed from the ship. As though rivetted to the floor, Giselle and Pierre stood at the window. A uniformed attendant approached. "Are you not leaving?" he asked.

"No," replied Giselle.

"Then I'll have to ask you for another ticket."

Pierre gave him the fare and he walked away. They stood without speaking while the boat reloaded, but when the ship was finally under way again and headed back to the city, Giselle broke the silence.

She spoke slowly, almost in a whisper. She told him of her fears, her hatred for the Movement and everything it stood for. She told him of her surprise visits by François, of her constant fear of Roger, and of her decision to give in to François' demands. To pay the price he demanded for their freedom. In dull monotones, she told him how horrible it had been with François. The reasons! The inside-out reasoning that allowed her to give in to him. What difference could it make? One more man to a body that had been used by so many before? And then she told him of François' laughter, his gloating. How he had planned the whole thing. Her fury. Her attack on him with the fork. The cut. The deep wound in his arm. Her flight. The race from the Hébert house in François' car. The refuge. The haven she found at Emile and Yvonne's.

Pierre's staring eyes bulged as he looked, without seeing, through the window. Could he believe her? Could it be possible? There was one coincidence in her story. François' arm. François had fallen against a curb and broken his arm. This was Roger's explanation and Pierre hadn't cared at the time if the whole world had fallen on him. He had felt sick about François at first, and it was only due to Roger's constant harangue that he forgave him. By the time Pierre was again speaking to François, over two weeks had passed and François no longer wore his arm in a sling. Pierre had never thought of it again.

"I want you to know," Giselle continued. "It's the most important thing I want you to remember, Pierre. I love you. I love you as I have never loved anyone. I know what I did was wrong. I did it out of cowardice. I thought I was protecting myself. I did not want you to know what I used to be." Her voice caught. "I wanted only your love. The way it was at the first. The way I hoped it would always be. But, Pierre," her voice pleaded, "I don't want you to feel sorry for me. Something wonderful has happened to me, knowing you. You've given me something more. You've given me a treasure that I will hold and protect forever." She stopped and Pierre wondered, but didn't ask, what it was that he had given her.

His thoughts were racing, racing wildly from one complexity to another. This quiet discussion, this confession, this farewell was certainly not the rambling of a crazy woman. It was a logical chronicle of events, and everything added up. If only he could believe her completely. But if he did, he thought sadly, then the whole situation would change. Instead of François being his friend, what would he be?

"Please try to believe me. I don't expect you can. I don't ask that you will. I only ask that you try. I ask it, Pierre, so that some day it will all make sense and you will know what was in my heart tonight."

The boat hit against the dock, and soon Giselle and Pierre were back in Lower Town. They stood together at the entrance. The moment of parting had come and as though the blood was drained from her body, the coldness of the night chilled Giselle to the marrow. It was like the coldness of death!

Turning to Pierre, she said simply, "I'm going away. Goodbye." The statement caught Pierre by surprise. Bewildered by his doubts, dumbfounded by her confessions, he grasped her arm and held it.

"You can't leave like this. I won't let you. We haven't talked enough. There's too much to say. Where are you staying? I must see you tomorrow . . ."

Giselle looked up at him and only the snowflakes and the steam from their breath were between them. "There's no use. It's all over. You don't believe me. You'll never forgive me."

"Phone me," he pleaded. "If we could only talk some more. Please see me." Giselle studied the hurt on his face. The snow covered his eyebrows and clung to his eyelids. He looked as though he was crying. She wondered if it was a snowflake that had caught in his eye.

"I promise," she said. "I'll phone you. But now, I must go."

"No."

She meant what she had said earlier. The words rang in his ears. "I'm going away. I'm going away and I'll never see you again." Suppose she was telling the truth? Suppose François was what she claimed him to be? He thought of her story of François' arm. Maybe she had done it. And then again, he thought sadly, maybe it was just another lie.

Then he remembered her story of Emile and Yvonne. She was there. She was a witness. This, at least, was what she claimed. But if this was true, why didn't she tell the police about Roger? Maybe it was because it was all a dream. A sick dream, like François said.

Suddenly, it was clear to Pierre what he must do. He must contact the police and see if what she said was true. See if she really was at the house. If that was true, then the rest would be more believable. He must phone tonight. Now. There was no use in more questions, more explanations. "You must phone me first thing in the morning. Will you promise?"

"I promise. I give you my word."

With a longing Pierre had never felt before in his heart, he watched as she turned and swiftly vanished in the swirling snow.

41

The wind blew in ever increasing gusts up the narrow streets, whipping the snow into a blizzard and sweeping it into irregular dunes against the ancient buildings. Giselle slowed down. She had hurried since leaving Pierre, taking the most direct route to the elevator which would carry her back to the Terrace, to Upper Town and home. She was confident they had lost Roger earlier, but even the thought of him made a chill sweep over her and she wondered whether she had been wise to leave Pierre. Perhaps she should have stayed with him until they had returned to Upper Town, but her pride had made her leave him. She had told her story and left him as she had promised, and now it was too late for regrets. There was just enough time to reach the safety of the elevator before the snow closed all the routes.

In the dim light of an old-fashioned lamp, she stopped to catch her breath. The snow swirled about, surrounding her, encompassing her, enfolding her in its bosom. She looked behind. At first it appeared there was no one there, but a second look said there was. Spectre-like, a vague and shadowy form bore down on her. She caught her breath in fear, then pushing herself forward through the snow, crossed the street. Panting like a hunted animal with the brutally cold air catching in her lungs, she forced herself on, but still the shadowy form besieged her.

The streets were deserted. Occasionally, a light appeared through the frosted windows of medieval houses which stood like sentries of the past along both sides of the narrow street, but no one could be seen or heard. Perhaps it was not Roger, but just another citizen going home. She must find out.

At the next corner, she doubled back. Then furtively glancing over her shoulder, she saw that the figure stalked her relentlessly, following her footsteps in the snow. It was him! It had to be him. But why didn't he race after her and get it over with? If he wanted to catch her, his strength, his stamina, far outweighing hers, would allow him to do so. He had only to put on a short burst of speed and he would have her. But he wasn't trying. When she stopped momentarily for a breath, he stopped as well, just far enough behind that she could not recognize him and yet, close enough that she could not fail to see he was there. Could she stop and face him? Challenge him? No! That was what he wanted. Her fear drove her on and she stumbled through the snow in what she hoped was the direction of the elevator.

Voices filled the air. Loud voices that sang a raucous song. Strong voices that came from a group of skaters returning from a party. Giselle raced after them as fast as she could, each footstep harder to take than the last, each one draining the strength from her. There were four of them. In bright, coloured toques with tassels, heavy woollen sweaters and mitts, they stood under the light standard at the corner, singing. She stumbled through the drifts until she stood before them.

"Help me!"

They stopped singing.

"Help you? Certainly, *mamselle*. How can we help you?"

"That man!" She pointed behind her. "He's been following me."

"What man?" She turned and looked. No one was there.

"He's hiding," she sobbed.

"Where are you going?" asked one of the men.

"To the Ascenseur."

The man laughed. "No wonder someone was following you before and no wonder he's gone now. You should have turned at the last corner. Here, we will show you."

Laughing and singing, the group led her down the street, retracing her steps. At the corner, one of them pointed. "It's just a short distance. You can't go wrong. Walk straight. Don't turn."

Giselle looked at them helplessly as they turned and disappeared. Moments later, she could see the bright lights through the driving snow. But there was someone standing at the entrance. Roger? Hoping it was not, she stumbled on while the figure stood there, statue-like, making no attempt to hide. In the bright light, there was no mistake. It was Roger.

Giselle slipped into the entrance of an antique shop which had a light burning in the back. Entering, she shook the snow from her clothes while the attendant, an odd-looking, old woman, sat on a chair at the rear. Giselle browsed for a few minutes, keeping her eye on the window. Finally, the woman spoke. "Is there something I can do for you?" she asked.

"Oh, no," replied Giselle. "I . . . I was lost. I thought I was going to freeze to death until I saw your light. Is it okay if I warm up for a few minutes?"

"Certainly," said the woman. "I'm glad of your company. I'm really not open for business. I'm waiting for a friend to come and pick me up. He's walking, the poor dear, so I don't know when he'll get here. Sit down and I'll get you some coffee."

Giselle was glad to get out of the store and into the back room where a pot of coffee bubbled on an old wood stove. She felt safe here, knowing that nothing could happen to her and knowing, too, that every moment she stayed, Roger would be more convinced she had escaped, would eventually give up his chase and go away. She took off her coat in response to the woman's invitation. Then leaning back in a comfortable chair, she felt good. "I'd love to work in a shop like this," she said. "It must be fun."

"Yes," agreed the woman. "It's a pleasant way to make a living."

"I feel so peaceful sitting among these beautiful old things." Giselle studied the collection of aesthetic trinkets. "That old clock," she pointed. "It reminds me of something back when I was a kid. I can't remember exactly. I don't think we ever owned one, but it does make me feel good just to look at it."

There was a rattling sound at the front door. The woman opened the curtains, separating them from the window. Giselle was quick to look over her shoulder. A man was stomping on the floor to shake off the snow. Then the door opened and the man called out. "You ready?" The woman put on her coat and Giselle followed.

Soon she was back on the street. The man and woman turned in the opposite direction while Giselle, with renewed vigour, hurried to the entrance of the elevator.

Success! She had waited just long enough. There was no one on the streets. She quickly passed the row of stores and her spirits rose.

Then, as though he was an apparition appearing from nowhere, Roger was suddenly at her side. He made no attempt to grab her. Instead, he just stood there, grinning at her. She stifled a scream and ran as fast as she could up the street. She entered the vestibule of the elevator where a man stood beside a fare box. There was a sign. "15¢ for the ride to the top." Giselle pulled a quarter from her pocket and put it in the man's hand. "Quick," she said. "I'm in a hurry. Keep the change."

The door of the lift opened and she hurried in. Seconds later, the doors closed behind her and jangled into the locked position. "Thank God," she whispered to herself, "Thank God." But her relief was short-lived. The noisy door began to open again. "Oh, no! God, no!" She pushed her body hard against a corner, wishing desperately to escape. But there was no way out except through the door where Roger appeared. He just stood there, smiling down at her as the cumbersome doors jangled shut again.

"Hello, Giselle."

"Hello," Giselle's voice betrayed her fear.

The elevator began to move.

"It's cold."

"Yes."

"I'll give you a ride. I have my car."

He said the words as though he were reading lines. Giselle didn't reply. Her hand hurt and when she pulled off her mitt, she could see her palm was bleeding. She had clenched her fist so tightly, she had cut the skin with her fingernails. Up, up the elevator rattled. Giselle looked out the window. Far below were the rooftops of Lower Town, vaguely visible in the heavily falling snow. What a hell of a night. What a hell of a rotten mess to be in. Cornered in here with this bastard. His lack of action puzzled her. He hadn't trailed her all day to carry on an idle conversation, and yet, now that he had caught up with her, he just stood there trying to smile. When they reached the top, she'd go the opposite way. She'd skip into the Château and stay there all night if she had to. Anything to get away.

The elevator clanked to a stop and the two walked out. Roger first, Giselle following. They passed the attendant, then through the doorway to the snow-swept Terrace.

"Come with me." Roger tried to lead her across the Terrace toward the Place d'Armes.

"Thanks anyway," she said, pulling away. "I have to go this way." Without another word, she turned and hurried down the Terrace toward the Glossier and the security she believed was waiting for her there. But instead of refuge, she found only a blinding torrent of snow and wind. The wind whipped around the Château, colliding with the frigid blasts which screamed up the cliffs to Citadel Hill. She pulled her coat collar tighter around her neck as she struggled to reach the skating rink and the far entrance to the Château. She felt a hand on her arm.

"Let me help you." It was Roger.

"No!" She tried to break away.

"I only want to help." His grip on her arm tightened as they continued along the Terrace.

The lights on the skating rink were out. The Glossier was deserted. It was only the swirling snow, the biting wind and the bitter cold that greeted them as Roger led her to the wrong side of the toboggan slide, the side that fronted the cliffs to Lower Town.

"We're going the wrong way." Giselle tried to run back, but Roger's grip stopped her.

"No, Giselle. We're not going the wrong way." Roger laughed. "I know a short cut. I have my car parked along here." His laugh rose. She flung her arm at him.

"You bastard," she screamed. "Let me go." Her breakaway was only momentary. He tripped her as she tried to run and she sprawled in a deep drift. Resisting his efforts to lift her to her feet, she fought her rising hysteria. To her right was the Glossier, to her left were the cliffs and behind her stood Roger, barring her way to the Château and freedom. In front of her was nothing. Nothing except the steps to the Citadel. The steps she and Pierre had taken that August afternoon. Perhaps she could run up the steps. Yes, that would be her plan. Run for the steps. But first . . . She looked up at Roger.

"If you put your filthy hands on me once more," she said in a firm voice, "I'll scream so loud, they'll hear me in Lévis."

Before he spoke, Roger laughed again, contemptuously.

"Scream as loud as you like, you little bitch. Yell your god-damn head off. No one'll hear you." Giselle pushed herself to her feet, then screaming as she ran, she tried to circumvent her tormentor. But her cries were answered only by the howl of the wind, while her passage was blocked by Roger.

Roger was having fun. Giselle backed off. "I'll jump over the cliff," she warned, still backing off.

"Good. That will save me the trouble of pushing you."

"I'm not fooling. I'll kill myself." She continued to back away.

"How obliging, Giselle!"

There were the steps, covered with snow and ice. She raced for them. For a moment Roger was taken by surprise. His hesitation gave her the advantage and she was determined to make the best of it.

When Roger became aware of her intention, he lost no time in chasing her. But luck betrayed him. He slipped and fell on a lower step and let out a cry of pain.

Giselle raced along the walkway and up the next series of steps and along another walkway. With no thoughts of the dizzying heights or the consequences of sliding from the icy perch and plunging down the cliffs to certain death, she raced on, thinking only of escape.

Panic drove her on. Up still another series of steps. She could see the sides of the Citadel looming above her, and behind her she could hear the curses from Roger as he pursued her.

And then it happened. Her foot slipped. It caught in a piece of chunky ice and she fell sideways, landing on her shoulder. Sobbing pitifully, she struggled to her feet but slipped again and there he was, standing above her. She crawled on her hands and knees across the steps and grasping the railing raised herself to her feet. It was then she realized where she was.

It was the same spot where she and Pierre had first kissed. The enchanted place where the bells had echoed along the valley and up the cliffs and held them in its spell.

Here she was, on the same ledge and the bells began to ring again. But this time, it was the mournful dirge of a funeral hymn. The ghostly sounds tolled up the cliffs and fought the wind.

Pleadingly, she looked up at Roger who stood over her. Raising her snow-covered mitts in prayer, she screamed for mercy. But his laugh rose higher and higher, defying the wind with its insane glee.

42

Sleep for Pierre was impossible. Like a seductress, she called, welcomed him to her bosom and then, betraying her promise, ran away. One after another, he smoked cigarettes. Time after time, he raised himself from his sprawling position on the bed, only to move like a caged animal about the room.

He cursed himself, willingly throwing the blame on his own shoulders. Blaming himself for everything! He censored himself for getting involved with Giselle in the first place. He reproached himself for having fallen in love with her, but worse than that, he should never have believed that she was in love with him. He denounced himself for having taken her seriously, but his most severe self-rebuke was for the unforgivable sin of introducing her to Emile and Yvonne. He knew this now. If it had not been for him, they would still be alive. The telephone call to Emile's friend, the police captain, had confirmed it.

His one compelling thought when he left Giselle at the river was to get to a phone, call the police captain who had investigated Emile's death, and find out if Giselle was lying. Had she been there at the time? Had Emile killed Yvonne and then himself? His questions were quickly answered. All doubts were removed.

"She was here," the police captain had said. "She was hysterical. Kept insisting that someone else had killed them. We turned her over to a doctor. He gave her a sedative. She disappeared the next day. We are anxious to contact her."

"Why?"

"A full-scale investigation has been completed. We brought in some outside experts. We need her testimony. Do you know her present address?"

"No." Then he added, "Are you going to arrest her?"

"Of course not," the policeman laughed. "We only want her help. We believe she knows some things that can help us."

Following the captain's request, Pierre promised to help the police locate her. Then, puzzled and confused, he had made his way to Giselle's apartment. His key would not fit; the lock had been changed. He waited in the lobby for hours. Shortly after two o'clock, the superintendent, obviously awakened from his sleep, approached him.

"She hasn't been here for weeks," he explained, after recognizing Pierre. "I don't know where she's been. She's behind in her rent. If it wasn't for Mr. Flynn, I would have sold her furniture by now."

"Roger Flynn?"

"You work with him, don't you?"

"Yes."

"Well, then, you better ask him. In the meantime, don't hang around here. The tenants are complaining. If you don't go, I'll have to call the police."

His mind in a turmoil, Pierre turned to go. The man called after him. "You'd better tell Flynn I'll give him only another twenty-four hours to pay me the back rent. Otherwise, I sell the furniture." With that he was gone and Pierre had retreated to his rooming house with the forlorn hope that she might call.

The long hours of the pitch black night finally turned into grey and still more endless hours seemed to pass before the sun, peeking its head from behind the Gaspé hills, spilled its rays over the St. Lawrence, the Citadel, the Château and the sleeping city.

By seven o'clock, he had run out of cigarettes so he rolled his own from the butts which overflowed the ashtrays. At least it took some time. The hands of the clock seemed glued to the face. By ten o'clock, he could stand it no longer. He woke the landlord and explained the urgency of taking a message if Giselle called while he was out. "I'll be back by twelve. If she won't leave a number, tell her to phone back at noon." The landlord reluctantly agreed and he left the house.

She was not at her apartment. The superintendent, tiring of his questions, spoke brusquely. "She's not here and I don't want you hanging around any more. One more time and I'll call the police." Pierre left quickly, anxious not to cause needless trouble for Giselle.

He returned to his rooming house. No news! No phone call. She said she would leave forever. She said she'd turn her back and never bother me again if I would only listen to her. I listened and now she's gone. Isn't that what I wanted? Yesterday that was all I wanted. But today? What the hell is so different about today? Nothing, except that I don't want her to go. But why? Why have I changed?

Why don't I do what I've always done? Phone François. That's it. That's it exactly. I can't phone François! I can't phone that conniving bastard or his pimply-faced helper. I can't phone them because now I know they've been lying to me. That son-of-a-bitch

Roger said he hadn't heard from Giselle. Then why is he so interested in paying the rent on her apartment? And if Roger is paying the rent, there's no question where the money comes from.
François! Then why does François pretend he knows nothing? And
why does Giselle insist they're trying to kill her, if she's satisfied
with the arrangement? The answer is simple. She isn't.

And what about the cops? The police captain who said she
might know something important. Christ! Why doesn't she phone?
I can't blame her if she doesn't phone me. She left me because I
didn't believe her. I've got to find her.

He left another urgent message with the landlord. "Tell her
I've got to see her," he pleaded. Then he left the house. He would
search for her.

First, through the narrow streets jutting off rue St. Jean, then
past the Ice Palace where their pact to dance together had never
been fulfilled, through the gathering crowds of merrymakers celebrating the final day of Carnival, to the Basilica where the candle
Giselle had lit yesterday still burned, to Place d'Armes, the lounge
at the Château, finally ending up at rue St. Jean again, and the
bar of the Victoria Hotel. He sat by himself and drank beer, gulping
it down at first and then, when it sat heavy and impotent in his
stomach, sipping it. The place was quiet, almost deserted and the
only sound was a radio noisily drumming out a rhythm.

As he drank, the three o'clock news was broadcast. "A by-
election in Ste. Rose produced no surprises yesterday. The seat was
easily won by the separatist candidate. This victory adds to the
enormous power of Jacques Ginette and the predictions now are
that they will sweep the next general election." The next news item
was brief, ghastly and to the point.

"About one-half hour ago," said the announcer, "the body
of a young woman was found by a group of youngsters in the snow
at the foot of the cliffs. She is described as about twenty-two years
of age, brown eyes, auburn hair and five feet, three inches in
height. Police are requesting the assistance of residents in identify-
ing the body."

Pierre heard the words as though in a dream. As though they
could not be real. It could not be Giselle.

He left the bar, crossed between the empty tables and along
the narrow hallway. Once on the street, he moved dazedly through
the holiday crowds, bumping into people, not uttering a word of
apology. There were people dressed in all types of costumes.
Unconcerned people, daring to enjoy themselves, when the world
had just ended. Many held long, white canes with screw tops and

on every street corner they could be seen lifting the canes to their mouths and drinking the refreshing contents. Others had flasks of liquor; some wore masks. Everyone was in a total holiday mood. Music filled the air. Bright, cheerful music that conflicted with the numbing realization of Pierre's thoughts as he pushed his way through the crowds like a man possessed, like a man no longer alive. Shocked and despairing, he moved as though someone was pushing him.

The corporal at the desk was impatient as Pierre fumbled for his words.

"There was a girl. A girl you found in the snow. Where is she?"

The corporal, schooled in the recognition of shock, ushered Pierre into an inner office where he introduced him to a detective. "Yes," said the detective, "we have her downstairs. What makes you think you know her?"

"Can I see her?"

The detective studied him for a moment. Then he rose. "Come with me," he said, and led him down a hall, a set of stairs and into a damp and cold basement room.

The body lay on a table, a blanket thrown carelessly over it. The detective pulled the blanket from the body. Pierre stared at it. He said nothing. He did nothing. But inside his tortured mind, thoughts in a raging torrent flooded through him. She had not lied to him. François had lied. She had not been sick; she had only been terrified. She had been true to him. It was François who betrayed him.

Silently, he stood, tears in his eyes. Tears of pain and remorse, they trickled down his cheeks. They poured from him and he made no attempt to stop them. No attempt to brush them away or to wipe them from his face. They were tears of understanding. The tears he should have shed just twenty-four hours ago when she, by the Virgin, swore that she had not betrayed him. When she had pleaded for his understanding. His answer had been silence then. Silence instead of forgiveness. Mistrust instead of love. And now it came. A river of remorse. A river of understanding, come too late.

"Who is she?" The detective's voice had no emotion.

"Giselle . . . Giselle LaFlesche."

"Are you sure?"

Was he sure? How he wished he weren't. That it was only a bad dream; that he had listened to her; that he had never let her go but that he had gone away with her and done as she had begged. Then none of this would have happened to her; the piti-fully cut and bruised face, the dishevelled hair, and the eyes, stark and glaring so blankly at the ceiling. And the fingers, pointing straight and covered with blood and hair.

The detective took him by the arm. "Come on," he said, "you've looked enough." He led him upstairs to the office, and then called an assistant who stood at the door.

"Take off your coat and strip to the waist." The policeman made no pretense of politeness. Not fully understanding, Pierre did not resist. Soon he stood before them naked to his belt. A man in a white coat entered the room. He studied the condition of Pierre's skin in minutest detail, paying particular attention to his head. Finally he was finished, leaving the room as abruptly as he had entered. The detective followed him.

"You can put your clothes back on," he said as he closed the door. Seconds later, he returned.

"Did she kill herself or . . . ?" Pierre's eyes were red-rimmed, but his voice was steady.

"Why do you ask that?"

"Somebody told me that she would. Somebody told me she was sick." Pierre thought of the dozens of lectures François had given him on the subject of Giselle's supposed sickness.

"A doctor?"

"No, a friend."

"It is not a question of suicide. It is a clear case of murder." The telephone rang and the detective picked it up. He listened but did not speak. "Thanks," he said finally. "Thanks a lot." He hung up. "What was your relationship with this girl?" He turned his eyes to Pierre.

"She was my friend. A very good friend."

"You mean her lover?"

"I wanted to marry her."

"Why didn't you?"

"She kept putting me off."

"There was someone else?"

"No," Pierre's voice caught. "No, I don't think there was any-one else."

"It doesn't make sense." The detective shook his head. "Did you know she was pregnant?"

"Pregnant? No, I didn't know . . ."

"Four to five months," said the detective. "You were her lover and you didn't know? She didn't tell you?"

Pierre shook his head. His thoughts hammered relentlessly in his mind. She had really told him, hadn't she? This was what she meant yesterday. "Something wonderful has happened," she had said. "Something I will treasure forever." She had said it so clearly, so definitely. She had said, "I gave away my first baby but never again. I'll do anything, but I'll never give up my baby again." She wanted his baby but she would not marry him because of her past. She tried to tell him yesterday. She had tried to tell him all along. He had been too stupid to listen to her. Instead, he had told her mortal enemy, François. He had betrayed his own flesh. Sorrow and overwhelming grief encompassed him and he wanted to cry again. But the tears could come no more. He had cried as much as he ever could. For in the place of sorrow and remorse, a more terrible emotion was taking place. Revenge!

"Was there anyone you knew that hated her enough to do this?" asked the detective point blank. Pierre shook his head. How could he tell them? How could he say it was François or Roger? They would have alibis. They would be covered. They would have their lawyers. They would twist and squirm and get out of it. And even if they were found guilty, they would not be hung or electrocuted. They would get a few comfortable years in a nice, clean cell. The years they had stolen from Giselle. This punishment was not enough.

"She had no enemies," he said. "I never met any of her friends."

"It was not the work of a friend," the detective mused. "It was a fiend. And he will be easy to identify if we catch him."

"Why?"

"She fought him. She fought him like a tigress. Her fingernails were covered with flesh. She scratched deep. We think mostly on the face, some on the head. Yes, whoever it was, she hated him. And by what he did to her . . ."

"What did he do?"

"He practically ripped every piece of clothing from her," said the detective. "If the fall had not killed her, she would have frozen to death."

"Can I go?"

The detective was surprised at the sudden question. "Yes," he said, "but don't leave the city. We will want to talk to you again tomorrow."

Pierre walked slowly along rue St. Jean. Encircled by the gay holiday makers, he was oblivious of them. There was only one thought in his mind, one demanding impulse that would never leave him. He would never let it go. He would nurture it, sustain and uphold it. He would perpetuate and prolong it. He would preserve it to give him the strength to do what he knew must be done. Obsessed with only one idea, he pushed his way through the crowds, bumping into people at every turn, only partially conscious of what he was doing.

But after a while, he straightened up and the gaze left his eyes. In its place was a look of purpose and determination. He felt in his pocket and pulled out a ten dollar bill. He had enough money. With quickening steps, he hurried to the corner where he spotted a taxi and flagged it. The cab stopped and he climbed in.

"Where to?" asked the driver.

"I'll show you. Just follow my directions."

43

It was dusk when the cab passed the Hébert house. There was only one car in the driveway. Roger's! Lights were on in the coach house. The main building was in darkness.

"Let me out here."

The cabbie looked around. "What house?"

"We just passed it. I'll walk back. Stop here." The driver did as he was asked. Pierre gave him the ten dollars.

"Keep it," he said as the cabbie tried to make change.

Skirting the front entrance, Pierre walked as silently as possible up the driveway, opened the door to the coach house, entered quickly and silently closed the door. He stood at the bottom of the stairs until he was satisfied that he had not been seen or heard.

Music drifted down the stairs, blaring, thumping music from Roger's radio. Pierre was satisfied that he had not been discovered. He removed his overshoes, then silently slipped off his heavy coat and toque and let them fall to the floor.

Then, just as silently and quickly, he made his way up the stairs, stopping only when he reached the top at the entrance to Roger's room. He listened. There were no sounds except for the radio. He put his hand on the door knob. It turned easily. The door was not locked. Roger was undoubtedly in there. Alone. He was probably, as usual, lying on the bed, daydreaming or asleep, or cleaning his guns. Pierre pushed the door open and walked in.

Roger sat on a chair, his head bent over a large bowl from which he applied a liquid to his face with a large swab of cotton. Pierre had barged across the room and stood directly beside him before Roger was aware of his presence. He lifted his head and revealed the existence of deep scratches stretching from forehead to chin.

"Hello, Roger," said Pierre.

He dropped the cotton pad and tried to stand up, but the pressure of Pierre's hand on his shoulder prevented him.

"Don't bother getting up," said Pierre, switching the radio off with his free hand. "I don't want to disturb you."

Roger's eyes flashed momentarily in surprise and anger. He tried to stand up again, but it was useless. Pierre's weight on his shoulders made it impossible. He relaxed.

"It's good to see you, Pierre." His voice was shaking.

"Those are nasty scratches, Roger."

Roger picked up a towel from beside the bowl and wiped his face.

"Did you have a fight?"

"No," replied Roger, trying to figure out what was the best thing to do. "I slid on the ice getting out of my car. I cut myself on the fence."

"It must have caught your hair. There's some pulled out."

Pierre knew! That was obvious. But what could he do? Just as obvious. Kill him. The automatic under the pillow, or the .38 on the wall.

"It must hurt," said Pierre in mock sympathy, as he rubbed his knuckles hard on the inflamed area around Roger's temple.

"Ouch!" Roger spun to one side, fell to his knees, and crawled to the bed. Reaching under the pillow, he found the automatic, pulled it from its hiding place, slipped his finger on the trigger and swung it around toward Pierre. But too late. A well aimed foot caught it, knocking it so violently from his hand that the bullet fired as Roger's finger jammed against the trigger. The bullet hit the ceiling while the gun spun across the room, hit the wall and fell in a heap of newspapers.

"Nice try, Roger, but you need more practice. Maybe you'd have done better if you'd spent your time practising with a gun instead of scaring girls. But that's your speed, isn't it? You pimply-faced bastard."

Roger sat on his haunches beside the bed holding his finger which bled profusely. The impact from Pierre's foot had cut it deeply against the edges of the trigger.

"I know what you did," said Pierre.

"What do you mean?"

"You killed Giselle!"

"You're crazy! You stupid son-of-a-bitch!" Roger jumped to his feet, but before he could move from the spot, Pierre had lashed him with his fist, catching him squarely on the mouth. He fell backwards onto the cot and lay there, feigning unconsciousness. Pierre stood over him for a moment and then lifting the bowl of antiseptic solution spilled it over his face. Roger suddenly came to life.

"What the hell's the matter with you? Have you gone nuts? What're you trying to do?"

"I'm going to kill you," said Pierre.

"Kill me?" Roger's reaction was a quick glance at the wall

covered with guns. Well oiled, immaculately cleaned guns in perfect shape. If only . . .

"Why not try?" taunted Pierre. "You have nothing to lose."

Suddenly, as though he, himself, was triggered from a gun, Roger rolled off the bed, bounded to his feet and ran headlong into another flying fist. This time the force was so great it knocked him across the bed to the floor on the other side. When he sat up, coughing and spitting blood, Pierre could see that his front teeth were broken.

"I'm going to kill you, Roger. You can't stop me anymore than Giselle could stop you last night. Do you want to confess to me first?"

"For Christ's sake, what do you want me to tell you?"

"Everything." Pierre backed away toward the door. Roger could see another chance coming. He watched as Pierre pulled the door shut and bolted it. Now was the time. Quickly he pushed himself from the floor and, bounding to his feet, raced across the room. He almost had the gun in his hands when he felt the sharp smash of Pierre's fist against the side of his jaw. He spun around and fell to the floor, only to feel Pierre's hand grasping his neck and dragging him across the room.

"How many times do I have to tell you, Roger? I want to hear everything. Every single thing." He lifted Roger to his feet and slapped his cheek with the back of his hand. Then he dropped him into a chair. Roger sat like an errant schoolboy trying to find a way out of being punished.

"I don't know anything about Giselle."

Pierre slapped him hard across the mouth. "Tell me first about Emile and Yvonne."

"What do you want to know?"

"Who did you kill first?"

"Neither. I didn't kill either one. I wasn't up there."

Another blow refreshed his memory. "François sent me up there to find Giselle, that's all. They were dead when I got there."

"Giselle knew differently. That's why you killed her."

"She was going to talk. They were all going to talk. She blamed you for everything. She was going to the cops."

"And so you killed her. You killed them all."

"No!"

"Then who did?"

"I don't know."

Furiously, Pierre lifted him to his feet and pounded him in the chest. Without the slightest attempt at defence, Roger screamed in pain, doubling up as he fell back in the chair.

"Who killed them?"

"François! François! François killed her," Roger moaned.

"How do you know?"

"He told me. He did it. It was François. He threw her off the Terrace." He spit blood on the floor. "He killed her and he's going to kill you. He told me that. He's just waiting until he gets the insurance money. Let me go, Pierre. I didn't hurt Giselle. I wouldn't hurt anybody."

"You're just a nice, clean-cut kid, aren't you? Then why did you kill Madame Hébert?"

"François made me do it. He forced me to kill her. He told me if I didn't, he'd kill me. For God's sake, get me a doctor. I'm dying."

"You're going to die," said Pierre slowly and clearly, so Roger could not misunderstand. "You are going to pay a just penalty for murder. For murdering Madame Hébert. Unless you tell me your other sins. If you tell me the truth, I may get you some help. Tell me the truth, Roger, and maybe I'll get you a doctor."

"I didn't want to kill Emile. He attacked me. I defended myself. Get a doctor." The words came between gasps. "For Christ's sake, get me a doctor."

"And Giselle? She attacked you too?"

"Yes."

"She scratched. She fought. You had to kill her."

"Yes, I didn't want to. Help me. I'm bleeding to death." He tried to stand up. A blow to the chest set him back in the chair.

"That's why you followed her, persecuted her. It was a good game, wasn't it? It was fun scaring the girl, wasn't it? But now, it's my turn. This time it is you that is the victim. This time you die. How do you like that?"

"You promised . . . get a doctor."

"Bastard." Roger tried to move but doubled in pain. Pierre forced him to a sitting position.

"She was helpless, Roger. And yet you had to kill her." He slammed him again across the face. "Say your prayers, Roger. If you've got any prayers to say, now is the time. You are going to die."

"I'm sorry." Roger was mumbling through his broken teeth.

"It's too late to be sorry. It's too late."

Roger began to cough, choking on his own blood. Moaning, gasping as he struggled against Pierre's unrelenting hold, until finally, his mumblings became incoherent. His body fell limp, the coughing ceased and he fell to the floor. Pierre rolled him over as he lay gasping until finally there was silence. His face turned blue, his mouth dropped open and his eyelids flickered upwards in the stare of death.

Pierre walked to the door, thought for a moment, then switching off the lights, he lit a cigarette and stood at the latticed window overlooking the driveway.

What a crazy waste! Why did there have to be people like Roger? Or François? Why did there have to be these power-mad, determined parasites? Were they the victims of a bigger power, as he and Giselle had been theirs? How many times had Giselle told him that Québec, his beloved Québec, was the real victim of their connivance? Why did they all have the same line? Hate everybody except them. Believe no one except them. He hated them and he hated himself for having been one of them. If only he had listened to Giselle. Travelled with her as she wanted. But no! He couldn't have. As she had so often reminded him, he was a prisoner of his own land, his own people and his own language. And, he thought bitterly, my people will always be prisoners as long as they lock their frontiers about them, as long as they allow themselves to be misled by psychopaths.

The moon cast its mystic shadows on the barren limbs of the trees bordering the driveway and made more strange, shadowy patterns on the snow. It filtered through the small window of the coach house and fell on Roger's body as it lay on the floor. Pierre had no remorse, felt no guilt, no sadness. He felt no worse than if he had killed a mad dog.

Lights appeared along the road and moments later, a car, its headlights flashing, turned into the driveway and stopped behind Roger's car. It was followed by a second vehicle. Pierre pulled back from the window and peeked through the edge of the curtains.

In the glittering moonlight, he could clearly see François, Jacques Ginette, Father Moreau, Henri Bédault and Jean Petrie. They followed one another to the front of the house, and soon all was quiet again.

Pierre moved across the room to the arsenal on the wall. He studied the guns. They were all loaded and well-oiled. He took a shotgun from its perch and the .38 calibre revolver from its holster. Tucking the revolver under his belt, he filled his pockets with ammunition he found in the top drawer of the bureau. Then, without a backward glance, he opened the door, walked down the stairs and, ignoring his coat and overshoes, stepped out into the frigid cold of the February night.

44

The gargoyles, their stupidly grinning faces encrusted with ice and snow, were the only eyes that watched as Pierre opened the huge oak door and entered the vestibule. The floor was sopping with water and melted snow kicked from the boots and clothes of the recently arrived guests.

There was no one in the great hall or on the stairs leading to the second floor. Sounds drifted lazily from the drawing room, sounds of laughter and excitement, sounds of celebration. Pierre remembered sourly the election victory of Ginette. Another seat won in a by-election. Another step up the ladder for François, another defeat for the people of Québec.

Without hesitation, without thought, he entered the drawing room and stood inside the door, gazing intently at the group noisily toasting one another. He kicked the door shut and switched on the lights of the huge chandelier. The sudden brightness and the noise of the banging door brought all eyes to bear on him. He stood there silently, the shotgun held at the ready and the revolver stuck in his belt. François was the first to act.

"Get out of here, you insolent pup," he roared, moving quickly toward Pierre. "Get out of here."

Pierre raised the gun and aimed it point-blank at François. "Shut up," was all he said, but the command was full of authority. François stopped dead in his tracks.

"What do you want?" he asked in a more subdued tone.

Pierre eyed the entourage before he spoke.

"I want you to shut your mouth. I want all of you to sit down."

Their eyes moved from one another, puzzled by this strange turn of events.

"Over there," Pierre said, pointing the gun. "Over there at the big table."

Without question, they did as they were told while Pierre propped a chair against the door leading to the hall. He looked about the room. There was no other means of escape. Only the windows. The windows behind the heavy drapes; the windows that were covered with snow and frozen tightly shut. He walked toward the table.

"Sit down," he said in a voice consumed with hate. "I want

to talk.'' They complied, with the exception of Father Moreau, who still stood.

"What's troubling you, my son?'' he asked.

"Sit down.''

The priest sensing the determination, obeyed while Pierre pulled up a chair. He sat at the head of the table far enough away that he could easily swing the gun. He eyed them for a long time. François, the king-rat and his front man, Ginette; Henri Bédault, the advertising agent turned propaganda minister. The news media usually termed him the logical choice for Minister of Education in Ginette's first cabinet; Jean Petrie, the hawk preying on the idealistic aspirations of the youth; Father Moreau, the man of faith, of trust, of connivance.

"You're having a celebration,'' Pierre said finally, "a celebration in a time of mourning.'' He searched François' face; François, who sat at the opposite end of the table, looking toward the door, obviously expecting someone to come and break down the door. Now he is the fool, thought Pierre. He thinks Roger is still alive.

No one spoke, so Pierre continued. "This is a time for mourning. You must all know that.'' Puzzlement marked their faces. "A time of mourning for Québec, a time of mourning for the Movement, for François, Ginette, you, Father Moreau, and the rest of you, but especially, it's a time of mourning for Giselle and Roger.''

François jumped to his feet. "I've had enough,'' he shouted. "Get out of here.''

Without a word, Pierre pointed the shotgun at François, held it on him momentarily, then slowly raising it over his head, pulled the trigger. The resulting explosion reverberated about the room as the blast ripped through the hanging glass of the chandelier, splintered pieces through the room and smashed the ceiling with such force that huge cakes of plaster broke its centuries-old hold and came crashing to the floor.

"The next one is for you, François. If you want to live out this meeting, keep your filthy mouth closed until you're asked a question.'' François sunk into his chair.

"My son,'' Father Moreau stretched his arms in an encompassing gesture toward Pierre. "You must not act like this. Violence is not the means to a just end. Put down your gun. There is nothing to mourn. We are celebrating a well-earned victory. A victory for our cause. Your cause.''

"Not my cause! I've changed since our last meeting, my good Father. Tonight, I am not one of you. Tonight, I am the judge and jury of your crimes.''

"Our crimes?"

"Yes, Father, I include you with the others. Your crime and the crimes of all of you."

"But a crime against whom?"

"Against your people. Against my people. Against Québec. Against me."

Pierre studied their faces. They were all trying to figure a way out, to find a way past this lunatic. If only I could talk as glibly as François, thought Pierre. If only I could talk them out of their filthy treachery. Only Father Moreau seemed genuinely interested in talking. "You can never accuse me of betraying Québec. You cannot say that I am against my own people."

"I can't?"

"Not with honesty."

"You and your Church always had the power in Québec, didn't you? It came easy to you. You agreed to co-operate with the English after they beat us if they let you keep the power. It was simple, wasn't it?"

"We did it for God. We worked for the souls of our countrymen."

"Who can argue with an excuse like that? Who knows why the Church did it? But you did get the power, didn't you?"

"We were a defeated people. We were beaten."

"And for two hundred years, you've never let us forget it. You've repeated that lie like a parrot. You've drummed it into every kid that was ever born in Québec. But why did you do it?"

"Because it was the truth."

"Your kind of truth. I think you used it to maintain your power. The power of the Church. And how did you use that power? Did you use it to help your people? To educate them? To teach them to travel and work with all the others? No! Sometimes I wonder whether you haven't got a special hold on deceit too.

"When I was a kid, I used to hear the women talk about the revenge of the cradle, Father Moreau. I used to hear the girls talk about the big families they would have, so that we would outnumber the English. I didn't know what they were talking about then, but when I got older, I did. What a hell of a way to use your own people. Breed them like rabbits just so you can keep your power. To keep the power that's brought such wealth to you and such poverty to your people. But it's backfired, hasn't it? The people of Québec are sick of you now. Your power has diminished and the reactionaries are taking over."

"If we hadn't been strong and steadfast," there was a quiver in Father Moreau's voice, "you would not have been speaking French today. You would have been overwhelmed by the English majority. We are the protectors of the language."

"What good is a language, Father Moreau, when no one else in the country understands it? We live on a little island in an English sea. We are five million people out of two hundred and twenty million on this continent. Are you going to teach each the other two hundred and fifteen million to speak like us? Why should they? What good would it do them to learn? No good! They would have nothing to gain from learning to speak your language. But what good would it do us to learn to speak theirs? If we did, we could engage in their commerce, we could learn from them, we could carry on contact with them, we could make money with them. But no, this isn't what you want, is it? You want us on this island. You want us to be different, so you can control us. Well, Father Moreau, you have controlled us. You've controlled us for two hundred years and now you've been booted out.

"How many luxuries could we have used in the last hundred years? How many things could anyone in Québec have wanted other than the luxury of a private language? When everyone has been crying out for a better standard of living, what do you throw at them? You tell them about their language and their culture and they've listened. But times are changing, Father Moreau. They've kicked you out and pretty soon they're going to get wise to the rest of this gang, the inheritors of your legacy. This gang that tells us about our culture, tells us about our language, but doesn't tell us how much this language and culture is costing.

"Just think, Father Moreau, if you had taught me a language that everyone else in this country could understand, I could have learned things, I could have had a better education, I could have been a more productive person. But instead, what have you done? What have you taught everyone in Québec? Fear? Fear! Yes, that's it. Fear that has turned to hate, and hate that has turned to murder."

"You speak heresy." Father Moreau shook his head. "You speak heresy, my son. You speak against your Holy Mother, the Church. You must repent. You must have absolution."

"Absolution! You want to give me absolution?" Pierre pointed his finger at Father Moreau. "You are the one that needs absolution, Father Moreau. You are the one that initiated this power struggle. The Church in Québec is like the seed. And this gang of criminals," he swung the gun around the table, "they are like the fruits of your tree."

Father Moreau looked at him coldly. "You must know that we have nothing to do with education in Québec. The power has been taken from us. You must know that."

"I know," said Pierre, "it's been turned over to people like this." He pointed at Henri Bédault. "Yes, it's easy to see what he's doing. He's taking advantage of the ground work you prepared for him, Father Moreau. He's going to continue this mania of perpetuating a language that is throttling his own people. And is he determined? God, how determined he is! Does he give a choice to his people? Does he tell them what kind of a prison he's locking them in? No!

"He's learned your lesson well, Father Moreau. He's seen the power you've had for two hundred years. And now he wants it. Success follows success. It worked for the Church. Why shouldn't it work for this bunch? So they've worked out a cozy little plan. Get the kids real mad. When they find out they're in a prison, a prison of language, blame it on the Americans, or the other Canadians. And will the kids swallow it? Yes, they will believe you. That's the real tragedy. They believe you when you tell them their precious gift, their language, is in jeopardy. The thought makes them afraid, and their fear turns into hate, and the hate turns into a reaction, and the reaction turns into a revolution. And then, it's too late."

Pierre looked wearily at the faces around the table. "If I had only listened to Giselle," he said, as though to himself. "If I had only listened to her, I would never have gotten involved in this stinking Movement. I would have gone away with her. We could have got married. But now it's too late."

"Nothing is ever too late, my son. You are a young man. You have your whole life ahead of you. Make peace with God, lay down your arms, marry the girl. I would be pleased to officiate."

"You don't know?"

"What?"

"Giselle is dead."

"No! That is impossible. Please forgive me, my son. But how?"

"François murdered her."

A moan passed through the group. François' voice raised above the others in a roar. "Liar," he screamed. "You're a liar."

"You shut up!" Pierre's eyes bulged as he pointed the gun at François. "When you speak, it will be to answer questions."

"You must be mistaken, my son. A horrible mistake. A. . . ."

"There's no mistake. There's no mistake. She's dead. She's lying on a slab at the morgue. And there's no mistake that François killed her. That he killed Madame Hébert, and my friend, Emile and his wife, Yvonne, that he murdered the crew on the American destroyer."

The rumblings increased. Henri Bédault shouted, "It was an accident, Pierre, we all know that."

"A well-planned accident," retorted Pierre. "I was on the Sans Souci that night."

François was about to interrupt, but his better judgment took over. Ginette sat beside him, calm and cool. He was pleased that the conflict raging about him did not really involve him. He had never had a problem with Pierre and wasn't likely to start one tonight. Not as long as I can stay out of the line of fire, he thought.

"This cannot be true." Father Moreau's voice was unbelieving. "You planned to have the accident?"

"Yes," admitted Pierre, as though he was going to confession. "The accident was planned. The Sans Souci was stacked to the gunwales with explosives. We rammed the destroyer."

"Is this true?" All eyes turned to François, whose face whitened as Pierre pointed the gun at him.

"Answer them," Pierre screamed. "You wanted to talk. Answer them now."

François was cagey. "How can they believe me if I admit to this deed while you point that gun at me?"

"Answer!" ordered Pierre.

"Yes, I did what Pierre said," admitted François. He searched out their eyes in turn and the knowing look encouraged him. Father Moreau, Bédault and Petrie didn't really believe Pierre.

Relieved, Father Moreau turned to Pierre. "We are more clear on that issue now, my son," he said. "Now tell us more about your friends and Giselle. What makes you think François killed them? Surely, you did not see him do it?"

"Roger confessed."

"Roger confessed to you?"

"Yes."

"What did he say?"

"He said he killed Emile and Yvonne for François."

"And you believed him?"

"Yes."

"Why?"

"Because Giselle knew. She was there."

"And Giselle? How did she . . . ?"

"The same. She has told me for the last two months that they were going to kill her."

"Impossible! I can't believe it."

"I have proof."

"Where?"

"In the coach house."

François realized Roger would never admit anything to anybody, this gang, the police, nobody. And Roger would act decisively when he came into the room. The talking would stop and the shooting would start. The first to hit the floor would be this young pup.

"Why don't you get Roger? We'll get to the bottom of this." François' voice was confident as he turned to Ginette. "You go, Jacques," he said. "Pierre seems to have no argument with you."

"No!" Pierre's gesture was menacing, as was his voice. "Ginette will stay." He turned to Father Moreau. "You go," he said sourly. "He needs you more than any of us."

François tried vainly to catch the priest's eye, but without success. Pierre backed to the door, removed the chair, opened the door and the priest was gone. François drummed his fingers on the table in agitation. Would that fool have brains enough to call for help? And if he did, who would they be? Pierre returned to the table after replacing the chair.

"And now we come to you, Mr. Bédault. What there is of you. For you are nothing but a parrot. A very dangerous parrot, but a parrot." Henri Bédault twitched nervously in his seat. "You distort the truth, you'd rather lie than eat. But what has it done for you? They say you're to be the Minister of Education in François' government. Well, forget it, parrot. François will never be the government of Québec. So you'll never be anything but a parrot. You've fed your last lie to my people. The people of Québec are waking up. Soon there will be counter-propaganda to dispel your lies. This propaganda will fill the radio and television like yours has done for the last ten years. It will be started by our own people. It will preach unity and co-operation, instead of hate and separation."

His gaze shifted to Petrie. "You're two of a kind, aren't you? You both yap like terriers. Yap, yap, yap! And your yapping is swallowed up by people like myself. But do you know why?"

Petrie looked at François, then returned his sheepish gaze to Pierre. "No," he said meekly.

"Because we have such a gutless government. We have believed you because we never hear anything else. Those gutless wonders will scream like a wailing woman about the wars that spring up in every country but our own. They will send aid to everybody including their enemies. But will they spend one bloody cent to counter your propaganda? To educate our people? To tell them the advantages of being a part of a beautiful, big country? To help them get into the swing of things? No! Instead, they hide their heads in the sand and believe these simmering hatreds that exist, only because you bunch of bastards keep the pot boiling. Our people deserve more than this. They will get more. Our people are members of North America. We will join the other North Americans. We have been imprisoned too long. Now we must free ourselves. And we'll free ourselves with the truth.

"And when the thinking people of Québec rise up against the real trouble makers, our problems shall disappear like fog before the sun."

"If you feel so strongly about this now," said Jean Petrie in a strangely humble voice, "why have you been such a good worker for the Movement?"

The room was silent as they waited for an answer. François kept one ear cocked for sounds of Roger and watched the door as much as he could without being too obvious. Finally, Pierre spoke.

"I've asked myself that same question and the answer is always the same. I've heard only one side of the argument all my life. I'm like most people in Québec. I've been scared out of my wits ever since I was a kid. I've been scared of everybody that isn't French. At first, I thought it was natural. I was taught that my language was going to be taken from me, my religion was to be denied me, that my culture was to be stolen. Isn't that what I was told when I was a kid? Isn't that what I was taught in school? In Church? Everywhere? Naturally, I was scared. Scared by a bogey-man. So when my best friend shows me a way to quit being scared, a way to get even with this bogey-man, why the hell shouldn't I listen to him?"

"But how could you change so completely?"

"The truth."

"That's ridiculous."

"Ridiculous! I believe there is no bogey-man out to get us, except a few gangsters like yourselves. Nobody has ever tried to stop me from speaking French, but I know I could get along better if I spoke English. I notice every one of you speaks English. Why you and not me? I don't believe anybody, except you, will stop my religion or culture or anything else. Look at François! He's the kind to be afraid of. Him and his silent partner."

He pointed the gun at Ginette, who looked up, startled. "They're the ones who will steal our heritage. The other people in this country are willing to let us grovel in our own muck. That's what's puzzled me for so long. Why haven't I heard the other side? Why hasn't the federal government, why haven't the Americans been on the radio, the television, the newspapers, telling me their side? The answer is, they don't care. They think I'd resent hearing from them. They'll never act to stop movements like this. They'll let you say and do anything you want and never raise a finger or say a strong word to stop you. They'll let you split up the country, start a civil war, debauch our people with an imported philosophy, and they'll just sit idly by until it's too late."

"Pierre." It was Petrie again. "You've never had much schooling, I can tell that, and yet you talk like an expert on the subject. How did you come to these conclusions?"

Pierre looked at François whose face whitened at his answer.

"Giselle," he said, and his voice caught with the sound of her name. "Giselle taught me."

"But don't you know what Giselle was?"

"Yes, I know. She was a lady."

"You didn't know her too well, did you?"

"No one could have known her too well. You see, you are a fool. You think of her as a prostitute. Take advantage of her, you say. Ridicule her. The same way you ridicule and take advantage of Québec. But you never knew Giselle, and you don't know Québec. You are only the filth that is contaminating Québec. You never knew Giselle."

Noises at the front door disturbed them. Heavy knocks, the door bell ringing and Father Moreau's cries. "He locked himself out," said François rising, "I'll let him in."

"Not you." Pierre's voice was stern. "You, Petrie, and you, Bédault, you two go and comfort the good Father. He seems to be upset."

Without delay, the two jumped to their feet. Pierre removed the chair from the door and they raced each other from the room. When they reached the front door, they unlocked it and brushing by the priest, ran into the biting cold outside, preferring it to their captive positions inside.

"See how the rabbits run," said Pierre, menacing François and Ginette who had risen from the table.

"He's dead! He's dead!" Father Moreau's voice echoed through the hall and stunned François, who dropped back into his chair. Roger dead? Impossible! He can't mean Roger!

The priest stopped at the door leading to the drawing room. "Did you kill him, my son?"

"Yes."

"It is a mortal sin. You know that."

"Punishable by eternal damnation, Father Moreau?"

"Yes, my son. Without confession."

"Is it the same hell that René was sent to?"

"René?"

"Yes," said Pierre, as though in a trance, "René drowned in the river after he stole some candies from old man LaCourte's grocery store. The priest said he went to hell."

Father Moreau had no idea what Pierre meant.

"Lay down your gun, my son. Come with me. We will talk. I will give you absolution. You are sorry."

"I'm not sorry, Father. I wish I had done it before, and as far as absolution is concerned, I think you need it more than me."

"Come, now! You must do as . . ."

"Get out! I'll count to three . . ." The priest began to speak, but the movement of the gun stopped him. Turning, he walked to the front door, opened it and was gone. Pierre quickly followed, kicked it shut and bolted it. Then, retracing his steps in long firm strides, he entered the drawing room just as François and Ginette had reached the door. They threw their weight at it and it slammed shut. But too late. Pierre was inside the room with them. They looked at him as they sprawled on the floor.

"Get up," Pierre said with authority. "We have things to discuss. Things like murder. And we haven't much time."

45

"There's no use watching the door, François. He won't come. You heard Father Moreau. What he said was true. Roger is dead. He can't do your dirty work any more." Pierre looked at the two men facing each other across the table. He stood at the end. They both sat.

"What do you want of us?" François' face was downcast.

"We're going to hold court, François. You know the way. The same way you used to. The same way you tried Giselle and the others. The only difference is that you are on trial. This time, I'm the judge."

"And you want me as a witness," Ginette broke in hopefully.

"No, Mr. Ginette. You are on trial too. You see, there have been some terrible crimes committed. But no one, except Roger, has been punished. Now, we can't put all the blame on him, can we? He was only a madman. He was not much more to blame than me."

"You? You think you're guilty?" François showed a momentary sign of his old self. "Let me assure you, Pierre, you are not guilty. You . . ." Pierre pulled the .38 from his belt.

The bullet hit the table less than an inch from François' hand. He pulled it back quickly, his face white with fear. A faint noise came from outside the house. It was Father Moreau. He was shouting something, but Pierre could not make out the words. "I told you before, François. You are to answer questions. You are not to talk unless you are asked." There were more sounds from outside. This time it was the distant wail of a siren. The police! Pierre noticed the slightest trace of a smirk on François' face.

"We must hurry," said Pierre. "We must hurry. I don't want to kill the wrong man."

"The wrong man? What the hell do you mean, Pierre?" said Ginette. "Why would you want to kill me? Haven't I always been your friend? It's been François who's made any trouble you're in, not me. I hardly knew Giselle. I . . ."

"Shut up! That's not the point. It's too late to think of the dead. My friends, my dead friends. We can only think of the living. The living people in Québec. Anywhere! Canada, the United States, everywhere."

"But what good will killing François do?" The question jarred François and he glared at Ginette. "If you kill him, someone else will only take his place."

"And if I kill you?"

"Me?"

"You are the politician. You have been elected. You have the power."

"But I did it for François. For Québec."

"Did you?"

"Yes, yes! If anyone's guilty, it's not me."

"What do you say, François? Is Ginette right? If he is, then you are guilty and I must kill you. Here's your chance to get out, François. You gave Giselle a chance. Remember? Well, now I'm going to give you the same chance. Prove to me that Ginette is more guilty than you and he shall die. Instead of you, he will be sacrificed for the blood of my friends."

"You told me not to talk," replied François, stalling for time.

"Answer. Tell me if your smooth-talking politician is more guilty than you. Is he in politics only to help you make deals with foreign powers? Is he planning to be the new dictator of Québec? Is it he that is using us to gain his ends? Is he keeping us in a language prison so we'll do as we're told? Does he want us to separate so he can own us? Rule us? Betray us? As we've been betrayed for all our history? Answer me, François, or I'll kill you, now." He cocked the shotgun and pointed it at François.

"Don't! I'll tell you. You're right, Pierre. Ginette wants power and personal wealth. He has it. You can see. He's in politics. Not me. Kill him if you must, but you and I must escape. Listen, Pierre, they're outside. The police. They have guns. Now look! You and I are in this together. We can still escape. We can run out the back door, across the field and escape. Escape with me, Pierre. We can do it together."

Cars honked. Sirens wailed. Outside the window, a man called out. "Give up, Pierre. We know you're in there. We know all about you. Give up."

Pierre fired a bullet at the upper part of the window and the voice stopped.

"You're right, François. The police are here. We must escape."

"Good," said François rising.

"But first, we must kill Ginette."

"Kill him?"

Yes. Right now. And you must do it. If we are to escape

together, you must prove your loyalty to me. Just as Giselle proved hers to you. You must kill Ginette."

"No!" There was panic in Ginette's voice. But François caught his eye. He winked. Ginette stopped. François had a plan as usual.

"How can I kill him?" asked François.

"I'll give you the revolver," said Pierre simply. "I can trust you."

"Of course. Give it to me." There was a rebirth of eagerness in François' voice.

"First, you must stand beside Ginette. Here, let me show you." Pierre motioned with the shotgun. François walked around the table and stood beside the shaking Ginette. François caught his eye and winked again. Ginette relaxed.

"Now give me the gun." François turned and smiled at Pierre, but the smile left as Pierre stepped back and, turning the chamber of the .38, dropped the remaining shells, except one, onto the floor.

"Turn and face Ginette," he ordered. "You have one bullet. If you miss, you get it in the back."

Beads of perspiration showed on François' forehead. This imbecile was serious. His plan to shoot Pierre instead of Ginette couldn't work.

"No," he said, spitting it out as though he were going to be sick. "I can't kill Ginette."

"Then I'll kill you."

"All right, I'll do it." He turned and faced Ginette, again winking.

"Ginette," said Pierre, "turn your back to François." Ginette looked at François for reassurance. He got it. He turned. "Now the gun," said François.

Pierre pushed the nozzle of the shotgun into François' back and, with his other hand, shoved the .38 along the table. François put his reluctant hand on it, knowing what he had to do. He raised it to Ginette's temple, while at the same time feeling the heaviness of the steel shaft between his ribs.

Ginette stood there like a department store dummy expecting, until the last fraction of a second, that François would think of something; that his clever mind would show him a way out. He had the gun, it was loaded. All he had to do was suddenly turn and fire it into Pierre. Then it would be all over, but something about the way François hesitated, something in the stony silence, made him realize that it wouldn't happen that way.

The bullet hit before he could turn. It made a neat, almost

unnoticeable hole on one side of his head, while it carried away half his skull on the other. He slumped to the floor.

"Come on," said François, turning to Pierre. "Let's go."

"I've changed my mind, François. You know, just like you changed your mind about Giselle. I don't want to run away with you."

"But I killed him. Just like you wanted. Look!" He pointed to the bloody mess on the floor.

"You didn't kill him for me. You killed him to save your own skin."

Outside, a loudspeaker blared. "We have the house surrounded. We're coming in. Give yourself up." The voice continued as Pierre checked the door leading to the hall. Someone had entered through the back and was sneaking along the hall. He opened the door and fired a blast into the hall. The scurrying sounds he heard told the story. The intruder had hastily retreated. But he would be back soon. He turned to François who still held the empty gun and was eyeing the shells Pierre had dropped on the floor when he was preparing the gun for Ginette's death.

"I'm going to kill you," said Pierre.

"But you promised. You must live up to your promise."

"I promised to avenge the death of Giselle, Emile, Yvonne and maybe even Paul. But that's not why I'm going to kill you."

"Then why?"

"Because of something Giselle said once. She said we were all victims of our own folly. She said our own leaders were making suckers out of us. She said the United States would never interfere in our affairs because they can't. She said our federal people wouldn't interfere because of our constitution. She said our only hope was for the French people in Canada to get rid of the parasites that are leading us down a one-way alley."

"She was one of us. She didn't mean us."

"She was one of us only because of fate, in the first instance. And later, only because you blackmailed her. Just like you'd like to blackmail the whole country."

The voice on the amplifying system outside was Father Moreau's. "Do not resist, my son, you will be slaughtered. The police will open fire if you do not come out in five minutes. Come out. I will help you." There was silence for a moment, then a projectile crashed through the window. It hit the draperies, ripped them, then fell to the floor. Vaporous fumes spurted from the canister.

"The only help that old man could have given me," said Pierre as though speaking to himself, "was when I was a kid. Now it's too late."

"We've got to get out of here, that's tear gas," yelled François as he started his dash to the door. But he was less than halfway there when the blast from the shotgun crushed his side. He spun around with an unbelieving expression on his face. His mouth dropped open as the second blast hit him. He clutched his chest and fell to the floor. Pierre walked to him, rolled him over with the pressure from his boot, and watched his spasms decrease into death.

"Giselle!" said Pierre. Then his eyes filled with tears and they flowed like a river down his cheeks.

46

One after another the canisters smashed through the windows and dropped to the floor, releasing their noxious fumes. The smoke became intense before it began to have an effect on Pierre and when it did, he moved slowly through the doorway, into the hallway and toward the front door.

The flood of lights from a dozen cars flashed on him as he opened the door. He stepped to the entrance and stood between the two gargoyles.

"Drop your gun," a voice commanded from the loudspeaker. But Pierre took no heed.

He looked at the gargoyles, grinning their stupid grins in the brilliance of the cars' headlights. They seemed to be laughing at him as much as to say, "You are only a pawn. You have always been a pawn. You will always be one."

The voice sounded again. "Drop your gun. Drop your gun, or we'll shoot."

What should he do? What could he do? Nothing. It was all done. He raised his gun and aimed it at the lights of one of the cars.

A volley of shots flew through the air. He fell sideways grasping the gargoyle, knocking it from its pedestal. Then he slumped to the ground beside it, the gargoyle's face still smiling, while Pierre's was masked with the shroud of death.

The police stood around him. Everyone talked at once. Finally, one of the policemen, a sergeant, ordered the gathering to disperse and threw a blanket from one of the cars over Pierre's corpse.

"Why did he do it?" asked one of the younger constables. "Why would he kill a couple of wonderful guys like Ginette and François? They were really going to do things for us."

"I don't know," said the sergeant, shaking his head. "I guess he was just plain crazy."